SWEET SEDUCTION

Lucy would have been horrified at Josh Dylan's actions and shocked by his kiss, had she been able to think once he'd kissed her. But his lips were warm and gentle, and his arms were the most comforting thing she'd felt in a very long time, and the scent of him was of the night and the fire and strong sweet liquors and spices.

When he deepened the kiss, she felt threatened only for a moment, until the unfamiliar touch of his tongue became an oddly welcome intrusion, if only because it withdrew as soon as he felt and heard her small gasp of alarm.

That was the way he wooed her, taking only what she offered, waiting for her response before he took more . . . until it would have been hard to say who was leading whom . . . this woman who knew so little of the flesh and this man who knew so little of the heart. . . .

THE GILDED CAGE

THE GILDED CAGE

by

Edith Layton

AN ONYX BOOK

ONYX
Published by the Penguin Group
Penguin Books USA Inc., 375 Hudson Street,
New York, New York 10014, U.S.A.
Penguin Books Ltd, 27 Wrights Lane,
London W8 5TZ, England
Penguin Books Australia Ltd, Ringwood,
Victoria, Australia
Penguin Books Canada Ltd, 2801 John Street,
Markham, Ontario, Canada L3R 1B4
Penguin Books (N.Z.) Ltd, 182–190 Wairau Road,
Auckland 10, New Zealand

Penguin Books Ltd, Registered Offices:
Harmondsworth, Middlesex, England

First published by Onyx, an imprint of New American Library,
a division of Penguin Books USA Inc.

First Printing, August, 1991
10 9 8 7 6 5 4 3 2 1

For Susie: for the face, the voice—and Duncan.

Oh better far to live and die
Under the brave black flag I fly,
Than play a sanctimonious part,
With a pirate head and a pirate heart.
Away to the cheating world go you,
Where pirates are all well-to-do;
But I'll be true to the song I sing,
And live and die a Pirate King.

For I am a Pirate King . . .
And it is, it is, a glorious thing
To be a Pirate King!
—W. S. Gilbert,
The Pirates of Penzance

Gentlemen. You have undertaken
to cheat me. I will not sue you—
the law takes too long. I will ruin you.
—Cornelius Vanderbilt,
"The Commodore"

1

August 1879

THEY CAME RIDING out of a glaring sunset, with the freshening wind at their backs—a coach and six mad horses, sending up clouds of dust to rival the high white ones scudding over their heads. The sound of their laughter could be heard over the noise of the laboring horses and the careening coach, so for all the onlookers thought they were as crazed as their foaming teams, in some small part of their souls they envied them, every one of them. Then, when they saw who was driving, their envy vanished. It was impossible to covet what was impossible for an ordinary man, after all.

"By God, Josh, you did it!" the younger man cried as the coach pulled up to the rail fence by the station, and it could be seen that there was no train even in the distance—and a sharp-eyed man could see for miles down that long track. "On time, and in no time, even starting out a half-hour late. Looks like you've even got a half-hour to spare," he exulted.

"And every one of the horses sober too," the driver said on a laugh as he held his right hand as though he were swearing to it, after he'd transferred the whip to his left, where he still held the six reins tight in his gloved fist.

His younger companion threw back his fair head and roared with laughter again, before he sat up straight and grew grave as he stared hard at the driver.

"Don't go, Josh," he said then seriously, his sky-blue eyes searching the dark gray ones that had turned to him with sudden and equal gravity. "This is your home."

"I haven't got a home," the driver said softly, his eyes losing their glow and growing like slate. "That's the whole point of it. It's time to find one, or make one, time and past it, and you know it. A man has to grow up sometime, and though the change in altitude can make him dizzy, that does mean settling down too," he added as he turned his attention to pulling the separate reins carefully from his fist.

"But you've always been grown up, Josh," the younger man argued. "Don't you want to have some fun?"

"One doesn't rule out the other," his brother drawled as he stood. "In fact, where I'm bound, I hear you can't have the one without the other. Now, is it brotherly concern or plain envy that's eating at you? Don't think I haven't seen that pile of *Police Gazette*s growing in your bedroom. So don't worry," he said as his brother tried, and failed, to look nonchalant in the face of finding out that his secret hoard of scandalous literature had been discovered, "it's not 'Sin and Excess in the Wicked City' I'm out to get myself."

As the younger man tried to compose himself after hearing his favorite, much-thumbed article named, his brother added as he handed him the reins before he let himself down lightly to the ground, "When it's 'Sin and Success' I'm after—and what I'm after, I'm dead-set on getting."

Joshua Dylan stretched his long body as he stood by the carriage; it had been a wild and far ride to town, and though he hated to admit it except in jest, the jolting he'd taken as he'd taken care to impress his little brother with his driving seemed to have driven his spine straight up into the top of his head. Getting older, he thought as he put two hands to the small of his back and flexed to straighten it, *past* time to get on with ordering my life.

But his brother didn't agree, and after he'd given the horses into the care of a helpful idler, he came to Joshua's side to continue the argument that had started weeks ago, when he'd first heard of his plans.

"A man can do business from his home," Gray Dylan protested. "There's letters and telegraphs. You done fine so far that way. No need to go to New York City, for that matter, neither. Chicago's nearer. It's good enough for your partners. And they're richer than I can count."

"And that's exactly why you're going back to school. To learn counting and conversation again. So there's no man alive whose worth you can't calculate to the penny, and no man you can't speak to like a gentleman. Lord, Gray, you've been with the horses so much this summer you're starting to talk like one," Josh answered, wincing as he shrugged his back into place. "God, I'm getting old. Time was, a buckboard felt like a feather bed to me, and now a coach gets me into knots. Almost thirty and halfway to Boot Hill already," he mused aloud. "And don't argue," he said quickly as his brother opened his mouth to protest. "I may be going to New York, but the ranch is stuffed with spies, and if you're not on the train to New Haven by the end of the month, little brother, I'm coming home and hauling you to school myself."

Gray had actually been noting the way his older brother's large tanned hands had met on his hips, accentuating the neatness of his trim waist and flat abdomen as he leaned back into his fingers to ease his muscle cramp. He'd been about to argue about the obvious fitness he saw, but mention of his most galling complaint erased other thoughts from his mind immediately.

"Now, as to that," he said in frustration, "you know I can speak well enough if I want to, but you know damned well I don't have to here, and not with you, and I've got enough education for any man—"

"Any man but my brother, maybe," Josh agreed, reaching up to the carriage and hauling down a bag.

The bag swung at his side as he took long strides into the little building that served as a train station. He opened a door to a small side room. His brother followed him in, limping slightly.

Josh noticed, and frowned, "Leg acting up?" he asked.

"No, no," Gray said quickly, "just that I was sitting in one place too long. It'll do. It'll be fine in a minute."

"Next time a horse will fall on your head, not your leg," his brother said gruffly.

"Then there'll be no harm, just like Doc said," Gray answered with a laugh, but seeing he got no response, he protested, "It was years ago, it only acts up when it's real damp out. Accidents can happen in the East same as the West—aw, damnation, it's not like I've got anything in common with poets—*poets* for God's sake, Josh," he went on plaintively, "or Boston accountants or Rhode Island clothiers' sons going into the family business," he said with loathing, "not when my life's going to be here, with the horses and cattle, and I know them better than most men, so what's a college degree going to mean to me . . . and what are you doing?" he asked, breaking off in the middle of his best argument.

His brother had taken off his cowhide jacket, kerchief, and soft shirt. As Gray watched, he took a white shirt, so stiff it seemed to have an invisible torso already in it, from the bag. He shook it out and began to put it on, buttoning it up to his neck.

"Your life can be here if you want. But your business is going to be the family business too—here and everywhere. I need a man with an education behind me. And I'm getting dressed, as any fool can plainly see," he added, raising his chin high to get the studs on his collar to snap tight.

"You've got more education than anyone I know, and you never went to school," Gray said absently, wondering at the unusual sight of his brother with a formal white shirt buttoned high as a noose, and looking just as comfortable. But Joshua's long muscled legs were bared beneath his shirttails. He'd stripped off his tight blue denims and sorted through his bag until he found a pair of gray trousers, and proceeded to pull them on.

"No, I never did have an education. Because I never could," Josh said. "Someone in the family has to get a sheepskin without a sheep in it," he laughed, and added, "and with a long Latin brand on it. If you stare at your classmates like that when they get undressed, it's no wonder you're having problems at school," he added lightly, buttoning up the pants and sitting down to pull on a pair of black wing-tip shoes.

"You look different," Gray said softly, with a note in his voice that sounded a decade younger than his nineteen years, and in a tone his brother hadn't heard for years.

"You said that after I shaved," Josh answered, suddenly feeling much younger than his own twenty-nine years himself. But for all that he'd looked forward to this moment, and for all that he knew it was right for him, it would never be easy for him to leave this boy. That was why he'd never done it before. He'd sent him away—yes. To get schooling. And he'd gone away himself. To earn their keep. But he'd never left him like this, without promising to be back. And he'd never let him know how hard it was, or he'd never succeed in what he was planning to do. So he rose and began to wrap a tie around his neck, and pretended he hadn't heard that note in Gray's voice just as much as he guessed Gray was now pretending he'd never allowed it to escape.

"Well," Gray said in a pointedly casual voice, but such a deliberately deep one now that his brother had trouble holding his face still, "it was a shock, seeing all that skin all at once. It looks good, now I come to study on it," he added, "but I don't understand, I thought it was the fashion for gents to have beards in New York too . . . I look at more than pictures of the ladies in my *Gazette*, you know," he said defensively.

"You don't get thumbprints all over them, though," Josh answered, gazing at the piece of mirror hung from a string on a nail on the wall before him.

Their eyes met square in the mirror. And then they started laughing. Because they never could stay sober around each other very long.

"I know fashionable men in New York have beards," Josh chuckled at last, "that's why I don't anymore. Because I'm just a lucky feller from the Wyoming Territory, in the right clothes with the wrong accent, rich as Midas and just as smart, like all us newly rich Western gents," he said in a burlesqued and thickened drawl. "Savvy?"

"Like when you're sitting down to poker in a strange town," Gray said, nodding. "Oh, I savvy. I do pity them New Yorkers, though. But ain't that going to be hard on you, Josh?" he asked gently. "I mean, never being who you are?"

"I'll be me as soon as I can be. But it doesn't pay to put your cards all out on the table at once, does it? Ah,

listen, little brother," he said, putting his hand on Gray's
shoulder, "New York's my home. Or was. I was born
and raised there, unlike you—you wild Westerner. But I
haven't really been back in years. So I'm worried—just
a little. And when you're not sure of your welcome—
like when you're with a new girl on the back porch—
trust me, it's best to go slow."

"I'm worried too," his brother said softly. "New York
ain't been that good to us, Josh, you know it."

"It's been bad and good," Josh said, "but it's a worthy
challenge. Mr. Greeley told you young fellows to go
west, but I've got to go east. You'd get back on a fine
horse even after he threw you, wouldn't you, Scout?" he
asked gently, smiling at the old name he'd used to placate
his fierce little brother all those years ago.

Gray remained still as his brother struggled into a
tight-fitting coat. "Oh, I see—since you're putting it into
terms even a cowboy could understand," he muttered,
abashed, as Josh finished dressing, turned, and asked,
"Now, how do I look?"

The slender young man looked hard at his brother.
Standing close as they were, it could easily be seen that
they were related; there was that in their lean wide-shouldered forms and finely chiseled features that claimed certain kinship. But they were only like enough to be
brothers, never twins. They were both tall. But the boy
was slender and wing-shouldered with the raw look of
rapid and fresh growth. The man was honed and hard.
It wasn't just their ages or stages of growth that
accounted for their differences.

The boy had a wealth of shaggy flaxen hair and eyes
the color of bluebonnets, while the man had thick tobac-
co-gold hair and his almond-shaped eyes were fog gray.
From high foreheads to high cheekbones and determined
chins, both had classical features, but the man's mouth
had wider lips, his chin had the hint of a cleft, and his
eyes turned down slightly at the corners, while his brother's tilted upward.

The boy stared in honest admiration at the face he
hadn't seen without beard and mustache in years. The
sun had evened the tan on that smooth gold skin in the
week since the beard had been shorn. In fact, Gray

thought, his brother could be the model for a statue of an athlete if it weren't for . . . His eyes slid away from what he'd been staring at. But it was a damned shame that shapely nose had broken so badly and set so unevenly, because the lump at the top of it was pronounced, and the way that once straight nose sat slightly askew ruined the perfection that once had been there. It wasn't comical-looking, or even so noticeable at first stare, but anyone could see it was off-center and damaged. Of course, the women didn't seem to mind, no more than Josh himself did. But then, Josh had a way with females; he'd appeal to them if he had no nose at all, his brother thought with prideful envy. It might even be an asset, since it probably made men trust him more than if he'd still had his perfect looks. But the fashion was for noble-looking men with chiseled profiles, and Gray resented anything that took any of the shine out of this brother, who'd been like a father to him.

"Now, now. The nose," Josh chided him, "has been out and up front for inspection for years—I never did find a way to grow whiskers over it. Aside from that, will I do?"

"Ah, Josh," Gray sighed, "you'll do. I just wish you didn't have to."

"This is all in your bones, isn't it?" Joshua asked seriously. "All of it—the never-ending sky, the openness, and the smell and sound of it. Take off your spurs and guns and you can't even concentrate on your books, can you?" he asked, putting out a hand to ruffle the wild light hair even more, as his brother ducked away and said with some belligerence, "That's right too—can't even wear your guns back east, Josh . . . how in hell will you take care of yourself?"

"They don't have shoot-outs on Fifth Avenue," his brother answered. "They kill a man in the back room of their offices—they get him with papers and pens, and he bleeds red ink until he's dead as surely as if it was blood—that's why you need an education if you want to help me. Still, I'll do all right. I want to go." He looked at his brother steadily and spoke softly but firmly. "When you go east, you suffer because of it, you die a little remembering the mountains and the prairies, I know that. But I don't. I remember the city wherever I go. Think of that when you think about me, eh? And think of why I'm going besides that. I can't consolidate our business from here. I need to be in the thick of things—where fortunes start and stop. I need to know what to buy, what to sell, what to trade, and what to steal, if I'm going to make us rich."

"We *are* rich," his brother insisted. "We've got the ranch, and the cattle, the railroad stock, the mine, and the shares in the rolling stock—even in this new refrigerator car you're riding shotgun on all the way east . . . and what all else. God Almighty, Josh, how much richer can we get?"

"Much, much richer. Really rich. So rich that we'll never know, or even remember, hunger or want, ever again."

"I don't," his brother said softly, as though ashamed for it.

"But I do, enough for both of us, enough for everybody in the world," Josh said, as though proud of it, even though, as they both knew, he was ashamed for it.

And that, his brother knew, as he straightened his shoulders and accepted his loss at last, was why he had to go. That was why his big brother, even now that he lived in luxury—no, especially now that he lived in luxury—would never be able to call anyplace home but the city he'd been driven from in poverty.

The younger man sought something safe and amusing to say so he wouldn't say what his heart demanded as they stood on the wooden boards outside the railway office and heard the first wails from the oncoming train.

"Gonna get yourself a wife now too?" Gray asked. "A girlfriend of Mrs. Astor's, now that you're dressed up like her pet horse? A New York socialite?"

"Just might," his brother agreed.

"Oh, too bad, I thought you were going to find out for me just what those New York actresses were like."

"Just might get one of those too," his brother answered, smiling, and then added, drawling, "After all, makes sense. Got two hands, two arms, and two eyes. And it is New York, you know."

"But you've only got one . . . brother," Gray said.

They were still laughing as the great black train rolled to a stop, shrieking so loudly they could hardly hear each other, spewing so much steam and cinder they could scarcely see each other's expressions clear even as they shook hands and then hugged hard and fast. Which was just as well.

"You'll write?" Gray shouted as his brother boarded.

"You'll read?" his brother called back to the young man who was his only family.

And they laughed so much as the elder got on the train and waved to the younger that no one watching who didn't know them could guess at how deeply they grieved at this parting.

Josh loved horses, and driving was his passion as much as it had once been his occupation. He'd learned at the hands of a master, and if his father had mastered nothing else, he'd known the ways of coaching as no other man he'd ever met had done. And Josh had met the best in his time. When he'd left his father's side, and had still been a boy with quick growth and enough quick wit to disguise his youth, he'd driven for Butterfield himself on the old overland route. As a man, he'd driven for Wells Fargo when they'd taken over Butterfield. But a man gets ahead by staying one step ahead of the competition. So then he'd driven coaches and horses across the jagged spines of mountains and limitless plains for any man who could pay him enough to live spare—and yet spare him enough left over to invest so he'd not have to drive so hard in the future. But now as he sat back like a gentleman and let invisible teams of iron horses drag him away from his home, Josh had to admit that railroads were better than good. They were the future, and the future was already here.

It hardly mattered if they sank steel roads down over all the West, or just half of it, or if every city across America put up elevated trains like the one he'd be arriving in had already done—it was here or it was coming. The horse was going to give way. Man or horse, flesh and blood would always be done in by cold steel. Maybe they'd have to carpet the land with cross-ties so every man could have his own personal railroad car to gallivant around in someday; maybe there'd be a major train stop near his front door; he didn't know how it would be done—that was one of the reasons he was going to New York, to find out—but he knew it would be done. And he intended to profit from it.

The days of coaching were over. He might rue it in a way, as he sat back at his ease in the railroad car carrying him effortlessly east, but he knew it was a good thing, any which way he looked at it. Progress always was. The past was comfortable only because it was known so well. It was the only way *his* past could be called comfortable, he thought wryly. That was the reason he regretted not coming back to New York the way he'd left it, the way he'd traveled most places in his life: working every inch of the way. A working man had to keep his mind on the present, the only thing he had to do with the past was to try to learn from his mistakes. Otherwise there was no profit in it. Only the rich or the old had time to relive the past.

That wasn't to say he sat back like an emperor on an elephant on this trip; traveling by rail wasn't that easy. He'd changed trains three times since he'd left Wyoming Territory, and if he wasn't jounced as hard as he might be on a high stagecoach seat, he still could feel the miles being eaten away beneath him. But he was protected from the elements, he could eat, sleep, and relieve himself while in motion, and that was still a miracle and a delight to him. He might be the only passenger on the train who thought so.

"By jingo!" a hefty, loudly dressed gentleman who looked like a drummer remarked to the passengers sitting in the club car. "Looks like rain! All we need, eh? Slick rails and we're off the track, one, two, three," he prophesied.

The other passengers nodded nervously and began to voice their own fears, trying to outdo each other with hair-raising tales of railroad disasters. Josh left the car.

His fellow travelers complained endlessly about the noise, delays, speed, their fear of accidents, and their difficulties living in a rattling, swaying train. But he was used to passengers complaining; that much hadn't changed. He suspected it never would. Half the pleasure

of traveling seemed to be in carrying-on about it, or so
he'd often thought when he'd heard his own fares whining on the easiest routes. The harder or more exciting the
journey and the more a man felt he was either exerting
or endangering himself—the more significant his travels
seemed to be, no matter how trivial they were. He didn't
need that sort of stimulation. A man who'd learned to
subdue fear long ago, to eat whenever food was offered
and sleep wherever and whenever he was left alone long
enough, this journey was sheer luxury.

· And so he prowled the cars as though he meant to
walk the miles since he'd left Wyoming Territory. He
was uneasy with luxury. It coddled his body, leaving his
mind too free to roam. A driver to his soul, he liked to
keep his thoughts in tight harness, moving smoothly over
ground he was ready to cross. If he were holding the
reins of six horses in his one hand and directing them by
whip with his other, if his body was braced against their
every movement and his eyes were on them and the road,
he wouldn't be able to indulge in memories of how the
road had felt before. Or wonder where it was taking him
now. But there was nothing else left for him to do. He'd
chatted with passengers, conductors, and engineers. Now
his thoughts were becoming as idle as his hands, and that
bothered him as much as all the other hardships of travel
hadn't. Daydreaming made a man vulnerable.

At the last he succumbed, as he sat looking out the
rain-smeared windows that distorted the sight of the out-
skirts of the city he was about to enter. It seemed he'd
always seen this part of the scenery in a blur. The last
time he'd come to New York, he'd come for a funeral;
the first time he'd left, he'd left in tears.

He'd been nine the first time. Nine, and alone in the
back of the wagon his father drove. He'd not wanted to
leave. His father sat up on the high seat, full of that
fervor he glowed with whenever he set out on a new
venture, crackling with nervous energy, talking sixteen
to the dozen, sounding so sure it seemed strange that his
wife stayed so solemn at his side, and his son tried not
to whimper in the back of the wagon. But they'd heard
his enthusiasm before, and this time they were leaving a
member of their small family behind them. Josh's older

sister was staying in New York with neighbors; she was
too fragile to be forced into this fevered dream.

Still, it might be as Bartholomew Dylan promised: that
she'd soon be sent for and delivered to the mansion he'd
build them in the West, drawn back to them in a golden
coach with milk-white teams. Or else, by then, when he'd
made their fortunes, they'd return to her in splendor and
buy a mansion on Fifth Avenue to hold their joyous
reunion in.

It might be . . . at least, it always seemed possible
when he said it. Anything seemed logical to his wife and
children then, when his incredibly handsome face lit up
with enthusiasm; anything seemed possible when told in
his rich, even voice, with his cultured English accent
making it sound clever and wise. He was an educated
gentleman, no less than the son of a viscount. Only he
was the third son, come to America when he'd come to
nothing but ruin in England, and come in the hopes of
surprising and dazzling his family with his success, at last.

All he'd managed to do was to surprise his wife with
his constant failure. It was as well that she hadn't married
him for his riches, for he hadn't any, or for his promises,
because they never came to anything. It wasn't that he
didn't work. He did, and hard. Nor was it that he drank
to excess, or spent his hard-earned money on other
women, or cards, or dice, or opium eating, or any vice
at all. It was only that he never made very much money,
and whatever he did make, he spent. At once. On things
that caught his eye, or that he thought his wife might
like, or knew he had to have. He appreciated beauty so
much, after all, that was why he'd married his fair,
orphaned bride, British generations back, but of ancestors too insignificant or illegitimate to be documented.
He'd never have been able to marry such a commoner
at home. But here he could do anything he pleased. And
that was what his life was all about: pleasure. Little pleasures that a gentleman might enjoy.

His wages might go for a snuffbox or a silver candle-
stick, a leatherbound book for his library, or an intricate
trinket for his wife's neck. When the rent came due, or
the grocer became hostile, he'd save to pay them and
then celebrate when he came into funds again—with a

fine walking stick to replace the one he'd gotten bored
with, or a bouquet of hothouse flowers of a sort he'd not
seen before. He could always find work, after all. His
father had been a great amateur coachman, and he'd
learned the art at his knee. He was beautifully educated
in everything but business. Because his greatest expendi-
tures were on business ventures, and they were always
the ones offered by men who promised the greatest gain.

On that day twenty years before, his father had been
sure his new venture in the West would bring lavish
rewards. As his son had wept and his wife had sat by his
side, believing him implicitly, as she'd always done, he'd
gone on about Mr. Greeley, and cattle and ranching and
railroads and mines and gold and silver in Oklahoma,
Nevada, California—talking about them all together, as
though they were all together, all waiting for them out
there—somewhere in that land called "West" they were
heading for.

Work waited for them. And more travel. Because they
moved on with every new rumor of riches. Sometimes
Bartholomew Dylan traveled alone—once as far south as
Nicaragua, as part of a grand scheme driving coachloads
of would-be prospectors across that benighted country to
get them to California faster so they could work the rest
of their hearts and health out seeking gold; once as far
north as Canada's prairies, partner in a venture to do
with rare furs. He made enough to live and a little more
to squander, but never gained the riches he expected,
only one unexpected one—another son—born when
Joshua was ten.

Josh was educated in the back of the wagon and at
home, because there wasn't much to be gotten from the
disjointed weeks in various one-room schools as they
traveled on in search of gold or silver or other treasure
at the rainbow's end. But his father had a lot to teach
him, aside from coaching. He never stinted on lending
his own books and buying more for his elder son to
devour. He was careless but not unkind or unloving. He
knew how one-sided his own memory was. Although he
laughed when Joshua groaned at the gaps in his own
knowledge, realizing he'd never learn Greek or Latin
because his father had hated those lessons, he knew how

his son grieved at his secondhand knowledge as he never did for his secondhand clothes. So the one bit of real luck he ever had, the one business venture that paid off, was presented to his elder son in a lump sum that stunned him, dropped on the kitchen table with a flourish—the exact amount needed to send him east to school that year he was almost past old enough to go.

But Joshua had seen more than his father's pride in that moment, he'd seen his mother's eyes. He'd seen how much work she did with no help but his. He'd seen the grocer's bills, and knew exactly how much rent was due, and precisely how much his father yearned to go into that partnership with Bill Gregor in that derelict silver mine they were thinking of trying to reopen. So he handed back the money as cool as you please. And with great enthusiasm, told them about the new job he'd got with the overland stage, now that he was, at fifteen, past the age and interest for formal schooling. And they believed him, every one of them. Because he'd learned the only things his beautiful, feckless, charming, and foolish father never had: how to plan ahead, how to see into other people's hearts, and how to lie.

But he never learned how to lie to himself, so even now there was no way to gloss over that pain and pretend it had all been for the best. Instead, he shook his head and gave up the far past and thought of the second time he'd come to New York. But that only made him remember his sister's funeral, and the way they'd never actually got to see her at it, after all, for all they'd hurried to New York when they'd got the news. Because it turned out they'd burned the victims of the smallpox epidemic as soon as they'd died.

Better to drag the damned train with my teeth, Joshua thought, rising and pacing the length of the train again, annoyed with himself, his leisure, and his memories. Yet when he tried to think about his future, he couldn't help remembering his father and all his mismanaged plots again. And though he'd never made the same mistakes, the thought of what was coming made him as uneasy as the memory of what had been. So he made his way to the front of the train, to talk to the engineer, or the conductor, or to have his damned thoughts blasted away by the train whistle as they came into Central Station in New York.

After Josh claimed his bag and had a final word with the conductor as he tipped him, he heard the man behind him laughing.

"Ha," the hefty man said, "that's rich. Nothing beats the crust of some fellows, eh? Thanking you for keeping *his* train in order and on time. Well, thanks for keeping *mine* on track too."

"You don't understand," the conductor answered, grinning. "It *is* his train. That's Joshua Dylan, out of Wyoming Territory."

"By God!" the man blurted, forgetting the presence of the ladies come to meet him. "And I talked travel to him, and never mentioned hardware at all!"

Way out of Wyoming Territory, Josh thought, hoisting his bag and seeking an exit before the fellow remedied his omission. But he slowed as he found himself gazing up instead of at the signs. He'd a vivid memory of the ceiling of Central Station from his last visit, but he'd thought he'd been impressed at its height because he'd been a boy then. Now he was taller than most men, but still the vaulted arched latticework of steel and glass above him seemed high enough to let clouds drift by beneath it. For a moment he paused, feeling somehow diminished.

The men in New York were no larger than the men in the West, and yet they'd built the station big enough to give headroom to titans. He was used to the low roofs of cabins and ranch houses; even the moderate heights of gracious houses he'd visited in Chicago and New Orleans were dwarfed by this vast space above him. If a man felt belittled by the landscape out west, at least he had the consolation of being the same insignificant size as one of the mountains around him, against the sunset. But here, a man was as nothing, the building seemed to be waiting for something that fitted it.

Then he understood. He squared his shoulders. Everything manmade had a meaning. This was New York, after all. The ceilings, he decided, striding forward, weren't to shrink a man—they were to give him room to grow.

After the cool of the marble vault of the train station, the late-August heat of the city struck him with force. He was used to extremes of temperature, but this was heat aggravated by an irritable city. The cries of drivers and pedestrians trying to cross the streets competed with the sound of horses clattering over the cobbles, and the constant rumble and creak of the many vehicles they pulled made the thick air throb with noise. It reeked with more than that. Joshua was well acquainted with the smell of heated horses and unwashed humanity, but not the stench of so many together. And then too, whatever small breeze their passage produced carried the statistics of how much waste and garbage the two species produced on its breath.

But he was nothing if not adaptable, and however unpleasant, the chaotic mix of noise and stench stirred small lost memories of his childhood to life once more. It was familiar, almost comforting . . . but not quite. Still, he'd endured worse, he'd dare more. He signaled for a hackney cab.

Though he'd wanted to stay at the Fifth Avenue Hotel, in homage to the lost boy who'd gaped at its elegance as he'd been driven out of the city, past it, so long ago, they'd no room; they rented by the month, not the day. At four dollars a day, the Broadway Central, where he was bound, was probably equally lavish. At those prices, it had to be. Even the hansom cab driver he hailed was impressed by the address. But obviously not by his passenger. Because when the driver immediately headed east instead of south, Josh realized he was being taken the long way round to his hotel. It was the oldest trick in the book, but today he didn't care. He couldn't be driven off Manhattan Island, after all, or even up so far as the fields above Sixtieth Street, and so much as he hated to feel he'd been cheated, he enjoyed seeing the city.

And maybe, he admitted, he was just a little unwilling to step out into it so soon. But he disliked being thought a fool. He tapped the ceiling. When the driver slid the trap back, he smiled.

"Thanks for taking the long way," he said as the driver's face grew still. "It's been a while since I was here. But let's not take all day. Down Third and then follow the elevated for a while, then cut west before the Bowery. Okay with you, friend?"

The brisk nod and worried look he got satisfied him. His accent was neither Western nor New York, but a mixture of both—unless he wanted to make a point. His clothes weren't unusual. But his sun-bronzed face was a sure giveaway to his being new to town. New York men, he noticed as the cab crept through thick traffic, were pale as lizards' bellies, even in August. And New York women—he noticed with dazzled delight as he stared out at the streets—were *there*.

That shocked him more than the height of the station's ceiling had, because he hadn't noticed that when he was a boy. There were so many females, of all sizes and conditions, everywhere. He pictured his brother's face if he could see so many breathing examples of his favorite subject, and all on the hoof. Gray, he thought with a smile, mangling a bit of his favorite poetry, thou shouldst be with me at this hour.

He stared in dizzy pleasure. A man just didn't see so many females in the West. Not on the street. Not even in the best brothels. There simply weren't so many there. But here they were, and in vast numbers. Herds of them hurrying along the streets; accompanied, alone, rich and poor, dressed like ladies or shopgirls, they every one of them delighted his eyes.

But as the cab inched downtown, Josh soon noted how many men there were too. He began to feel uneasy for the first time. He'd survived blizzard and storm, he'd fought with fist and guns, he'd thought he'd acquitted himself as well as he could each time. That wasn't to say he didn't know the tinny taste of fear. But he'd swallowed it down each time and gotten on with his life. Now, as he saw how the monster city breathed waves of humanity up and down its crammed streets, he felt trapped along with the hansom cabs and wagons and horse buses, in its clogged arteries. He acknowledged fear, wondering if he was going to be just another bit of grit in its cement gut someday. Josh Dylan grew still and thoughtful as his cab carried him to his hotel.

He was a strong man and a stoic one, but only an idiot didn't have doubts. If they grew too big, it was time to pay attention to them. This move was an enormous one. He'd plenty of money, and though the thought of coming to New York to increase his fortune seemed as sensible as putting sheep to grassland before—now it seemed a presumption. This city had chewed up smarter men than himself.

It wasn't just a gamble for himself; he was all Gray had. Their father had died in a coach accident a decade before: the twin pities were that he'd gone before the money had come in, and that he hadn't been driving the coach that day. Their mother died two years after, while her elder son was nearly breaking his neck trying to keep her in comfort and her younger had been cursing the doctor for not having anything in his bag for the cholera but advice and regrets. If this venture failed, not only would Joshua prove the Dylans were all nothing but doomed dreamers, Gray would have even less than Josh had had at his age. At least he could drive. Gray was, for all his graces, too wild by half to drive professionally, and still too untrained to make the living he should, and could, when he'd finished his schooling.

Well, it wouldn't come to that, Josh decided; he'd too much money to lose all at once, unless he lost his mind too. He'd give the city a trial—six months . . . maybe three. He'd see, he thought angrily.

Uncomfortable with himself and his fears, he gazed out the window again, and chanced to see his own reflection in the glass. He grimaced. He reckoned the accident that had toppled him from his driver's seat that long-ago day the best thing that had ever happened to him, because it got him to thinking seriously about his future. It had broken more than his nose; it had ended his childhood. It made him invest his next week's wages, and it began his climb out of poverty. The accident had changed him physically too, of course. He shrugged it off most of the time as proof of his passage into manhood. His mirror told him more. He wasn't vain. But he wasn't blind. He'd no problem finding female companionship, but once his looks had been like his father's, and had been much remarked on when he'd been a boy. He seldom thought of what had happened to his profile, but it was also true that when he did, he regretted it. Now he disregarded it, focusing on the outer world again.

As the cab crawled onward, he occupied himself with studying the women he saw with a frankness that he'd never have dared back home, or in the streets here. But so many people massed together actually reduced intimacy. He discovered he could stare at a woman no more than a foot away, as she stood on the pavement and his cab paused in the street. Because invariably, she, used to the way to preserve privacy in the big city, never raised her eyes enough to notice his presumption. It gave a man the courage to be rude. It also gave him the eerie feeling that maybe he wasn't there at all.

The women seemed to appear in similar flocks in each different neighborhood he passed through, like the fine-feathered birds they reminded him of. He saw covies of drably plumed shopgirls in their white, gray, and black costumes, along the streets of shops. The ladies among them gleamed and shone out from them, like cardinals and jays in with groupings of sparrows. Their fantastically ornate hats, parasols, and beautifully colored gowns distinguished them at a glance. The plain uniforms of the housemaids and nannies, making them seem as similar as bands of chickadees on a winter morning, began to appear as he moved on past the brownstone fronts of elegant town houses. By the time the cab reached the theater district in the Twenties, he saw few women, which disappointed him, if only for the sake of Gray's expectations. Wherever they were found, whores and actresses always sported the most brilliant plumage.

But then he recalled that the Bowery was where both nighttime professions flourished. Even there, few actresses went about by day. Here in the newer theater district, he couldn't expect to see ladies either, since few patronized the theaters. It was just as well; his game had begun to pall.

It was when he'd begun to brood again, as the hansom stopped in traffic, that he saw the girl. She was paused in a doorway to a theater just a few feet from him. It might have been the way the sun struck her hair, causing the cascade of long curls that showed from beneath her hat to gleam like gold over amber, that caught his eye. He loved the look of light-haired girls almost as much as he loved the touch of light ones. It might have been that whatever was making her hesitate at the door made her turn that pretty head a fraction. She, of all the women he'd seen today, was actually looking at the world around her. That was why she caught him staring at her.

She wore a bottle-green dress in the new close-fitting style he'd seen since he got off the train. No matter how high-buttoned it was, the way it swagged up in the back and clung close in the front showed off a figure to match the lovely face that turned to him. He'd a quick glimpse of white skin, light-filled eyes, and the pink of a plump and pouting mouth that made him draw in his breath. What pleased him the most, though, was that her eyes actually met his.

He didn't look away, as a gentleman should. He smiled at her with frank pleasure. And was astonished when he saw her blush. Because she stared back at him for a moment, and then, before she swung her head away and marched into the theater, he actually saw patches of ragged color fly up in her cheeks. If the carriage hadn't lurched forward at that moment, he wasn't sure that he wouldn't have leapt from it to further their acquaintance. Instead, he settled back, laughing to himself. An actress, blushing! Nothing was impossible in this city, after all.

The cab moved down the avenue, and by the time they came in sight of his hotel, he couldn't remember much about the girl but her coloring and that blush. But the city had shrunk back to a wonderfully human place again by then. A man and a girl, a leer and a blush—a chance encounter had returned his problems to a normal, and so surmountable, size.

Still, before he stepped out of the cab and into the new life he'd chosen, Josh drew a deep breath. The incident had lightened his mood, not his burden. He was back home at last, just where he'd driven himself so hard to be, and for all that it had taken a long time—his lifetime—he wondered if he was really ready. Too smart to have to work with his hands anymore, too rich to drive a stagecoach, but too ignorant to be a true gentleman, and not half rich enough for what he wanted to be—and maybe not quite smart enough to know what that was. . . . But he had to find out, didn't he? Anyway, it was too soon and too late to turn back.

He remembered his father's books, and as his hand clenched on the door handle, in a moment of whimsy he looked out at the city and thought: *En garde!*

But then he remembered his own hard-won knowledge, and where it came from. He opened the door and stepped out.

He planted his feet apart on the pavement and looked around.

"Well, all right, then," he murmured, grinning, "have it your way, you big cement bastard. Draw whenever you're ready."

And then, finally, he laughed. Because, finally, he reckoned he was ready.

2

SHE HEARD the sound of singing, so she knew she'd come to the right place. And although she'd never meant to walk in so quickly, she exhaled and relaxed a fraction. At least she hadn't barged into the wrong place, and that was something; any small thing that went well today was a blessing. Nothing else had: the ferry had been late, the heat of the day had grown intense, so now her dress clung to her skin in uncomfortable and possibly indecent ways, her hair had sprung into Medusa coils, that horrid, vulgar man had leered at her, frightening her into leaping into the theater . . . Lucy Markham swallowed hard. All the rest was as nothing as she realized she was actually inside a theater now.

For all that she'd traveled all morning to get here, there was every possibility she might never have stepped over the doorsill if she hadn't been molested. Well, she amended as she stood in the dim entryway, it had felt like being molested. Bad enough that she hadn't been able to sleep peacefully for a week, worrying over the step she'd just taken, the look on the man in the hackney's face had confirmed every one of those fears that had kept her up half last night. She couldn't remember his face, except for its having been ruggedly attractive and distinctly male, because there was no getting past that broad leer it had grown when he saw where she was standing. She didn't blame him in the least, although she'd fled in an instant. After all, who else but an actress would be alone in the doorway to a theater? No respectable female, certainly. What she'd gotten was exactly what she'd feared, expected, and now deserved.

Because she'd gone into the theater at last, and she knew now that she wouldn't go out until she'd tried for

the position. To fail because you'd never had the courage
to try was bad enough. A hundred excuses could, in time,
cover over it, she supposed, renaming it wisdom or dis-
cretion. But to flee just before your trial was to lack
spirit as well as courage. No excuse would ever forgive
panic. Or judge it anything but cowardice. Lucy Markham was very glad she hadn't laced her stays too tightly
today, because the thought of what she was about to do
made her feel faint enough. And for all her resolve, there
still was every possibility that she would have stood in
the alcove at the backstage of the theater, congratulating
herself on stepping inside and preparing for her coming
ordeal until sunset, or until the audition was actually
over, if a man passing with a notebook in his hand hadn't
noticed her and, inclining his head, absently said, "In
there, missy. They're all in there."

Because then she knew she would have looked even
more conspicuous ignoring him and continuing to stand
there dithering.

"Thank you very much," she said bravely, although
he'd already disappeared around a corner, and she
gripped her handbag hard and made her way toward the
crowd of people she could see milling about on the side
of the stage.

"Lilac, my darling, my heart, my only love," a smooth
and charming tenor voice called from the darkness of
the empty audience, "*do* remember that the gentlemen
beyond the fifth row deserve to hear you even if they
did pay less for the privilege. Now, again please."

A petite young woman with a hairdo so shockingly
yellow and frizzed that it looked like a dandelion's and
not a woman's, glared back into the darkness. Even if
she hadn't stood center stage, she would have commanded the eye. Her ample frame was packed into a
gown that was maroon with red festoons and she wore
so much paint upon her face that it looked too theatrical even on the stage. Lucy halted in her steps behind
a huddle of other women who were watching, and her
eyes grew wide as she stared at the actress. They grew
wider when a piano took up a tune and she began to
sing it.

Refrain, audacious tar,
  Your suit from pressing,
Remember what you are,
  And whom addressing!

Then, just as Lucy, wincing, was about to step back
to get away from all the dogs she was sure would come
rushing from the shadows to respond to such high-
pitched wailing, the singer stopped abruptly and continued, after a broad wink to the unseen audience, with a
singsong recitation: "I'd laugh my rank to scorn in holy
union, if he were more highly born, or I more lowly!"

Then she stopped, looking triumphant, as a tall bored-
looking woman to her left side, whom Lucy hadn't taken
in with her first stunned glance, sang back, in a passable
alto: "Proud lady, have your way, unfeeling beauty! You
speak and I obey, it is my duty! . . ."

"No!" The man's voice came from the darkness again,
cutting off the tall woman's recital. "Not 'in holy
union'—'in union holy'! I know it means the same
thing," the voice said wearily, "but it does not rhyme.
The words rhyme, you see—'holy' . . . 'lowly'. Rhyme.
Like 'cat,' 'bat,' 'hat.' That's that whole point. Go on.
No, not you, Jewel. Lilac. Take it all over again."

The young woman he'd named Lilac placed one hand
to her brow in a gesture of exhaustion, while, Lucy
noted, she planted her shiny little high-heeled shoes apart
militantly.

"I have sung it twice already and I am fatigued," she
said.

Although Lucy was profoundly grateful to hear that,
there was a muttering, and a moment later a young man
put one hand on the stage and vaulted up to it from the
empty audience. He stalked over to Lilac, and though
he wasn't very tall, he seemed to tower over her. It was
his attitude, Lucy decided, as well as the fact that his
opponent was tiny, that made him seem so large. He was
willowly and slender to the point of emaciation, although,
Lucy conceded, Lilac's swelling bosom might be causing
that impression by contrast too. But he was long-faced
and white-skinned, with soft billows of ink-black hair that
he threaded his long graceful hands through before he

spoke. And when he did, it was in a silken voice all at
odds with his ferocious demeanor.

"You do not have a contract yet, I remind you, my
sweet Lilac," he said.

"*You* do not have an audience without me, I remind
you, my dear Kyle," the young woman answered with a
smirk.

"I do not ask for very much," he answered, gesturing
toward the onlookers as if for their agreement. "I am
not a hard fellow to get on with . . ."

"Oh, not hard at all, I daresay," Lilac said sweetly,
glancing from beneath her heavily kohled eyelashes
toward the sidelines for reaction too, as he went on piti-
ably, "All I ask is that we begin to do some work. A play
cannot be mounted without work—nothing, actually, can
be mounted without *some* effort—present company ex-
cepted, of course," he said charmingly in an aside to
Lilac.

"I did the damned thing twice," Lilac snapped, as
Lucy drew in her breath at the profanity, "and I didn't
have luncheon yet. If you want me, Kyle, you'll let me
alone now. Go bother the chorus," she said, turning, as
if dismissing him, although she added, "Or chase your
tail. It'll be good practice for when you try humans," as
she stalked off the stage with as much majesty as such a
plump young woman could muster in a dress that hobbled her at the knees.

The young man's long-fingered white hands clenched
at his sides as he watched her leave. But then he wheeled
around and fixed the assembled women watching him
with a cold stare.

"All right," he said dispassionately, "we'll run through
it until the queen finishes stuffing herself again. Sopra-
nos," he called, gesturing to stage right, "here. Alto's
. . . there"—he indicated the left—"come along, I told
you what you were yesterday, move along."

The mass of women began to separate in desultory
fashion, some going into one cluster, others walking into
the other. There were, Lucy noted when they'd done it,
about ten in the "soprano" group, some dozen in the
other. But once there, they did nothing else. Except,
she noted with sudden terror, to stare back toward her.

She was, she realized, left standing alone at the side of the stage. The young man regarded her with a weary eye.

"Baritone, I presume?" he asked in laconic tones.

"Miss Frances!" she blurted.

When the silence began to drag on, she spoke all at once. "I didn't know that you'd already done it . . . cast the play, I mean. I came to audition. I thought it was today. Well, it is the twenty-fifth, isn't it? Oh, I daresay it's the twenty-sixth, there you are," she said, realizing she was running on at the mouth now, as she always did when she was nervous, but no more able to stop than she was to pick up her skirts and run away, as she longed to do. "I've got the date wrong again, as I always do. How disappointed Miss Frances will be, but there you are, the twenty-sixth, still, after all my worries and preparations, such a long trip on the ferry, and so hot today too, but the twenty-sixth, who would have thought it?" she said as her voice faltered and she heard, with enormous gratitude, that she'd stopped talking.

"It's the twenty-fifth," the young man said, before he stepped nearer and looked at her more closely. Then he smiled, and as he slowly walked around her, studying her, asked mildly, conversationally, as she shrank back, without moving a step, "Who is Miss Frances?"

Her eyes grew wide in consternation. He smiled again, this time, at how lovely they were.

"The other chorus instructor. At the church," she said. Someone sniggered as she went on, babbling again, she thought with horror as she heard her voice explaining, "She said she'd heard you were casting for a production of *Pinafore* here today, and as I had said, ah, rather say, that as she knew that the wages would be welcome, more than that, actually, and that I might be able to overcome my compunctions . . . well, *HMS Pinafore* after all, is not precisely 'theater' . . . ah," she said with great effort, wrenching herself out of her convoluted explanation, "I was going to try to see . . . I was going to try out for it."

"We can always use a singer," the young man said, and as Lucy wondered why a man who was going to present an operetta would say such a queer thing, he reached out, took her hand in his, and led her like a sleepwalker to the front of the stage. "Now, tell us what you'd like to sing and Mr. Bascombe over at the piano there will play it," he said, and as she continued to look at him, he added softly, "Do relax. I used to stammer, impossible as it is to conceive, I grant you, but so I did, myself, once upon a time."

"Ah," she said, but as he sighed and started to shake his head, she surprised him and herself by saying without preamble, " 'Little Buttercup.' Oh. And I'm a soprano, Mr. Bascombe, so the key of C, please."

She didn't need the music in front of her. She'd committed it to heart. It wasn't because of her quick ear, it was because it was on everyone's lips. The tune floated out from church choir lofts as well as from behind the swinging doors of every tavern with a piano; it was trumpeted by every German band in the street, just as every organ-grinder's monkey capered to it as it was cranked out for the children to dance to. New York was *Pinafore* mad, and had been from the moment it had first been heard last winter. Even the newspapers said so.

Lucy Markham heard the opening notes and closed her eyes. The young man said he used to stammer, and she knew that some stutterers could sing without a pause; she'd taught some children with that affliction how to do it. Song was a thing apart from speech, a thing quite removed from that sort of conscious thought. It was a thing entirely of its own, and it was everything to her. She heard the music and forgot all her trepidation, and sang.

Kyle Harper's smile slid away as he heard her. He forgot to gloat over the fact that he'd got such a boon as this little beauty for his production. He'd been staring at her, assessing her physical attributes with growing excitement. But, he thought, her skin was as clear and free of stain as if she'd already put on makeup—that faint color in her cheeks was only her own warm blood beneath the skin, not rouge over it. Her eyes were almond-shaped and wide and clear and lightest brown, ringed with lush lashes. Her nose was small and straight, her lips too full for anything but kissing or the stage. But the balcony couldn't see that. They'd see that glorious hair, the way it curled in long separate strands, as though she'd spent an hour crimping it, although, from the way it shone, he doubted she had. They'd see the color—the way it ran red to gold around each twisted curl. Then they'd see those lovely high breasts, the neat waist—he'd wager it could be nipped in even more with the right corset—the flippant curve of her saucy derriere that green dress was swagged up upon—she scarcely needed that bit of bustle—and then the legs . . . well, some things remained to be seen.

He considered her without lust, or at least without the sort of lust he knew in more intimate circumstances. He was seized in the grip of a blinder desire, the need for acquisition, and he counted over her charms with the glee of a miser sorting coins. But he stopped cataloging her attractions when he heard her sing.

Kyle Harper stood absolutely still and forgot his plans as well as himself as she sang, and that was extraordinary for him. But her voice was lovely, pure and sweet: it dipped, it trilled, it rose to thrill, and gracefully rippled down again, and, he realized with growing excitement as sense began to filter back to him as she came to the close of her simple song, it was pure English that she sang.

The applause when she was done brought Lucy back to reality, and though she glanced to the admiring ladies who'd given her tribute, then she turned her eyes to the silent young man for his reaction. He was, she noted with some return of her anxiety, not clapping. Instead, he stared at her, disbelieving.

"You're English!" he said, as though it were an accusation.

"No, no," she said, shaking her head as he persisted, pointing a long finger at her.

"You sang English."

"Well, yes," she said, mystified, "it is an English opera and I thought it sounded better that way and—"

"It was real English," he persisted, but in a lower voice as he took her by the elbow and drew her aside so that he could speak with her privately.

"Oh. Well, my grandmother, on my mother's side, you see, was British, and she raised me. My other grandmother, however, was not, and often mocked me for it, but I always—"

But he'd taken the measure of her speech and realized that she usually put her answer in her first reply, and so simply cut her off to ask, over her ongoing explanation, "Can you speak English too?"

As someone who had the utmost difficulty explaining herself, she was quick enough to understand someone else's attempts at communication, however odd.

"Yes," she said, smiling, speaking up in her grandmother's well-remembered clipped and high arched British accents. "Well, of course I can, although, mind you, I was brought up right here in New York City—Brooklyn, in point of fact, and—"

"You're hired!" he called out, laughing, relief and wild joy in his dark eyes. "Too young to be Buttercup, no matter how sweetly you sang it, but . . . perfect! . . . Oh, yes, dearest Lilac," he said merrily as the small blond woman appeared onstage, her purse in hand, as though she'd been about to step out, but had returned for the applause, as any actress would. "Have a nice luncheon, do. You may take as long as you like with it— an hour, a week, or a month. It's all the same to me. Behold!" he said as he turned Lucy around to face the other woman. "Our new Josephine!"

"She won't get you the audience I can," Lilac cried.

"I daresay not," he answered. "They'll be sober."

"*I* have a reputation," Lilac screamed.

"But she'll earn one for *singing*," he countered.

"You moved heaven and earth to get me," she persisted. "You're an unknown, I was doing you a favor."

"Do me another one, dear, wave good-bye," he said, never looking at her, as he continued to stare at Lucy.

"I'll never work for you again," Lilac vowed, her eyes wild.

" 'Again' is hardly the correct word, is it?" he asked. "Or do you remember our last discussion? Fare thee well, Miss Landau," he said dismissively, waving his long hand at her back as she sailed from the theater.

He broke the silence after the back door was slammed hard enough to cause the stage curtains to sway.

"Now, then, you may take a break, my dears," he said

absently to the assembled singers. As they began to talk among themselves, he put his hands behind his back and smiled at Lucy.

"Let's just see what we have here, aside from the right voice and accent," he said with great merriment, but then, Lucy had noted that every one of his many moods seemed accentuated. "A face that Rossetti would weep for, although," he said with mock seriousness, "the nose is a trifle short," and as her hand flew up to that small nose, he went on, "a figure that would make Venus de Milo want to scratch your pretty amber eyes out for—if she'd hands, that is," he said laughing. "Now, then, Miss Edwards," he called, "come out here, we've some costumes to alter."

Lucy stood silently, stunned, as the young man waited for the seamstress to join him onstage. She scarcely dared breathe. It was beyond her every expectation, and she knew it wouldn't do to start thinking about it now. She tried to still her thoughts lest she listen to the small voices already clamoring to be heard. She'd only overcome her repugnance at the immorality of appearing on the stage in the first place because she needed the money, and in the most important place, by convincing herself that she'd never be noticed in the chorus. But now—to be offered a starring role? She wanted to do it as badly as she was terrified of doing it. So she held herself still and refused to consider the matter just now, because the more deeply committed she became before sanity and conscience reasserted themselves, the harder it would be to stop herself from going through with it. She tried to listen to what the man was murmuring to the white-haired woman who had come to his side.

"Now, then," he continued, speaking to the seamstress, who was studying Lucy with him, "we don't have to just show the top, she hasn't got much height, but she's got the length too, you see, which Lilac sadly lacked. Bother. Josephine doesn't wear tights," he muttered obscurely.

Lucy thought she must have heard wrong. He seemed to brood before his mood brightened and he said, "But ingenues can have knee-length skirts, can't they? Something that flounces up when she bounces, yes. Don't you think? Perfect. Absolutely," he answered himself, before he addressed Lucy, "Raise your skirts, miss . . . ah, what is your name, dear?" he asked, laughing at himself this time.

"Raise my what?" Lucy said.

"Your skirts, dearie," the seamstress said through the pins she'd popped in her mouth.

"Good heavens, no," Lucy said, backing up.

"Come now," he said indulgently, "this is no time to be kittenish. We've only a few weeks until opening. But we do have a big rental fee and a small budget. The sooner we can get you girls in costume, the sooner we can begin."

"I can't show my *legs*," Lucy said in a fierce whisper, looking furtively around her, although, clearly, he was the one who was mad.

"Come, come," he said patiently. "Unless there's something wrong with them, I can't see why not."

She gaped at him.

"What a bother," he said. "Here, what's the problem? None of the other girls mind in the least. And half of them will be in tights."

"Tights?" Lucy asked dumbly. "Why would they be wearing tights if they're in *Pinafore*?"

"Well," he said on a rich chuckle, "sailors can scarcely come out singing lustily in *skirts*, can they? . . . It's an all-girl cast, after all, miss . . . Ah, whatever is your name, dear?"

"Good-bye," Lucy said, and was halfway to the door before he could comment on what an odd name that was.

"There are at present in New York six versions of *HMS Pinafore* for the astute theatergoer to chose from," Kyle Harper lectured. "At this moment, that is. Last week, there were seven. By next week there may be ten or a round dozen. For highest quality, there's the production at the Standard, but there's another good one a block away, and two passable ones competing down in the Bowery. That is not all. You look kindhearted, Miss Markham," he said, with the sort of condescension that made Lucy squirm. "Do you like children? Ah, then you can see a troupe of the most cunning little dears this side

of seasickness doing their version of *Pinafore* just down
the street this very afternoon. I do not wish to press the
point," he said with growing agitation as he paced back
and forth in front of the chair Lucy was anxiously
perched upon, "or to make undue inquiries into your
religious feelings, but I will add that if you are of that
persuasion, you might be interested in a yet another mar-
velous production of *Pinafore* that is in Yiddish—yes, the
language of the less ancient Hebrews—not a half-mile
from where I stand. No doubt," he said bitterly, "there
is one in Sanskrit being rehearsed even as I speak.

"My point," he said, wheeling about and looking down
at Lucy, "is that at least no one else is doing an all-
female production at the moment. Yes, one, as you so
deftly put it, with 'legs.' Although," he brooded, "no
doubt our deposed Queen Lilac is already using her own
squat little limbs to hasten to another producer's office
to try to steal my fire. That is why I can no longer delay.
Surprise and novelty are *everything* in the theater. I gave
you the role, Miss Markham, before witnesses. I dismissed Miss Lilac for you. I raised your salary over what
I'd offered her," he lied, as the other girl in the room
coughed. "Four dollars a week is unheard-of for an amateur," he said with more force, that being true enough,
pausing to glare at the now-straight-faced girl before he
turned back to regard Lucy with glittering eyes.

"Come, this reticence no longer serves a purpose," he
said impatiently. "May we now begin to rehearse?"

Lucy swallowed hard. The salary was beyond her
dreams. But so was this conversation. The only reason
they were having it was that it would have been unlady-
like to struggle, and also completely useless. If Kyle
Harper had not bodily swept her up and carried her to
this tiny office of his when she'd begun to leave, he might
just as well have done so. He'd insisted she come, and
had promptly ordered a girl from the chorus to come
along for the sake of propriety to still her last protests,
and now they both stared at Lucy, waiting for her
answer.

There were a great many things she could have
answered. If it had been hard for her to imagine how
she'd nerve herself to appear on a stage in a chorus, and

harder still to accept that they wanted her to appear, alone, merely singing pretty songs—the idea of appearing and showing her legs was absolutely unthinkable. She might as well walk naked and be done with it. Actually, she thought miserably, showing her legs on a stage was worse than walking on the street without clothing. Because a nude woman in public would only be considered a madwoman. But a semiclothed woman onstage was a . . . harlot. An actress.

If she were to lose her mind and abandon decency, she'd just as surely lose the respect of anyone that mattered to her. Most of all, of course, she'd lose her own for herself. Respectable young women did not do such things. But she knew that Kyle Harper wouldn't understand. He glowered at her and she was afraid that if she tried to explain, she'd soon be nattering in nervousness again, and fail to make her point. But somehow, she knew he'd be able to coerce her, and then she'd have to do it, and then, with all her decency gone, there'd be no choice left but to run away from home or end it all in some awful way, as the wayward girls in the novels she read did. . . . There, she thought miserably, she was already babbling in her mind, just trying to think of how to answer him. But he was so formidable-looking.

He wasn't above average height, but he had a gift of making himself look larger. Close as they were now, she could see no wrinkles or lines on that intense face, and she realized he might not be any older than she herself was. But he'd the ability to appear to be any age from those twenty years to double or triple them. And she was sitting on a chair and he was standing, and the other girl was staring at her. Worst of all, she admitted, deep down she knew that the money offered was beyond wonderful and she wanted to accept it so badly she had to let him know how impossible it would be for her to accept it.

"You didn't see my . . . legs . . . when you let Miss Lilac go and offered me the position. They might well have been odd-looking anyway, so I don't feel guilty and I don't think I owe you anything, no matter what you say," she said, and stopped for breath, very proud of the way she'd come around an unexpected corner to make an excellent point.

"There's nothing wrong with your legs, and if there was, we could always pad out your stockings," he said.

"Oh," Lucy said miserably, before she murmured, her eyes growing bright with unshed tears as she tried to explain, "But only actresses . . ." She darted a look to the impassive girl watching her, and couldn't go further with that thought and so ended feebly, ". . . but I am not an actress, I only came to sing, you see, preferably in a chorus, where I'd be unremarked upon. Miss Frances said nothing about legs," she muttered, and then grew pink at the thought, because she couldn't imagine Miss Frances ever saying that word, much less knowing about that requirement.

Kyle Harper stopped his pacing and considered Lucy as she sat, distinctly wilting, fumbling in her handbag for whatever someone might be seeking so that she wouldn't have to look up. But when he spoke, his voice was so warm and soft and comforting that she did look, and saw that there was such understanding and tenderness in his dark eyes that his thin face looked less feral and ratlike— as it had moments before—than it did princely and patrician now.

"There is nothing wrong with showing limbs," he said gently, "onstage. As there is nothing wrong with being an actress. The word," he said majestically, "is not synonymous with 'whore.' " As she gasped, he went on in his velvety voice, looking sternly at her, "It is in the dictionary, Miss Markham, and if ministers say it in their sermons, why should I not? I wish to make it clear. I'm not just speaking of Lydia Thompson's song-and-dance reviews—which everyone agrees are decorous, and have been for years now, even if they glorify female limbs. No, I'll not even bother to discover if you find that controversial, as some fire-and-brimstone types still do. No, Miss Markham, I speak of art.

"Acting is a noble profession, brought low by little minds. Would you have Mr. Shakespeare not have written Viola, Rosalind, or Portia?" he accused in a thunderous voice. "They dress as men on the stage, after all. And dressing so, appear in tights. Should those immortal lines be struck from the language and lost forever, then?

The theater is a place for fantasy. Art must go on, it cannot stoop to accommodate filthy minds."

Lucy grew still. Even the girl from the chorus seemed as impressed as Kyle Harper himself did. He'd made an excellent point. But for all of it, and despite his bombast, after she'd gotten over the effect of his performance, Lucy remembered that they were really discussing girls in tights playing at being sailors in an operatta that would sound much better if the sailors were men, after all. She thought a moment longer. Kyle Harper began to smile. But then Lucy's chin came up and she surprised them both again.

"Legs," she said, "will not profit your *Pinafore*."

She went on quickly, before the vagrant thought stole away, without rambling, because she wasn't so much nervous as thoughtful now. "*Pinafore* sounds better with men, after all. And singing is what it's all about. If you think men will come to see this production because of girls, I don't. I think the one with children, or even the Sanskrit one, would do better, actually. Everyone knows *The Black Crook* has two hundred female legs in it. And everybody goes to see that if they want legs . . . and other parts on view. Or they go see *Evangeline* or something else just like it at Niblo's Garden. They've got girls in tights and short trousers and what-all. Well, I know all about that because I do teach music at a church—and it's what the minister talks about every Sunday," she said defiantly. "So, a little production of *Pinafore* done by all women may be different, but more bizarre than profitable, I'd think. Yes," she said with some spirit, as the truth of what she'd said was borne in upon her, "if I'd three legs, I don't doubt it would be the first time Josephine was sung by a three-legged soprano—but I don't think it would be particularly attractive."

The ensuing silence was as profound and filled with the sound of her own rapid pulse as an empty seashell held to her ear might have been. And then Kyle Harper started laughing. When he stopped, he looked to the other girl, his eyes dancing, excitement and elation evident on his expressive face.

"Leave us," he said to the other girl, "and close the door.

"Now," he said, smiling at Lucy as the girl left, "we'll see what you can do for four dollars a week."

"You will have to kill me first," Lucy said, sliding off the chair, crouching, and backing to the door.

He stopped, and seemed puzzled. Then he laughed again, but in a tone which chilled her.

"Good heavens," he said, looking down his thin nose at her as though she'd left something nasty on the chair, "your virtue is the last thing you have to worry about. I do not buy my pleasures—or I wouldn't if I could afford them," he sighed. "Oh, do sit down, will you? See here, Miss Markham, money is precisely what it's about. There's a great deal of it to be made in the theater, art is all very well, but it's money makes art possible. If no one ever paid to see Shakespeare's plays he wouldn't have been able to eat enough to live to write them—he was a dreadful actor, you know. Or at least, he must have been, all he ever played was ghosts, I understand. . . . But what has that to do with anything? My Lord! It must be catching. Now you've got me doing it," he said, frowning.

She laughed at that, and that seemed to be what he'd been after, because he grew serious again.

"I needed a device," he said, "a hook, if you will. A quirk. Something that would make people come to see my *Pinafore*. It's the perfect thing to produce now, everyone loves it and there are no royalties to be paid. Mr. Gilbert and Mr. Sullivan are in England, and they've no American copyright. It's not just the music that makes it as popular with producers as it is with the public," he said wryly. "And everyone loves legs now, they're the rage. It seemed perfect: original . . . profitable. But, alas, you're right. So far as legs go, I can't compete," he sighed again.

"I'm terribly sorry," she said, standing up again, "but I'd never have been able to wear tights onstage anyway."

"Of course not. Josephine doesn't wear them. You've tights on the brain, my dear," he answered absently. "But you will play Josephine. I'll hire on some gentlemen who can sing. We'll do our *Pinafore*, even so."

"I won't show my legs," she said nervously, because she knew there had to be something other than *Pinafore* he was thinking of doing; he was beginning to smile and notice her again.

"Of course you will, you're not an idiot. In fact, you're very, very clever. But the finest productions have the ladies in fetching costumes—it's part of the fun. A bit of leg's expected on the stage, after all. You'll get used to it because it will make you a great deal of money. Because you will be my star. My bright and shining star."

"Oh, yes, of course," she said. "Me. Lucy Markham, with her name on a handbill outside, no doubt. 'Come see Lucy Markham and her legs.' Good-bye, Mr. Harper."

" 'Come see the English Rose, and hear her magnificent voice. Straight from . . .' Where did your grandmother come from?" he asked as she stopped and cocked her head to the side, listening to him.

"Ah. Cornwall . . . and then London," she said hesitantly, because an idea was beginning to take shape in her mind.

"Exactly," he said, beaming upon her. "Everyone's mad for Europeans. Always have been. If it comes from there, it's better than here, everyone knows that. Everyone with money goes abroad—from Barnum to Vanderbilt, it's over the sea for culture and class. They hire French chefs and English nannies, and try to get titled European anythings to marry their daughters. The poor would too, if they could. American is boring, if it isn't second-rate. Why, there isn't a theatrical troupe floundering in cow country that doesn't say it's performed before crowned heads so as to draw the locals in. I've been in a few," he muttered.

But he brightened again. "Just think!" he said, gesturing as though she could see the whole thing printed out on the wall. "A *Pinafore* with a beautiful English girl as star. One who can sing. And one with mysterious relatives, which is why we can't be too specific about her past with the press . . . maybe even with a royal in the woodpile, eh? *You* can speak in British, as well as sing in it. And," he said as she paused, thinking of all he said, "Miss Lucy Markham's legs will never have to go on public view. Not when it will be Miss . . . Rose! Yes, a lovely English Rose. Miss Rose . . . Merchant . . . no, Mason . . . no, no, Miss Lucy Rose will be the one exhibiting her shapely limbs. They'll love it, they'll adore it. And we, sweet Lucy, will love it even more. For we shall be rich.''

"But that's a lie," Lucy said in a small voice that dwindled as she spoke, as the idea and its ramifications grew larger.

"No," he said imperially, "that's *theater*."

She'd rehearsed her lines so carefully that, of course, she got them wrong when the time came. But that may have been because the time hadn't really come. Because instead of rejoicing to find the house empty when she got home, and taking advantage of it by going directly to bed, Lucy had hung about the kitchen fretting and anticipating events. So naturally she blurted it out the moment she saw her grandmother. She hadn't even been asked. That could have been precisely why she'd spoken, because of a last vagrant hope that she'd be talked out of her decision. Or maybe, she admitted to herself before her mind skittered away from the idea, because of exactly the reverse.

But instead of saying it smoothly, in a confident recitation, she simply blurted, "I secured a position in New York City today, and so of course I can't continue to live here and travel to and fro every day, I'd be late, and coming home too late, and so I'll have to move to rooms in the city, Grandmother."

"Doing what?" her grandmother asked, looking up from the teakettle she'd put on the stove.

"Ah," she said, forgetting every plausible lie, as she always did when faced with an unblinking stare, "singing . . . in a theater, but really it is entirely proper. It'll be light opera, after all . . ."

"How much are they paying you?" her grandmother asked.

Then, of course, she remembered, too late, that this lady would never object to her appearing onstage, or living alone, or doing anything at all, actually. She was her grandmother, but not her "Grandmama," and it was foolish to keep pretending she was. Lucy gazed at her grandmother sadly. The woman she looked at was large and sharp-featured; she'd been dark-haired in her youth and was light-eyed, not at all like herself. They didn't think alike any more than they looked alike. Sometimes Lucy found it hard to remember they were really related, except for the fact that Mrs. Markham did let her live with her, and at a reduced rent. It was the title "Grandmother" and the fact that it was historically true, at least, that made Lucy forget that. That, and the fact that she so badly missed her "Grandmama."

"I'm being paid quite nicely, very well, in fact, generously, actually, ah . . . four dollars a week," Lucy admitted, as she always had to do when matters came to a point and she was dealing with someone who knew what her wretched verbal stumbling meant.

A spasm of pain crossed over her grandmother's face.

"Four!" she exclaimed. "Lord, if Gwennie could only have been able to sing," she sighed.

Well, there it was, Lucy thought, biting her lip and looking away. Aside from the fact that this grandmother found nothing wrong with her granddaughter appearing onstage, and thought it shocking only in that it paid so well, she couldn't even think about it without deeming it a pity it hadn't happened to her other granddaughter. It was reasonable, if regrettable. Lucy and her sister had the same parents, but no one ever pretended they had the same grandparents.

Seven years separated Lucy and Gwendolyn, but they might have been seven centuries, their upbringings had been so different. When their father had deserted their mother, his elder daughter, Gwendolyn, had been sent to live with his widowed mother. And when Mama had taken up with Mr. Denning a year later, her parents, appalled and mortified, had swooped down and delivered the baby, Lucy, from the scene of the immorality. By the time their father had gotten his divorce and his new bride and settled somewhere in the wilds of New Jersey, Gwendolyn had been too firmly ensconced with his mother to pry loose, even if his new bride had had any intention of letting her set foot in her new house. And when Mama had finally married a Mr. Richards, she mightn't even have mentioned her two daughters—they'd never know now: Mama had died as she'd left them, without sending a word.

Gwennie had known all this from the start, and she'd let Lucy know. They'd lived at different ends of Brooklyn, and it might have been different planets, but they'd visited now and again, here and there, down through the years. Otherwise, Lucy mightn't ever have known all the truth; her grandparents had been too mortified by their errant daughter to speak of it directly. Which wasn't to say they'd been prissy, as Mrs. Markham always said. It was only that they'd been people of firm morals, as Lucy always tried to explain. And from England, after all.

So Gwennie grew up as her grandmother's adored delight: saucy, pert, and indulged in everything. And Lucy grew up as her grandparent's chance to right a wrong. Which was never to say she hadn't been loved equally well, she always thought defensively—just differently. Gwennie might have been able to win a new frock for every frown, but Lucy had been taught she could win approval for her smile. Neither family was well-off, but Gwennie had tutors at home for piano and dance, so as to secure a husband in time. Lucy was allowed to finish high school, so as to secure an education for herself. Gwennie had got treats and luxuries, cosseting and compliments all her life, so it was only reasonable that was all she'd looked for from a husband when she'd chosen the draper Mr. Hodges—aside from his bank account. But as for herself, Lucy thought whenever the loneliness became too profound, at least she'd gotten genuine love, earned and returned with interest. Which was why she'd no interest in settling for anything less now, and was why she still had no husband.

That—and the other reason Lucy understood, but tried not to think about. Which was that Gwennie was never more than flippant on the subject of their parents and what they'd done, and Lucy had never been anything less than shamed by it. She didn't have Grandmama or Grandfather to console her any longer either. They'd been old when she was young, and were gone now; Grandfather years before, Grandmama just two years past. It was two years of living with Gwennie's grandmother that had sent Lucy to the city to try to find a way to support herself other than marrying.

"With her looks and a voice too . . ." Grandmother

left off dreaming of even more spectacular grandsons-in-law than Mr. Hodges, and fastened her watery blue gaze on Lucy. "Where?" she asked.

"Ah, they haven't got a theater yet," Lucy lied with astonishing speed and ease, proving to herself that Mr. Darwin was right, nature did help the weak evolve in order to protect them.

Clearly her grandmother didn't believe her, but just as obviously, she didn't care. Lucy didn't contribute much to the house. As her sister always jested, Lucy's grandparents hadn't much to leave her except for some furniture in storage, some trinkets in Lucy's jewel box, and a lot of useless clutter in her head.

"When?" her grandmother asked, her thoughts already turning to the pleasant notion that there'd be a room to rent out now.

"Monday," Lucy said promptly. "I'll be staying at a very respectable boardinghouse, I assure you," she added, wishing that she could assure herself of the same thing, despite what Kyle Harper had promised.

Her grandmother nodded. If this had been Gwennie, she thought, she'd be having a good laugh with her about it. About the gentlemen she'd be meeting, about her chances for making her fortune and finding a rich man. Having a laugh? Lord, wouldn't she just have been halfway upstairs already, packing to go with her, to share with her as well as to protect her? But this wasn't Gwennie. She sighed, causing Lucy to brace herself for a question or comment that never came. After all, Mrs. Markham thought, if it had been Gwennie, she'd have cared.

3

"DEAR GRAY," he wrote, "Just a quick letter to let you know all is well with me. I've only been settled in two days, but the hotel's a good one, and I'll stay here until further notice. Today I'm meeting Litton again, and he's taking me to his club for lunch. He wants me to join."

Joshua Dylan stopped writing, lost in wonder at the thought of himself a member of a New York gentlemen's club. Then he shook his head and wrote again; he'd no time to marvel. Still, with all he had to do today, this came first. Gray would worry until he heard from him. But after only two days in New York City, there wasn't much to tell. He had to be inventive. A three-line letter was as insulting as it was proof of an arid brain. He grinned and wrote again.

"I went to the theater last night. Strictly for you, old scout. There was some music, which I didn't remember long enough to hum in the lobby. But there also was an incredible display of feminine charms. Don't grip this page so tight, you'll tear it."

He laughed aloud as he blotted the lines before he put pen to paper again.

"But I didn't get to do that research you were so interested in. I'd never have believed it," he wrote, "I know you won't. But there can be too much of a good thing. One girl in a room with a man is exciting, but believe me, Scout, one hundred is daunting. A glimpse of ankle is enough to get a man thinking. A look at two hundred shapely ones kicking together isn't—at least to get him thinking about the same thing. It's like trying to hoot and whistle at a centipede. You're too young for this letter, I think, so I'll end it. I'll write again soon. Start packing, understand? My next letter will go to New

Haven, and if you aren't there to get it, I would not wish my dearest enemy to be in your particular boots. With much affection, yr. brother."

He signed his name. But then he frowned and added a scrawled postscript.

"And don't test my theory with the Peterson sisters, as I expect you're itching to do. Moses Peterson is a man of strong convictions. They mostly concern shotguns and preachers. Which is why those two are still not married."

Good brotherly advice, he thought as he sealed the letter. But better, he thought, that autumn and the school term were beginning. He wouldn't wager two bits on how long good brotherly advice would be able to stand up to Gray's current obsession—or against the Peterson sisters' enticements. The girls might not be raving beauties, but they were healthy, young, and breathing ones, and so were prime articles on the marriage market back home. It said a lot for Gray's charms that they were casting out lures to him. Men outnumbered women four to one at home, but Gray was a particularly handsome and, most especially, rich one of them. And poor men outnumbered rich ones by much more than that, everywhere. Except maybe, Josh thought when he reached the lobby of his hotel, right here in New York City.

Every man he saw there was well-dressed, and every one of them could obviously afford the luxury of this hotel, where the nightly room rent for a suite equaled most men's wages for a week. Josh had checked himself in the mirror in his room, and knew that his double-breasted jacket and straight-cut trousers fitted closely and without a wrinkle, and that his new white linen shirt glowed blue-white with cleanliness. Still, as was his habit, he tugged at his hat brim before he stepped out the door, and only then really understood his transformation. Back home, a man shaped his hat like he shaped his destiny, and his hat made a purely personal statement about himself. A man played it closer to the vest here in the city, and his stiff-brimmed top hat said only: I'm here to do business. But so he was, so he left off remembering what had been, satisfied himself by tilting his hat forward, and went on up the avenue to be on time for his luncheon appointment with his New York manager.

English and Western manners might be as different as English and Western methods of riding, but there were some things they agreed on. A gentleman, Josh's father had taught him, never showed an excess of emotion. The men Josh had met and most admired in the West agreed, and further told him that a man who showed his emotions to strangers was likely to be taken—for a fool, if he was lucky, for a lot more if he wasn't. He was glad of his dual training when he was shown into the brownstone mansion on Fifth Avenue and led to Henry Litton's table. Because without it, it would be clear he was so impressed, he was almost struck dumb.

The club was furnished in a style that Josh had been told about by his father—surely this was how his unknown grandfather, the great viscount, must have lived. Before today, the finest homes Josh had ever seen had been the famous houses in New Orleans he'd visited. They'd seemed to him then to have been the epitome of style. Yet by contrast with this club they were reduced to exactly what they'd been: overdone and overly decorated houses of pleasure. Now he could see what he'd believed to be the height of elegance had been pretentious accommodations for men who didn't know the difference between true and false goods—just exactly like the tarts they'd showcased.

Here the high ceilings lacked a trace of gilt, but their creamy carved moldings lent an air of grace and symmetry to the spacious rooms. The long windows were framed, not dominated, by their heavily embroidered draperies; the thick, rich-hued carpets were as soft underfoot as they were easy on the eye; the furniture was old and substantial, but it was as hard to remember the room's colors as it was to recall the subjects of the many ornately framed paintings hung on the stretched-silk-covered walls. Everything spoke of money and taste, but it murmured rather than shouted it.

Josh Dylan, tall and broad-shouldered, trim and immaculately dressed, his ruggedly handsome face as bronzed by outdoor living as his heavy gold hair was, seemed perfectly in place and natural in his surroundings—and because of more than his princely bearing and his aristocratic features. He was grateful for his training as he strode across the dining room, easily threading his way past tables full of gentlemen, to meet his manager, Mr. Litton.

When Josh reached the table, the middle-aged man there put him at his ease by asking him about business a moment after he'd bidden him good afternoon and inquired after his health. It wasn't long before he was no longer wary, and was enjoying himself entirely. So it seemed to him that the five-course luncheon took less than an hour to finish. Although when they arose from the table to take coffee and brandy in an adjoining room, Josh, who could read the lateness of the afternoon in the shadows outside the long windows faster than he could count the muted chimes struck by a nearby mantel clock, was amazed at the passage of time.

"Yes, that's one of the pleasures of this place," Henry Litton agreed, when Josh mentioned it, as he leaned back in his leather chair. "It's an oasis in the city. So, I'll put your name up for membership at our next meeting then, shall I?"

"I suppose you may as well," Josh said as he crossed his legs and accepted a light for his cigarillo. "The food's good, it's conveniently located. Might as well."

A faint smile crossed Henry Litton's face, but it wasn't a condescending one. For all that the soft-spoken young man seated next to him was correctly dressed and well-mannered, he knew the clothes were new and the manner cautious—as was only natural for a man newly come from the wilderness. But he never made the mistake of thinking Joshua Dylan a bumpkin. He knew only too well that any man could feel out-of-place on another man's land.

In fact, he recalled that was exactly what Josh Dylan had said to him, with only the trace of a smile, after Litton had suggested they look for a hotel as the sun began to set that day Josh took him riding to the western limits of his grazing land. He'd said it much later, when they'd both been lying near to their campfire, wrapped in saddle blankets, beneath a terrifying limitless star-shattered night sky.

Now Henry Litton simply said, "Clubs for food and

privacy are all very well. This one isn't for that purpose. It's for business."

"My father used to say that a gentleman never talks business at his club," Josh said softly.

"Ah, but then, your father was a gentleman. And an Englishman. It's hard to be a gentleman in New York without money, so most of us don't make that distinction. I'll show you what I mean. When you want company here, you've just to look up and find it—and it's usually either interesting or profitable to you . . . Ah, young Peter. Perfect."

Gazing across the room, Henry Litton caught the eye of a short, fresh-faced young man with thinning light hair, who'd been looking at them every so often with ill-concealed curiosity. Now he smiled in response to being noticed, and immediately rose to join them.

"Hello, Peter," Henry Litton said. "May I present my guest, Joshua Dylan, from Wyoming Territory? Josh, this is Peter Potter. His claim to fame is that his ancestors were here even before yours began sending pilgrims over."

"Before the Indians too, if you believe my grandfather," Peter said as he shook Josh's hand. "He says we sold Manhattan to them in the first place, before we saw the business possibilities and bought it back. . . . But Wyoming Territory!" he said with great satisfaction as he seated himself. "You must have a tale or two to tell!"

"I was hoping you'd tell him why he should join our club," Henry Litton said.

"So we can hear his stories about the West, of course," Peter said eagerly. "I've always wanted to go there."

"Why haven't you?" Josh asked.

"Something else usually comes along to distract him," Henry Litton answered promptly. "Usually female, and always expensive. Isn't that so, Peter?"

"Just so," Peter answered without a trace of resentment. "Are you rich, Mr. Dylan? If so, I can show you how to spend your money in amazingly interesting ways. Think of me as the opposite of old Litton here. He's in business to increase your fortune, while I, I'm pleased to tell you, can get it down to pocket size in no time, and then show you how to spend that. My family's very rich, that's why I'm allowed to belong here. Because every so often," he confided, "I amaze them by something I've heard, and make a few guilders to keep up the family name. And my membership, of course."

They laughed. It was as if their laughter were a signal, because before long they'd attracted other men to their circle. It was Josh Dylan's new face—and expensive new clothes—Peter said, to more laughter, that did it. Before long Josh met several amiable gentlemen. They seemed as proud of their occupations as they were of their success in them. Some were in manufacturing, some in the larger aspects of trade, more than a few in investments, and only some, like Peter, born to fortune. A few stood out in Josh's mind apart from their stated professions. Peter, because he was the youngest and most amusing. Cyrus Polk, a thickset gentleman with white hair and impressive white beard, because he was the oldest. And Edgar Yates, a dark-eyed, dark-whiskered, balding gentleman with an exaggeratedly friendly manner, because he seemed, to Josh's experienced eye, to be trying to sell him something, though he'd no idea what it might be.

"So, then," one of the men said, "I've heard 'cattle' and 'railroads' and something about 'refrigerator cars' too, I think. Just what business are you in, Mr. Dylan?"

Josh hesitated only an instant. Then he remembered that these men couldn't know that they'd violated both rules of conduct he'd been raised with. No English gentleman would speak about trade, and neither did any sane man in the West ask another how he earned his keep. But this was New York, after all, and they'd all been open with him, and he couldn't see a hint of aggression or mockery in their faces as they awaited his answer. Still, as always when he felt he was on thin ice, he answered in exaggerated accents. Out west, he could sound very British. Here, he drawled.

"You make me sound like the old Commodore himself," he protested, "but I'm no Vanderbilt. Out where I come from, a man with two cows can say he raises cattle, and he's right. And a fellow with two stocks framed over his fireplace can say he's invested in a railroad—and a lot do, we've got over fifty railroads layin' down track now, just in my county. I'm not that paltry, or I wouldn't be here. I guess you could say I've got a little bit of a lot of things. I'm mainly in the business of business now, gentlemen. If it sounds like it might pay, I'm listenin'."

"Andrew Carnegie says a man ought to put his eggs all in one basket—and then watch that basket carefully," another man said over their laughter at Josh's answer and a few cries of "Hear! Hear!"

"Well, now, Mr. Carnegie's a genius. I'm just a cowboy," Josh said humbly as Mr. Litton tried to swallow his amusement and smile only his narrow smile.

"Then what are you doing in New York, cowboy?" a man asked.

For the first time Josh heard that small, sharp edge to a man's voice that made him remember he wasn't wearing his guns anymore, and made him regret it. He answered slowly, his accent much thicker, even as he heard some murmurs of disapproval for the question.

"Well, now, I agree. If a man's got a callin', he should stay with it." Josh's soft but dangerously steady voice silenced the others, as he went on, his face impassive, but his eyes narrowed and glinting like steel. "Still, a man's got a lot of time at night out on the range, and I got to thinkin' . . . Mr. Rockefeller knows oil, but he's got to know more, 'cause he needs Mr. Carnegie's steel to make tracks to get it anywhere. Just like Mr. Pullman knows railroad cars, but they wouldn't do him much good without tracks to put them on, neither. Mr. Swift's amazin' with what he does with my cattle, but he's also figured out a way to take his meat to market, over those same tracks. And Mr. Gould and his friends know railroadin' and are layin' down that track from here to the Pacific—along routes that they find out the others need."

Josh sat back and regarded them all with lazy good humor in his eyes.

"Seems they all found a use for Andrew Carnegie's 'eggs' somewhere along the way, didn't they?" he asked gently. "That basket of his wouldn't be worth his watchin' if they didn't, I don't think. And no matter what they're expert in—railroads, cattle, oil or steel, or even dry goods . . ." He seemed diverted, then continued with a grin, "The cleverest businessman I ever met out west was a fellow named Levi Strauss. Why, he made more money out of men's pants than a dozen dance-hall girls on a Saturday night ever did." He paused as they all laughed, before he went on quietly and seriously, ". . . because he knew how to use the rails and the stages and the roads to get them where they were needed.

"No, sir," he said, shaking his head, "no matter how good you are at your callin', you need to know more than that, I think. Rockefeller, Carnegie, Gould—they can find uses for each other, and profit in each other, *if* they know each other. One hand washes the other. I'm just a cowboy with callused hands. But I'm interested in a whole lot of things. I figured that coming to New York might help me too."

"Oh, well said! Let me shake that hand, sir!" a robust gentleman cried as the others called their agreement.

The hostile gentleman left soon after. Long before Peter asked if Josh was going to join their club after all, and the other men grew still, awaiting his answer.

"Well, thank you, seems I will, if you'll have me," Josh said, as Peter, eyes alight, remarked, "As the old maid said to the salesman," to get them all chuckling.

"But it will seem strange to be a member of New York society," Josh mused after flashing him his ready white-toothed smile.

The laughter that greeted that was even louder. Loud enough to make Josh Dylan's smile freeze and make him wonder if he'd read them right. Until one of them spoke up.

"Good heavens!" a gentleman said merrily. "We're not all members of the 'Upper Ten'—the ten thousand that are Society with a capital S, Dylan. Never think it."

"Peter, here, was born to it," Henry Litton explained, "but many of us were not. Society's more than mere money these days. It's acceptance. Why, I do believe William Henry Vanderbilt could buy and sell Mrs. Astor, and yet she won't have him in her drawing room, and everyone knows how that galls him."

"Why not?" Josh asked, leaning forward to listen closely.

"Because her father-in-law, John Jacob, made his money a few years earlier—and obliged her by dying much sooner," Peter answered. "The old Commodore was still spitting and cursing and scratching his unmentionables, and mentioning them too, when old John Jacob was long gone, half-forgotten, and already being dressed in angel's robes by his descendants," he added as they all laughed and agreed.

"No, I doubt you or I will get into the 'Four Hundred,' " Edgar Yates said on a sigh.

"Some call the cream of society the 'Four Hundred' because they say that's how many will fit into Mrs. Astor's ballroom," Henry Litton explained. "She and her clique rule New York society."

"Well, then," Josh said on the merest smile, "I might just see if it can hold four hundred and one."

There was a moment of silence as the other men heard what he said and studied him. There was no derision. Not after they'd heard his tone of voice. They were men of business, and a large part of their business was summing up other men. It wasn't easy in his case.

He was young and strong, trim and athletic, with features almost fine enough to make him look embarrassingly good-looking—except for his nose, which saved him from beauty and made him a man another man could feel comfortable with. Obviously successful, and clever. Well-mannered, soft-spoken, and yet forceful, with a quantity of hidden power behind his soft words. Because for all the quiet charm he radiated, they didn't know what he was thinking or what he was capable of. He was a man who could be threatening, and yet they felt he could be trusted. Whatever he really was, he was entirely unique, and would bear watching, and befriending. Not one of them laughed at him when he said "four hundred and one," although it was a laughable thought. Because they started to wonder if they should doubt it.

"But first," he said, "I think I'll join up here."

Many of the men stayed on to chat. But as the afternoon drew on, the friendly circle around Josh slowly dwindled. Gentlemen checked their watches and cited their obligations to wives, or friends, or other dinner companions, and presented their cards to Josh before they left, professing themselves eager to see him again.

"I have to remember to get some printed up," he said,

tucking another into his vest pocket, "just as soon as I
know where I'll be staying. The hotel's fine, but I need
permanent lodgings."

The men around him grew silent and he looked up to
see their strained expressions and quickly said, "Please.
I've just come in off the range. If I saw one of you about
to get on an unbroken horse back home, I'd speak up
fast enough. Is there something wrong in what I said?
Someone ought to tell me how to get along here, you
know. In my town a man can break his neck riding over
something he doesn't notice. But I suspect he can break
his heart here on something completely invisible—to him."

"Ah, a gentleman is expected to have calling cards,
Josh," Henry Litton said, "to leave when he goes calling on
ladies or families, or to give to other men. It's almost his only
proof of his respectability," he said apologetically.

"I see," Josh said, nodding, absorbing, learning. "So
I'll have some done up with the hotel's name on it—until
I get settled."

"I know how hard that can be—my wife kept me looking for the perfect address for a year," Edgar Yates said.
"Does your wife know our city, Dylan? My wife would
be glad to show her around town."

"Thanks for the offer," Josh said, "but first I have to
find one. I'm not married."

It seemed to Josh that Edgar's eyes lit up when he
said that, so he supposed the fellow had a litter of ugly
daughters, and was bracing himself for a dinner invitation, but the older man only laughed.

"Is that another thing you're looking for in New
York?" Cyrus Polk asked.

"Ah . . . eventually," Josh said.

"A wise man," Peter said. "Then you'll want to come
along with me tonight. I never go near any wives unless
they're other men's, and other men with bad aim, at that.
I'm going to the theater after dinner," he said. "How do
you feel about actresses?"

"It's funny you should mention that," Josh said,
smiling.

He didn't head back to his hotel to dress for the evening after he'd left the club. Instead, Josh strolled down

the broad avenue, deep in thought. Then he paused, and only then began to search the houses he passed for their street numbers. When he found the one he sought, he stopped, took a deep breath, and then quickly mounted the marble stairs.

The butler was appalled. The only reason the heavy door wasn't closed directly in his face, Josh thought, wasn't because his clothes and manner might be a gentleman's, but because the butler acted too much the gentleman himself to make that sort of scene. It was amusing, but it was also getting late. A hard edge crept into the clipped tones Josh had been reasoning in.

"I've no card because I just arrived in the city two days ago," he said with the sort of bored annoyance in his voice that his father would have been proud of, because a true gentleman never lowered himself enough to lose patience with an inferior. As the butler blinked, he went on, "Just tell your master that Josh Dylan, from Wyoming Territory, is here. And add that Bartholomew Dylan is in a far fairer and more distant place than Nicaragua now, or else he'd be with me too."

"Mr. Vanderbilt does not see persons in off the street, sir," the butler said in less chilling accents, "but if you would like to leave your name and current address with me . . . ?"

"I should like to come in and see William Henry," Josh said plainly, "and I suggest you tell him so. Now."

The butler hesitated. The man he faced was clearly disgusted with him, his every nuance of expression showed it, and yet he showed no other outward sign of distress, and made no great fuss, despite making it plain that he very much desired entry. But neither did he make any secret of the fact that he thought himself too superior to dispute with a mere servant. Something in the butler's heart thrilled. It was homesickness and sweet remembrance of his youth and training. This man was possibly an American. But he was obviously a gentleman.

"At once, sir," he said, and only fretted that the house rules insisted he leave the gentleman standing on the doorstep with a pair of footmen to watch over him.

But not for long.

"Josh!" William Henry Vanderbilt said as he took his

visitor's hand moments later and led him into the house. "What are you doing here? You didn't mention it in your last letter. Well, whatever it is, it's good to see you. I only wish the Commodore were still here too."

"So do I," Josh said. "I'm here because I finally found the West too small for me, just as he always said I would."

"You haven't changed," the older, heavyset man said on a laugh, leading his visitor to his library, to the side of his great entry hall.

"I hope I have, sir," Josh said. "The last time I saw you I was poor and scared of the big city. Now I'm just scared of the big city."

The older man paused. Tall as he was, still he had to look up slightly to see directly into the dark gray eyes above him. He shook his heavy, heavily side-whiskered head. "You've never been afraid of anything. That was what was so enviable about you, always. You were just a boy when you came that first time with your father after he'd talked his way in to see mine, with some wild scheme about a new overland express line. All along, the Commodore could tell he hadn't the price of fare across town. But you were proud of him. The Commodore never forgot that. That's why he hired him to do that stagecoach work for us, he said. But he knew Bartholomew would never hold on to a cent he earned from it. And you—you never took a cent in charity," he said wonderingly, before he went on quickly, belatedly remembering none was ever offered, "And look at you now. Although I'll swear your father never left you a penny, you managed to get that penny from somewhere and parlay it into a fortune."

"With your father's advice," Josh reminded him.

"Advice is cheap enough," the older man scoffed.

He was answered soberly. "No, sir, it was invaluable. And continued to be so. He saw me when we came back years later, and counseled me, and always had time to answer my letters. My father taught me the value of work; your father showed me how to put that work to work."

The florid-faced older man turned his head. It might have been because he remembered how his father had been amused to send scraps of advice to the proud pauper boy from the West when he'd been asked for them, before he became genuinely interested in the growing fortune the young man was amassing. That was when the Commodore had named the relationship friendship: because no rich man, he always said, could ever afford to ignore another. But William Henry could also have turned his head aside just then because he was acutely aware of how little this young man had been given by anyone, and how grateful he was for whatever little it had been. Or it could have been because he was too aware of how much he himself had been given, and too worried about what he'd do with it now. Though Josh Dylan was a generation younger than he was, he both shamed and inspired him.

He lightened the moment. "Your father was a gentleman and a dreamer—the most convincing orator I ever heard. The Commodore used to say it was too bad he was born in England or he could've been President."

"And the country would've been in debt unto the fifth generation," Josh said on a sigh.

"But not if you were, eh?"

"Oh, I've no interest in politics. No, sir . . . Damnation, look at the time. I've a dinner engagement," Josh explained as he declined the glass of brandy he was offered. "Got to be moving on. I only came to pay my respects and let you know I plan to stay on awhile."

"Is there anything we can do for you?"

"No, sir—aside from letting me know if there's anything good in the wind. I'll be staying at the Broadway Central until I find other lodgings. But I'm joining the Atlantic Club, so I'll get any message left there. By the way, sir," Josh added as he walked back to the door with his host, "is there anything I can do for you?"

"No, Josh. Nothing—nothing but come to dinner when I ask you, that is to say."

"You sure?" Josh said as they shook hands, and he lowered his voice to ask softly, lightly, "Not even get you an invitation to come with me to Mrs. Astor's house?"

"So it's out, eh? Well, I'll admit it rankles. For Willie and Alva's sake, as much as mine. My children and I are not admissible . . . . Damned woman thinks she invented society. Well, maybe she did," he murmured before he said, "I'll believe you can tame wild horses and ride straight up the side of mountains, Josh. But there are some things even you can't do, thank you anyway."

"You think not?" Josh asked, inclining his head to the side.

And though he laughed as they parted, the older man soon sobered when he'd gone, because he wasn't that sure.

The refrain of "Little Buttercup" was the first thing Josh heard as he entered the darkened theater, but it was the last intelligible thing heard from the performers after he'd taken his seat.

"Doesn't anyone here come to listen to what they paid for?" Josh asked Peter after the noise from the audience made him give up trying to make sense of what was happening onstage.

"What they paid for, my good man, is a look at some fairly good women . . . only not *too* good, you understand," Peter answered absently before he sat up straighter, pointed, and said excitedly, "There! There she is, see? The one . . . one . . . two . . . the third from the left, in the back, with all those yellow curls. Good Lord," he said fervently, "I didn't know they made them that sweet, did you? Look at that little face . . . look at those big . . . Damnation, look at that redheaded one, stepped right in front of her and cut off my line of vision . . . Oh, well, we'll see her later, at dinner."

"Then why," Josh asked, looking at his seatmate in the box they'd rented, "did we come to the theater?"

"She's an actress, she'd have been insulted if I hadn't. I have to watch my step, I've only had her twice, you know. Her line is coming up in about a half-hour. That's how I found her: heard that line and lost my heart, and then my week's allowance. And how else can you pick the one you want? Yes," he explained as his new friend stopped laughing and listened carefully, "pick anyone you want. That's what you're here for. If she's not married or already taken or indisposed, I'll have my sweet little Millie ask her along with us for dinner.

"Just have a look," he said, passing along his opera

glasses and indicating the stage and the dozens of scantily clad young women dancing and singing upon it, with a sweep of his hand. "That's what they're there for. Oh, good," he said, never noticing the curious look that had come over his friend's face, "they're doing the number from *Forty Thieves* now. You'll get to see more of them that way, in every way—that's the best part of a revue. Just as well, you came so late, you almost missed it all. What kept you so long? Did your hackney driver see the hay in your hair and take you to Brooklyn first and not the Bowery?"

"I stopped off to see my old friend William Vanderbilt before I changed clothes for the evening," Josh answered absently, raising the opera glasses.

"Well, I suppose I deserved that," Peter sighed.

Josh was too busily watching the stage to answer. And too involved with realizing how nervous he was at the thought of actually having dinner with an actress. The idea was as astonishing and exciting as being asked to appear onstage himself. Gray wasn't the only one who perused the *Police Gazette*, although his older brother was satisfied with a glance at the beauties it featured. Just as he didn't bother passing hours sighing over them, he'd never seriously thought of becoming familiar with one of those mythical creatures.

But he loved the theater, and always had. Ever since he could remember, whenever he'd a spare half-dollar in his pocket that he'd decided he could afford to squander on himself, he'd gone to the theater. Any kind, wherever there was any sort of touring company performing in anything designated as a theater, wherever he'd found himself in all his wandering days. There was something about the theater—the drama, the language, the intelligence of it, and the way he was included in it just by being in the audience—that made him feel his lack of education less keenly. A book might enthrall him, but a play could absorb him into itself.

If the theater was magical, the actresses who performed in it enchanted him. It was hard to believe they existed in real life; he'd never met them there.

Tonight he was seeing musical comedy; the actresses were only here to amuse. He focused his opera glasses on a particularly interesting-looking one, a girl who managed to look haughty even in her costume of spangled tights, and doubted she'd consent to meet him. Peter was clever, and as wellborn as he was well-dressed, Josh supposed. But it was hard to think of him being familiar with actresses. For all his advantages, Peter was, after all, undeniably short, his fair hair all but vanished from above his round, bland face, and his fashionably tight clothes revealed a growing paunch beneath his vest. Back home, a man had to really be something special to stand out from the crowd—especially around women. And actresses were leagues above women.

But New York was a city of miracles, after all. Because Miss Bedelia Ames was delighted to come to dinner. She was so warm and friendly that within moments after their acquaintance had been made, Josh felt as though he knew her very well. And that wasn't the only thing to disappoint him so badly.

Distance had lent her more than enchantment, it had enhanced her in every way. Her eyes weren't as blue as the paint she'd worn onstage had suggested, and though her curls were just as yellow, close as he was now, close to her as her champagne glass on the table they sat together at, he could see that her hair had been born almost as black as her brows had been painted. The illusion of beauty was only a part of it. His ears were soon cheated as his eyes had been. Because as dinner wore on, he found that the silly songs she'd sung onstage had made a lot more sense than her own unrehearsed dialogue did.

"So then, see, quick as I can, I says to her, I says, 'Well, Miss Miller, I remember seeing that bracelet right here on that table, and so where—I'd like someone to drive up and tell me—do yiz think it's gone, huh?'" she asked, looking triumphantly about her. Before anyone at the table could answer, she picked up her fork, along with the threads of her story, because the pheasant had been removed and the waiter had just delivered the lobster and she wasn't going to miss a morsel of what was being served, any more than she'd dream of letting them miss a detail of her story, Josh thought unhappily.

"Very true," Miss Millie, Peter's lively companion

commented when the story finally wound down. But she added, "Don't you think so, Mr. Dylan?" as she'd done every so often all through dinner, with much dimpling and fluttering of her eyelashes.

So Josh wasn't surprised when Peter stood as soon as the vivacious Miss Millie demolished her dessert, to announce that they really must be going. But he was astonished at how deserted he felt as he watched them walk away, leaving him alone with Miss Ames and her interminable gossip about all the other actresses who'd stolen either her lines, or bits of her costumes, or her opportunities for betterment. He wondered how soon he'd be able to take her home and leave her. He'd been with many women before, but a man didn't take a woman out to dinner where he came from. His business with her was either at her place of business or at her home, depending on what sort of woman she was, and just exactly what her business was. Different rules applied here. And he didn't know them. But a gentleman always waited on the lady; he'd take his cue from her. He almost didn't believe it when it came.

"Right upstairs," she answered his startled question. "Where Millie and her gent went. Only not the same room," she giggled. "What d'yiz think I am?"

He thought he knew now, but he didn't believe it, so he went along with her to make sure. Certainly her face, form, and manner didn't spur him to, and her conversation argued loudly against it. That is, when his disappointment wasn't speaking louder. But it was what she expected of him, what his good manners insisted, and his body, as always, went right along with the suggestion.

At least, her figure was every bit as astonishing in private as it had seemed on the stage. She was big-breasted and round-bottomed and with a waist he could hold, and did, in his two hands. It was incredible. That which he could see or feel of it, that was.

"Honey," he said finally at a very crucial juncture of their newfound acquaintance, "aren't you going to take that damned thing off?"

She didn't answer in words, and she resisted all his efforts. And because he wasn't a man to use force, even if he could've figured out how he could accomplish what he wanted with it, the act was performed, over and done, and all with her black-laced corset still on. Nothing he'd said or done had persuaded her to remove all her clothing after she'd dragged him down to their hastily rented bed in the room above the restaurant. Just as nothing she could say or do now would get him to stay a moment longer.

So he supposed, as he counted out enough bills to make her try to detain him after he'd dressed to leave, there'd been something different about the night, after all. He'd never made love to a woman in a corset before, for all that her every other move was like every practiced saloon girl's back home had been. Except that she'd insisted on calling it "making love," when anybody at home would've known the shorter, more appropriate name for what they'd done. Or actually, he thought after he'd started down the stairs, after what *he'd* done. Because for a girl who'd been so remarkably vivacious, prattling her way through dinner, she'd been uncommonly silent and swift about her business in bed. And business it was, he decided. It was a good thing his imagination was as easily triggered as his body or he'd have completely wasted his time tonight.

His anger was more at himself and his foolish expectations than it was at Miss Bedelia Ames, whose performance in *Baron's New Revue*, however inadequate, had been better than the one she'd given in his arms. Actress? he corrected himself: she'd been only a foolish, trivial, and entirely commonplace whore, with nothing theatrical about her other than her paint. Even after he'd accepted that, he'd expected something different, at least more exotic—she'd named herself an actress and the word still held its magic. But though she was better-looking than some, she was no more interesting than any other, and far worse at her job than most. It wasn't really her fault, he supposed at last, accepting his folly. When a man expected to taste an apple, it was bound to feel odd to bite into an orange, no matter how good it was. And this one, he thought grumpily, hadn't even been very good.

"Why did you call her an actress?" was all he asked

Peter when he noticed who was walking at his side as he left the restaurant and stepped out into the night.

"Because she is," Peter said sulkily. "Yes, you can stare, I thought I'd be leaving later. I should've known better than to bring you along. Millie couldn't stop talking about you all night, any more than she could stop looking at you all through dinner. Yes, even *then* she did," he said, and laughed despite himself, as Josh chuckled.

But Josh didn't feel like smiling. It was more than his disappointment at finding a whore where he'd thought he'd find a cultured lady. He'd been, he realized, a little lonely tonight. It was a new city that seemed almost a new world. He wished he could've had a caring woman tonight, and not a woman of business. He'd known both sorts, and was sorry sometimes—times like tonight—that he had. Women were scarce in the rough land he came from, so a man usually settled for what he could buy, since there was little chance he'd get what he wanted without marriage. He'd been too poor, if he hadn't been too busy working, to look for that.

But no matter what he was looking for, he did look and speak the way he did, and women seemed to like it, so there were always exceptions. Always lonely wives, widows with needs that matrimony would only rob them of, and women who were interested in settling scores with other men. He'd thought he was lucky when he got involved with Holly Slocum, when Jim Slocum went down to Mexico to drive overland there—and took up with some Mexican girl, they said. Holly was as warm in bed as she was out of it, and though years older than he was, and no beauty, she became almost as much of a friend as a lover to him. And a patient, generous one, at that. He'd been sorry when Jim came back, but since he'd already gotten over the first flush of his infatuation and gratitude to her by then, he'd left her with thanks that he'd been fortunate enough to have shared some time with her. But now he wasn't so sure he'd been lucky at all.

Because if Holly Slocum had delighted as much as she'd educated him in bed when he'd been nineteen, she'd just as surely kept showing him the emptiness to be found after thoughtless pleasure in other women's arms down through all these years. There was more to what he'd done tonight, and the problem was he knew it. There was even more than that, he suspected, and the problem was he didn't know if he'd ever find it. The biggest problem was that he knew his own hungers by now, and understood that whatever his feelings in the matter, his body didn't give a damn.

"Slow up, or call a cab," Peter complained. "Didn't you like her?"

It took Josh a second to come back from where he'd wandered in his mind. He almost answered: For an actress, she could've used a few lessons. But the jest died on his lips. No matter who or what she was, and he'd already forgotten her face as well as her name—in fact, remembered only her tight-laced black corset now— Joshua Dylan had been brought up not to discuss what he did with women with other men.

"I didn't mean to be a cause for disagreement between you and your lovely . . . lady," he answered evasively.

"It hardly matters," Peter said airily. "I never noticed she had so little conversation before."

"That's why you seek out actresses—for conversation?" Josh asked as he strolled on.

"Aren't you going to call a hackney cab? Of course not, that's why you don't get fat even with all you eat," Peter grumbled as he tried to keep up. "No, of course not. Actresses are there for entertainment."

"Of all sorts," Josh said. "And here I thought they were there for art's sake."

"I don't know about him," Peter said on a sidewise smile, "but if I want culture, I go to a museum. If I want something busy and warm in my bed, I go to the theater and find an actress."

"At home we call them something else," Josh said softly.

"Well, here we call them what they want us to."

"Oh," Josh said, nodding. "Well, now I understand."

4

"OF COURSE, this is a theatrical house, you understand," the landlady at Kyle Harper's boardinghouse said.

Lucy didn't, but she wanted to be polite, so she nodded.

"I doubt she understands as well as she thinks she does," Kyle put in. "Things are different in England than here, you know."

"Not so different," Mrs. Fergus said comfortably. "Didn't Chauncy Howard himself stay here when he first came to our shores? Didn't he say it reminded him of home? Never mind, my dear," she said to Lucy, "it's very simple. We take in only those in the theater."

Mrs. Fergus paused. Everything about the lady, Lucy thought, from her angular face to her correctly dressed tall, thin frame, looked to be dignity personified. Now she seemed almost regal as she added grandly, "I was myself a performer, an actress. As was, or is, everyone in this establishment, even Mr. Fergus, who works backstage. So we try to cater to our clientele's needs, which we so well understand. We live by the performer's clock. Breakfast is at eleven, not seven. Dinner is available hot at six, cold at midnight. Rent is due every Friday night, whether our boarders are employed or not, since even in the theater, there can be no admittance without a ticket," she said, and paused for laughter.

"No pets, please, Duncan wouldn't like it," Mrs. Fergus continued, "and as for other rules—I hardly need to tell a young lady such as yourself, but this is a respectable house, so you understand what that means."

Lucy nodded again, and felt safer than she had since she'd left Brooklyn.

"Yes," Mrs. Fergus went on, smiling at Lucy in a

friendly, conspiratorial way, "so if you have a friend stay the night, please keep him to your room. His breakfast will be extra, of course. If he stays on with you, the rent will increase," she said, and noting Lucy's widened eyes and paling face, added kindly, "Only a little, but two cannot live as cheaply as one, at least not if I'm doing the cooking," she laughed, "although, of course, I'm not. Well, then, my dear, I take leave to tell you it will be quite an honor for us to have an English person in our home again. Now, is everything satisfactory?"

"Certainly," Kyle said smoothly, before Lucy could speak, "and, oh, Mrs. Fergus, we've suddenly a dearth of male leads, I'll be auditioning for them today and tomorrow. I know Mrs. Hasgood and the Santoro brothers signed up with Bates and are going on tour, could you hold their rooms open a few days, just in case there's a need?"

"For you, Mr. Harper, I shall. Now, Miss Lucy, please make yourself at home. It's so early, no one's available at the moment, but you'll meet them at dinner. Ah, but Duncan's here, and as he'll be the one you'll have to watch out for when you come home late, it's as well you meet him now. Duncan! Oh, Duncan!" Mrs. Fergus caroled.

Lucy tensed. Mrs. Fergus had stirred her strongest doubts and made her wonder about the respectability of this "theatrical" boardinghouse, and now she heard even more ominous words. Kyle bent his head and whispered, "It's not what you think, I promise you."

They waited, Mrs. Fergus looking distinctly displeased, but no one entered the parlor where they stood.

"*Duncan!*" Mrs. Fergus shouted so loudly several porcelain figurines on assorted shelves in the crowded parlor shivered in their places, as Kyle whispered, "Wonderful projection, take note."

Mrs. Fergus smiled and said apologetically, "He's getting on, a bit hard of hearing, you see."

Lucy looked to the door with apprehension, but no one entered, except for an old, slow-moving, decrepit-looking shaggy yellow dog. He paused when he reached the doorway and stared at them.

"Ah, Duncan," Mrs. Fergus said. "You may pat him, my dear, he doesn't bite, I assure you."

"He scarcely breathes," Kyle said as Lucy shot him a quelling glance and went to pat the dog, for she did love dogs and had never been afraid of them. Her only fear, as she ran her fingers through the dog's scruffy hair, would be of seeing this poor old creature expire. It seemed her landlady felt the same way.

"Good, he has your scent now," Mrs. Fergus said, "and you've met him. If you come in late, my dear, please take care not to step on him, won't you?"

"He's a great deterrent to crime. Burglars would break their ankles stumbling over him, since he sleeps by the door," Kyle said sweetly.

"He's not a watchdog," Mrs. Fergus said at once, drawing herself up. "He is, in his own small way, an artist himself," she explained, as Kyle had hoped she would, "and when Mr. Natwick, late of the Borden Minstrels and the variety stage," she added for Lucy's benefit, "passed on, he was left in our care. Watch closely," the landlady said as she raised her hand, pointed her forefinger at the dog, and said loudly enough to make Lucy startle, "*Bang!*"

Duncan collapsed.

"You are dead, sir!" Mrs. Fergus said.

Duncan rolled over, waved his four fringed feet in the air, and grew still. He lay there so stiffly Lucy began to worry, until Mrs. Fergus cried, "Bravo!" and then he slowly rose to his feet again.

"Remarkable," Lucy said, smiling, all her trepidations forgotten in her amusement, just as Kyle had hoped they'd be, but then he frowned as she went on with enthusiasm, "Why, he's wonderful! Why doesn't he go onstage anymore?"

"There isn't much call for his abilities," Mrs. Fergus said, but then frowned and asked, "My dear, you did say you were British?"

"Miss Rose has that most remarkable of gifts," Kyle said swiftly, "the ability to parrot others' voices. I've told her again and again that American audiences will accept her as she is"—he gave an outsized sigh—"but she worries about it endlessly and has been trying to perfect an American accent."

"Oh, never!" Mrs. Fergus cried as Lucy flushed. She'd forgotten her British accent in her amusement with the dog, and Kyle had told her only an hour ago when she'd met him at the theater that she must keep it up from that instant on.

"Why, Miss Rose," Mrs. Fergus said, "you mustn't! There's nothing lovelier, more cultured, or delightful than your accent. Our audiences will eat it up, believe me!"

"Oh, thank you," Lucy said, feeling terrible.

"Half our actresses wish they'd been born where you were, my dear," Mrs. Fergus insisted, "because then they could get work. It's all the rage. How very lucky you are."

"How very kind you are," Lucy said, feeling worse.

But her room had a bed, a night table, a washstand, a wardrobe, clean white lace curtains, and a wide rag rug. It was spacious enough to hold all of Lucy's own possessions and was clean, and the two windows that caught the afternoon sun looked out over the street. There was a room down the hall with a bath in it, and the necessary was just down the stairs and to the back. It was everything she could have wanted, and if she could only forget she was there on her own, and the room was in a house where the most depraved behavior could be considered acceptable, Lucy might've been able to accept it and be pleased. As it was, after she'd unpacked she wondered how soon she'd be packing again.

Kyle had said that if she roomed in a house where everyone overate, she wouldn't have to be monstrously fat, would she? Then, when she didn't laugh, he'd said that Mrs. Fergus was respectable but she'd a house to let out, and landladies, however decent, had to be realists, and not everyone had morals, even outside of the theatrical world. Then, when Lucy said that maybe everyone in the theater had no morals, but she certainly did, and so she wondered if she belonged, he'd said, "of course" and "certainly" and did she think every great opera singer and fine actress in the world was depraved? That had silenced her. Because, of course, she did. But he insisted they weren't. And she very much needed to believe him. Well, and but, and we shall see, Lucy thought as she put the rest of her things away.

But she couldn't put her past away as neatly. She had to go to the theater to rehearse, but she wondered if she weren't really going straight to perdition with herself instead if she took a step in that direction. Kyle promised her fame and fortune. Her grandmother had spoken enviously of both. But all Lucy wanted—had ever wanted—was respectability. Going on the stage was a strange way to gain it. Still, she'd little other course.

In order to marry a respectable gentleman—and Lucy could think of no other or finer way to win respectability—one had to come from respectable beginnings, and she did not. It was that simple, just as her state hadn't been at all difficult for her parents to achieve for her. Her father had only to leave his wife, marry another, and never see his daughters again. A gentleman might understand divorce—it was 1879, and not the Dark Ages, after all. But her mother had done worse, taking up with a few men, and none of them gentlemen, before she'd abandoned her children altogether. It was how she and her first husband had abandoned standards of decency that affected their daughter more.

Lucy had to admit it was only the one daughter they'd troubled. Gwennie, after all, had found herself a wealthy husband, and never seemed to mind her past. But then, Grandmama had always considered Mr. Hodges unutterably vulgar. Although Lucy thought him amusing, she'd never have thought of marrying anyone remotely like him. She did think of marriage, though, and often, and even oftener now that she was so lonely. Her friends were all married and occupied with their new families, and she thought it would be wonderful to have a new friend who was also a husband. But nothing would happen unless she acted on her wishes; she knew that, for all the good it had ever done her.

She'd walked out with several young men. Only four had ever interested her for even a little while. John Davenport went to Virginia when he inherited his uncle's farm, and he'd increased its size when he'd married his neighbor's daughter. Lucy still had his last letter—it was both a tribute and an insult to her, depending on which day she reread it. Then there'd been John Benson, Howard Smith, and Tom Warren. John had eventually bored her, Howard had pawed her before she sent him on his way, and Tom had interested her very much. They were very different. One was a clerk, another a greengrocer, and Tom a druggist. One had been dark and heavyset, another as middle-sized as he was middling-looking, and Tom as handsome as he was charming. But for all their differences, they were all from the neighborhood and cared what their neighbors thought of them, and knew all about Lucy's family too. And so they'd all eventually thought her a risky sort of wife to take, even though they'd all just as obviously decided she would be a perfectly delightful armful to take somewhere else, preferably dark, and certainly alone. Tom was the only one who'd almost succeeded. But he'd had no chance against Grandmama's training.

But that sort of training didn't catch a husband. Not for a girl with her family history. And she wouldn't lie about it, because she'd a code of honor—and couldn't anyway. Aside from it being common knowledge, she feared terrifying consequences if such truths came out after marriage. Respectable young men had a certain code of honor too: girls with unstable family backgrounds were only for dalliance. The apple, everyone knew, didn't fall far from the tree, and even though this particular apple had rolled away from it as far as she could, it didn't matter.

She was also missing that other social requirement: money in the forefront, to gloss over the decent background she lacked. Grandfather had been a horsecar conductor. Grandmama had a bit put away, but it hadn't outlasted her. And her other grandmother had neither money nor interest in Lucy.

Still, if respectability couldn't be earned in the usual way, perhaps it could in another. And so if she could earn money as Lucy Rose, Lucy thought, she could maybe someday afford to wed as Lucy Markham.

Some girls, she decided, sang for their supper. I shall sing for my wedding breakfast, Lucy thought defiantly as she threw a light shawl over her shoulders and went out to rehearse so that she could do it right.

He was an astonishingly handsome young man. Slender and elegant, with patrician features and shining brown hair. Lucy was half in love with him before she even heard him sing. Which was, Kyle said with a weary sigh when he came upon her watching from the wings, perhaps the only way to fall in love with him.

"But he *is* scenic," he added as she blushed, "which is why I hired him. Yes, I've engaged them all. The pretty one you were mooning over is Bayard Skyler, he's your love interest, poor girl," he said softly as he walked her to the stage. She shot him an offended look.

"Trust me," he said, unnecessarily, because she didn't in the least, before he went on, "The old man's Ned McCullogh, he may be playing your father and he may look like your grandfather, but that's not the kind of fathering he'll be interested in, in your case, believe me. Lester Claxton, the one with the nose, will be our Right Honorable Sir Joseph, he's a very funny man, but a thirsty one, that's why I got him so cheap. Darren White's our Deadeye Dick, he's all right, he's all business. And the new girl, that older redheaded lady, is Fanny Gill—our Buttercup—and very grateful to you for it," he said obscurely.

She didn't have time to question him. He presented her to the huddle of persons onstage with a grand flourish, as though he was presenting royalty.

"Here she is, ladies and gentlemen, Miss Lucy Rose— the English Rose!"

They actually applauded. Lucy curtsied because she didn't know what else to do. She didn't dare think of what he'd told them about her.

"Welcome to our shores, my dear," the fatherly-looking old man said, taking her hand in his and placing his arm about her waist. "I am Ned McCullogh, and as I'll be your new 'father,' allow me to get used to the role. Here, my child, let me introduce you to these others."

She could hardly not. But Kyle had been right, it wasn't very fatherly for that hot hand on her waist to keep clenching her, sliding up or down an inch every so often, and he didn't seem clumsy enough to explain why he kept bumping into her as he walked her the few steps to each new cast member.

"Now, then," Kyle said when Lucy had met all the new principals, "time's a-wasting. We open very soon—sooner if we can. You all know your music, so do you think we can have a read-through with it now, my friends?" he said as he pulled a spindly chair to the side of the stage. "Here, Lucy, have a seat, you don't come in until after Fanny and Ned and Bayard have had their solos. Next time," he whispered as he seated her, "slap him hard. Otherwise he'll think you're charmed by him."

Lucy was thinking of several more good reasons to pack, when she heard Buttercup's song. Then the thought went out of her head, along with the discomfort she felt at the damp spots Ned's hand had left on the sides of her dress.

Fanny Gill sang beautifully, her voice rich and warm and colored with feeling for her words. Lucy couldn't help but clap when she'd done, and won herself a warm smile from the older woman for it. Ned didn't so much sing as recite, and in a quavery sort of voice at that. But it suited his role, and despite her dislike of him, she conceded he was effective. She struck her hands together, because since she'd already applauded once, she had to show some enthusiasm for his performance too.

But she'd no desire to applaud when Bayard finished his first song, even though she did, because he looked over to her for it. He sang very nicely, when he found the key, she thought, but the main trouble was that he acted before and after he did. Maybe such large gestures would look better from further back in the audience. He might improve with practice. After all, he was only reading for the first time, she decided, giving him every benefit of the doubt because he was as handsome a man as she'd ever seen so close.

But he wasn't, she decided, when she got even closer. Then she noticed that his eyes were small, and his nose far too sharp, and his lips too thin. And she saw his nose and mouth a great deal, because it seemed to her that he put them much too close to her own during their duet. She thought Kyle might suggest she slap him too. But

for all that he kept as close to her as the ends of her
eyelashes, it was odd, because it seemed he didn't notice
her at all. Instead of feeling uncomfortably aware of his
masculinity, she only felt oppressed by his nearness—as
though he were a dentist, not a lover. Kyle explained it
as he corrected it.

"No, no, my dear Bayard. How will they believe
you're stricken with love for her if they can't see her?
They'll be trying to peer around you to get a glimpse of
the girl you're swearing to adore, won't they? They won't
be paying attention to you at all. They'll see you much
better if you back up two steps and look down at her
. . . no, angle your head left . . . a little more . . . there!
Now your backdrop is a bit of scenery, not living beauty,
and it shows you up much better. Very nice. Now everyone can see your profile perfectly."

Bayard seemed gratified by this, which made Lucy
decide that his nose was actually funny-looking when you
came right down to it.

Lester Claxton's nose was very much funnier to see,
but so was his whole large, flexible face, and she thought
he was as good as he was professional in his role, even
in this first reading. It was impossible to guess his age,
because he was like no one else she'd ever seen. He had
dark and springy hair and an olive complexion, and every
feature on his mobile face looked as though it had been
fashioned from birth to have been seen from the balcony.
When others made mistakes, he laughed them off or
made them laugh at themselves. If it hadn't been for
him, Lucy decided, Kyle would have gotten angrier much
sooner than he did. As it was, he lost his temper only a
few times during Fanny's first scene with Ned; became
enraged a few more times during the male chorus's greeting to Lester, and didn't fly into a real passion until her
duet with Ned.

"My friends," he declared when he'd screamed the
proceedings to a dead halt, "my dear friends," he went
on, pacing the stage, running his hand through his hair,
before he stopped and faced them with a weary expression, "I realize that *HMS Pinafore* is different from what
many of you are accustomed to. In Britian, as our
English Rose can tell you, its performers are all trained

in the opera. I realize few of you are. I understand, I comprehend and sympathize, I do," he said in unsympathetic accents as he glared at them. "Some of you are from the variety stage, some from the drama, some lately from the minstrel stage, or riverboat or pantomime, or even the church chorus, no doubt," he said scathingly as a few nervous giggles were heard and Lucy stopped breathing, "but all of you, I hope, are performers! If you are not, you may leave now."

There was silence, aside from the sound of shuffling feet. "Ah, then," he said, "it's agreed we may be a motley crew but we are a professional one. So we'll get on with it. Now. Ned, you are merely drawn to Buttercup, not about to ravish her. A little less leering, please. And on that subject, kindly remember Josephine is your doting daughter, not your concubine. Gentlemen of the chorus, you are jolly tars, but you are also supposed to be singing ones. No doubt you're all very fine vocalists, but I remind you that none of you have been hired to do solos. Kindly begin and end together, if you please. Bayard. This isn't the theater for the blind, restrain some of your gestures, will you? And on that head, Lucy," he said, spinning on one heel and turning to face her, "you and Ralph Rackstraw are in love. You are not wondering whether to admit him to a leper colony. Do you think you might generate a little warmer emotion?"

The others only nodded glumly at his suggestions; Lucy colored and stammered, "Yes, yes, but of course, I'll try." But it would be hard to simulate love on the stage, because she wasn't an actress, and she didn't even like Bayard, and was embarrassed at how close she had to stand to him as it was. And because it was hard to pretend to an emotion she'd never felt. But she didn't explain that last to Kyle when he called a recess from their rehearsal, although she tried to tell him the rest. And would have, she thought sadly, if she hadn't gotten all tangled up in her explanations again, to the point where he had to remind her he'd called only a half-hour break from work.

She watched him cross the stage to have a word with the male principals and wondered if she'd leave the company this evening or tomorrow. The thought was suddenly a terrible one. It was one thing to think of giving up the stage because it was immoral and dangerous to her fundamental decency. It was another altogether to think of being asked to leave because of her ineptitude and lack of basic talent.

"Don't fret," Fanny Gill said. "Kyle roars, but if he was really unhappy with you, he wouldn't bother. He's very good, you know. I should know," she added, "I've been in many productions under a great many directors. He's young, but he's good, I assure you."

Lucy was about to explain that she hadn't been in *any* productions, and was glad she'd stopped to summon the words, since Fanny's next words reminded her that hers wouldn't have been in the right accents, because she wasn't thinking about her offstage masquerade just then at all.

"You may not be used to our ways," Fanny said, "but I think this will be a fine production. I'm happy for it, and for you too," she said, smiling sadly. "I know this started as an all-girl show, but because Kyle's been lucky enough to get you, he's trying to do it the way it ought to be done. I'd never have got Buttercup in that other production—too old, you see. Thank heaven the voice lasts longer than the face or figure."

Lucy stared. Fanny Gill was tall and buxom and pleasant-looking. Only the unrealistic color of her hair and the powder and paint on her face made her seem theatrical. Even that looked very well on her—so well that Lucy began to wonder why all older women didn't use such artifice. But behind the paint, Fanny *was* an older woman. As Lucy foundered, trying to think of something comforting and polite to say, and trying to remember to say it in an English accent, Fanny went on.

"Even though he's young, he reminds me of the director of the company I was in. Yes, I was in Vincent Charles's company," she said proudly, "until it disbanded after he died. I suppose you haven't heard of it in England, but it was a fine troupe. I don't know how it is there, but I can tell you," she said softly, so they wouldn't be overheard, "you'd do well to join a company here. They take care of you, you see. It's steady work, and like being in a family—they look after their own.

There's Wallack's, and Daly's, and Palmer's . . . but you have to be very good to get into them, and they like to start you young, you've a chance, but I . . . Ah, well," she said, patting Lucy's hand, "who knows? Maybe Kyle will start his own troupe if we're successful in this. We can always hope," she said, smiling sadly, making Lucy realize she always smiled that way, unless she was onstage.

Kyle saw Lucy occupied with Fanny and told his three male leads to come with him. When he'd gotten them to a more private part of the backstage, he let out a long breath.

"Gentlemen," he said, "we've a problem. I'll make it brief, and I most strongly suggest you make it private. Our English Rose is . . . ah, very British. That is to say, she's a prude. In short, your gallantries scare the stockings off her. She can't act or sing or think if you're trying to entice her. So don't."

"Aha," Ned answered knowingly, "hands off the director's dolly, eh?"

"Hands off the director's purse!" Kyle shouted, before he lowered his voice and hissed, "My bed is busy enough, thank you, I don't have to rape my production to fill it. We need her. She's got class, looks, and she's new—she just might turn the trick for us. Offstage you may do as you wish, though I doubt you'll get much for your efforts but the back of her head—or hand. But I remind you that a woman who hates you offstage can make your life a misery on. That's your business." He shrugged before he stared them all down and said emphatically, "This production is mine. Hands off. And I do mean that literally."

"A prudish actress," Bayard said, amused. "Now I have seen everything."

"No, you haven't," Kyle promised. "Wait until you see me if you don't behave."

"She's new to the country, I expect she'll change," Ned said, as though the thought gave him some comfort.

"I expect she will," Kyle said, "but the show must go on until she does. Now I hope none of you have dinner plans?"

*   *   *

"The theater again?" Peter asked. "Good God, Josh, don't you have anything better to do at night?"

"No, in fact, I don't," Josh said thoughtfully, stretching out his long legs and laying his head back against his leather chair. "That's true. At home, I'd be so tired after a day's hard riding, I'd sleep. But though I've had meetings down at Wall Street and up at Madison Square, and walk everywhere in between, that's not the kind of day that exhausts a man. I'm not used to feeling so lively at night. Or being where there's something to do after dark. What do you do at night?"

"Dine. Drink. Go to the theater. Find an obliging girl to do that and more with," Peter answered, and cut off his new friend's laughter by explaining, "Just my point. You go to the theater, and yet you don't play there after the play—which is the whole point of going."

"Too bad Shakespeare didn't know that," Josh said on a smile. "He could've saved himself a lot of ink. I don't like your kind of theater, Peter. I prefer an honest crib girl to the actresses you've introduced me to for that kind of sport. They're better at it, and I don't have to buy them dinner and pretend to admire them before I get what I've come after."

"My theater is New York theater," Peter replied haughtily. "You won't find it different anywhere."

"If you'd ever lift your eyes from all those thrashing limbs—and I mean the ones on the stage, not in your bed," Josh said, "you'd understand."

"What did you see last night?" Peter said, sitting up straight in his chair and staring at Josh.

It was a gray day, a slight rain was falling outside their club, they'd just finished luncheon, and they'd been chatting in the idle, teasing way of friends with nothing urgent to do. Now, from the look in Peter's eye, Josh knew he'd stumbled across something in conversation that had kindled his interest. He sighed. He'd known Peter only a matter of weeks, but he'd become a friend. For all the fellow was as indolent as he was fascinated by the trivial, he was also educated and well-bred as he was good-natured. Josh liked him as well as any man he'd met anywhere, but he knew him enough by now to suspect there was a wager being born somewhere. Only food, females, or a good bet brightened him that much.

"*Twelfth Night*," he answered cautiously.

Peter winced before he asked, "And who was the best actress in it?"

"Mrs. Howard, of course."

"I mean, the best actress under a hundred years old," Peter said.

"So you do know something other than legs." Josh laughed, before he answered, "Emma Woodward, of course. She was grand."

"She'll be grander," Peter said happily. "Twenty dollars on it!"

Josh whistled at the amount, causing some of the other men to look up, before they realized it was only that long-limbed young Westerner, and they smiled and got on with their own conversations again.

"You're crazy," Josh said softly. "She's a fine actress, a famous one, and a lady."

"And just who would that be? And would you introduce me to her?" a voice interrupted, and they looked up to see Edgar Yates beaming down on them.

"Just talkin' about the theater," Josh answered lightly.

"How convenient!" the older man exclaimed. "I've a pair of tickets to *The Black Crook* for tonight, and my wife can't go. Would you like to come with me, Dylan? I'd ask you, Peter," he said when he received no immediate answer. "But I'm sure you've seen it."

"Memorized it, actually," Peter murmured as Josh said slowly, "Well, I thank you kindly, sir. But Peter and I've made plans already. Some other time, if you don't mind."

"Not at all, not at all," Edgar said heartily, and looked pointedly at the vacant chair near to theirs.

"I'd ask you to stay and chat awhile too," Josh said, rising, "if we weren't about to be on our way."

"If you were a girl," Peter said as they walked down the street moments later, "I'd tell you to be careful of that gentleman. He seems to have designs on you."

Josh nodded. "Smiles and tickets and dinner invites. Everything but flowers. The man sure has taken a shine to me."

"You've noticed. Is that why you get so 'Western'

when he appears?'' Peter asked curiously. "That convenient accent is protective coloring, is it? Right out of Mr. Darwin's book. Interesting. I'll be sure to be alarmed whenever I hear you drawl. But you're right—and probably ahead of me. But it's not your handsome body he's after. There've been rumors. He has a penchant for attaching himself to young men—those newly arrived in town. He's in investments. And they're in pawn shops, and then out of town, after they get to know him.''

"Out where I come from, they get greenhorns into card games or sell them stocks in the gold mine that's about to be discovered under Granny's washline," Josh mused.

"No sense warning you about anything," Peter grumbled, before he brightened and said, "But you don't know everything. This will be almost as great a pleasure for me as it will be for you. You'll have to spend a few dollars in order to win me my twenty, but 'a fine, famous lady' costs more than a dinner and a bottle of wine on the Bowery. Is it a bet?''

Josh paused and then laughed. "You think I can buy Emma Woodward? Maybe her autograph.''

"Everything in this city is for sale. Especially actresses, most especially unmarried ones," Peter insisted. "Are you in?''

Josh shook his head and grinned.

"There are actresses and actresses, son," he drawled. "Never draw against a full house, and hers always is. You're on.''

She received four curtain calls, and it would've been five if Josh had had his way. Miss Emma Woodward, just as the posters outside the theater claimed the papers said, was "Superb!" "Enchanting!" and "Enthralling!" And so Josh felt foolish loitering outside her door with a bouquet of flowers, as Peter had instructed him to do. Except, he thought as he stood staring over the top hats of the other well-dressed gentlemen who waited at the stage door, he supposed that if it netted him a word with the lady, he'd be satisfied.

It netted him more. His card with his new address took him to her dressing-room door. His smile to her maid got him an audience with the lady herself, and his flowers brought a smile to her lips, even as the long look she took at the lean, muscled length of him brought another sort of light to her eyes. And before he could explain away the bracelet that Peter had insisted he wrap around a rose, faster than it disappeared into a pocket of her dressing gown, it got him an invitation to her rooms. And then, of course, it lost him his bet, which didn't pain him a fraction as much as did the loss of his illusions.

It wasn't that Emma Woodward wasn't attractive. He admired her dark, strong-featured face and queenly form as much offstage as on. Nor was it that she wasn't accommodating; she dismissed her maid and offered him iced champagne and caviar, and he didn't have very long to wait before he was offered even warmer accommodations. And it wasn't that she wasn't as fine an actress offstage as on—because he knew that in no way could their brief and impersonal encounter account for all her muted cries of pleasure. Knew it entirely when she cried, "Now, oh, my dear, now!" 'way before time, because he'd deliberately held off for her sake, having known more honest, if less famous, women before. It wasn't even because she was older than he was by many years more than he'd thought from seeing her onstage, because what he could see of her body was as well-preserved as her face.

It was because she'd been not very different from Peter's Bowery actresses, after all, for all that she did Shakespeare and they had trouble with complete sentences. He'd been stimulated by her flattering attentions, but every hasty thing after that had been produced only by his body's automatic reactions. He was as disappointed with her behavior as he was irritated with his own reflexive cooperation with it. She'd been as efficient as a parlor girl, and it had been about as intimate as a session with a barber, and less rewarding. Because all he'd really wanted to do was chat.

But he never told her that. He only gathered up his things, which didn't take very long, since he hadn't removed very much. He put on his hat, and wished she'd not given him her last performance even as he thanked her for it. Because he felt as foolish as he did used.

He never told Peter that either, when he appeared on his doorstep the next morning. But Peter didn't ask for a review. He only smiled and held out his gloved hand, palm-up.

"I saw you leave the theater in a cab with her," Peter said, smirking. "I've won, haven't I?"

Josh turned and went back into his suite. He ran his hands through his sleep-tangled hair, and yawned to buy himself some time. For once his dual upbringing failed him. A gentleman never discussed what he did with a woman, but a man never welshed on a bet. New York City had already taught him one lesson; now he learned another. He was set on living here, after all. He compromised.

"Well, and was it worth it?" Peter asked after the twenty dollars had been placed in his hands.

He was answered with a question. Josh had read the book by Mr. Darwin that Peter had mentioned the day before. He might have to evolve, he thought, but he wasn't changing his species entirely if he could help it.

"Tell me," he asked lightly, "do all the women in New York wear their corsets *all* the time?"

"Be glad if they do," Peter said as he folded his money and put it away. "They're laced up so tight, they expand in frightening ways when they're loosed. It's a shock to see a waist that looks like a willow become one that's like an oak. And the marks those whalebones leave on the skin . . ." He shuddered. "They look like they've been given twenty lashes."

"Must cut off their circulation too," Josh mused, feeling a bit better about his prowess when he realized how numb the lady must have been from the waist down in that contraption.

"So, you'll admit that money can buy a man anything?" Peter asked, taking his mind off his hatred of corsets.

"Can't buy my dog's love or my brother's respect," Josh drawled, still refusing to put the deed into so many words.

"If they lived in New York, it could," Peter said.

And Josh had the unpleasant feeling that might be true.

5

WHENEVER SHE FELT a twinge of guilt about her new profession, Lucy would think of how hard she was working and feel much better about it. Of course, every now and again, in the few moments when she was left to herself, she'd begin to think that no matter what she'd been taught, hard work wasn't necessarily virtuous. After all, she supposed a harlot could have busy nights too. . . . But then she'd drop the matter, worrying whether even that train of thought had been brought about by her new circumstances. Then she'd comfort herself with the realization that no matter what she'd been told about the stage, there simply wasn't enough time to get up to no good. In her case, at least.

She rehearsed all day, and sat up memorizing all night, because she dreaded being scolded by Kyle as much as she hated to hold up rehearsals with her mistakes. Everyone was kind, but she knew she was the only one without stage experience and was determined not to show it anymore than she had to. She might do things wrong, but she refused to do so because she wasn't prepared. Her other time off was filled with singing practice or costume fittings. And her few hours of leisure were taken up by sleeping. The only scandal in her life was that she was living in a decidedly immoral sort of place, surrounded by wanton people, and she enjoyed living there, and liked most of the people.

Because no matter how nice Mrs. Fergus was, she was as full of advice about Lucy's career as she was about how she could find some congenial masculine company for each of her lonely nights. Bayard Skyler, Lester Claxton, and Ned McCullogh had taken lodgings in the same house, and when they weren't hinting the same things, only more furtively, they were coming home at dawn with tales of their nights that Lucy usually managed to shut out at breakfast. Just as she tried to ignore the fact that Jewel Allan, who'd been elevated from the chorus to the small but distinctive role of Cousin Hebe, shared more than gossip with Kyle in his room every night. Well, but, Lucy thought with the blinkered thinking she was getting so good at, there was no way of knowing that for a "fact," after all, unless she saw it for herself, which she wouldn't care to, thank you. Just hearing it from Mrs. Fergus and everyone else in the boardinghouse except for Duncan wasn't certain proof, after all.

But however little time to herself she had, a girl needed a friend. Ada Jessup, another girl from the chorus, was just her own age, as merry as she was kind, and was a very good sort of friend to have. Especially since she lived several streets away from Mrs. Fergus', so Lucy didn't have to be on guard with her false accent every waking hour. And more important, since that accent had become second nature to her now, she didn't have to know just how Ada lived, and could change the subject whenever it got dangerous for their friendship, which was often.

"What you don't know can't hurt you" was becoming Lucy's favorite adage. Ada strongly disagreed. What Lucy didn't know about the stage, New York City, and what a girl had to do to get ahead were all exactly what Ada hoped to teach her new friend before it was too late. She was as impressed by Lucy's knowledge of music as she was at her ignorance of their world. And she was amazed at how quickly Lucy could change the subject from gentlemen friends and the sort of gifts they could give a girl to advance or hinder her career, from jewels to babies, whenever it was brought up. Which was whenever they spoke.

"That's a peach!" Ada said now as she stood back, the better to take in Lucy's completed costume for Act One.

"No, no, I can't go onstage in this, not me, you see, it's . . ." Lucy stopped speaking and inhaled sharply. Kyle had taught her how to immediately silence herself when she knew she was going to blather. She held her breath. Just when she thought she might turn blue, and

Kyle, the dressmaker, Ada, and other assorted members of the cast began to wonder who was going to have to be the one to pick her up from the floor, she spoke on one mighty puff of released air. ". . . drafty," she said.

"Well, it is," she complained, because Kyle had been right: if you could stop the nattering when it began, you could speak more reasonably after. "Too low here and too high here and too tight everywhere. Kyle," she whispered, "I can't sing if I'm laced this tight. Because I can't breathe enough to speak, much less sing."

It was a time for holding breaths, Kyle decided, because he almost said she didn't have to sing at all if she wore that costume. It was a compromise, worked out after hours of argument. He was glad for every second of it now. The bright pink-and-white frock had been lowered so as to show almost all of the high jutting breasts that the tiny nipped-in waist showcased so dramatically. The skirt was long, but drawn up high in front to show her shapely legs from knees to high-heeled slippers. Everything crucial had been covered, just as Lucy had demanded, but because only those portions of her curving body were draped, they were only hinted at more loudly.

Lucy, strategically covered, was more tantalizing than she could ever be in less. Now, at last, Kyle saw the value of modesty. The costume was sensational. Prudery had been bowed to, but lechery was satisfied.

"Take shorter breaths," he said bemusedly.

"I can't even swallow!" she complained.

"I can loosen her up a little between numbers if you can find a way to get her backstage before each one," the dresser volunteered.

"It hurts," Lucy insisted, though it didn't really, since everything had gone numb from her ribs to her hips since she'd been strapped into her corset. Her waist was small enough to be proud of when it wasn't artificially drawn in, but it was so unnaturally tiny now that a glance at it in the mirror frightened her even more than seeing the tops of her breasts did. Her eyes were just widening at the sight of them, when Kyle forestalled her next comment. It was better to concede the little things, he decided as he watched what her eyes saw in the mirror, so that you could remain fixed on the big ones. He managed to tear his own gaze from those larger issues before he spoke.

"No, too complicated. All right, loosen her up enough to reach the low notes, but keep her well-laced even so. It may look odd from here," he said to Lucy, "but I promise it will look wonderful from the balcony."

"Yes," Lester agreed, "I'm beautiful from there. And even more handsome from across the street."

"Nuance is certainly not your forte," Bayard agreed.

Lucy didn't listen, it was all too familiar to her. Bayard resented the attention Lester drew from him onstage, and with good cause. Ralph Rackstraw would never get so much laughter as Sir Joseph Porter, the ruler of the queen's navy; he wasn't supposed to. But Lester managed to steal every inch of attention whenever he was onstage—even Lucy had trouble not looking at him when she was supposd to be sighing over Bayard. It was getting harder to do that every day, because Bayard also resented the attention she took from him. She didn't mind when Bayard held his face in front of hers, or stepped in front of her, or even when he stepped on her lines, because she considered him the only concealment she had onstage. But everyone else did mind. If *Pinafore* was a one-man show, as Lester said, Bayard would have been in heaven. As it was, he sulked, and sniped, and made everyone very sorry they were opening so soon, too soon to get themselves a new Ralph Rackstraw.

Opening as soon as tonight! Lucy remembered, her head jerking up from contemplating how she could pull her top up a jot without Kyle seeing it.

"You look a rouser," Ada said sorrowfully. "And don't go tugging at that bodice," she added, "if you want reason to bawl, just look at me."

But Lucy thought Ada looked charming. Kyle had decided to keep some girls in the navy, just for the amusement of it, only he took the high road, now that he had such a high-class cast, and let those few girls appear dressed exactly as the men were—in baggy middy blouses and bell bottoms. Ada, being small and straw-haired, looked wholly adorable, and so Lucy tried to tell her, forgetting her own discomfort as she did—just as Kyle had hoped.

The costumes had been given out at the last minute because the director had a fair intuition that his leading lady would have altered, hidden, or refused hers if she'd been given time to think about it. That was the only thing left to the last minute. The script had been drummed into everyone's heads, the music played and practiced until it was as familiar to them as their names, their stage places had been nailed to the floor, their cues and takes and exits rehearsed until they ran as smoothly as notes played up and down the scale. Now it needed only that someone come to see them.

There were seven other *Pinafore*s playing tonight. But only one was opening tonight, only one had papered the town with posters, only one had given out free tickets to half the house so that any real paying customers wouldn't get lonely in the auditorium. Because only one was being done in an unfashionable theater, budgeted on a shoe-string, and with a cast composed of cast-offs, would-bes, once-weres, might-have-beens, and may-bes. And only one featured the mysterious English Rose.

Kyle Harper had paid a great many urchins to distribute handbills, he'd paid more to various gentlemen of the press just to make mention of the elusive "Rose" in their papers. He paid more for what was on paper than he'd paid for any other part of his production. It wasn't that much money—only every last penny he'd earned and could borrow. He knew it was his only chance; success in the theater was always only a matter of chance. Born to the business he was in, he knew too well that talent was second to publicity, ability a poor third to notoriety. If there had been a shrine to P. T. Barnum, he'd have worshiped at it; he sometimes wondered why the man wasn't President, and decided it was probably because it was a position beneath his abilities.

The New York public was always seeking something new and different. Lucy was different enough. There was a surfeit of pretty girls, even pretty girls with talent. But there was something about her, Kyle thought. Something that showed through all the stage makeup and the personal history he'd invented. She was delectable, but it went beyond that. It was ineffable, and he was superstitiously content to leave it that way. He almost was afraid that if he could define it, he might lose it, and he needed it to make his production a success—it was that rare. It could even be the thing that had given him the most trouble with her from the start: the primness, the innocence that seemed to really be there. That was why he frightened her costars away from her offstage, and why he'd never let her see a look of anything approaching desire for anything but the show's success in his eyes. That was why he hadn't let himself admit it either. Success was his consuming passion; mere passion couldn't be let stand in its way.

There was a fortune and a half to be made by the right man in this city; the wrong men were making it every day. Theater was as good a way to make it as any; at any rate, it was the only way he knew.

"Anything the matter?" Lester asked him when he noted his director's uncharacteristic stillness.

"Nothing," he said, and was believed, since he wasn't lying, having so long since blurred the line between truth and fiction for himself that he never knew when he was.

"We'll do fine," Lester said more quietly than usual for him, but then, stage fright on opening night took a different guise for every actor. "Bayard can emote to the hilt—it's a comedy, after all. Ned and Darren are professionals, and Fanny's so grateful for the work, she'll outdo herself—and that ain't bad. Our little Rose is a stunner. And I," he said very softly, "will not drink until closing night, not a drop, I promise."

"My dear, dear Lester, thank you," Kyle said.

And I believe you, he thought as he smiled as though he hadn't a care in the world; the only trouble is that I greatly fear that even with all our work, you just might be able to appease your great thirst—this very night.

Lucy discovered that an actual performance was nothing like rehearsal, although the words and the music were the same. But they didn't seem to be—the working theater deceived her just as it did the audience. She knew the stage was small, so small she could pace around it in the space of a minute. But tonight, lighted only by its borders of flaring gaslights, it seemed too big to compass, it seemed to encompass a whole world. A world she and the others in the cast were creating. She also knew, too well, that their costumes were cheaply made, and looked tawdry by the day's honest light; but tonight, in the shadowy glare they pranced in, they seemed, even to her eyes, rich and ornate. The sets, partial and painted as they were, no longer hinted at the sea: they became it. Most magically of all, Bayard and Ned, Lester and Fanny, and all the chorus were gone. In their places were the crew and characters of the *Pinafore*.

It was impossible for Lucy to be shy or frightened now, not only because it wasn't Lucy Markham onstage, only Lucy Rose—but because it wasn't even Lucy anything anymore. From the moment she stepped out on the stage, she found she was only, entirely and utterly, Josephine, the captain's daughter.

Most incredible of all—that audience out there that she'd worried so much about, wondering if the sight of them would freeze her, had simply vanished. They'd become one entity, and not entirely human at that. The dark at the edge of her bright new world contained an unseen but breathing presence—a thing—that watched and listened to a story it was being told. Now and then it laughed, sometimes it coughed, and best of all, when it was happy, which was often tonight, it beat its hands and feet and cried out in pleasure.

At the end, Lucy stood before all the people she could see had been that audience, and yet even then she couldn't feel shy. As she slowly returned to herself again, the approval and gratitude of the audience flowed over her. She no longer worried about shame or respectability. How could she with all that love pouring out to her? For she found that though she'd never known it, it was everything she'd ever wanted.

"Last night," Peter Potter reported as he came to the table, "was incredible. Astonishing. An entirely new experience for me. You should have been there."

"You stayed home, read a book, took a bath, and went to bed alone," Josh said.

"I went, ignorant savage, to the theater. To the opening of *HMS Pinafore* that everyone is talking about."

"It opened a while back," Josh said absently around the steak he was chewing, "You know Peter, don't you, Jacob?" he said to the man he was lunching with, before he continued with his conversation as if his friend hadn't just dropped down at his table, "You sure do need our cattle, Jacob, this stuff is saddle itself, not saddle of beef," he said.

The man he'd called Jacob nodded, and said as soon as he swallowed, "Everyone knows Peter. But the point is, Joshua, can you get it to us fast, regular, and cheap?"

"Sounds like a girl I once knew," Peter commented, but was ignored as Josh said, "Can, and will, Jacob. If you'll sign on the line, I'll deliver."

Peter became silent and his eyes widened. Money talk took precedence over anything else at the club, as it did everywhere the rich gathered together in New York. Other men in the dining room were sliding looks at their table. Joshua's guest, Jacob Van Horn, was both wealthy and fashionable. Although his family knew Peter's, it was a coup that he'd come to visit someone at the club; a greater one that he already called Josh by his first name.

"Easy enough, with those new refrigerator cars," Josh said. "Done and done. Give me a quantity needed, Jacob. And I'll give you quality, my word on it."

"You've got mine," Jacob said.

All the men in the vicinity relaxed after the two men shook hands over the table; they'd just seen a major business triumph pulled off before their eyes. Van Horn's distributors serviced the East Coast. His share in hotels was as great as his interests in markets. If the deal had been what they'd thought they'd overheard, the handsome young Westerner had just sold several thousand dollars' worth of beef. But as such business was commonplace, and often done at lunch, and oftener by a few well-placed words, by the time they'd removed for brandy and their cigars, joining some other gentlemen in the lounge, they were all chatting together. Soon some railroad stocks and oil futures had changed hands, and there'd been some serious hints of interest in the gas company Joshua Dylan was asking about. It hadn't taken long for the other men to show interest in anything he asked about. A seat at his luncheon table was rapidly becoming as coveted as tickets to any plays his friend Peter always tried to lure him to. And once talk of business was over with, he tried again.

"I've seen enough *Pinafore*s to sing in one myself," Josh said now, as Peter tried to persuade him his life would be wasted if he didn't come along this very night to see the new toast, "The English Rose." "If I could sing, that is. Think I've had enough of actresses for a while too."

"But you said you loved the theater," Peter protested.

"I do," Josh said, "but you're the one that taught me that's not the same as loving actresses."

As the men laughed, Jacob Van Horn nodded approval.

"Just what do you do for entertainment then, Josh?" he asked.

"Well, mostly I look for it," Josh answered, grinning. "There's no problem at night, except maybe for too much choice. But day's another story. That's when I'd like to find a different kind of exercise."

"And we all know Peter's idea of exercise," Henry Litton added as Peter tried to look insulted.

"Exercise? Capital!" Jacob said, sitting back and studying the end of his cigar. "You'll find New York offers a great deal to an athletic man. Do you sail, Josh? A lot of us thank the Commodore for starting more than his fortune in New York, you know. The old man was a keen yachtsman, we still hold races up on the Harlem River, near High Bridge, every clement Sunday. Could we interest you in that?"

Josh smiled. "Prairie schooners are a little different from the ones you sail, Jacob. Not much opportunity to sail a yacht out where I come from, sir."

"I should've realized that," the older man laughed, "but we also scull on the river there. Maybe you did some oaring at college?"

Josh's smile remained, but it left his eyes as he said with a shake of his dark gold head, "Never did go to college, sir."

The older man seemed unfazed, as he went on, "Lacrosse? Polo, then? We play at the field in Jerome

Park . . . no? Well, there's always coaching. All the young fellows are mad for it. I find it hard to keep up with them. My daughter's friends are always yammering about driving tandem, unicorn, and four-in-hand. As to that—the Four-in-Hand Club and the Coaching Club are the latest craze—just try to take a pleasant drive in the park on Sunday, and you'll see why you can't anymore. The roads are clogged with rigs, and not just victorias, landaus, barouches, and pleasure carriages, which I could understand. Some of them drive stagecoaches too, just for the show."

Josh's dark gray eyes opened wide. For once, Peter thought, his friend seemed genuinely surprised.

"They drive their own coaches, and just for pleasure?" he asked.

"No one would pay them to make such a spectacle of themselves," Jacob said as another gentleman put in, laughing, "They drive for fashion. Almost impossible to join the Coaching Club, though—takes more than money, takes social position." He paused, belatedly remembering that Jacob Van Horn sat with them, and hurried to add, "Still, whatever club they belong to, costs a pretty penny to build and furnish those monsters, and all so that the ladies can climb up and parade down Fifth Avenue with them on a Sunday."

"You seemed pleased at that," Jacob said, watching Josh's bemused expression. "Have I finally hit on it? Do you like driving?"

"No, sir," Josh answered, grinning, "I purely love it."

Peter hung back in the entry hall, waiting for his friend to say good-bye to Jacob Van Horn. Once the older man was out of earshot, Peter spoke. "I suppose you're going to tell me you're going to join the Coaching Club as soon as you become Mr. Four-Hundred-and-One. Don't even think about it," he said. "You can't. You have to be invited in. It's more than society, or I'd join up. The girls that ride with them are the cream of the crop. It's how much you can impress them with your driving. That means more than being an ace with a prairie schooner or whatever you rustics drive. It means knowing all that English-style driving, and knowing it to an inch. Don't worry, I still love you. Come along, we'll have dinner and then I'll take you to something you'll love more.

"Wait until you see her!" Peter caroled, happy to be on his favorite subject again. "This one's made for you. English and cultured—an out-of-sight beauty! Fresh as a little rose too—imagine finding her at the Stratton Theater—it's so run-down. No one's heard of anyone else in the company, either. Why, if some friends and I hadn't wandered in last night because of nothing better to do, half of New York wouldn't be trying to get in to see her tonight. And what they'd have missed! Come on, Josh," he said as he saw his friend shaking his head, "living like a monk is bad for anyone but a monk."

"I'd rather take the habit than another of your actresses," Josh said with a smile to take the insult from his words. "Thanks anyway."

"A man of taste," Cyrus Polk said as he stopped to adjust his top hat in a wall mirror. "Not every able-bodied man wants an actress for a companion, Peter. I tell you what, Josh, come along with me tonight, as my guest. We've let this gay blade show you the wrong side of our town long enough. Meet me at Delmonico's for an early dinner, and then I'll show you how a gentleman enjoys the company of some real ladies for the evening."

Peter made a face. But Josh nodded. He'd turned down a great many invitations offered by Edgar Yates and others because they'd been too transparent bids for business advantage. But Cyrus Polk had both money and position, and Josh respected his wisdom in business and out of it. It wouldn't be so bad, Josh thought. Though he mightn't have much fun, he'd get a chance to see how the upper crust lived and meet some real ladies. That wasn't possible in the places he'd been frequenting. There was always the dread possibility that there'd be a spinster daughter lurking in the woodwork, but life was full of chances a man had to take.

"I'd be pleased," Josh said.

"Oho," a voice said before Cyrus could reply, and they turned to see Edgar Yates collecting his coat and walking stick behind them. "Tell me," Edgar said with forced brightness, "what did you offer the lad, Cyrus? I can't get him to so much as budge to my favorite tavern. Next time . . ." he said, waggling a gloved finger at Josh, and it was hard to tell if it was a threat or a promise.

Cyrus, correct to his fingertips, wagged his own heavy head as Edgar Yates left them.

"You're a wise young fellow," was all he said about the departing gentleman, "except in your choice of diversions. *Actresses!*" he muttered, before he added, "Six, then, at 'Monico's. Till then," he said, going out the door, swinging his walking stick.

"You're killed with jealousy," Josh said, waiting for Peter to call him a fool.

But Peter just smiled slightly and shrugged. "Here," he said, handing Josh a ticket. "Keep it in your pocket. For when you change your mind. You will, I think."

Peter certainly would've, Josh thought, when Cyrus signaled for their check after dinner. They'd done nothing but dine and talk, but he'd enjoyed himself. It wasn't just because he'd been close to his father and still missed the company of an older gentleman. It was true Cyrus was old enough to be his father, and almost as educated, but he was nothing at all like Bartholomew Dylan. Cyrus was an American gentleman, and they, Josh was beginning to see, took lessons in dollars and cents along with their Greek and Latin. Certainly his father would never have been able to speak so wisely about business. As much as he'd yearned for it, he'd never felt comfortable with the idea of making money. There was another marked difference. Maybe just because they were of a new class in a new country, American gentlemen valued what they considered "respectability." Josh doubted his father ever thought of it. It had been part of his inheritance, a thing he'd considered as ultimately useless and unimportant as his discarded title of "Honorable" had been. But it meant a lot to Cyrus Polk.

Although their conversation had been about horses, business, and politics, Josh had been permitted glimpses into Cyrus Polk's personal life. Not only was he relieved to discover that Cyrus' two daughters were already married, he also heard the proud references to the "gents" they'd married, the "good" addresses they lived at, and the "best" school the grandchildren were sent to. And the absent Mrs. Polk had been a "Johansen" before she'd married—something, Josh decided from the tone of Cyrus' voice, on the order of having been a "Hanover" on the other side of the ocean.

"Well, now then," Cyrus said, digging his watch from a tight fob pocket and blotting his snowy mustache on a napkin, "time to move on. No, no, my guest, remember?" he asked as they walked to the door and he signaled for the doorman to call a hackney cab.

"You'll like this next, Josh," he said comfortably after he'd settled himself into the cab. "Had I a son," he said, patting Josh's knee, "I'd introduce him to this place. Actresses! Young Peter's a good lad, but *actresses*, on my word, *really!*"

Cyrus was still lecturing on the evil physical and moral consequences of having to do with actresses—he seemed unsure of what was worse for a young man consorting with them: exposure to bad upbringing or social disease—when the cab rolled to a stop in front of a neat brownstone house not far from the Fifth Avenue Hotel. Then he stepped down to the street and trotted up the stairs to the house, looking jaunty and spry for such a portly old man, and with his white beard and wine-reddened cheeks, very like an illustration of St. Nicholas Josh had once seen.

They gave their hats to the butler—that was a custom Josh found it hard to get used to, because where he'd passed the last several years, a man took off his hat for only two things: one of them was a funeral and the other unmentionable in mixed company.

"My dear Mrs. Hotchkiss," Cyrus said, bowing over the hand of the older lady who greeted them in the crowded, ornately furnished salon they were shown into, "allow me to present my young friend Mr. Dylan. He's my guest tonight. He's from the West, and doesn't know our fair city."

"I do hope you enjoy it here, Mr. Dylan," Mrs. Hotchkiss said, "and then find it possible to come back often."

Josh doubted it. He'd read about literary salons often enough, but if this one was a fair example, he thought he'd pass in future. For the time being, he stood, obligatory glass of sherry in hand, listening to Mrs. Hotchkiss

gently chide Cyrus for being absent the previous week.
There were more women than men in the fashionably
overdecorated salon, but this, however delightful, was a
thing Josh had almost gotten used to since he'd come to
New York. He was less delighted than usual, though.
Although these ladies were mostly young and all well-
dressed, they weren't unusually good-looking. And though
they stole glances at his tall, broad-shouldered form, they
did so furtively, and then pretended they hadn't. They
seemed so chillingly refined, they made him as uncomfortable with his size and gender as the room filled with
delicate, expensive knickknacks did.

They were soon joined by a plump and charming
young lady named Miss Kidd, who seemed to be an old
friend of Cyrus', and she waved some of her friends over
to chat with them. Miss Tone was an opinionated young
lady with black hair, Miss Reese a shy young woman
with a lisp, Miss Peabody had a musical bent, and soon
sat at the spinet and played for them as the bony Miss
Dineen sang accompaniment. After a while several of
them flirted discreetly with Josh. The other men in the
room remained in their own conversations with other
ladies, and Cyrus excused himself to sit with Miss Kidd
to continue their discussion. Time seemed to stumble by,
and Josh began to steal glances at his watch, until Miss
Tryon appeared, smiled at him, and engaged him in
conversation.

She was a slender brown-haired young woman with
neat, even features and long-fingered thin hands that she
fluttered to emphasize her conversational points. She was
too fragile and mannered for Josh's taste, but her voice
was even and melodious, and her conversation light and
clever. He liked her well enough for the time and situation he was in, and chatted easily with her, answering
her questions about his life in the West. It amused him
to play the cowboy to the hilt; Miss Tryon enjoyed it
enormously—Easterners usually did.

But he tried to keep the conversation general because
he doubted he'd come calling on her in the future, and
didn't want to raise her hopes for anything more. He
didn't consider himself a lady-killer, but he'd seen how
women reacted to him often enough. So he was as sur-

prised as relieved that she didn't seem to expect more from him. But even more pleased when he glimpsed his watch again to see that enough time had passed for him to make his farewells without insulting either Cyrus or Miss Tryon. But he couldn't seem to find Cyrus anywhere in the room, and that was odd, because most of the other men were gone now as well.

"I think," Miss Tryon said to his unasked question, as she lowered her voice and her eyelashes, "that it is time to go upstairs, Mr. Dylan, don't you?"

What he immediately thought was so patently ridiculous that he was ashamed of himself, and so he couldn't answer her for a minute.

"That is," she said softly, "if you want me to, of course."

Josh could handle the right fork at a dinner as easily as he could the reins of an eight-horse rig. But he was at a loss with the finer points of Eastern society. Still, a gentleman always took his cue from the lady.

"Nothing would please me more, ma'am," he said.

She nodded, swept her skirt up in one hand, and taking the mincing steps her gown allowed, went up the long staircase in front of him. He'd walked up similar staircases in the same manner, he mused, as he kept his eyes firmly on the back of Miss Tryon's tiny high-heeled boots, but never in such doubt as to where he was going, and never with such nervousness about what might lie ahead—no, not since he was sixteen and following Misery Annie up to her rooms above the Five Star Saloon. But that was a ridiculous, unworthy comparison that he was instantly ashamed of himself for.

She led him to a door and opened it. It was to a bedroom, just as he'd hoped it wouldn't be.

Miss Tryon closed the door and came to him. She stood on tiptoe and began to unbutton his high shirt collar. He felt a strange combination of horror and amusement at what was happening, and hoping he'd neither laugh nor shudder, he caught her two hands in his. Her mild brown eyes searched his as he searched for something to say that wouldn't sound as foolish and trite as what one of the heroines in one of Gray's hidden pennydreadful novels usually said in similar situations.

"Don't you want me?" Miss Tryon asked.

He sighed. He owed her nothing. But he was tired of doing what the professional women in this city expected of him, weary with being a witless pawn in a game they all thought he'd love, and even so, as confused as he was anxious not to hurt her.

"Darlin'," he said softly, drawling as he always did when in deepest doubt, "I purely just did not know. You see? I came to keep Cyrus company. Now I see that would be ridiculous. I thought this place was a salon. Not a bawdy house. Honest."

She winced, but it was, like all her other actions, a faint reaction, a mere flutter in her composure, immediately corrected.

"We don't call it that," she admonished him, like a teacher calling an errant student to order. "We do supply . . . that . . . but we are mainly in the business of providing gentlemen with educated, cultured young women for . . . company of all sorts."

"Lord," he said, sitting down on the edge of the bed and shaking his head, "I didn't know, I swear it. Cyrus— why, he's the height of respectability . . ."

"Yes, just so, so you see then," she said.

"But, Miss Tryon," he said, trying to buy time to extricate himself with the least damage to her feelings, "how should I know? You're a lady. How in the world did you get into this line of work?"

"Ah," she said, smiling, as at ease now as she'd been downstairs, "I was raised in a good home, sir. But I was foolish enough to be unwise, so very young, you see," she said, as he noted with growing alarm that she was unbuttoning her gown. "I believed the seductive reasonings of my tutor, a gentleman, or rather, alas, *not* a gentleman, who was teaching me watercolors. My father caught us at one of our trysts. I was sent from the house. My tutor disavowed me and disappeared. You know the rest. A young woman without reputation and dowry has only one occupation open to her. I was fortunate to make the acquaintance of Mrs. Hotchkiss. She treats me very well. And indeed, I meet many charming gentlemen here, since this establishment caters to persons of taste and refinement. I speak three languages. Most of the ladies here are similarly accomplished. As Mrs. Hotchkiss says: we come from good homes, and so are employed at a superior house. Come here, my dear Mr. Dylan," she said, reaching for his hand as she sat down on the bed beside him.

She, at least, wore no corset. He wished she did. He'd never seen any woman more naked, and he'd seen a great many without their clothes. But her body looked like it had been shut away from air and light for all of its young life. Her skin was blue-white and oddly slack where it lay over her ribs, for it bulged at her waist, although she wasn't at all fat. Her breasts were small and infantile, with small brown nubs of nipples that seemed to stare down sadly to where she'd coyly arranged a corner of her gown over the apex in her lap. He was a lusty man who'd never dreamed of disappointing a woman in her condition. But now he thought he finally understood just what all those heroines in Gray's novels meant, too—because he'd rather die than go ahead with her suggestion.

Aside from her lack of appeal, he felt no tug of attraction on her part. He doubted she appreciated anything of him but his conversation, and now he'd doubts about her fascination with that. In his wide experience, a woman interested in a man would look at him a certain way, and if she'd done it just once, he'd have caught her at it before she'd looked away. That was part of the game. But Miss Tryon played no games; she offered herself as a lady conferring a great honor. It wasn't his conceit so much as his sense of self-preservation that made him feel nothing but an immediate desire to leave. He sensed that a man's manhood could be withered by such a lady's idea of favors: he's sooner bed down with a blizzard.

"Thank you, honey," he said, "but I just can't. It's not your fault, darlin' " he said, his drawl thickening as he stood, genuinely glad he'd played a hayseed oaf—he'd have been embarrassed to be himself in this situation— "it's just that I didn't know that was what this was all about, and you remind me so much . . . in the face, that is . . . of my poor departed mama." He breathed a silent prayer that if angels could eavesdrop on conversations in bawdy houses, his pretty doll-like mama would forgive him, as he asked Miss Tryon, "You do understand?"

"Oh," she said, sitting up as though she'd been pinched and wrapping her dress around herself, "you poor man. Of course. Shall I introduce you to another girl? Oh, dear," she said, genuinely moved for the first time since he'd met her. "But that would hardly do—the whole point of our establishment is to have some hours of civilized conversation first, some getting acquainted before a . . ."

"Honey, I had that, and I thank you for it," he said as he strode to the door. He stopped and reached for his wallet. "But I don't want you to go wanting because of my problem. How much is it? I insist on paying for time taken."

She drew herself up, angry for the first time.

"We do not discuss money. Mrs. Hotchkiss takes care of that, sir. But it's fifty dollars, and you'll find her downstairs in the parlor."

"Fifty dollars?" he asked, genuinely astonished enough to be rude: fifty dollars could buy him an actress and her understudy and her sister-in-law.

"Of course," Miss Tryon said proudly, "we *are* ladies."

It turned out that Cyrus had paid for him already, and was nowhere to be seen, so Josh could only stalk out into the night, angrier at himself than at anyone in the house. It was childish to feel so disappointed in Cyrus; the old man had thought he was doing him a favor, and it was none of Josh's business what arrangement Cyrus had with his wife. Hadn't he been told that everything in New York was for sale? It was the law of supply and demand. Here, where women were in such great supply, he guessed a man's vows to one, even if she was his wife, meant nothing.

How could Cyrus have known that he came from a place where women were revered and virginity didn't mean as much as loyalty? A place where a father who found his daughter sweet-talked out of her britches would reach for his shotgun and open the door to fetch a preacher, instead of throwing his little girl out of it? He couldn't expect Cyrus to know the man he'd taken to his fancy whorehouse was one who'd be contemptuous of him for it, because he came from a father who wouldn't cheat on his wife any more than he'd cheat another man. Even if the old man had known, did it matter any more than Miss Tryon's poor foolish history did?

Josh paused, frowning, his gray eyes dark as the night around him. A man had to live for here and today. And the question was whether he was going to stay here for all his tomorrows, after all.

He walked a long way before he calmed himself. A man of his size and experience never worried about where he walked. Still, it was a city at night, so along the way his thoughts were interrupted every so often by an assortment of women who stepped out of the darkness to offer him themselves for a fee, and he thought every one of them was more eager than Miss Tryon had been. He refused them all, gently but firmly. For once, he wanted nothing to do with any of their sex. He'd bought women in the wildest city in the West and the most sinful one in the South, but neither Dodge City nor New Orleans had ever filled him with such disgust as this great whore of a city he found himself in now.

Still, his whole life had been aimed toward this goal— success in the city he'd been exiled from. It was too soon to give up just because of a few weeks of days filled with good business and bad nights. Nothing good was easy, or ever had been in his life. Except for the love of his family, and he'd had to work to hold on to them too. The prairie was lonely at night too, he reasoned, until a man learned how to live with it. New York had to have a heart, and he'd find it, he decided.

And if he fleetingly realized that if he gave up he'd have to arrange his whole life anew—and if that thought chilled him by the emptiness that it left as he wondered what it was that he was seeking—the unwelcome thoughts were silenced when he plunged his hands into his pockets and found the forgotten theater ticket. Because then he thought gratefully of the one thing this city excelled at: diversion. He raised his head, and then his hand, to summon a hackney cab. There was still time.

"I thought you'd never get here," Peter murmured as Josh folded his long body into the seat next to his. "You missed the overture. I'm surprised. Mrs. Hochkiss' place didn't seem the sort of house that would appeal to you."

"Why didn't you tell me?" Josh demanded in a harsh whisper.

"About the home for well-bred, demure, and fallen virgins that Cyrus loves to donate to? I thought you wanted some rest tonight," Peter said innocently.

"I don't understand. I thought he was a happily married man," Josh answered, low.

"Very happily. No one minds whatever he does outside of that marriage as long as he does it discreetly. Why else do you think we have so many houses like that? And actresses, for that matter? It's just like it is in your father's country," Peter said softly as the music struck up and the lights dimmed, "only here we marry to match up fortunes, not bloodlines. You should see what they've got picked out for me. Wide as the door to the safe all her money's in. I can hardly wait. Now, hush," he whispered.

It was an amusing production, Josh thought. He'd seen far worse, but he'd heard much better. His attention wandered as the Stratton Theater *Pinafore* wore on. He was just starting to wonder how to refund Cyrus his money when he heard the sudden silence, the audience growing still with anticipation. Onstage, the rubbery-faced Sir Joseph had stopped talking. A girl walked out from the wings as Sir Joseph and the captain left it.

Her hair was gold on amber and its long ringlets glowed ruddy in the stagelight. Her form was exquisite, but his eyes went to her face after his first startled glance at her lovely body, to see if it matched such perfection. She wore paint, but he sat close enough to see that it didn't exaggerate, it only traced the contours of her face and pointed up her best features—which were all of them. She looked familiar to him. But then, that was only natural, since he'd seen her in his dreams so many times since he'd come to manhood.

The hours creep on apace,
　My guilty heart is quaking!
Oh that I might retrace
　The step that I am taking . . .

He listened to her sing, so enchanted that he only dimly heard Peter's muffled murmur of triumph at his expression. Her voice was pure and sweet and British, as familiar to him as his father's, and just as suggestive of his lost empire of elegance. Her costume hinted at everything her innocent smile did not. She moved with grace and sang with joy and seemed totally unaware of her tremendous appeal. She was obviously as wonderful an actress as she was a contradiction, and one he wanted to solve as soon as he could.

Josh sat back and watched her performance, planning when and how he'd buy a private one for himself. He was getting used to the ways of New York; he was endlessly adaptable. He decided that he'd more than survive this damned city, he'd enjoy it. Money could buy everything here. He had money. And he'd just discovered what else he wanted to have, for now.

6

"NEVER AGAIN! Never, never, never *ever* again!" Lucy cried as she came in the door, slammed it behind her, and almost tripped over Duncan in her haste to get into the house.

"Very good," Kyle said approvingly as he watched his new star fling her cape off and march into the sitting room. "But no, a weak ending, I think," he added as she dropped like a stone into a chair opposite him. "Much better to go upstage three steps, lift the decanter, pour yourself a drink, toss it off, and then toss the glass into the fireplace. It'll shock the temperance set and set up a nice mood for the rest of the audience. It's a murder scene you're doing, is it?"

"I wish it was," she sighed, her anger fading, being replaced by guilty anger at herself.

"I went out to dinner with him, as *you* suggested," she said, before she added wearily, "Oh, I know—not by name, but you said I should get out at night after performances, get my name in the news, and he was so rich and gentlemanly, and old enough to be my father . . ." She let her voice trail off, noticing that Mrs. Fergus had come into the room, as had the other lodgers: Jewel, Ned, Lester, old Mrs. Fairfax and her friend and onetime partner in a magic act, Miss Hampton. Lucy was grateful that Bayard was out, at least, as she grew silent, realizing the scene she'd made. She only bent to ruffle Duncan's ear as he collapsed at the side of her chair, obviously having forgiven her for startling him so badly when she'd stormed in so late, just when he'd gotten settled for the night by the door.

"You might as well go on," Kyle said on a yawn. "We've all been waiting up for you. After a week of being a raving success, we all wondered how our little girl would fare on her first night out with a gentleman."

They were all watching her, and for all her sense of outraged privacy this night, these people were at least her friends, and Lucy had begun to see the world held a great many enemies. "It was dreadful," she admitted, "just terrible, he started out so nice, but there was something, well, sneaking about him, I thought, but then I thought: 'How am I to know?' so I just kept smiling and he ordered so much food I couldn't eat half of it, these laces, but you insisted I can't be one size offstage and a different one on, but if I can't eat I'll be no size in no time—"

"Draw a breath," Kyle interrupted. "A long one."

After a silence, she exhaled and went on, on a long sad sigh, her accent as firmly in place as her thoughts now, "Delmonico's was very grand, and the place we went to for dessert was even more plush, but no one told me restaurants had private parlors and no one told me what that old monster would try to do once the waiter left."

They all stared at her. It seemed even Duncan did.

"Well, he didn't!" she said when she realized what they were waiting for. "But he tried."

She shuddered, remembering those damp and grasping hands the kid gloves had concealed, the wet and searching mouth that mustache and beard had revealed when she'd been dragged close. Worst of all had been the thickly muttered endearments tumbling from those damp lips, so unexpected and inappropriate coming from a man old enough to be her grandfather—which was why she'd gone with him in the first place. Her own lips trembled, remembering.

Her hair was tousled, her fine amber eyes filled with tears; her complexion looked as white as it ever had on stage, without a hint of powder to assist it; there wasn't a woman in the room who didn't want to brush back her hair and rock her, or a man who didn't wish to take her into his arms to comfort her in other ways. That was part of her amazing power, Kyle thought as he restrained himself from rising to go to her: her ability to project her every emotion so clearly, even off the stage. What she generated now was almost too much for this small room, and they were all actors themselves.

"Badly done," Mrs. Fairfax announced, her thin nose reddening in outrage. "A gentleman should ask first."

"Exactly," Mrs. Fergus said. "Imagine, a man of his years not knowing better! No lady should have to give out free samples."

"Jumped the gun and frightened the dove, did he? Old fool," Ned chimed in, with nevertheless in his voice a certain gladness at an old man's folly not being his, as Jewel folded her arms and smirked at Lucy's reaction to the sort of comfort she was getting. It was sympathy, Lucy supposed, but not the kind she wanted, and it only made her curl deeper into her chair and observe them all with widened eyes.

"Gentlemen friends are not unheard-of in the theater," Kyle said slowly, frowing at Lucy's response.

"Our English Rose isn't ready for a liaison, and who can blame her?" Lester put in. "She's the toast of the town, and doesn't need to be anybody's honey yet. Come, ladies, it's good news, isn't it? Just think, John T. Wellman himself has been spurned tonight—both him and his millions. Now, come on, don't any of you want to try to fill his empty love nest?"

John T. Wellman, the gentleman Lucy had wrenched away from to leave standing sputtering in his rented private booth at the restaurant, was several years older than Mrs. Fairfax, who everyone in the boardinghouse said was three years older than God. But the older women giggled like girls at the flattering foolishness of the idea of their trying to entice him. Old men never looked at old women, and a woman over thirty would be considered too old for J. T. Wellman or any other man of his sort.

"But I like wine aged in the bottle," Lester said gallantly, "so since I'm on the wagon for the run of the show, you lovely ladies can feel safe with me in the kitchen now. And I'll keep randy Ned under restraint," he promised as some of the women tittered and cried "Oh, no!" and "Spoilsport!" before he added, "So will you join us in a cup of cocoa, if there's room for all of us in there?" He winked at Lucy, as he and Ned led the three older ladies off into the kitchen, as Kyle had signaled him to do.

Kyle shot a significant look to Jewel, and she shrugged and turned and went up the stairs to their room.

"It's no use your asking me," Lucy said defiantly, once she'd seen he'd cleared the room. "I won't. You talked me into being 'Lucy Rose'—and I'll admit it's very pleasant. Then you said I ought to be seen about town, and I tried. But I won't be . . . I cannot . . . I am not . . . an actress," she finished weakly, hating herself for her inability to say the word she really meant.

"But you are," he said simply before he rose and stood before the fireplace, looking in moodily. Lucy stiffened; when Kyle Harper stood, he was about to act. She dreaded what he'd say next. She didn't know why he didn't go on the stage instead of behind the scenes, because when he spoke, he was the most convincing actor she'd ever seen. At least, he always convinced her—but not this time, she told herself, whatever it was he was going to try to persuade her to do.

Kyle was thinking deeply about how to say what he had to say in order to get her to fall in line, just as she thought. But unlike she imagined, he wasn't angry with her for not selling herself to the old man tonight. He didn't much care what her state of morality was, so long as it didn't interfere with her work. But still, a little publicity was a lovesome thing. And so he said, so deep and mournfully that even Duncan's ears pricked up, "It's all very well to be very good," he said, stressing the "good" so she could take it either way, "but goodness onstage gets only applause, and badness in public gets the audience in to give you that applause. I am not a procurer, I am a director," he said grandly, wheeling around and accusing her with a steady stare of all the things she'd only thought. "I'm merely trying to get you to see you ought to be seen with powerful men, to get the notoriety. Your name on everyone's lips means cash in the box office, and the more I get there, the more you eventually do too. What you do with that money is your business, as is what you do with your influential beaux. It doesn't always have to be bad business. Do you see?"

"Oh, yes," Lucy spoke up. "Mr. Wellman and I ought

to have gone to the aquarium instead of Delmonico's, is that it? Oh, silly me!'' she said with a great show of spirit, because Kyle's theatrical manner was catching and she found matching it easy and distracting enough to be fun once she began. "I should've known! Maybe we could've discussed the weather instead of my charms, or his grandchildren instead of my price. Should I have asked about his opinion of President Hayes or his rheumatism instead of slapping his face?"

He smiled, diverted by the thought of one of the richest men in America being slapped by this little girl. Then, as he thought about how the spoiled old fool would probably carry on about it, Kyle's smile grew broader as he imagined the publicity—and the horde of new suitors it would bring into the theater to see his English Rose.

"Something like—yes," he said slowly as she fell still and stared at him. "You don't have to pick an old lecher—there are a lot of foolish young men out there too. A great many who might want you—yes. But who'd be content to be seen with you for the glory of their reputations just as much. Men-about-town very often aren't about anything *but* town, you see," he said, but a look at her face showed him that she didn't.

To explain that concept would take educating her to an extent that would probably embarrass her out of the room. He stared at that lovely and confused young face and noticed that she couldn't quite take her eyes from his. Not for the first time he thought what a pleasure it might be if he could educate her in other ways, and not for the second time he thought he might just be the man who'd be able to do it. But it was too risky to try. At last he had an attraction people would pay to see. He couldn't afford to do anything that might jeopardize it.

He closed his eyes, burying his desire for more and settling for the less he needed most.

Lucy felt relieved as well as lost when Kyle dropped his searching gaze and stared back into the fire. He wasn't a handsome man, nor one she entirely trusted. But his vivid, dramatic, strong-featured face reflected his personality. And his personality was like none other she'd ever met. There were times when he looked at her that she felt uneasy as well as breathless. She didn't know quite what he wanted from her aside from her acting, and wasn't sure she wanted to. He was too unpredictable for her to think of as a brother, too young to depend on as a father, too capable of sudden cruelty to imagine as a friend, and the few times she'd dared entertain the notion of him as a suitor she'd been too frightened to continue the fantasy. He was her employer, but far more. Because even though she didn't trust him very much, somehow she found herself relying on him more than others she trusted more. Whatever else he'd ever done, he'd never hurt her. And for all that he sometimes disturbed her, she doubted he ever would.

"How do I find such gentlemen, then?" she asked now, pretending great interest in Duncan's upturned furry belly, to avoid Kyle's dark and penetrating stare.

But he continued to look into the fire as he answered, "Trial and error, but trial in such a public place that error doesn't matter very much. Daytime is better than night, a museum's preferable to a restaurant, teatime to a late supper, a fancy-dress ball to a tête-à-tête. Avoid his rooms and closed carriages. Be most in sight and make the world the stage for your courtships."

"Oh," she said, smiling at the way Duncan's left leg scratched at the air if she scrached his belly in just the right spot, and the smile reached her voice as she went on musingly, "Oh, yes, I see. And you think I can find a young man who'll be pleased to court me ardently in broad daylight in the middle of a crowd, in the center of Manhattan, and be just as pleased to fade away when twilight comes?"

"If he's after fame, yes. If he wants to build his reputation as a dashing fellow, yes. If he's anything like a dozen other young idiots who clutter up the alley backstage after each performance, yes, yes, yes."

"And how shall I know him when I see him?" she asked.

"You won't," he said. "You'll have to experiment."

"Will I?" she mused.

He wheeled around and glared at her.

"What do you want to do after the *Pinafore* sails?" he snapped.

Her eyes opened wide. "I don't know . . . I thought

I'd go back home and . . . well, no, I thought that with money I wouldn't have to go back home, because I really don't have one, but I wanted enough money so I could make my own future—not as Lucy Rose, but as Lucy Markham again . . . an American girl who doesn't even know she resembles that English actress that used to sing in *Pinafore*—just like you said, and I . . . I . . ." She took in a breath and didn't hold it very long before she blurted, gazing at him helplessly, "I want to marry. I want to marry someone respectable, Kyle. I want to be entirely respectable, and happy."

"Oh, yes," he said, "one does guarantee the other— I'd forgot. Well, listen, my dear, in your case, as in mine, money will buy you happiness. Success as an actress will make you rich, and respectable or not, as you please. And fame is the only measure of an actress's success, isn't it?"

She became silent, and remained so until Duncan wriggled, recalling her attention to her abandoned task.

"How often do I have to go out?" she asked softly.

She recognized him immediately, and swung her head around to pretend that she didn't.

"Oh, please, ma'am," he said, putting his hand to his hat brim, as his other held the horse's reins so that his handsome high light carriage kept even with her, even though she'd picked up her pace. "I know it's not fittin' to accost a young lady in the street—I may be from the West, but that much I do know, I promise you. I may be lackin' in my manners right now, but I do know them. My mama would kill me for flirtin' in public like this," he said with a slight grin that won a roguish glance from Ada, although Lucy kept walking, head up, eyes straight ahead.

"But I'm a stranger to New York, and I surely don't know what else to do to get you to listen to me, Miss Rose. I wait outside the theater, just like I'm supposed to do. But you wind up chattin' with Mr. Nichols one night, or Mr. Larkin the next, and you look right past me as though I was made of glass," he said as they all, the two ladies on the pavement and he, in his light carriage, paused at the corner for traffic. "Why, I've taken to checkin' to see I've still got my shadow, 'cause you just don't seem to see me," he complained softly.

But she did, Lucy thought rapidly, as she kept her head high, although she yearned to take a clear look at him in daylight. Surely, she thought, he wouldn't be as attractive then, and she wouldn't feel the same rising panic she did every time she'd glimpsed him in the shadows at the theater. His voice was as different and exciting as she'd thought it might be each time she'd seen him staring at her, towering above all her other stage-door admirers in every way. He sounded as different as he looked from the rest of them. That was just the problem.

She knew him amazingly well from just a few glimpses, though from the first it was as though she'd seen him before, although she couldn't remember having done so. Maybe it was because he was the kind of man most girls wished they could see. His clean-shaven face was lightly tanned and his nose was irregular, but for all that, he was, if not more handsome precisely, then certainly more attractive than any man she'd yet seen in New York. He'd more and longer hair than the other gentlemen too, and it seemed to glow dark gold in the night. She couldn't guess at the color of his eyes, but the shadows always emphasized his high cheekbones and determined chin, and the perfect cut of his mouth. Oh, yes, she'd noticed him.

But only that. Precisely because he was as different from her other admirers as his deep, Western-accented tones were.

She'd take one look each night, and look away. One glance was enough to tell her that this was no eager and manageable young puppy like John Larkin, or as effeminate and frivolous a gentleman as Fred Nichols. And she'd bet he wasn't as patient and tolerant as that nice old Mr. Price. He was nothing like those safe gentlemen she'd allow herself to be seen with at luncheons and afternoon teas at fashionable places in the city. No, and from the way even her skin tingled when she glimpsed him, she wondered if she'd be disgusted with him if he lured her to a private parlor and . . . No. That was the problem. She feared nothing that the gentleman might do to her in public; it was what he might make her want to do with him that absolutely terrifed her.

Lucy had never met anyone like this man before, but she could do without the experience now. She thought of herself as a decent, reasonable girl, and despite all the dime novels, she didn't know if any man really had the power to sway a decent girl—but she'd rather not test that theory. She'd always suspected that half the trick to remaining virtuous in an evil world was in avoiding situations that tried that virtue. Otherwise nuns wouldn't have convents, would they? But she didn't have such a refuge. She saw right through him whenever she saw him because she simply couldn't afford to see him, whoever he was, and that was that.

These days she passed in the theater were only for the money, before they faded to dim memory and she could begin her respectable life again. And few men, however respectable, expected anything respectable from an actress—unless they were less than masculine, as her approved suitors were. Nothing had tempted her in this new life but money before, and if she was careful, nothing would.

That would be hard to explain to Ada, who was smiling and eyeing him as they waited to cross the intersection. It would be even harder to explain to the amused and interested onlookers who'd begun to notice their odd conversation.

"It can't be my flowers," he said as they started walking again and he picked up the reins as his horses trotted beside them, " 'cause I sent every which kind in the shop. Aw, please, Miss Rose, take pity on a poor wayfaring stranger. I've been in New York only one month. When I came it was August, and now it's getting chillier—much chillier. Oops," he said as she walked on, stumbled because she didn't see where she was going, and collected herself as Ada giggled.

"I know you've been here only a little while too. My name is Joshua Dylan, ma'am," he said respectfully, tipping his hat just as she dared a glance, and the sight of his shining gold hair and intent gray eyes caused her to wrench her eyes back to the street before her as her cheeks burned.

Ada was poking her in the ribs, under her handbag, just beneath where she was holding her arm, as he continued, "All I want is to tell you how much I enjoy all your performances, and I've seen almost all of them since I first saw you. I thought we might meet for some dinner. Or luncheon? Or tea? Or coffee, or milk . . . anything you want. I'm respectable, ma'am," he said so longingly that despite herself she was just about to stop and smile and begin to speak to him. But then he spoke again.

"In fact," he said more enthusiastically, "we might have a lot in common. My father was English too. From London and a place called Arundel."

Her head shot up. He was danger on danger, with danger as a side course.

"I don't consort with gentlemen I meet in the street. Good day, Mr. Dylan," she said in her haughtiest British accents.

"But you do with those you meet in the alley backstage?" he called after her incredulously as she dragged a clearly unwilling Ada down a street she'd never intended to walk, just to get away from what she most wanted to do.

He was there again that night, of course, only this time with a mocking grin to show that he knew she remembered.

And the next night, when he didn't grin as Fred Nichols complimented the way her hat matched her gown and fussed over the new way she wore her hair—though even in the dim light she could see that his eyes agreed, and more.

And moreover, she told herself the next night, as she tried and failed to fall asleep, it was cowardly to run away. And yet, she argued as she flipped over her overheated pillow in order to rest on the cool side, it was only sensible to run away from a fire.

By the next night she was getting weary with her nightly arguments with herself, and Kyle looked at her sharply when she hesitated over a line she knew as well as her own name. Then, when she agreed to take tea with Mr. Price, and she saw him watching her from where he lounged against a wall, she wished that she was just a little girl again and that someone would settle the matter for her, taking it out of her own two hands.

So when she was ready to leave for home the next night, as she always did after her performance, and she met up with Ada as she was about to go out again for the night, as she always did after hers, she was as relieved as angry when Ada's fashionable new beau, Mr. Peter Potter, bowed over her hand and said, "How do you do, Miss Rose. I'd like you to meet my closest friend, a highly respectable fellow. Miss Rose, may I present Mr. Joshua Dylan?"

"What more can I do?" he said as he took her hand. "I'm sorry, but I was gettin' desperate. I tell you what, Miss Rose. Just come out with me once. Just once. For a drive in the park, nothin' could be safer or simpler. In the park, in the daytime," Josh said quickly when she didn't answer. "On a Sunday," he added. "Now, what could be wrong in that?"

She looked up into eyes she couldn't see too well in the dark, and wished she could meet him in the dark too, so that he wouldn't know what she was thinking any more than she knew what she was doing. But she did. And she knew that there was only so much running she could do. He could turn out to be a fool, or a boor or a nasty, lecherous man, or even one of those perverts girls were always warned about. She hoped so. Then she'd never have to see him again. But she doubted it. She knew her own luck. It had just been too good for too long a while.

It had all been like a glorious dream until now. She'd left Grandmother. She'd become an actress, and a successful one, with no effort, and in no time at all. She was growing used to applause, and soon she'd be getting used to a full purse. Because the house was full each night too, and Kyle had promised a raise in her wages within weeks. It had been wonderful, exactly like a dream, in that none of it had ever really touched her. Everything had been going so well, and then, just as with a dream, real life had come along and complicate things.

She sighed. And raised her eyes to meet his directly. And remembered her British accent just in time when she saw what she imagined she did in his eyes. But she had to meet the challenge.

"Very well, Mr. Dylan," she said, raising her chin, "Sunday it is."

"But not at dawn, with pistols, ma'am," he said gently. "So don't fret. I'll be a perfect gentleman, I promise."

Since that was exactly what she feared, she only smiled, and being an actress, and a good one too, she said, "Wonderful. I shall look forward to it, sir."

7

IT WAS A perfect day, warm and clear and sunny, with only just enough clouds flying in an azure sky to give it some contrast, only just enough coolness in the soft breeze to show that autumn was coming. It was Lucy's day off, and she was riding in a fashionable carriage with a handsome gentleman, and in all, she'd have considered it all a part of the amazing dream she'd been having since she'd left home, if she wasn't so vividly aware of the danger lurking in all the pleasure. And, of course, she thought, if her corset wasn't laced so tight she had to sit up straight as if she were on pins instead of a comfortably padded seat.

"You can relax," Josh said, sliding a glance to her as he maneuvered his curricle into a slow-moving lane, "I've got the horses under control. It's so crowded here, they couldn't get far even if I didn't," he added. "If I don't know much about New York, I do know horses. So just sit back and enjoy the day."

"Oh, I am," she said somewhat breathlessly, the way she always had to speak if she'd eaten while laced into her new dresses. That was why she preferred eating at home, where she could sit down to breakfast in a dressing gown, or have dinner after the theater in similar comfort. She'd found it always took a few hours for the food to go down, or resettle, or do whatever it had to do until her stomach, however flat it had been before she ate, deflated enough to be tightly laced into her corset in the highest fashion again. But Josh Dylan had arrived at noon, exactly on time, and insisted on taking her out to luncheon before their promised ride in Central Park. She'd toyed with her food, but it looked so good she'd swallowed some, and that was what made her so breathless, of course, she thought, and not just the knowledge that she rode in a handsome high curricle amidst all the fashionable of New York. And certainly not merely because she rode at the side of a gentleman who, to judge from the looks he was getting, took the breath away from all the women watching him from other carriages too.

But she got her own share of stares. She wore a dashing green-and-rust floral-figured promenade dress, high at the neck and tight all the way from her chest to her toes, with a ruffle she sat on that made another cushion beneath her, and her hat had a feather as green as grass to show up the burnished red shining in her long spiraling gold curls. Fine as she looked, she decided she was stared at because she was recognized as "The English Rose." Because she saw other girls dressed finer, and many she thought were prettier, and all of them, from what she could see of their slight smiles and supercilious stares, were more used to such treats than she.

Central Park was filled with carriages, and most were bigger than the one she rode in. There were great open black victorias and glossy broughams and town coaches with whole families in them, driven by smartly liveried coachmen, attended by uniformed footmen, with small boys in similar but miniature costume proudly and precariously perched in back like charming afterthoughts. There were dozens of smaller stylish coupes and other curricles, and a few lone horsemen and women on the paths, as well.

"Peter told me it would be crowded, but I didn't know the half," Josh said. "It's my first day out in this new rig too. Now that I've moved to the Fifth Avenue Hotel at last, I've got carriage space. I thought this was a mite small, but it's a nicely handling runabout. The team's got a better pedigree than most people I know. But it isn't a patch on what I see now. There's thousands of dollars on the hoof here today. Are you as impressed as I am? No," he answered himself immediately, before she could agree, "guess not. My father told me Regent's Park was mecca to English coachmen, and I guess you've seen more and better before."

"No," she said after a second's hesitation, "never like

this," and that was true enough and just honest enough
to please her as much as it seemed to please him.

He wasn't dressed differently from the other gentlemen, she noted, but then, in all fairness, gentlemen
couldn't dress *that* differently. He wore checked trousers
and a tight-fitting Norfolk jacket, and she was secretly
pleased to see he had a green vest, as if to match her
own outfit. But even though the gentlemen dressed the
same, they looked as different as the various horses they
drove. Josh was like his own matched chestnut team, she
decided. He was bigger than most men, and although
lean, his clothes didn't conceal his athletic form any more
than the sleek gleaming hides of his horses hid their own
smooth musculature. His overlong golden hair blew in
the breeze just as their own windswept manes did. And,
she mused, his tanned skin contrasted with the pale gentlemen around him so as to make him stand out from
the lot of them too. He was, Lucy realized, wrenching
her wayward thoughts from comparisons between strong
males and strong horses, even more disturbing in full
sunlight than he was beneath deceptive gaslight.

Josh waved to some gentlemen here and there, and
they all stared, which would please Kyle very much when
she told him, Lucy thought. After he'd saluted a few
coaches, Josh answered her unasked question with a
laconic, "I belong to a gentlemen's club. Seems they all
drive out on Sunday. They'll be mad as fire I didn't stop
and introduce you, but I'm just as glad there's no way
to, because I don't want to share you. Well, I only have
this afternoon, don't I? If I don't please you, I guess I
don't get another chance, do I?" he sighed. "It's too bad
you couldn't choose another day—or another night. . . ."
He slid a glance to her and laughed, showing strong,
even white teeth.

"Don't worry," he said before she could explain about
her days or lie about her nights off again. "I won't nag,
or I'll ruin my chance for another Sunday. But they told
me there was a nifty concert on the Mall here yesterday,
and there's less traffic most weekday afternoons. There's
supposed to be a fine collection at the menagerie, if
you're interested in tigers and camels—but from the
looks of the crowd here, it'd probably be a real caution

there today. It looks like the day for parading in circles in coaches too—though there's supposed to be some real driving, even some racing up on Harlem Lane. Want to try it? Not the racing, of course," he said quickly, "but the ride to see what's happening there? This creeping in line's as frustrating for me as for the horses. I'd like to let them out a little. And I'd like to be able to talk to you without watching to see we don't ride over some- body's foot. Some of these fellows are driving snails. Don't worry, I know there's a squatters' town in the park. I've got directions, we'll ride past them. Any which way, I'll take care of you. Shall we?"

She hesitated, toying with her parasol, wondering if he knew it was precisely his care she was worrying about. Was it any wiser to go somewhere less crowded to talk with this man than it would be to go somewhere dark with him? As she began to imagine as many pitfalls lurk- ing in conversation as in the possibility of physical con- tact, he added sadly, "Maybe not, huh? Guess you want to be seen as well as see the crowd."

"I'd love to go," she said, preferring to face danger rather than have him believe she'd such vanity and ambi- tion, never wanting him to think she was using him as she'd used the other gentlemen she'd been out with.

It took a while to wheel the curricle out of the press of fashionable vehicles, and then they were off on a smooth trot along a long, winding paved lane. They were surrounded on both sides by trees, and while they were by no means alone, there was a dramatic change in the atmosphere. The air smelled sweeter; it was quieter, birdsong could be heard aside from the steady beat of hooves, as could their own voices, giving their words more consequence than they'd had in the noisy, cluttered heart of the park. So Lucy was very careful about what she said, and the accent in which she said it.

"I like New York very much, from what I've seen of it," she answered in response to his first question, "but as you say—with six night performances a week, plus a matinee, I haven't seen as much as I'd like to.

"I've an older sister, and she's much prettier than I," she answered quickly as soon as he'd posed his next ques- tion, "but alas for you, she's married. My parents are both gone, as are my grandparents—the ones who raised me when my parents passed away. I've only one grand-mother left at home," she said, lowering her lashes as she thought of Brooklyn, and biting her lip as she realized he was thinking of London, because her deception lay heavy on her when she spoke with this genial, threatening, charming gentleman.

So she spoke up quickly, before he could form another question: "But come now, sir, I know all about me. What of you? I've never met anyone from the American West. Tell me about Indians and buffalo and outlaws, please do, we haven't any of those where I come from—not like your Mr. Jesse James, at least, that is to say," she added, ducking her head in wretched confusion, remembering all at once that England had highwaymen and that the tabloids said that Billy the Kid actually came from Brooklyn too.

He chuckled, and answered, and began to tell her wild, impossible, and impossibly funny stories about his life in the West. She breathed a long, trembly sigh. It was just as Kyle had said. It wasn't so bad if she stayed close as she could to the truth, and evaded whatever became too specific. But she discovered it was much easier to ask him questions, and more interesting too.

"No," he went on musingly as his eyes seemed to see much further than the team he was guiding, "I've never had any real trouble with the Indians. Which doesn't mean that there isn't any anymore. No, I've lost friends to them in my time, and I worry about some others I know up at Fort Laramie. But, shoot," he said, giving one wide shoulder a brief shrug that didn't go so far as to confuse his team, "can't hardly blame them, much as I'm willing to fight them for what's mine. What's mine *now*—that's the thing. Well, it was all theirs, once upon a time, and then we came pouring in and took it without a by-your-leave, didn't we?"

"I hadn't expected a Westerner to say that," she said in genuine surprise.

"You can bet I don't say it back home!" he answered on a laugh, before his face grew grave again. "It wasn't like it was with the Romans and the Britons back where you come from: we didn't take over their houses and ask to be their emperors. They didn't have houses, exactly—that might be the whole problem. They just range the land like the buffalo they live off, taking what's there, moving on to another patch when it gives out, with the seasons. We're just like two different species, I guess, and it couldn't work—like trying to run sheep and cows on the same acres. Our kind put up houses and fence them in, and they move like Arabs across the desert. . . ." He glanced to her, and saw how still she'd become.

Taking her serious expression as boredom and her silence as disapproval for his dropping his flirtation, he added on a grin, to change the subject to one he thought she'd respond to, "Now, maybe if the A-rabs had discovered America, instead of us Westerners, everybody would've been happy. They live in tents, and have a couple of wives apiece too—why, just think on it, ma'am, belly dancers and squaws, camels and bison side by side on the prairie!"

She was not diverted, as he'd wished, but neither was she in the least bored. There was as much interest in her voice as in her eyes as she spoke.

"I never thought of that," she said slowly. "Oh, not that foolishness about bedouins and braves together—although that's a fantasy fit for the stage," she admitted, nevertheless waving the notion away with one little gloved hand, "but the idea that we claim and hold the land they only want to wander through. All the penny novels I've read only paint the Indians as savages and black villains, you see."

"No," he laughed, "can't say I ever have. They paint themselves in brighter colors than that when they go on the warpath."

But then he added, sobering, "And it's not a pretty sight, no matter how colorful it is. No, for all a man may feel sorry when he thinks about what he and his kind have done to them, it's hard to keep it going. As I said, I've lost too many friends to them. I've just been lucky myself, I guess. Or traveling too fast to interest them, or maybe interesting them too much by traveling fast for them to take a shot at me—they purely do love speed, and horseflesh, almost as much as I do. That's not all we both love," he said wryly. "I generally lose several head

of cattle to them on my farther ranges in a bad winter.
Come to think of it, I haven't seen that many buffalo
lately . . . there were thousands when I was a boy,
too. . . .

"But I was born here in America, just like they were,"
he said forcefully, as if she'd argued the point. "I can't
go back to where my father came from any more than
they can leave the land now . . . and a man's got to
live."

She sat very still, and he silently cursed himself for
getting so serious. But she'd seemed so genuinely interested that he'd forgotten his aims, and her nature. Now
he remembered. He lowered his voice to its most seductive level. "A man's got to live," he drawled, "but not
bore a lady to tears with talk of Indians and moral
rights—not when he's lucky enough to be sittin' next to
a lady who looks as pretty as a poster outside her theater.
Forgive me, ma'am."

"For what?" she demanded, looking as angry with him
now as he'd thought she might be for his philosophizing
instead of flirting. "For speaking to me as though I might
understand something more than compliments? I know
what I look like, Mr. Dylan, and while I can't agree with
all your praise, I appreciate your opinion in the matter—
but I'd much rather hear some things I don't know.
Truly," she added, looking so sincere that, actress or no,
he had to believe her. And so set out to entertain her
with increasingly fanciful stories of the West.

It was while he was telling her a wonderfully tall tale
about driving a stagecoach and eight horses down a
snowy mountain in the dark that she began to become
distantly aware of something more unusual. She listened
closely to something he wasn't saying.

"I agreed, if only because I'd agreed, and a man's
word is his bond in the West," he went on as he let his
team out a little more, as though the story were carrying
him away as well, "so I unplugged my bottle of whis-
key—and after the horses all had a drink, there was
enough left for me too. Then I closed my eyes, picked
up the whip and the reins, and tried to remember the
exact words to all of 'Amazing Grace. . . .' Well, you
needn't laugh," he said with great mock annoyance, fix-

ing her with an affronted gray stare. "Not everyone can
remember them all."

It was as he was noting her show of even teeth and
the way her eyes crinkled up at the corners as she
stopped giggling and burst into laughter—just as if she
were any girl alight with merriment, and not a sought-
after stage actress, he was thinking—that it finally
occurred to her. She stopped laughing abruptly. She sat
up straighter than her corset demanded, and her eyes
grew tawny in the reflected sunlight. He stopped admiring the effect when he heard her words.

"Why . . . you're no more from the West than I am!"
she cried.

When he looked at her in puzzlement, she said very
haughtily, the more so because she'd been feeling so
guilty about her imposture while all along he'd been
deceiving her, "When I met you, you drawled like a
music-hall cowboy, and dropped all your G's. 'I'm goin' '
. . . 'You were sayin'.' " she mimicked him. "But now
you speak as well as I—well," she said, a little more
quietly, remembering the truth was that she didn't even
speak as well as she did, "at least as well as any man in
New York, and better than most. I don't believe you're
even from Wyoming Territory. Just who are you, Mr.
Dylan?" she asked, all at once too aware of how far
they'd driven and how far she was from home.

She'd never walked out with anyone whose name,
address, and family she didn't know, before she'd become an actress. Nor had she appreciated how good an
idea that was. Now she realized she could very well be
in the clutches of a terrible man: all the lectures, adages,
and sermons about women who dared life on their own
that were never far from her mind might be true. Such,
she thought, eyeing him nervously as he gazed back at
her, oh, such might well be the wages of sin.

"I am from the West," he said gently, "and I'm not.
I was born right here in New York, and left when I was
nine. My father was English. So I can speak like him, or
like any Easterner. But I've spent most of my life out
west, so I can speak that way too. It's just that I thought
I'd have a better chance with you if I was more exotic
than most of the other fellows who were after you. I was

right, wasn't I? And then too," he said, shaking his head and smiling slightly, "playacting sometimes saves feelings, I guess. Win or lose. It's easier to be bold when you're not being yourself, and a darned sight easier being turned down if you're just a poor wanderin' cowboy," he added with his deepest drawl, before he said sofly, "You're an actress. Can you understand? And forgive me?" he asked, his head to one side.

She did immediately, for the look on his face. She did, because of his sad smile. And she did, for reasons she didn't dare think of just now, when he added, "It's not as though I actually *lied* outright and cold."

"No, no, it's not," she said, turning her head away. "I do understand . . . so then . . . How do you do, Mr. Dylan," she said, recovering, and holding her head high as she held her hand out to him.

"Fine, now," he said on a smile, and briefly took her hand, and briefly considered holding it longer, before he felt her tug it away and he attended to his team again. "Better now that we're starting with a clean slate, now that I can stop being on guard. I can be myself. Imposture starts to become permanent after a while—you can forget who you really are. I don't know how you actresses do it."

"Ah, but," she said with a bright, nervous smile, "it would be difficult to believe I was Josephine, wouldn't it? Ned's not the most fatherly of men."

"You know," he mused, "I sometimes wondered about that. I think they'd have locked him up for the way he looked at you if he was."

"As transparent as that?" she laughed. "And here I thought leers couldn't be seen from the fifth row."

"Oh, good," he said, "then you didn't see mine."

As she was trying to decide whether to take that as a compliment, an insult, or an invitation, he changed the subject to her feelings about America again. And so she murmured something inconclusive and asked about his homesickness for Wyoming, and he replied by asking her about London weather. It was several minutes before they stumbled onto the subject of books they'd read. When he registered surprise that an Englishwoman had read not only Charles Dickens and Jane Austen but also

Mark Twain and Louisa May Alcott, she countered by
exclaiming in wonder because a Westerner had read not
only Mark Twain and Bret Harte but also Jules Verne
and Victor Hugo. They were so engrossed in conversation they were almost disappointed when they reached
the long broad drive they'd sought.

But not quite. He'd all the rigs and teams to look at,
and she'd so many fashionable people to try to recognize.
It wasn't as crowded as the heart of the park had been,
but the carriages here were more streamlined—even her
inexpert eye could see they were built for speed as well
as comfort—and there were a great many of them. There
were more gentlemen than ladies on the broad long avenue, but those ladies present were as elegant and expensive as the rigs their gentlemen drove. No woman
acknowledged Lucy's presence at all, and that was odd,
for all the gentlemen did, and a few nodded to Josh as
they drove past. Some spoke to him.

"Miss Lucy Rose . . . Mr. Edgar Yates," Josh said,
and Lucy didn't need the slight stiffness in her escort's
voice to warn her from Mr. Yates. There was too much
speculation in his smile, far too much presumption in the
way his eyes traveled over her, assessing her. She was
relieved when Josh begged off from the older man's invitation to try his high curricle, more so when he declined
another invitation to supper before he drove away.

But, "His team didn't look up to it," was all he said
in explanation for the first refusal, and his second remark
made her forget his first, when he added, "and if I get
the chance to take you to supper, I do not want
company."

Then his face lit up as he seemed to recognize someone
else in the crowd, but by the time he'd angled his team
and got to the place he sought, whoever it was was gone.
"Odd," Josh said, frowning. "I thought . . . But never
mind. Doesn't matter. See here, Miss Rose, speaking of
supper, I've had enough fresh air. I've had years of it,
remember? It's getting late. You don't have a performance tonight. And I'm still not used to eating alone. So
will you, could you, won't you, please come to supper
with me?"

The curricle was stopped. And such was the power of

his intent gray gaze and such was the pull of the
attraction in his handsome hard face, that she knew, in
that moment, that she could never go with him tonight.
Because supper would be in some dark restaurant, and
then it would be darker, and there was only so much
experience she had of such things, after all. But she
didn't want to hurt his feelings. She didn't want to lose
him entirely. And if for a moment she wondered what
she'd have to do to keep him, or what she'd do if she
did, she decided to think of that later, some other, much
later, later.

He watched the expressions play over her face. Amazing, he thought, for an actress to have such transparent
feelings. If she did. But she wanted him, he'd swear it,
as much as he did her. Her eyes, almost golden in the
reflected late-afternoon sunlight, had been clear a moment
ago, but now they clouded with doubt—with fear? No,
impossible, he thought, as intrigued as he was drawn to
her. He wanted to know more. From the look on her
face, he doubted it would be right away. Still, from the
look in her eyes he knew it would be, someday. He was
content with that. She was playing games. He was very
good at games. So he was ready for her answer before
it came.

"I can't," she said softly, the English stresses of the
"cahn't" causing him to smile. "Tonight, I can't. But
some other time?"

"Some other night?" he asked, leaning toward her, the
width of his shoulders blotting out the sun, making her
forget they were surrounded by people, making her
afraid she'd forget to say no.

"Not yet," she blurted, and asked hurriedly, "Next
Sunday?"

She seemed so sincerely anxious, he relented.

"Next Sunday," he agreed, picking up the reins and
heading his team back downtown. "Where would you
like to go?"

"I don't know New York," she reminded him.

"I hear we can walk across the ropewalk they've strung
up between Brooklyn and Manhattan, where they're putting up the bridge . . ." he began, only to see her flinch.
"Guess not, no head for heights, I see. How do you feel

about water? There's a boat we can take out from the Battery along the shore all the way to the Rockaways and back in a day. If the weather holds, would you like that?"

"Fine," she said. "Good," she said. "Lovely," she said, because it sounded all of those things, and safe besides.

"Good," he said, because he'd enjoy a day with her almost as much as he expected to enjoy the night he'd soon have with her. She had conversation and charm as well as those incredibly good looks. She was the first woman he'd ever met who looked as lovely by day as by night, and was as good to listen to as he believed she'd be to touch. When it came, he believed it could be more than a hasty hour—much more than they'd bargain for. But being no stranger to disillusion, he decided to enjoy the anticipation of it even if it weren't.

He wondered if it was jewelry or cash she was after, and because he was tired of simple games, was pleased he didn't know yet, very pleased to wait to hear her price. He congratulated himself; it was the most interesting decision he could have made. Women were so easily come by in this city, the best way to have them was the way he was doing it now—to pretend to doubt he could.

"Next Sunday," he said contentedly.

He drove her downtown, chatting lightly about a dozen little things that made them laugh, as he smiled at her, wondering if she'd leave on her corset too, and she smiled back at him, relieved at the week's reprieve she'd won.

"Then it *was* you I saw!" Josh said. "But you were gone when I got there," he complained.

Jacob Van Horn smiled. "Joshua, my young friend," he said into the thin cloud of cigar smoke he blew at the ceiling of his clubroom, "Henry Litton was right. I'm glad I listened to him, or I'd have made as big a mistake as you almost did. No, bigger. Because I like you, young man, and wouldn't have wanted to sever our relationship in error."

His thin patrician face showed traces of genuine warmth as he said mildly, "You know a great deal about overland travel, railroads, cattle, oil—and God knows what else to make money from. I respect you in such matters. But you don't know New York yet. Please, listen. I saw you coming and was astonished. I escaped by the skin of my teeth—how you got through that crowd! You can drive like the devil. I could have been . . . dammit, I *was* angry—but I asked you to lunch today because I believe in my first impressions of a man: I thought it might be that you didn't know."

"Joshua," he said sternly, "I couldn't acknowledge you yesterday afternoon. I had my daughter with me."

Josh's face grew cold and still, so that the insult he felt was disguised by unspecified anger. It was enough to cause his companion to catch his breath and remain in his seat only by reminding himself of the comforting, civilizing background of his club, and all of his fellow members, as well as servants surrounding him. Josh's dark gold eyebrows rose when Jacob spoke again, as much for his words as for the supplicant tone of them.

"You were with an *actress*, my good fellow. That Englishwoman everyone's speaking of. A gentleman keeps his . . . diversions far from a lady's eyes."

"She's not my . . . diversion yet," Josh replied.

"However. She's still an actress," the older man explained. "My daughter can see her at the theater—if she's in something suitable, Shakespeare or such. Never socially. But I want her to meet you. Let's forget yesterday. I know you don't sail. How would you like to try? I've a small yacht. We live near the water on Long Island, but we meet up near High Bridge. I'd very much like you to come with me, as my guest, next Sunday."

It was lightly said for such a great honor. But such men of power, like ancient kings, were used to giving their heaviest tributes in casual voices. There were men who'd give up much more than a promised appointment with an actress for such an opportunity. Jacob had more than social position: he'd stock in a railroad Josh wanted, he'd real estate Josh needed, with his connections he'd an ear to all the things rustling in the depths of the financial pages that Josh would dearly love to hear. And just now, he'd said he had a daughter. It was possibly more than an honor. Incredibly enough, it might even be the prelude to an enormous opportunity for more than a business merger. If the young woman with him yesterday had been his daughter, Josh thought, remembering the glimpse he'd got of an elegant, slender girl on the high seat next to Jacob . . .

But he remembered a soft voice saying, "Fine, good, lovely," and he couldn't forget the look in those eyes. An actress could pretend to many things, but not, he thought, that particular look. Or if she could, he wanted to know of it; that kind of deception might even be better than truth. Still, he was no boy, to put lust above opportunity; no fool, to cast away years of ease for moments of pleasure.

He sighed as he realized none of this mattered. Because he'd given his word. He might be throwing away a golden crown in order to pick up a gaudy trinket, but he'd given his word.

"Thank you, Jacob," he said with honest regret, "but I'm busy that day."

"How about the following Saturday, then?" Jacob asked without pause. "Or, if it rains, then that next Sunday?"

Josh blinked. He was, he realized, like Caesar, being offered the crown thrice. He liked the number.

"Fine. Good. Lovely," he said, smiling.

The thing Lucy would always remember the most was the laughter. Maybe it had begun because she was so very nervous, and when she was on edge like that, she was prone to giggle. Maybe it was because she'd gotten up so early she wasn't entirely awake when they'd left Mrs. Fergus', and so her dignity hadn't been firmly in place yet. Or it might have been just that he was so funny, or the world looked funnier through his eyes, or that she was so happy to be with him. But after a long week of work, and worry because he never appeared at the stage door—not once after any of her performances— he appeared, on the dot, when he'd said he would, at the boardinghouse door on Sunday morning.

He'd stared at her for a speechless moment, taking in her new violet walking dress and the great floppy violet hat she'd tied over her hair. Then she'd introduced him

to the only other person awake in the house at that hour
of the morning, and he'd shaken Duncan's paw with such
gravity that she'd begun to laugh. They'd laughed after
he'd helped her into his curricle and she showed him the
lunch Mrs. Fergus had packed, and he silently produced
another straw hamper from behind his high seat. And it
seemed, as the sun climbed higher and they got to the
slip where the boat awaited, that they couldn't stop
laughing each time they were offered fruit and sand-
wiches and cakes by all the vendors that swarmed about
the passengers awaiting the ship on the dock.

But then she caught her breath, and paused, staring.

"I've never seen such an assortment of people," she
whispered, looking at the waiting passengers. There were
whole families, from grandmothers to infants, and young
couples, and children by the score. They were dressed in
their Sunday best, and that best, she realized with widening eyes, varied considerably. There were people from
every social stratum in New York preparing to board—
every one—except, obviously, for the very rich and the
very poor.

"Would you like to leave?" he asked quietly. "We can
picnic in the park or go somewhere else."

"Oh, no!" she said at once. "I never meant that. I was
just surprised. And actresses have to get to know many
types, don't they? Although," she admitted, watching the
passengers beginning to board the ship, "I never knew
there were quite so many types."

He laughed, and offered her his arm.

"Prepare to learn," he said, leaning close in order to
have a private word with her, and so almost causing her
not to hear what he said as his warm breath touched her
ear and, seemingly, her wits, "valiant little sailor."

The ship was huge, or so it seemed to be, since the
wildly wide assortment of people had room and to spare
in which to stroll its decks beneath its towering sails.
Even if it had been crowded close, Josh and Lucy would
have been very much alone. Because people in New
York learned to ignore each other beautifully, even if
they were forced to be cheek by jowl, and today they
weren't. And their fellow passengers were well-occupied.
From the moment the ship left the dock, all the mamas

were occupied with keeping the children away from the rails and out of the water, and the papas with holding their high hats on their heads and keeping their families in line.

The water was clear and blue as the sky, the wind sent the ship slicing and bobbing through the froth, and Lucy discovered to her delight that the motion made her nothing but exhilarated as the ship strode on beneath her. Josh discovered, as he told her, that it was much less difficult than staying upright on an unbroke horse or on any mule. They staggered along the deck under the snapping sails until they got their sea legs, and clung to the rail to point out things on the horizon, and breathed in the salt wind as it carried their laughter away.

At noon they went below to dine, but the sound of the children wailing and the parents shouting and the sight of some few being dramatically ill sent them out into the sunlight again. They found a place to perch on a bulkhead near the cabin, and ate their chicken, pâté, ham, cakes, fruit, and bread while sliding along their improvised seats; and drank their champagne and gasped and giggled when the ship sent it down their throats on the outside, as well as in. Something in the air made them finish every scrap, even though Lucy's laces, not so tight for this pleasure trip as for her job, made her fill up so that every extra bite was as much pain as pleasure, and Josh, too, never noticed what it was he ate.

As they ate they eyed their fellow passengers and commented on them in low voices, trying to guess their occupations from their appearance and snips of conversation that came to their ears. She only stopped laughing when he congratulated her for getting so many of their New York accents right.

"Well, but I'm an actress, after all," she managed to invent, on a gasp, before he made her incapable of anything but laughter again as he envisioned the boatload of holidaying New Yorkers as the crew of the *Pinafore*, and began to cast characters from the assortment of people before them.

An old fellow with a cane and two middle-aged sons to guide his teetering steps across the deck became his captain of the *Pinafore*. As she was giggling at the thought of what Ned would think of that, he picked a small man, an immigrant father of what seemed to be several dozen children, as his Sir Joseph Porter. She was puzzling over why when she saw the man begin to shout at his unruly horde, and saw the way he waved his arms and contorted his face into bizarre expressions Lester would love to have copied. A buxom lady with a head of ginger hair that the wind made into a fuzzy halo became a suddenly credible Buttercup. A gentleman with a long and bothersome strip of hair that the wind kept lifting off the top of his otherwise secretly bald head was chosen as his Ralph Rackstraw.

"Oh, never, not *my* leading man," she chided him between giggles.

So he promptly pointed out another gentleman for the part, this one so fat that she had to immediately turn her head away into the privacy of Josh's wide shoulder so that the poor stout fellow wouldn't see her laugh so soon after looking at him. When she suddenly realized how close she was to Josh, so close that the lemon and sandalwood scent of him was stronger than that of the sea, she looked up to see his eyes, as gray as the foam, gazing down, serious now, at her.

She straightened and looked everywhere but at him.

"And so, who," she asked, flustered, "shall be me . . . Josephine?"

The sea breeze had pushed her hat to the end of its strings and it fluttered at the back of her head. He saw the long wind-fingered shining amber coils of her hair twining about her face like those of some beautiful sea creature he'd once seen illustrated in a book of myths, and it seemed exactly right to him, because with her wind-chafed cheeks and light-drenched eyes, he'd never seen such human beauty. He gazed at her lips and not her eyes as he answered slowly, "No one. No one but you."

Her laughter fled. She stared at him a heartbeat longer and then lowered her eyes, and hurriedly began to gather up the remains of their luncheon to pack away in the hamper. She carefully avoided touching the strong tanned hands that helped her, but nevertheless felt them guide her as she made her unsteady way to the railing once more when they were done. He leaned on the rail and looked down at her.

"Here, the sun is turning your nose pink," he said on a half-smile, and helped her tie on her hat again, as her cheeks grew even pinker than the tip of her nose. Then he stood by her side, between her and the sun, and before the wind, blocking it from her, as he blocked all other thoughts from her mind, even though she pretended a consuming interest in the wild shores they were passing.

"Imagine," he said softly, turning so that he could gaze at her and the horizon, "just imagine the world we're passing over now. They say the ocean's like the plains, seething with life—unseen by us—and that fishermen are the ranchers of the sea. I suppose they are: they herd and corral the creatures of the oceans. It must be much the same as it is on the prairie, for all it's so different, not only because of the hard work but also because it seems just as lonely here. I told you some tales about the West, but I don't think there's any way I could tell you about the loneliness of it, and what it does to a man."

"Ah," she said on a sigh, "but I know."

"What would you know of loneliness?" he asked, and she could hear, if not see, his gentle smile, as she continued to gaze out at the sea.

"You don't need a prairie or an ocean to know loneliness," she said slowly. "If the circumstances are right, you can be just as lonely here in New York, or in any city, however filled with people it may be. In fact, in some ways," she said, tilting her head to the side as she considered it, "it may be worse here. Because on the sea or the plains, you know it's only geography that's keeping you apart from others. When you're with masses of people, but ones you don't know and have no reason to speak with—why, then you can be even more alone, I think."

She spoke freely because they were alone—but as she'd said, not at all alone—and so he could hear her words, but she stood in no danger of his acting on them.

"That's true. But it's hard for me to think of someone like you ever being lonely," he said, and meant it.

Then she dared look up at him.

"Admiration is not company," she lectured him solemnly. "Flattery is not company. No, and neither is anyone's desire for my company, if I don't feel the same way. I assure you praise is not company. Applause is not either—but it *is* very nice," she added with a spurt of honesty.

She joined his laughter. The more so when he began applauding.

"Isn't there something else I can do to make you feel less lonely?" he asked plaintively after a moment. "Not only are my hands starting to smart, but I'm being stared at, and I'm not used to it."

"Oh, I doubt that," she laughed, before she added, "but you needn't do that—I don't feel in the least lonely now."

Nor did she, even though they fell silent. She stood at his side and watched the sea and the land, strangely confident that he knew what she neither said nor could say. It seemed he'd caught her mood. He spoke only to point out, smiling, that her home was just over that stretch of water, and she agreed, frowning, realizing how right and wrong he was. The only move he made was to put his hand over hers on the rail, and since it was daylight, and as the ship was rocking, and because there was no way on earth or sea that she'd move her hand after one brief involuntary spasm of startlement, they stayed so as the ship turned around. Then they watched the waves parting to take them back to a more familiar shore. And only then, seeing their afternoon ending as the land came closer, did either of them feel discontent.

"Now, then," he said as his curricle carried them back from the Battery and the late-afternoon shadows faded to early evening, "we'll be passing my hotel. Shall we stop in for some light supper?"

"I couldn't eat another bite," she said quickly.

"Then maybe so as to freshen up? The wind made you lovely. But we're on dry land now," he said gently, looking at the wonderful tangle of her hair.

"Oh, no," she said, "I've a comb, and it will take hours, I'll have to wash the salt air out of it anyway before I straighten it—that is, I don't want to straighten

it, just fix it . . ." She took in a breath, and held it until
he spoke again.

"Oh. Then would you like to stop in to see my rooms?
They're very fine . . . No," he said, frowning, "enough
subterfuge. Especially after a day like today. It's not worthy of you, or me. Would you like to stop in to spend
some time with me, Lucy?"

"I just have," she said, but he cut in, not smiling at
all now, or watching his team, only staring down at her:
"*Alone* with me. Now, and tonight, and for the rest of
the night."

"Oh," she said in a hurt, pinched voice before she
said, "Oh, no," and he added: "It will be my pleasure,
and I hope yours, and to your profit, I need not say."

She held her breath and stared up into his steady gray
eyes and then said all at once, "Oh no, you need not
. . . Oh, how I wish you had not! No, no, of course not,
no. I am not . . . I do not . . . I don't expect you to
understand," she said at last, defeated, "although, especially after today, I thought you did. . . . But no, I only
sing and act, and nothing more. Please take me home
now, please."

His horses didn't even slow as they passed his hotel,
and he didn't speak again until they had.

"My friend Peter, and your friend Ada—" he began,
but this time she cut in, without raising her eyes from
her gloves in her lap: "I'm not like Ada."

"I see," he said, though he didn't.

But if she didn't want him, that was her prerogative.
He'd never insist or cajole. She might be no better than
she should be, but she was gifted and lovely and sought-
after. And any woman had as much right as a man to
make her choice. He was as sorry as he was hurt that it
wasn't him, because he'd more than wanted her—he'd
admired and liked her. It went beyond vanity, and was
more than frustrated lust. It made him feel he'd failed
her in some unknowable way—unknown because he was
unlettered and undereducated, very much like the crude
cowboy he'd portrayed for her. It wasn't a new sensation.
Yet because of his twin codes of honor, none of this
showed in his face any more than it would in his actions.
He remained silent.

But when he stopped his team and looked at her again so as to hand her down to the street in front of her boardinghouse, he saw her eyes. He was astonished to see how red they were, and curiously hurt to see how bad she looked when crying.

"I'm truly sorry," he said when he stood with her in front of her door.

"I didn't want to make you angry," she said, her chin trembling as she tried to keep her voice level.

"Then it isn't me?" he asked.

She only shook her head.

He stopped that by placing his hand to the side of her cheek. Her mouth was warm and trembling and tasted of salt from the sea and her tears, as he tried to discover what else it offered. In slow time, it began to hesitantly offer him far more. She relaxed against him for that long delicious moment, only long enough for him to curse the style that encased that slender body in steel, before she pulled herself away and stared up at him. He knew what he'd do then, as did she, because it was in his eyes, as it had been in the hunger of his kiss. She was wondering how she'd react, when the door opened before them.

There was silence for the space of time it took each of the three people to assess their situations, and then Kyle spoke.

"Odd . . . it didn't seem blustery from inside . . . ah, but I remember, you were at sea, weren't you, my dear? Of course, just see what it's done to your hair and your eyes."

"Oh, Kyle," Lucy said distractedly as Josh and Kyle stared at each other, "this is Mr. Dylan, from Wyoming, the gentleman I was telling you about. Josh, this is Kyle Harper, my . . . ah . . . employer."

"Director, producer, manager," Kyle said smoothly as he saw the other man misunderstand Lucy's hesitation and description of him and his title, and complicating it further, he added sweetly, ". . . and good friend, I hope."

"Of course," Lucy said.

"How do you do," Kyle said.

"Well enough, and how are you, 'friend'?" Josh drawled.

They all stood silently until Josh put on his hat, and taking Lucy's hand, said, "Thank you for a lovely day, Miss Rose, I'll be in touch. Good evening, sir . . . ma'am," and smiling, turned and went down the short marble stair.

But he didn't show up at another performance that week, although she hesitated at the stage door each night, scanning the shadows. Nor did he send a message. And she didn't stop thinking about him any night as she lay in her bed and relived that day, searching through every well-remembered word for shadings of meaning that could tell her why he didn't come again . . . aside from the fact, as she reminded herself every night: that he'd thought her a prostitute, and didn't want her if she wasn't, and even if he didn't think so, thought Kyle was her lover.

Still, even if Kyle had apologized as insincerely and convincingly as he did everything else, she wouldn't, couldn't, dared not call on him at his hotel, as Kyle suggested she do if she were that disturbed. Which she wasn't, she also told herself every night, remembering Josh's words, his kiss, his laughter, all the way down into all of the rest of the night.

"You're a man of unexpected strengths, Mr. Dylan," Gloria Van Horn said admiringly as she saw how he stood firm on the deck of her father's sloop although it sloped with the waves that danced the ship out into the bright sunlight.

"No. Just, 'Josh,' " he answered. "Please."

8

"DEAR GRAY," Josh wrote, "I'm glad to hear you're settling in at school. No, I'm purely relieved, because I didn't feel like going home and dragging you there by your ears. That's why I haven't come to see you yet. I wanted you established there first, and to tell the truth, I didn't want to put up with you pleading to come home until you were. So I'm pleased you're tolerating the place. Now, if you're coming down for that football game against Columbia College, you'll be in my backyard. So, yes, you can stay with me. I've got these fine new rooms at the Fifth Avenue Hotel, and will be more than pleased to have your company. I get homesick too, sometimes— even if I *am* home now."

Josh dipped his pen into the ink again, and remembering his brother's fondest dreams, grinned as he set down the next line.

"Knowing of your interest in the modern drama, I'll even arrange to take you to the New York theater while you're here. If you're good, I'll introduce you to some friends I've made there too."

His face grew still as he wrote that. It was a gamble he was taking, and he hadn't called for his opponent's high card yet. He hadn't been in touch with Miss Lucy Rose since that strangely wonderful day they'd spent together on the sea. He wasn't sure of her relationship with that dark, sardonic "manager, director, and producer" of hers. She said she wasn't for sale, and she'd almost convinced him, but that, after all, was the best way for any clever dealer to get the ante up. The fact was that she was an actress. Still, he was in the game now, for good or ill. It was his move, and he knew enough about his fellowman and woman to know that a week's dead silence served him better at this point than appearing to languish at her doorstep. Now the week was up, and after he wrote and sent his letter, he'd dress and go to a party, and however pleasant it was, he'd end up at the theater. Because no matter how sweet life had been for him this past week, he couldn't get the taste of salt out of his mouth. And he didn't want to.

But thoughts of brine made him remember something else.

"Now, hold on to your hat, Scout," he wrote, "but your big brother went out on a yacht the other day. A private one, too. I ate caviar and oysters right over where they live, and drank French champagne while I chatted up a genuine American beauty . . ."

The pen left a spot where his hand paused, and he blotted it quickly. "Beauty" was an overstatement. Gloria Van Horn was handsome enough, but no beauty. Everything about her claimed she was, but she was more impressive than lovely. Her clothes were the finest and most expensive. But she was too slender for the sort of looks that would get her more than a nod back home, and her thin face was too much like her father's for the sort of feminine grace such a lean frame needed to soften it. Her smile was polite rather than spontaneous, but, he thought, maybe that was because it showed as much of her upper gums as her teeth. Her hair was shining clean, but straight and of an uninspiring, indeterminante color, and she moved, even balanced on shipboard, as though she were wearing the stiff corset she obviously never needed. That reminded him of something else.

"By the way, there's a thing about New York women your magazines only hinted at. Our women back home have got backbone. These ladies wear theirs outside."

Just thinking of the puzzlement on Gray's face cheered him. Then he frowned, trying to think of something else to say about Miss Van Horn, because he planned to introduce Gray to her when he came down for the weekend, and wondered if they might have to get to know each other a lot better than that in the future—because he thought he might be getting to know her much better himself.

Gloria was well-mannered and well-spoken. She might

even be intelligent; it was hard to tell, since her conversation had mainly been about her own circle of friends and her activities. All of which, having to do with cotillions and society people he didn't know, had bored him blue. But it was only fair, he thought, since his talk had all had to do with the questions she asked him about Wyoming. He concentrated, and tried to explain her attraction to Gray, who was the closest thing he had to a living conscience. It wasn't only because he was a younger brother who looked up to him. He'd never spoken down to Gray, because despite his youth, the boy had as much wisdom as candor. Josh picked up his pen again.

"It was Jacob Van Horn's yacht I was on. Yes, *the* Van Horn that's got the piece of the Iowa and Ohio track we need if we're ever going to get that spur to the Union Pacific we want for the cattle. If we get that, we can cut out a couple of hundred miles of droving and get less stringy steers to Chicago. Aside from improving the quality (the thing you're always going on about), I see now that it'll mean saving big money on the drive, and on the freight—*if* I can negotiate with him. He's also got some land needs looking into down south and out west, and an ear to the ground where the bulls and bears roam. And don't fool yourself, Scout, they're the only cattle worth a damn here in New York. He's got a daughter named Gloria, and she's as handsome as she is educated. I can't figure why she seems to like me. She's a . . ." He paused again, and not wanting to make another blotch on his letter, added quickly, ". . . real lady, and went to some school up near where you are. I hope you can meet her soon."

Thinking about that yachting excursion recalled him to memories of the sea again. Memories of another day of clean wind and salt air and sun and laughter. He shook them off and wrote about his day with the Van Horns again.

"I ran into William Henry V. and his wife at the dockside. He made some noise about having me to dinner, which gave some of my new friends a turn—yes, I've been playing the lonesome cowpoke again. Not with Miss Van Horn, of course, because I never set out to fool her pa. He's honest as he can afford to be, so I didn't have to be on my guard with him," he added as explanation, not mentioning that from the first he'd also seen that Van Horn's daughter wasn't likely to respect him for ignorance, whether because of geography or innocence, and moreover, had probably been trained to avoid contact with such a man.

"I'm getting to be quite a sailor," he wrote. "By day, I'm riding on yachts, and I'm spending my nights on the *HMS Pinafore*. I'm near the sea and the theaters, and there's a whole lot of both kinds of ships, real and theatrical, in the port of New York, but I think you'll like the same one I do best. If you're good, I'll take you too. Guess which one. See you soon, Yr. Big Bro.—Josh."

The room was more lavishly decorated than any he'd ever been in, and bigger than any as well—except for Central Station—and it was almost as crowded. What he could see of the floor was gleaming polished wood, the ceiling was high and painted over with an assortment of overweight gods and goddesses who seemed to be peering down at the company from between their toes, and even though a dozen musicians were playing in a corner, they could scarcely be heard. An army of uniformed servants bearing food and drink glided in and out among the guests.

The guests had sorted themselves out into natural groupings: the older ladies and gentlemen in two distinct clutches; the younger, of assorted sexes, in assorted interest groups. The invitation had said "soiree," so Josh hadn't known just what to expect. But if, as he suspected, the room had originally been built for dancing, it was clear that would be impossible here now.

He'd never been at such a party or even in a ballroom before, but nothing in Joshua Dylan's face or attitude betrayed that. He wore a beautifully fitted cutaway coat over a silver brocade vest and well-tailored straight-cut trousers. He stood tall and spoke softly, and ate the things offered to him from off silver trays, and drank out of crystal goblets, and no one could have known he didn't recognize or particularly like most of the things he was swallowing. Any more than they'd have guessed he didn't know half the things the other guests were talking about. The guests his age, that was.

"I did love Venice, but Dr. Johnson was entirely right: see Naples and die!" one young lady gushed, and another answered with amusement, "If you stayed at a hotel, I suppose. Father insisted on renting a palazzo for us."

"But Scotland! How can you forget Scotland!" another lady caroled, while the eager young man at her side said, "Yes, of course, for raw beauty. But how can you compare that with Italia?"

Since the young ladies were stealing glances at him from beneath their eyelashes, Josh had a feeling they'd soon be emboldened enough to ask his opinion in the matter. He wasn't surprised when the first question came.

"What do you say, Mr. Dylan?" a small young woman all in blue who worked hard at vivacity asked him. "For sheer beauty? Italy? Or Scotland?"

"Why, Miss Crandall, I couldn't say," he said gently, "since I've never been further east than where I stand—except for the day when your father," he said, smiling down at Gloria, at his side, "took me out to sea."

There was a moment's stillness. Well, he thought, not allowing himself to sigh, there it was. He'd played at being a rustic when it amused or protected him. But there was no sense in deception here. He wouldn't live a life of lies. This city was going to be his life. And his young hostess? Well, not hardly likely now, he thought ruefully, adopting the accents in his mind that he'd not used in his speech. Jacob had invited him. Gloria was standing by him, but that was a hostess's duty. He was only sorry he'd just made it harder for her.

Her friends had been chattering about their European travels for long moments now, and he'd envied them seeing everything he'd only read or heard his father talk about almost as much as he'd regretted how soon he'd be discovered. These were the favored few. They were wealthy and well-bred—too well-bred to immediately shun him for obviously not being of their kind. But they'd turn away; he was prepared for it. There were other roads to acceptance; he'd find them.

But he couldn't see himself; even his mirror never told

him what others saw. Tonight, in his new black evening suit, he stood out from the press of men. His size and form, and the steady eyes in that handsome face, had drawn the other guests to him.

"Josh is from the West, Wyoming Territory," Gloria said calmly, as she said all things. "He lived on a ranch, and actually drove the overland express stagecoach—for Wells Fargo, did you say?" she asked him.

Nothing in his face moved, but his muscles tensed. It might even have been that she could feel them bunch beneath the gloved hand she'd laid so lightly on his sleeve. It was hard to tell if she was putting him up to ridicule; he could see no reason for it. Even if she were, he could hardly remain silent. But before he could answer, one of the younger men reacted strongly.

"No!" the young man said. "The Wells Fargo Company? Why, that's wonderful. Did you really drive over the plains by night? Were the Indians troublesome? And buffalo. Gad—I've read and read about them. What keen hunting that must be! Hundreds of them out there, they say."

"Hundreds?" another young gent scoffed. "Thousands, I heard. Right, sir?" he asked Josh.

"And how would you know?" a young lady put in. "You've never been nearer to one than the Central Park menagerie."

"Thousands, it is," Josh said softly, and they fell silent. "There were thousands more when I was young. Even so, when they're on the run, the ground beneath your feet trembles. It's like they say—like a great brown wave coming over the prairie. Hard to say whether you scent them or hear them or feel them first, as they come rolling toward you over the miles. Hunting?" he asked on a shrug. "It's done, that's why there are fewer of them every year. But not much sport in it, I'd say. Not with a rifle. Like shooting ducks in a barrel. Ah, but with a bow and arrow, from a horse, or on foot . . . if you're in almost as much danger as your prey is—why, that's my idea of sport."

Quiet came over that part of the room as the young people in their group, some eight or nine of them, stood staring at Josh Dylan. It might have been the little pocket of silence, or the fact that Jacob Van Horn, as a practiced host, kept an eye on all his guests even as he chatted with some, but he looked up just then to see them there in their sudden hush.

By the time he'd maneuvered halfway across the huge, crowded room, there were two dozen young persons around Josh Dylan, all talking at once, trying to claim the tall young man's notice. By the time Jacob reached Josh's side at last, the group, twice as large now, was silent again. But that was because Josh was speaking.

"Why, yes. I did know Hank Monk. Hope I still do," he said with mock alarm, to their laughter. "He was fine enough when I saw him last, and he claimed he was almost a hundred then. Yes, he did give his horses liquor that night, just as it says in the song. But any driving man has done it in the past, if he's had to. It's the things they didn't put in the song that made his name. Now, let's see . . . what are some I can tell you with these lovely ladies here?"

The ladies cried their disappointment as one, and one bold one took the opportunity to strike him lightly with her fan, and won herself the instant hatred of the other young ladies for it, because it won her his smile. And then he answered their questions and told them about the celebrated stage driver Hank Monk and the old overland stage, and the winter of the Great Blizzard that stopped the trains, and other stories about the perils, rascals, and sorrows he'd seen and met in his days on the trail. Soon he had them all laughing, wondering, or gasping, as he wished, even Jacob. He played them like an actor might, and when they congratulated him, he protested that all he'd done was to tell the truth—a little.

"As little as possible, eh?" Jacob asked.

"No, sir, actually as much as possible. I only left out the truest parts because they'd be taken for lies."

"You should have been an actor," Jacob said happily, clapping him on the shoulder before he excused himself and went to visit with his other guests.

"Perhaps so," a striking-looking young woman with huge eyes said sweetly, glancing to Gloria, "I understand you do love the theater, Mr. Dylan. *Very* much . . . at least certain parts of it," she added, in case no one had caught her innuendo.

"True enough," he answered unhesitatingly, before any of the others in the group could become more uncomfortable than he felt. "But," he said softly, gazing down at Gloria warmly, "that was before I realized that all the world's a stage."

His hostess's eyes had been narrowed at his interrogator, but now they widened and the expression in them softened, suiting her very well. It suited her even better when the young woman who'd challenged Josh flushed and fell silent. Then another guest asked him about outlaws, and he was pleased to entertain them all so thoroughly that no one but himself noticed when the brash young woman stepped away.

Or so he thought until a while later. Gloria mentioned it after he'd excused himself from further questioning, bidden them all good night, and was taking a quiet leave of his hostess in the outer hall.

"That was well done, Josh," Gloria said simply.

"Your friends like tales of the West. Might be some money in it," he mused. "Outdo Buffalo Bill. Get myself up in buckskins, prop myself up on a rifle, and tell tall tales by the hour. Maybe I ought to see Mr. Barnum about it."

"I mean the way you silenced Elizabeth, after her rudeness," she persisted.

"Oh. Well, I could hardly spank her, could I? She's a lady. I couldn't insult her either, she's your cousin."

"Half the people here are," she said on a shrug, "and you are a gentleman. Thank you. Are you sure we can't persuade you to stay? Late supper will be served shortly."

She looked very handsome in the dim gaslight. Her gown was of an old-gold color, its train as regal as the jeweled coronet she wore in her high-dressed hair. In that vagrant light her hair's absence of color didn't matter any more than the neutral color of her eyes did. The shadows caressed her cheekbones and softened the too-exact line of her nose and chin. She looked very well. And if nothing in her aspect was more than properly hostesslike, there was certainly enough invitation in her low-pitched voice to encourage him.

But he had other business, and pleaded a previous engagement, although he never mentioned it was only one he'd made with himself. He took her hand, and might have dared to try to take some other liberty as well, but Jacob appeared from the ballroom, striding across his marble hall like a man on some strong and urgent errand.

"Ah, good," Jacob said as he came up to them. After casting one oblique look at his daughter, he nodded as though they'd spoken in that one silent glance, and said, "Caught you before you left us. You've entertained us roundly tonight with tales of your stagecoaching days, and I'd like to impose on your good nature further. You seem to know what you're talking about. I've joined the Coaching Club, and just got a new landau and two new pairs of gray Maine trotters. Would you mind taking a look at them and telling me if my driver knows what he's doing?

"Oh, not now," he said, before Josh could speak. "I don't keep my whole stable here anyway. They're home—on Long Island. What a fine idea! It's getting too chilly to sail, at least the ladies complained fiercely about the wind last time. Even Gloria, my most stalwart companion, refuses to set foot on deck again until spring. So how about you coming out to stay with us this weekend? I can send a carriage for you, the railroad's not far from us. Or you can drive and take the ferry—it should take only half a day. You'd have the weekend to recover from the journey. What do you say?"

They both looked at him. He didn't need more light to see their anticipation. He felt some of his own.

"Why, Jacob," he answered, "if I needed a weekend to recover from a half-day drive, I'd call the doctor double-quick. Can't I have the weekend to enjoy, instead?"

"Of course," Gloria said. "We'll look forward to helping you to do it."

Lucy didn't have to listen to the dialogue or the singing to hear her cue. By now she could feel it coming, the way she felt hunger just before dinnertime, the way she began to wake just before Mrs. Fergus' maid knocked on her door each morning. Maybe it was the vibrations of the "tum-tum-tum" of the sprightly music that cued her, or the time passed in her dressing room trying to forget that it was Lucy Markham about to step onstage, trying to become Lucy Rose each night again. She didn't care. It was part of her by now. Now she could stand backstage in the greenroom with the others as the play went on, listening to Kyle as he paced and worried aloud, and never worry about missing her cue, no matter how his words alarmed her.

"Are you sure?" Lester asked, his excitement magnified, as all his emotions were, by his stage makeup.

"Could I but be sure of anything in this rude life, I'd surely be a millionaire by now," Kyle said fretfully. "I only know the rumors are omnipresent. And so we must be on our guard."

"What does he look like?" Bayard asked.

"Again, if I but knew!" Kyle sighed. "The reports are that he's a dark, handsome little person. But I've never set eyes on him. They sent him to scout, you see. The worst of it is that the rumors predict they themselves will bring their own company here to do *Pinafore*. And that will leave us out in the cold."

He looked up from his pacing to see that his words had caused his audience of players' expressions to range from darkest despair to deepest thought. He wheeled around and said bracingly, "Of course, the best of it is that they may only be looking for an American cast. After all, why should they spend all that money to bring their own players to America?"

"To get back some of all that money we're stealing from them?" Lester asked innocently. As Kyle stared at him, he said reasonably, "After all, we pirates don't pay Mr. Sullivan or Mr. Gilbert a cent, even though their play is filling eight houses here in New York alone."

"That's show business and American endeavor. They'll have to get used to it. If they didn't open it here, they don't own it here." Kyle shrugged and added, "But it's vital to remember they may want *you* if they do decide on their own production here. So be in your best voices, my children, and on your toes every night. Because we

don't know what night it may net you fame and fortune.
Whatever you do, scan the audience—look for Mr.
D'Oyly Carte, and play to him if you think you see him,
because he's the one that calls the tune . . . and has the
ears of those who created the tunes: Mr. Sullivan and
Mr. Gilbert themselves.''

His words had a thrilling quality that silenced them,
and all that could be heard in that backstage room were
the sweet echoes of the overture and Buttercup's plain-
tive song.

"I hear," one of the male chorus ventured, "that
they're definitely coming here and that they're going to
present not only *Pinafore* but also a new opera. So as to
get the copyright," he explained, "so as to prevent . . .
ah, copying," he added, his voice trailing off as he met
Kyle's glare.

"This is a free country, the land of opportunity. Nothing can prevent copying. There are forty-two ways to skin
a cat, and not one to silence music or to stuff up trained
ears," Kyle said blithely. "A new opera only excites me.
But not knowing is not good, rumors breed error," he
added, before he said, "too many rumors. Too much
speculation. Ah, well, we'll find out more Wednesday at
Tony Pastor's, I expect.''

"Oh. Right. I was going to ask, can I have an extra
ticket for my girl?" the bold male chorus member asked.

"No," Kyle said abruptly. "There are going to be eight
casts there as it is. We can't hang from the rafters.''

"Lester's taking his landlady," a male voice grumbled.

"Might has its privileges," Kyle said haughtily. "Principals may take a guest. Those of the chorus may take
themselves. *May*," he said as he glowered at the hapless
chorus member, before he shooed them all away. "Now,
remove yourselves and get ready to sing, or you won't
even have the right to that one ticket, my dear fellow.''
Then he said, as Lucy was about to step to the wings to
await her cue, "You're coming, Lucy? It's amusing, but
you also might learn something other than gossip there.
After all, although it's an audacious thought—having all
eight companies of *Pinafore* in to see a burlesqued version of it—it's an honor to be invited. Afterward there'll
be a party—you'll be able to meet the seven other Jose-

phines: black, white, child, woman, and the dear knows what other kinds. It should be as entertaining as it's educational."

He gazed at her steadily, his dark, dramatic face singularly unreadable, as he wished it to be, although his voice was midnight on black velvet as he added, "You won't have to sit next to Ned. I'll see you're safe at the party afterward too—unless you won't be alone?"

She was always alone these nights; she'd even abandoned the charade of going out to be seen with her over-age, underage, and effeminate escorts. The only male she spent her nights with was Duncan. She thought of him as she smiled and whispered, "Oh, you never know," before, with the same wistful smile, she took her cue, picked up her head, and strolled out onto the stage.

". . . Heavy the heart when hope is dead,/ When love is alive and hope is dead," she sang.

It was lucky that it was on that, the last verse of her first song, that she saw him. Because the surprise was so great she would have forgotten the next line, had it not been Ned's. Since Ned made the most of every syllable he had to utter, she'd a few seconds to recover her wits. Kyle had said to search the audience. Although she'd preferred to think of the audience as one entity, now that she was more sure of herself onstage she was able to scan the separate faces she could make out in the flickering glow beyond the footlights.

And there he sat, in the center of the fifth row. Not a strange, dark, and handsome little gentleman. But a familiar tall, wide-shouldered, slightly smiling man, who would stand out from any crowd, even if she hadn't been looking for him every night.

That night Kyle Harper's company gave their best performance of *HMS Pinafore* ever. Lester had the audience aroar, Fanny made them drop a tear or two, Ned emoted to the farthest reaches of the balcony with no effort, the chorus stayed entirely on-key, as did, for a wonder, even Bayard Skyler. And the English Rose sang like a nightingale. She charmed them into calling her out four times, begging for encores. She sang so well, she was so much on her best and highest style, that every member of the cast believed the producer and business manager of the official Sullivan and Gilbert company of England was in the audience, and they performed to the hilt, as well.

They never realized they were following her lead because of her joy at seeing, not Mr. D'Oyly Carte, fresh out of London, but Mr. Joshua Dylan, late of Wyoming Territory.

He asked to be permitted backstage after the performance, and she sent word that he was to be admitted to her dressing room. It was such a small cluttered room that for a moment Josh looked for the door to lead him beyond it to her dressing room. But he left off when she emerged from behind a screen and smiled shyly at him.

"I'd have been here sooner, but I've been busy with foolishnesses that I had to do," he said before she could ask.

"Ah, but I've been so busy myself I scarcely . . ." she began, so he wouldn't know how very much she'd noticed, but actress that she was and was learning to be, still she couldn't go on and say "noticed, myself," and so simply stopped and gave him a tremulous smile.

He was surprised again by her loveliness: the purity of her complexion even when all her stage paint was washed off, the lovely shades of color that she was, from hair to eyes to lips, the fact that she was just as seductive in her simple dress, covered from neck to toes, as she was in her artfully improper costume onstage.

"I was going to ask you to walk out with me again this Sunday," he said, "but something came up . . ." He waited for her invitation for another day, but when it didn't come, because she just stood and stared at him helplessly, he went on, "Tonight, then? Or do I have to wait a week over again, until next Sunday?"

Over a week sounded like over a month . . . a year . . . a lifetime to her now. She'd missed him even more than she'd realized. His living presence was better than any of her day or night dreams. It was remarkable how he filled up the room, how he'd grown taller and more handsome—or else, she thought, she'd got used to smaller, more ordinary men. Even though she'd been listening to trained actors' voices all week, it seemed they were mere penny-whistle chirpings compared to his deep, rich tones. Worst of all, or best of all, for all that he frightened her, she knew no one—not even Ada—who seemed to know her better. No, not "know her better," she thought guiltily, but perhaps "understand her more." It might have been precisely because he wasn't from the theater—or because he was as much of a stranger to New York City as she, or because he seemed as alone as aloof, or for reasons she'd yet to discover . . . and wasn't sure it was wise to.

Because she couldn't go with him tonight. What, after all, she thought frantically, could she do with him tonight—except dine, and be alone with him, and be as afraid to say "yes" as "no" to him? She wanted to see him desperately, but not tonight—not unrehearsed. But she didn't know how to tell him that, any more than she knew how to justify it to herself. That was why she stood holding her breath so she wouldn't babble a jumble of nonsense at him. She stared at him as he patiently awaited her answer.

"Yes?" he prompted gently.

"No!" she blurted. "I can't now . . . not tonight . . . but, after Sunday? Oh. Wednesday night? There's a performance we're all going to," she said, letting out her breath, enchanted because she'd thought of it, "Tony Pastor's Vaudeville is presenting a burlesque of *Pinafore*—the whole audience will be made up of the cast of every *Pinafore* in New York right now. They've done it before. They say it's delightful. There's a party afterward. . . . Would . . . would you like to come as my guest?"

He grinned. Two much-desired invitations from two delightful women in one night. One for the money, two for the show, he thought.

"I'd be pleased and delighted," he said.

And he would be, he promised himself.

9

ONE'S SUCCESS at a house party, Josh's father had once told him, was in the servants' hands. Fill them with enough silver, he'd said, and you'd be assured a delightful visit. Then, when he'd stopped laughing, Josh had seen his eyes had that softened, distant look that meant he was remembering his earlier days. But he'd felt his son's eyes upon him and recovered himself and said with absolute sincerity, "A gentleman is always welcome—in a gentleman's house. It's a two-sided street, Joshua. Take advantage of it. Judge, as you will be judged."

Judging from the house he was in now, Josh thought, Jacob Van Horn was a wealthy man who spared no expense for his comfort. His home was the size of other men's dreams; his grounds reached from the forest to the sea, his servants were many and subtle, his guests were treated like family. And his family wanted for nothing, except, perhaps, some of his guests.

Because Josh doubted that many men were given the invitation he'd gotten, even though he was certainly not the only male guest this bright September weekend. But from what he'd seen when he'd arrived a few hours ago, he was the only single one of an age to interest the youngest lady of the house. One of his first surprises had been that there was another lady in the house. He'd assumed his host was a widower, but the Van Horn mansion also contained a Mrs. Van Horn. She was a tall, lean, fluttery woman the years had leached the color from to the point that it was difficult to remember her when she'd left the room. If she'd left it, that was, he thought, shaking his head as he buttoned his shirt and struggled into his formal jacket. Because all he'd seen was Gloria, and she

156

hadn't left any public room he'd been in from the time he'd set foot in the house. And that was interesting, he thought.

It was also the reason he didn't mind dressing up tonight so much as he usually would. He could see the point of formal clothes when a man went on the town, but it was one of the hallmarks of his Western heritage that he resented constricting himself in them when he was at home. Anyone's home. His father had jestingly called him a "savage" for it. He supposed he was. Compared to his father, he always was. But he liked his comfort above his style. Still, he could understand getting dressed up for wooing. And whether it was to be for Jacob's favor in business or his daughter's in more intimate business, he was, he decided, eyeing himself ruefully in the long mirror in his room, now as ready as he'd ever be.

His tight-fitting, long-tailed evening jacket had velvet cuffs and a velvet collar, and its high-cut front showed his waistcoat and shirtfront. It didn't show how caged he felt by the fashion as he tried to flex his arms and shoulders. It showed, instead, the remarkable width of those rolling shoulders, and that, unlike most gentlemen who could afford such dressing, the difficulty he'd had with the buttons on his waistcoat was because of the muscled strength the material had to stretch across, and not the result of overindulgence in good living. He even resented the constriction of the snug black trousers as he strode to answer the tap on his door.

A man who spent half his life in the saddle was used to wearing clothes that fitted like a second skin, but not when that skin was purely for show. There wasn't a gunbelt or chaps, or even a nice wide studded belt to drape over his lean hips; he felt as though he were on a stage every time he took a step. That might have been why he was frowning, and could've explained the look of alarm on the man's face that stood there.

"Mr. Van Horn wondered if you required my services, sir," the elderly man said softly. "I'm Ridgely, his valet," he explained. "I'm terribly sorry I didn't arrive earlier. I'd no idea you would go ahead without me. Please

accept my apologies, sir. Dinner is not for another half-
hour, and so I thought you would be—"

"No bother, Ridgely," Josh said, cutting across the
torrent of words that suddenly reminded him of someone
else who also ran on at the mouth when she was nervous.
"I'm used to doing for myself," he said. Seeing the distress on the valet's face and remembering more of his
father's advice, he added, "But you can do me a favor,
if you would. The train got my shirt full of soot and
made my jacket a deeper gray. Do you think you might
be able to do something with them?"

"Be kind," his father had advised, "but firm, and
remember: servants and children expect direction, along
with a measure of fondness. And though they don't know
it, your distance, to enhance their vision of your superiority. It would be, after all, as unendurable to be ordered
about by an equal as it would be by an inferior, wouldn't
it? That goes for women as well as servants, of course,"
he'd said, and then ducked, yelping and laughing merrily
as Josh's mother had shied her dishcloth at him. But it
was good advice, for all that. It had never failed him, and
from the gratified look that came over Ridgely's face, did
not do so now, when he most needed it. Because he very
much wanted to make the best impression he could.

He assumed he did when he entered the salon sometime later. Jacob greeted him at once, and immediately
introduced him to the other guests. He forgot about his
constricting clothes when he met them. One was a man
who had moved more steel in the past year than anyone
but Carnegie, another had shares in an oil company that
made Rockefeller nervous, another had a string of banks
Morgan had an eye on. The others' names were unfamiliar to him, but he soon heard of their investments. All
of them, like himself, were men who used money to buy
money. And all of them were men to listen to as carefully
as they attended to him when he spoke.

But he remembered his training, and was careful not
to get too involved when he spoke, because a gentleman
never discussed business in any house but one of pleasure. And so he wasn't as chagrined as some of the other
men when Gloria came drifting over to take her father's
arm and chide him for forgetting the ladies again. He

never minded standing and chatting politely with the ladies either, and minded less when he realized all of them were married, except for Gloria. It confirmed his conclusions about the weekend, and once sure he was right, he could go on and do no wrong.

They dined and chatted, and he made sure to speak no more to Gloria, on his left, than he did to the woman on his right. After dinner the ladies left the gentlemen, and Jacob sat back and sighed. As he had his footman offer cigars, he said, "It's an old custom here in the East, Josh, to let the ladies repair themselves while we men have our port and talk."

"My father said it was the same even further east in his home in England," Josh answered on a smile.

"Oh, but I thought you were from the West," one of the men said.

"Yes. But my father was English, he came here when he was a young man," Josh answered, accepting a cigar.

"Oho, remittance man," the man said knowingly.

Josh's eyes grew to the color of the thick smoke he'd exhaled, and his smile froze. The words stung. He'd met a few remittance men who'd sought his father out for company over the years, claiming kinship of nationality. And he'd come across a few on the trail. Most were no good; that was why their noble or wealthy fathers had sent them out of Britain to the American West, to toughen them up. But most just wasted their remittances, or allowances, and remained as soft as they'd been when they came. Climate never changed a man, any more than location did. The only geography that mattered was that of the heart. His father had had that, if nothing else, in plenty.

"No, sir," Josh drawled. "It was my father who ran away to America rather than to remain a drain on his daddy's purse. He was the third son of a viscount, and so it was either the church or the law for him. And he said he preferred to make his money, not pray or sue for it."

They laughed, but Josh saw the looks of speculation leap into their eyes, and saw the spark of pleasure in Jacob's as well.

"Now, that's something I didn't know," Jacob said softly. "Should we address you with a title, Josh?"

"Yes. Please do call me 'Mister,' " Josh said. "My daddy left his honors with his childhood, and I wouldn't have a tooth left in my mouth if I had grown up with airs. Why, as it is, even though I was born here, look what the English accent he gave me got me before I managed to lose it," he complained, running a finger over the bridge of his nose, lying to make them laugh, and so causing them to drop the subject, as he wished.

It was more sensitive to him than the loss of the perfect line of his profile had been. Not the matter of the title—that meant less than nothing to him. But his father, the third son and the weakest one, as he knew too well and regretted too often, had spoken of his old home as much as he'd spoken of his new one. His dream had been to return someday, trailing successes as his brothers trailed their many honors. He'd missed his family all his life, but cut himself off from them ruthlessly, vowing never to get in touch with them until he'd made his millions. And so now Josh would be damned if he'd mention them. Because it still hurt that he'd made all the money for his father—too late.

When they joined the ladies there was conversation, and some music at the piano, and singing. And then tea and cakes, cards, and an early good-night, because it was a country weekend.

Saturday dawned clear and unseasonably warm, and Josh dreaded leaving his room for more obligatory visiting. Discussing business with the men was fine, talking with the older women was bearable, because they were all so civil and charming. The house, the company, even the excessive dinner was pleasurable—if only for the way it signaled his arrival at a goal he was sure his father would have approved. But it also was, even after only a half-day of it, boring. And so when he came down to breakfast, he was delighted to find he'd dressed wrong. Because as he noted Gloria's riding habit, she eyed his morning suit and asked if he would prefer to go change and come riding with her.

The trail ran through forested acres; they rode beneath towering oaks, maples, and pines. Gloria showed him the pastured acres where he could let his horse out for a gallop if he wished. But he remained beside her, sedate and bemused. The pleasure of having a clear morning, an able horse, and the free outdoors around him again was somewhat muted by the magnificence that Jacob had managed to impose on the natural country surrounding him. Because every turn in the trail showed some artificial surprise to add to the wild beauty of the estate. Here a hidden corner revealed a statue weeping over a hidden pool, there a massive grouping of three marble Graces beneath a thicket of topiary trees, and everywhere hidden grottoes and fancies and follies.

She reined in her horse by the side of an immense glass-and-iron house with a ceiling arched high as a cathedral's. He was about to ask if it was an orangery, a hothouse to produce fruit out of season, such as his father had told him about, when she asked, "Do you play tennis, Josh? This will be our tennis house when it's done. Father heard it's all the rage."

"No, never tried," he said quietly, and thought: But I'll learn.

"Ah, you'll have to learn," she said. "He'll be looking everywhere for partners."

They rode on, and she explained the various settings and the whims that had caused them.

"There's where father intends to put down track—if we ever get the spur he wants from the railroad. We've a great many mouths to feed here, a good deal more building to do. Shipping the material and food directly to us would be simpler than having to bring it from the station," she explained, and he stopped himself from asking where all the people were, just in time.

The house held three people, but he'd already seen more than three dozen servants, and the grounds must require many more. He'd seen the indoor servants, but he never could catch their eyes, though they surely saw him well enough to serve him so well as they did. His water glass never ran dry at the dining table, the fire never went out in the grate in his room, and his clothes were hung and folded every day, even as his bed was readied for him each night. But those who served him never looked directly at him. He'd discovered that not

being able to see another man's eyes made him less than
a man in his own eyes. His father had told him that his
family had known and valued their servitors, but in other
noble houses they chose to pretend that, like Sleeping
Beauty, they were catered to by invisible hands. So it
seemed to be here. He'd lain in his bed last night thinking of all the guests asleep while the invisible staff
scrubbed and cleared, only to disappear, like modern-
day brownies, by dawn's first light. There was something
about it that bothered him, but not enough to ruin the
pleasure of the comfort of it.

"And that's the tunnel for the railroad track?" he
asked as he stopped his horse to stare at a cavernous
gaping brick mouth of a tunnel cut into the side of a
gentle hill.

"Oh, no," she laughed, and it was such an unfamiliar
sound, he turned to look at her. Because for all her gentle smiles, she seldom laughed full out. But there was
more pride than humor in her voice, and no disdain at
all as she explained, "It's just a foot tunnel for the servants. It connects to the basement of the main house and
goes to all the guest houses nearby. We're almost a mile
from the main house here, and so you see it's hard when
our guests want breakfast in bed. This way rain or snow
doesn't make for cold morning chocolate or even tepid
coffee."

"Guest houses?" he mused. "Should I be pleased or
insulted to be in the main house instead?"

"They're used only for enormous parties," she said,
turning her mount, "but you'll always be welcome in our
house."

It was too soon to say anything more; he turned his
own horse and followed her.

"This," she said, when she spoke again, "is why Papa
built our house here."

There was no way he could speak immediately.

They'd come out of the forest and sat their horses on
the rise, and looked down and out to the sea. Beneath
them, the grassy rise eventually gave way to sand, and
then, far below it, all along the U-shaped peninsula, a
long and high concrete wall held back the shore that
stretched out to a wide and tranquil sea.

"That's Connecticut there," she said, indicating the further shore he could barely make out in the distance even on such a crystalline day. "We sail here in the summer—the sound is usually calm. Sometimes we ride along the shore at low tide, where the sand is packed hard. It's growing late now, and it will take us time to get back for luncheon. If the weather holds, would you like to try that tomorrow morning?"

"Sounds delightful," he heard his voice say. Because he was beyond speech. He'd ridden in cities and on plains, through forest and over snow, but the thought of racing along beside the sea filled him with an indefinable joy.

That was nothing to what he felt two mornings later. He'd known many pleasures—few to equal this. He raced against a small seagoing breeze, the gulls overhead wheeling and crying him on, the water around him, about him, flying up from beneath this horse's hooves, the salt stench of low tide a rare and pungent perfume. He slowed only when he realized how far he'd left his hostess behind. When she came up to him, he slid from his saddle to the pebbly shore to walk the horse until it cooled, stopping only to help her down from her mount as well.

They walked in silence for a while. She didn't speak very much, and he wasn't inclined to yet. The weekend had gone by quickly. It seemed to him that it was a blur of conversation and cards, music and riding, feasting and fashion. Yesterday's drizzle hadn't affected anything but their promised ride. Gloria had been his hostess in all but name. Her mother appeared at dinners, but evaporated into the shadows, and then her room, soon after. She suffered, Jacob said, from numbing headaches. The lady had passed him closely once, and though he'd got no whiff of alcohol, he judged from her eyes that she was partial to the popular sort of bottled medication that had as much opium as it did sugar syrup. Those syrups claimed to cure everything from spavins to chilblains, and if they didn't, as the joke back home went, at least no one cared. In the Van Horn household, no one seemed to notice. Gloria was her father's hostess and was excellent at her job.

And yet, for all he'd seen Gloria every day, he'd spoken to her very little, or so it seemed, since he couldn't remember a word they'd said. And for all he'd seen her every day, he looked at her now and only now remembered what she looked like again. No raving beauty, not very entertaining, but a comfortable girl. That was it, he thought. At least, she was so for him. From the way her eyes flashed every so often when a servant fumbled or appeared where one should not be, and the way her voice sharpened when she spoke to other women, he doubted she was always so amicable or endlessly obliging. But then, he thought, he wasn't another woman. And he was acutely aware of that here, alone, with her.

"Must you go today?" she asked. "We thought to picnic down here tomorrow. The Andersons and the Robbinses are staying for the week, and the Wyatts are coming tonight. Seldon Wyatt is in banking, but he was also a friend to President Grant, and so has several other interests. I know he was looking forward to meeting you."

That was different, then; staying on wouldn't commit him to anything but advancing his business interests.

"Well, then, if it's no trouble . . ." he said.

But the next time they rode out on the beach, he again said he must be leaving.

"I've overstayed by two days. I'll have to go before my weekend becomes a week," he said.

She looked up at him as they walked their horses. The sun turned his gold hair into bronze, his skin glowed gold from his recent exercise, and she gazed at him until he turned his eyes away to look out to the distant horizon and she saw they were the exact color of the sea mists covering over that far shore. Curiously, his broken profile added a dimension to his handsomeness that emphasized it.

She surprised him then.

"Ah, I see. You can't wait to call on all the daughters you were asked to meet, is that it?" she said on one of her rare, small laughs. "Oh, I know. Miss Bates and Miss Robbins and the two Misses Anderson. Seldon would've had you call on his daughter, but Miss Wyatt is only seven years old."

He avoided answering; he wasn't sure he'd call on the

young ladies as their fathers had urged him to, but he hadn't known she'd know of it, and didn't want to discuss it with her. "I expect it's that mysterious title," he joked.

"Among other things," she agreed, "yes, it is. They're all the rage now."

"I haven't got one," he said.

"But you're descended from one. And you're not impoverished, as most of the gentlemen that have them are," she added. And, she thought, still gazing at him, you're not old or homely and foolish as most of them are too. Or for sale. But she said none of this, because she'd noted how he withdrew when she spoke of such things. His chivalry was not the least of his attractions. Her father admired his business sense and other things men could see to respect. She saw what other women did, and knew he was a great catch. New to town, wealthy, handsome, ambitious, and clever with it. But there was that charming old-fashioned chivalry and honor to get through. She was the pampered darling of an enormously rich man, and had been educated and indulged since birth. But she was very much her father's daughter too. She knew her value and spoke her mind. She did so now.

"Are you ever going to kiss me?" she asked. "Do you want to?"

He'd thought his way around quicksilver decisions about life and death before; it was odd that this took him a second longer. She was looking at him expectantly. There wasn't another soul on the long beach. The wind whipped her long straight hair into a misty veil across her eyes, her thin face was neither unattractive nor repellent. She paused in her tracks and waited.

"There are a great many things a man might want to do," he said quietly, "but back where I come from, a kiss is more than just a pleasure—if a man takes one from a decent girl."

She understood. And smiled.

"I am that, I hope. But I'm not a servant or a shopgirl. Or a shopkeeper's daughter. I expect no more than a gentleman does from a friendly kiss, either. Ladies are not so old-fashioned here, in my set, Josh. Neither is my papa. How is one to know what one wants, after all, unless . . . ?"

Her lips were cool, and never opened beneath his. She went into his arms and held him close, and he could feel the lean steel beneath the grace of her, even though it seemed she wore no stays for riding. It was not unpleasant. But it lacked passion on his part, abandon on hers. She didn't seem displeased when he pulled away. Nor was he, for that matter. He'd not pushed for more than she'd given him, and wouldn't, because he wasn't sure he wanted more yet. There was much more for him to learn about her. He'd been alone a long time; a matter of months more wouldn't matter. It seemed she understood that too.

"The gardeners say tomorrow will be glorious. Father says you've inspected but not driven his new rig. Four days isn't a week, Josh, and who knows how soon the weather will turn? Do stay."

"I've an engagement," he said, remembering, even though the noise of the city seemed far away here on this free and murmuring shore. Even though the thought of gaslit fantasy was alien to this seaside setting, improbable as the painted waves that rocked the cardboard ship on that distant stage.

"It's a black landau, with crimson velvet interior, and silver fittings . . ." she teased.

He smiled. This playfulness was charming, and very unlike her. Or, he corrected himself, at least unlike what he knew of her so far.

". . . and not only did he get that team of matched grays you saw, but he's got a rare pair of Cleveland bays coming tomorrow," she said, "all the way from England," she added.

He grew still, his eyes alight.

"From England?" he asked.

"You go on without me," she said.

"My dear Lucy," Kyle said in his most determined fashion, "I shall not. *We* shall not."

There was a stifled sigh from someone in the small group assembled around him. Kyle stood in the entry hall, opera hat on, black cloak swirled about himself, as if he were playing the villain in a road company *East Lynne*, just as Lester had said before a venomous glance from Kyle silenced him. He was surrounded by Lester, Ned, Jewel, old Mrs. Fairfax, and Miss Hampton, even Bayard—the entire contents of Mrs. Fergus' boarding-house, all dressed to the teeth, about to go to Tony Pastor's, excepting, of course, for Duncan. And Mr. Fergus, who had decided to spend the night with his troublesome lumbago for company.

"It is bad enough that Fanny cannot come tonight. I can't appear at this gala *Pinafore*-fest without so much as one of my leading ladies. How would it look? It is not done. Especially not because my English Rose is mooning over some bounder," Kyle insisted.

"I'm not mooning," Lucy cried, "and he's not a bounder—he said he'd come, and so he will, you'll see. And I'll wait, because I said I would, and I won't be a bounder, and I would be if he came and I wasn't here, because—"

"A gentleman that makes and breaks an appointment without notice is no less than a bounder, and in my opinion, more than a cad," Kyle said loftily, but with a warning glance that subdued Lucy, because her accent had slipped in her agitation. Fortunately the others were too busy disputing the point to notice.

"Not necessarily. There may be an excuse. He may have been killed," Mrs. Fairfax said kindly. "Remember the last act of *Orphans of the Bowery*, Mr. Harper? The male second lead was slain by the villainous earl on his way to the lady in the town house in that one."

"Yes," her crony Miss Hampton agreed, "but it was the wicked count that slew him, remember, Betty? Hamilton Egremont played him."

As Mrs. Fairfax nodded, Lester noted Lucy's arrested expression and said something about how few earls and counts there were in New York this time of year, and as Jewel agreed, Bayard put in sweetly, "Maybe it's a different sort of death he's met, a littler one—he might have met a likely lady on the way . . . these society swells aren't very constant."

"But who, pray tell," Ned said grandly, "could be likelier than our blooming Rose?"

They all fell still at that. Because for all her dismay, there was no denying Lucy had never been in higher looks. Her hair was combed back high, only to be allowed to ripple down to her shoulders, like the princess in a tower, just like, as Kyle had said, Mr. Rossetti's dream of a princess in a tower. Her distraction had raised a lovely crimson color in her pale cheeks, and her eyes shone with unshed tears of defiance. She wore a close-fitting golden-green gown with a charming hint of a back bustle of darker green, and it was hobbled at the knee with contrasting bows. It was low-cut enough to make Ned resolve to entice her to a darkened corner somewhere at the party they were going to, despite what Kyle had said, and yet high enough, and covered over further now by her trembling hand, to make Kyle hesitate before he spoke again. There was a curious note of sincerity in his voice when he did, so new to their ears that they all remained silent.

"Lucy," he said softly, "we've got to get to Tony Pastor's now. They won't wait for us. Everyone will be late, to make an entrance, they've allowed for that, so it won't start till an hour past program time anyway, but there is a limit. He's not here, for whatever reason. I would be only too proud to take you in on one arm, and Jewel on the other. I will be, I promise you, the most envied of men. Come, my dear, honor me, and make me so."

She bridled. She stiffened. And then he reached into his fob pocket, pulled out his watch, and held it up for her to see. She wilted, and sighed. As she did, there was a knock on the door that made them all jump and Duncan wag his tail.

"Oh," Josh said as the door swung open, taking off his hat as he saw them all staring out at him, as though he had been admitted to a convention of eyes, "how do you do? I'm Josh Dylan."

He stood in the doorway, his hair glowing even in the dim light, in full evening dress, tall, impeccable, as theatrical as any of them in his handsomeness, and yet, in a way, both less and more real to Lucy.

His eyes went to her, as though the force of her own gaze had summoned them. "Hello, Lucy," he said more softly, forgetting everyone else goggling at him, gazing at her as though he couldn't take in enough of the sight of her. "Sorry I'm late. My train was delayed. I had to hurry to change and, of course, broke two shoestrings in my haste. But I would've come here barefoot if I had to. I did get here on time . . . didn't I?" he asked as the silence grew.

Lucy could only beam at him, her happiness was so profound.

"Indeed," Kyle said, "in the nick of—just like the cavalry, Mr. Dylan."

The two men locked glances, and then Mrs. Fergus spoke up flirtatiously. "Oh, my, Lucy. Won't you introduce us to your young man?"

"Ah . . ." Lucy began, wondering how to explain that Josh wasn't her young man, for all she wished it were so, for all she wished he didn't think she wanted it so badly she'd have forgone the night's entertainment if he hadn't come—and abandoned her faith in mankind for far longer than that.

"Mr. Dylan is our Lucy's escort tonight," Kyle said simply, and then added, "unfortunately. A moment later, sir, and I would have been the happiest of men."

"A moment later," Josh said, "and I suppose I would have been the most wretched. Now, please, may I have that introduction, or shall I ask Duncan to do the honors?"

"Duncan!" Mrs. Fergus commanded gaily, pointing a finger at him. "May I present to you . . . ?"

Duncan threw back his head and howled.

They all did. Except that Josh and Kyle were looking at Lucy as she laughed, and each startled when he noticed the other doing so, and so neither was smiling as he laughed.

After hasty introductions, Josh hurried Lucy to his waiting carriage as the others piled into the convoy of rented hacks they'd engaged for the night.

"I'm honored," he said as he took up the reins. "Am I to be the only nonperformer there tonight?"

"I can't say," she said. "I've never been. But it won't matter."

Nothing matters now that you've come, she thought, so grateful that he'd not abandoned her as she'd begun to think he'd do, so satisfied now that he'd come that she fell silent. She relaxed even as she sat forward in a thrill of happy anticipation she'd not allowed herself to feel before, as their trap clattered on into the night.

He hurried his team, as anxious as she was for the night to begin. It would be entirely different from the last nights he had passed. That was why he'd hastened to this meeting, despite all the temptations to stay where he'd been. He'd left behind a promise of pleasure that would need time to ripen before he could see if he really wanted to partake of it.

This promised to be an entirely different sort of treat, one he needed as much as wanted, he thought as he glanced to where she sat enfolded in her cape at his side, like a dancing girl wrapped in all her seven veils. Variety was the spice of life, they said, and she, he thought, grinning to himself in the night, was the tastiest bit he'd seen in a very long while. And if he wasn't mistaken, he decided, watching her face as they passed under a gaslight, now ripe enough at last to try.

10

IT WAS A perfect audience: high-spirited, handsome, and eager for the curtain to rise. In fact, it was too perfect. Josh had never seen one like it. It looked as if someone had cast it as carefully as the play they were prepared to see. But the odd part about it was the replication of it. For every fine-looking distinguished silver-haired gentleman he saw, there were at least two others of the same type in each long row at the theater. Every pretty innocent-seeming girl had her quadruplicate, not duplicate, not far from where she sat. And at that, he'd never seen so many beautiful women all in one theater, on or off the stage. That was the point.

There were dozens of Buttercups and captains of the *Pinafore*, and of Josephines—as Kyle whispered to Lucy—there were a multitude. But none lovelier than she, Josh thought. Still, even he took his eyes from her in order to marvel at the remarkable audience. They were all of a type and all from the stage, and all from the same operetta, although from several theaters, and so he alone seemed singular. But because he loved the theater as much as they did, he was soon roaring with laughter as they all were, and laughing at the same jokes, even though they relished it because this time the joke was on them.

At first Lucy was lost in awe at the theater itself, not the crowd. The Stratton was the size of a hatbox compared to it, she thought with sudden humility. She noted the graceful sweep of depending boxes hung high over the mezzanine, not the people crammed into them, and craned her neck to see, not the other Josephines who were studying her, but the tier after tier that was the grand march of the balconies as they swept up to the

171

roof of the high gilt ceiling. The Stratton's orchestra numbered twenty-one on a good night. The orchestra here, she decided, after she gave up trying to count them, almost outnumbered a sold-out audience at the Stratton.

When the satire began, she gasped at the scenery as much as at the burlesqued version of her play. Because they'd not only painted drops for scenery, but huge ornate and clever movable pieces that really looked like ships and decks, all on that great stage. And more than footlights, they had limelight spots, so many of them there was scarcely a shadow where they didn't want one. And swinging pieces that fell into place neat as you please for a change of scene. And a glistening blue sea that moved behind all the action.

So she didn't laugh so much at first because of the shame, the realization that what she'd thought was a fine theater in which to perform was by comparison no more grand than the basement choir room at the local church had been.

But no one could remain solemn for long tonight, and soon she was snickering at the way the Ralph Rackstraw onstage was so very much like Bayard in his extremely good looks and extremely bad acting. She giggled at the way the captain emoted, and blushed to her hair as she laughed at the dreadful, uncouth, and exquisitely funny things he proposed to do with the man playing the dandelion-blond, overly developed, and overamorous Buttercup. And doubled over with laughter to the point that she needed Josh's handkerchief to clear her tear-filled eyes to better see the stupidly naive Josephine, all seduction in her voice and scanty dress, all impossible innocence in her words.

Josh enjoyed her reaction fully as much as he did the riotous satire he was seeing, and felt curiously proud because Lucy positively roared with mirth at the mockery of her stage role, even though several other Josephines in his line of sight grew stiff-faced watching it. Her laughter rang out so freely, he wondered if he'd have to pick her up from the floor when the stage Josephine tripped on a length of rope and fell into Ralph's arms, and heard her breathless gasps of laughter that had gone beyond laughter when the unfortunate ingenue's dress caught under Ralph's shoe—and came off entirely, showing her in an absurdly and delightfully vulgar state of undress.

"Oh, my," Lucy wheezed at the first intermission. "Oh, my . . . oh, my."

"There's more. Do you think you can hold up?" Josh asked her, eyeing her with sympathy and amusement, for she dabbed at her eyes, and her face was pink with her emotion.

"Ah, but she'd better," Kyle put in, leaning forward so as to see them from where he sat a seat away. "Now's the grand intermission promenade, when she gets a chance to actually meet her fellow performers. Are you coming, Lucy?"

"But . . . there's the party after for that, isn't there?" she asked, suddenly feeling more shy at the thought of meeting other performers, and all of them professional, than she'd ever felt about appearing onstage.

"Indeed," Kyle said in the falsely bored tones that meant he was growing impatient, "but parties tend to grow corners and cliques, and I want everyone to meet my company. The chorus will soon be descending from the heavens"—he tilted his head toward the balconies—"but I want to show off my principals. Even our reclusive Deadeye Dick is here tonight, and he never socializes. But this is not social. It *is* all business, for all it looks like pleasure, do you see?" he asked. "Personal appearances are free publicity. Or is it that your escort doesn't wish to stroll with us? Never mind, then, Mr. Dylan, I'll be glad—"

"I'd be pleased to stretch my legs," Josh interrupted him to say, before he added, "*if* you want to, Lucy."

She swallowed. They were waiting for her answer and there really was only one she could give. She hadn't been discovered yet. So she smiled and arose and said very grandly, "Yes, of course, certainly, shall we?"

And so, of course, she thought, resignation almost overcoming her instant terror, the first thing said to her as she left her seat was the last thing she'd wanted to hear.

"Why, it's the English Rose," a great-bosomed woman all in spangles trumpeted so that all the others in the aisle swiveled round to hear. "I've been perishing to meet you, luv. But my performance, at the Criterion," she said even more loudly, her kohl-black-fringed eyes slewing to see who listened to her, "is at the same time as yours. At almost the same *moment*," she laughed, "for all that I am Buttercup and you Josephine. But how *delightful* to meet a countrywoman at last. I'm from London, dearie, and you?"

Lucy wore no paint offstage. So everyone could see how pale she grew. Her eyes opened wide, as did her mouth, but all she did was stammer, "Ah . . . well," before she whispered, "near to . . . Castle Rising . . ." as she recalled her grandmother's mother's home, ". . . or at least, not so very far," she added lamely, because she saw Josh gazing at her curiously.

"Oh, pray do not ask her more," Kyle said in a great stage whisper that carried to the second balcony, "for she has sworn to say no more. Indeed, she only said as much as she did . . . mistakenly, I fear," he added, giving the buxom actress a strange and significant look.

The English Buttercup's eyes flew as wide as they could with all the paint that had been applied to their lashes to weigh them down. She grew rosier than the blush she'd painted in circles on her cheeks. Then one heavy eyelid fluttered down and she gave the most alarming wink.

"Ah," she cried, "say no more. Her secret's safe with me. But I could see it at once in the shape of her mouth, the color of her hair, and—"

"Shhhh," Kyle said with a sibilance that hissed clear in the silence that had come over the area they stood in. "Please, madam."

"Oh, to be sure," the woman said, gazing at Lucy in a hungry but gratified way, "it's a pleasure to meet you, my lady," she said, and shocking Lucy to the core, she dipped into a curtsy before she stepped back to let her pass.

As the woman turned back to murmur excitedly with her own companions, Kyle took advantage of the narrowness of the aisle to lean forward and whisper for Lucy's ear alone, "Courage. The idiot thinks you're a countess or royal or something, in disguise, just as we hoped. Wonderful."

But Lucy didn't think it was so wonderful when she reached the lobby and looked up to see the speculation in Josh's eyes. Out of one fire into another, she thought, biting her lip, and so then dashed into the next one without hesitation when Kyle introduced her to another group of actors from yet another *Pinafore*. And then, to keep Josh from framing the questions she imagined he was thinking of, she became so animated they had to pry her away from a horde of interested admirers when the boy struck the chime for curtain time again.

Josh said nothing when they sat, but his raised eyebrow was eloquent enough when she looked at him, so Lucy buried her nose in her program until the stage lights went up again.

So the lady has another secret, Josh thought as he settled down to watch the show. Good and good again. He loved a challenge. Now he'd several treasures to unearth before this evening was out. He could hardly wait for the show to be done, even though he was enjoying himself enormously. But all good things come to an end, and with any luck at all, there were new good things to come after. At least, he thought, so it seemed this remarkable night.

"The party, ladies and gentlemen," the producer of the burlesque *Pinafore* announced after he called for a break in the thunderous applause at the finale, "is just down the street. At Powell's Famous Beer Garden. And if you don't hurry," he added as they began stamping their feet for another encore, "you'll miss all the food. Because it's already begun."

Josh was astonished at the sudden silence, and then the mad charge the audience made for the aisle. He'd seen more orderly stampedes.

"If you want to clear the house," Lester told him, seeing his plain astonishment, "mention food to actors. It's better than shouting 'Fire!' "

There was more than food at the beer garden. There was music and laughter and dancing and some of the most entertaining conversation Josh had ever heard. It was a partygoer's dream and a theater lover's fantasy, he mused as he sipped his champagne and listened to a particularly clever storyteller. All of the guests were entertainers, and all eager for any kind of applause. All of them, he thought, looking down to see Lucy's enraptured face, except the one who was one of the most sought-after. The mystery, like everything else tonight, only enhanced her.

She wasn't the only listener at the party who was in demand. A great many actresses cast glances at the tall golden-haired, well-dressed, and well-proportioned rugged-looking gentleman in their midst. Although he remained at Lucy's side, in a knot of people from her company, he soon found himself in the midst of what seemed to be an instant harem. All of the lovely young women had a tale to tell, and eyelashes to flutter. He smiled and said nothing, but thought of poor Gray and the next letter he'd write to him. He'd gotten past the first paragraph when the old fellow from Lucy's company who played the captain sidled up to him.

"This is the place to stand, all right," he whispered, digging an elbow into Josh's side. "Not next to Bayard. He's mad as fire because he can't hold a candle to you. He couldn't get little missy to partner him tonight, and he couldn't get half these pretty little dears to mob him. You can't take them all on, so I'll just give you a hand, eh?"

Always observant, Kyle, who'd been listening to another Deadeye Dick, inclined his head to say, low but clearly, "Calm yourself and lower your . . . hopes, Ned. It's the evidence of money as well as the lack of a thespian career that's enticing them to him. Starving actors attract only creditors, no matter how handsome they may be."

Josh grinned, which amused Ned, disappointed Kyle, angered Bayard further, and encouraged several more young women in the vicinity.

The mountains of cold meats and aspics, the wheels of cheese and loaves of bread, barrels of oysters and platters of chickens, seemed to have been spirited away within an hour. Then the champagne corks popped with regularity and more beer barrels were wheeled out as more were rolled in, to applause, before they too were tapped into.

Then, above the laughter and chatter and music, they heard someone singing, and grew still. It was a lovely voice and the musicians quickly stopped their own tune and picked up the familiar melody. Before long everyone in the hall was singing along and swaying to the sound of "Little Buttercup"—all the verses and three reprised choruses. When they had done they applauded themselves, and immediately took up another tune, and another. When they got to "For he's the captain of the *Pinafore*, and a right good captain too," they automatically separated themselves into parts, with the ladies and tenors singing, "What, never?" and the altos and gentlemen responding with a hearty, "Well, hardly ever!" After that they laughed, roundly pleased with themselves and everyone else.

It was one of the best evenings Josh had ever passed. He'd never imagined such fun, not even when he'd sat alone in the night on the trail, gazing up at the stars, more alone than most men had the courage to be. Lucy felt foolish tears in her eyes and an obstruction in her throat at the thought of being part of such a wonderful world in such merry company, after all her years of being apart. Josh looked down into her face just then, just as she gazed up to see his reaction. He smiled down at her with such warmth and understanding, she responded with the same knowing, comradely smile, without reservation. Until she saw his eyes, and then she looked down, around, and everywhere but at him.

But then there was a stir and merry cries nearby to them. A small thin man was tossed up to the top of a table, and his friends cried "Now!" and "Yes, go!"

"Ladies and gents," the man cried in a surprisingly rich, resonant voice, "my friends say we've exhaused the poor *Pinafore*. And the night's young. What's to do?"

Shaking off several rude suggestions, he bowed, and straightening, said, "Allow me to introduce you to John de la Farge, my friends, currently Sir Joseph Porter from the Regal Theater *Pinafore*, New York's second *Pinafore*, which, like the farmer's daughter, is now going into its ninth month! No, no more advertisements, I promise you," he cried to their catcalls. "Before I set sail, I was with the Christy Minstrels, and before that, with Piper's Variety Show. And before that, I performed on the ark in high animal spirits, . . . ah, don't throw your beer, put it where it matters most . . . but I wonder if you remember this one?

". . . We all do like pretty girls,
   We see them day by day,
And how at first sight fall in love
   Whene'er they pass that way;
But a charming girl the other morn,
   I saw come walking by,
And as she gazed, I saw she had,
   A dark and roguish eye . . ."

Soon the whole hall was singing the chorus of "The Dark and Roguish Eye" along with him. When he'd done, they applauded, and he shouted before he leapt down from the table, "Ladies and gents: I invite you to sing for your supper!"

In a moment, another performer was handed up to a table top on the other side of the room, to lead them in another old song. And then a lovely little Josephine enchanted them with "Ask Papa," followed by a stout older blond woman who silenced the laughter begun when they'd struggled to get her up on a table, with her heart-wrenching version of "No Name."

One after another, various members of various troupes volunteered themselves or a fellow performer to sing. The drinking kept up with the singing. So Lucy shouldn't have been surprised when she felt two hands around her waist. Then she felt her feet leave the floor as first Kyle, and then Lester and Ned, joined together to put her up on a tabletop to sing. She looked down at them, as angry as she was embarrassed. But there was no backing out. She had pride in equal measure to her fear.

But she wondered what to sing, and looked down to see Josh staring up at her, a slight smile on his face, and recalled a sun-drenched day with the music of birdsong set to the rhythm of horses' hooves. She remembered a question he'd asked her in jest after she'd scoffed at one of his tall tales. Yes. She smiled back at him, raised her head, and sang.

The musicians were wise enough to know they weren't needed as her pure sweet voice rang out with an old song. When she was done there wasn't a sound in the room. But soon there was more than enough to make up for that lapse. Because they roared out their approval and applause.

"Thank you," Josh said as he lifted her down. "I apologize. You surely do know every word to 'Amazing Grace.' "

The look they exchanged made Kyle frown. But it caused Bayard to spring up to the top of a table.

"Ladies and gentlemen," he shouted, and though his voice was slightly slurred with wine, it was fine-edged with spite, "Bayard Skyler, Ralph Rackstraw at the Stratton, at your service—with a song in honor of a guest of *ours*:

"To others I will leave the praise
    Of being useful men,
It's ornamental I would be,
    One of the upper ten.
I daresay when it's at your foot,
    It's right to kick the ball,
But I always see he's most admired
    Who nothing does at all.
For I'd like to be a swell,
Yes, I'd like to be a swell,
With his drawling talk, affected walk,
I'd like to be a swell. . . ."

Bayard ended his song with a flourish, and took his applause. Josh's face was still, although Lucy looked up at him fearfully.

"Now come," Bayard called merrily, "Mr. Dylan, don't you have a song for me? Sing for your supper!" he cried.

Others in the vast hall took up the cry, half were drunk and half were only merry, and few, after all, knew who Bayard's challenge had been issued to. They pounded their feet and their beer glasses, and chanted, "Sing for your supper! Sing for your supper!"

Bayard smirked as Lucy cried, "He's not a performer!"

Josh looked hard at her and then up to Bayard's triumphant face.

"Oh, I don't know about that," Josh drawled. "I've kept the cows happy on restless nights. But I'd need a guitar."

"He says he's kept the cows happy with his songs. But he needs a guitar!" Bayard crowed to the crowd. "Safe enough, then," he said softly to Josh, sneering as well as a very drunk man could manage to do.

"Here! Here! Coming through," someone shouted from the musicians' end of the room. "Never say die, the banjo player in the band had one in a case. Come on, sir, sing for your supper! Sing for your supper!"

Lucy sincerely wished she were the sort of woman who fainted. But all she felt was ill at the thought of the embarrassment he'd face—she'd face. Because Josh took the guitar and bounded to the top of a table. He ought to have refused. He could have assaulted Bayard. She'd not have blamed him. If he sang, everyone else might be amused, but she doubted she'd be able to see him again. It was hard to see such a man make a fool of himself, impossible to take him seriously after. She wondered just how much he'd had to drink. She'd been too busy drinking to notice.

"I'm no performer, like the little lady said," he said with his most profound drawl, and his low, deep voice carried well enough to stop the chanting and the sporadic laughter and conversation, "just a man far from home. I'll sing you a song that we sing back home about how that feels."

Men had got up and sung with beautiful trained voices, some had recited more than sung, and some few had simply done recitations in meter, as music-hall comedians do. But Josh actually sang. When he did, she and the others no longer saw the golden-haired man in his evening clothes, they were that caught by his song. They heard a deep, carrying, true voice singing a slow sad plaint—so spare in its sorrow that they ached to hear him:

"I'm just a poor wayfaring stranger,
　Traveling through this world of woe,
There ain't no sickness, no toil or trouble,
　In that fair land to which I go.

I'm goin' there to see my mother,
   I'm goin' there no more to roam,
I'm just a-goin' over Jordan,
I'm just a-goin' over home."

It was very simple really. Very slow, but short. So she
didn't know why she was crying when he'd done. But
she knew why everyone else was cheering, even though
they'd wept.

He bent, but not to bow. He put a hand on the table,
swung down with easy grace, and handed the guitar back
without looking at whom he handed it to. He looked
only to her.

"Didn't shame you like you thought I would, did I?"
he asked.

She could only nod.

"I never do anything if I can't do it," he said softly.
He touched a tear on her cheek, and said even more
softly, "Come on, you've drunk yourself maudlin. You
need some air. That is, if you've had enough music?"

"Oh, yes," she said, and took his arm.

They left, just as the crowd was joining in "My Old
Kentucky Home" with a tall tenor. Lester said that it
was too bad they were going so soon, as they'd miss the
fun of seeing Bayard being spectacularly sick in a potted
palm. Everyone else smiled at that, but Kyle was still
frowning as they left.

"We'll walk," Josh said after he told the man he'd
hired at the beer garden to keep his rig pacing alongside
them as they did, "until your head is clear enough to
ride."

"I didn't know I had drunk so much," she said.

"I don't think you did," he said, "but it doesn't take
much for you. It's that thing you're wearing," he said
conversationally as he paced beside her. "It leaves no
room for anything to go down, so it all goes to your
head."

She gasped. "You're not supposed to mention my corset," she said with dignity.

"You're not supposed to mention that I mentioned it,"
he answered, "and I don't think you would if you were
thinking clearly. So, let's walk."

They walked in amiable silence for a while. The evening was cool and Lucy soon felt her dizziness fading along with her inchoate sorrow. She noted that Josh curbed his long strides to match her own mincing ones. Noticing how her shadow under the gaslamps seemed to sway like a mandarin's concubine, she finally spoke.

"This walking is very good," she complained, "but if you gentlemen had to walk with your legs tied together at the knees, I doubt you'd recommend it."

She saw his white-toothed smile in the uneven light. "You think we keep you hobbled so you can't run away?" he asked. "But you ladies pick your own fashions. If I had my way, you'd wear far less."

Before she could upbraid him for his effrontery, he added with great innocence, "You wouldn't be worth much back home. Couldn't do a lick of work togged out like that." And then he laughed at her expression. "But I guess if you're clearheaded enough to complain, you're ready to ride now. But where shall we ride to?" he asked. And her smile slipped.

She couldn't answer at once, with him so near. It could have been that he knew that, because he turned to signal for the coach to stop. Only after he'd helped her to her seat, paid the man who'd held the reins, and taken them himself did he look to her for her answer. She was still struggling with it. If she said "home" as her first impulse was to do, she'd have to ask him in for a few polite moments that could become some more dangerous ones. Because they'd be alone there now. The occupants of the boardinghouse were all still at the beer garden, except for Mr. Fergus, the maid of all work, and Duncan. Mr. Fergus would be asleep at this hour, or puttering about with his true love, the water pipes, in the basement. The maid would be asleep. And Duncan loved Josh. Not that she expected Josh to lunge at her if he discovered himself alone with her, she thought quickly. But if she didn't expect that, as a wicked little question insisted, why should she fear going anywhere with him now? There was no way she could resist his next suggestion while she was arguing with herself. Or so she told herself.

"Would you like to come and see my new place for a little while, until the others get back?" he asked lightly.

"I'm at the Fifth Avenue Hotel. It's luxury itself. You should see it—I'd like you to—and," he said gently, "I won't do anything you don't want me to do."

What could be fairer? she thought. Too confused to answer while such a monumental battle was going on in her own mind—with Sunday-school forces at sword's point with the impulses of the night and his nearness— she could only nod. Up and down. It seemed he sighed as he picked up the reins. But then he grinned.

There were only a few people in the elegant lobby, but their presence kept her from pulling back and running away. Because once in the light again, she thought of how it looked for her to walk into a hotel with him at this hour. Then she caught a glimpse of herself with him in one of the gilded mirrors, and barely restrained herself from pelting off into the night. They looked so sophisticated together, she thought as she automatically followed him across the thick carpeting; they resembled a picture of "Vice and the Downfall of the City Woman" she'd once seen in an illustrated Bible Society tract.

"Here we are," he said after the gilded elevator had taken them to his floor and he unlocked his door. "Please do come in."

She felt as though she was stepping into one of the circles of hell as she went over the threshold, and was so terrified by what she was doing that she only peripherally noted the wide, high-ceilinged rooms with their tasteful furnishings. He showed her to a sitting room, took her cape, hung it away, and then, after seating her on a sofa, bent to light the fire in the grate. Once that was done, he turned to see her sitting bolt upright, with an expression promising strong hysterics rather than sensual bliss.

"I thought I'd show you the rest later, when you're rested—or thawed," he said. "Ah . . . do you think you can bring yourself to speak with me?" he asked. "I haven't really done anything, you know. Would you like some more wine—or I can send for coffee or tea—or would you prefer a gun?"

That made her head shoot up, and so he added, "Well, it did look like you were staring at me as though I was a rattler. A snake, that is. I'm not, you know," he said softly, "I'm just a lonely cowboy."

"*That* you are not," she said at once, her rigidity fading as his voice brought the normalcy of the situation to her. "You're no more a cowboy than I am an . . ." She faltered, realizing what she'd almost said.

". . . immoral woman?" he asked, and as she gazed at him he said, "But I never thought such a thing. I just wanted some company. You don't want mine, is that it? Maybe it's not my morals—maybe you're just worried that associating with me will be bad for your diction . . . you're starting to pick up some of the awful 'American slur' my father used to complain about—or was that only the wine?"

It was astonishing, he thought, how she'd gone from fear to humor and now seemed gripped by intense horror. He didn't know what was bothering her; he'd just been trying to make conversation to put her at her ease. Maybe, he realized, watching her closely, that was the trouble. If he didn't know what to make of her tonight, she might be having the same trouble trying to figure him out. He wasn't behaving at all as a lover, or aspirant one, ought to. There were men with strange desires, he knew that, and as an actress, she certainly must. He was struck by the sudden idea that she thought him one of them. After all, she'd done all she could to encourage him in a ladylike manner. She'd come to his rooms, it was darkest night, she was an actress, he a wealthy admirer; she must be wondering just what it was he was after.

He decided it was time to show her.

He sat down next to her.

"I agree," he said softly, placing his arm around her shoulder, his voice thickening to a drawl as he watched the rapid rise and fall of her breast, and then focused on her lips as he scented the faint lilac in her hair. "Talkin's a waste, when there's this kind of tellin' to do."

She would have been horrified at his actions, and shocked by his kiss, had she been able to think once he'd kissed her. But his lips were warm and gentle, and his arms were the most comforting thing she'd felt in a very long time, and the scent of him was of the night and the

fire and strong sweet liquors and spices. His hand was
large and warm, and when he placed it at the side of her
head, she felt protected. When he deepened the kiss, she
felt threatened for only a moment, until the unfamiliar
touch of his tongue became an oddly welcome intrusion,
if only because it withdrew as soon as he felt and heard
her small gasp of alarm.

That was the way he wooed her, taking only what she
offered, waiting for her response before he took more,
even though the touch of her mouth was more delicious
than any he could remember, even though the feel of
her smooth skin made him forget that he'd ever felt anything like her before. He grew more involved as she grew
more pliant in his arms, and his mouth sought more of
hers as she gave him more than he'd expected—since
he'd never known such sweetness.

All the women he'd known had been experienced ones,
because those that weren't didn't fool with single men,
or those favored men wouldn't stay single, or live, for
that matter, for very long. This little actress had a strange
new quality of innocence that fed his desire, even as he
withheld it for her sake. It seemed to be what she
wanted, and so it was what he did, because it was working to achieve what they both wanted. It was a game, he
thought as his lips touched her neck, her shoulder, and
moved lower as one hand buried itself in the coils of her
streaming silky hair and the other sought to clear a path
for his lips. The best game he'd ever played. His gratitude for it met his desire to win it, as he, ever the gentleman, continued to take his cue from his lady, and she
was soft and yielding in his arms.

She was, he began to realize a moment later, but her
gown was emphatically not. Because though he could
stroke at the top of her breasts, they were encased in
what seemed to be chain mail, and his hand at her waist
touched what appeared to be canvas laced with bone,
and his hand at her hip might have been resting on a
concrete wall. His mind began to veer from pure pleasure
to tactical reasoning.

She clearly wasn't going to help him, and he'd the
oddest notion that with all her acquiescence, if he paused
to ask, she'd take flight. Frustrated as he was eager now,

he decided to progress another way. If she were in a cage, he'd have to spring it from a different angle. Holding their kiss, he bent her back against the couch, and, encased as she was, she lowered to it all of a piece. It was oddly like easing down a sapling. But then he was able to slide his hand up a shapely silken leg that could be nothing else but a woman's, inching along that smooth sweet curving line until he sighed against her lips and began to think of better things than tactics—and she erupted like a wild thing from his arms.

"How dare you!" she cried, standing and shaking, her hair all down about her face, though nothing else but her kiss-reddened lips and the faint blur of a blush from his late-night growth of beard on the white skin at her neck and her breast showed any disarray.

He let her go as soon as she'd begun to struggle. He'd never force a woman, and couldn't imagine why he'd have to do so with this one. She wanted him. He might be unsure of many things with her, but of *that* he'd been convinced. This, then, was a game he didn't know. And he was too annoyed and irritated with the cessation of it to mind his words.

"I dared because it is . . ."—he sighed, and tried to pretend to a calm he didn't feel as he reached into his fob pocket to consult his watch—"two o'clock in the morning, ma'am, and you are here alone with me in my rooms."

"How could you?" she hissed with convincing despair.

"Well, I couldn't," he answered. And then the humor of it came to him, and he started to laugh. "Lord, lady," he said between chortles, as she stared at him, "no man could—'less he had a can opener with him. I don't think Sir Galahad went clanking out with half so much armor as you've got on. You'd be safe as an oyster at the pussycats' picnic—you're locked up as tight as a drum."

She looked as though she were going to cry.

"What have you got on?" he asked, as he tried to sober himself.

She couldn't tell him how improper a question it was, because of the impropriety of the situation that had provoked the question. It was late, and she was weary, and as unaccustomed to leaving off at the beginning of such

rapturous lovemaking as he was—if for different reasons.
Because she'd never gone half so far in a man's arms
before. But then, too, she'd never felt such a man's arms
before, she thought, and, confused as she was disturbed,
she answered unthinkingly and honestly.

"My corset, of course, and a corset cover, and a camisole . . ." She saw his lips twitching, and her own began
to curve upward as she found it was more amusing than
degrading to go on speaking what she'd been taught was
purest, sheerest pornography—at least in front of a male.
". . . my camisole, and oh, yes, my underskirt with a
crinolette in back, and . . ." Now, incredibly enough, she
was trying as hard not to laugh as he was—she must have
had a great deal of wine, or else he'd gone to her head,
she thought—but she plunged onward: "and my . . ." She
was too far gone to hesitate more than a second. It was
true, she thought before she banished the thought, that
decadence became easier the more you got used to it.
". . . d-drawers and suspenders," she said in a rush, "for
my stockings."

They both began to laugh. But she stopped when he
did to ask, and he may have been serious: "Tell me, did
you feel *anything* I did?"

"Too much," she thought, and was amazed when she
heard she'd said it.

"Then why did you stop?" he asked, and he was
entirely serious.

"I don't do such things. I may be an actress, but I'm
not . . . an actress," she explained, feebly even to her
own ears.

"It's all right if you tell me it was me," he said quietly.
"I won't ever force you to anything, and I'll still take
you home. It's just that I'd like to know the truth."

It was time for it, she thought. He wondered at how
the starch seemed to go out of her. Her shoulders
dropped, as the rest of her would have done if it were
freed from the supports he'd tried to prize her from.

"My name is really Lucy Markham," she began.

It wasn't until the fire had burned lower, and she'd got
to the part about her mother leaving for good the second
time, that he finally accepted she wasn't really English,
just as she'd said, after all. Because her voice had

dropped its arch accent so completely he wondered how
he'd ever believed her. It was a strangely familiar unfamiliar voice he heard now. He knew he'd regret the loss
of his illusion; he'd loved the way she said everything,
from his own name, "Josh-wa," instead of the "Josh-u-
a" he usually heard, to the way she pronounced Gray's
real given name, "Graham," as "Gram," the way his
father used to do, and not as the Americanized "Gray-
ham" that had given him his nickname.

She was an amazingly good actress, he thought as she
told him all the rest. He'd never seen a lovelier liar. He
listened without interrupting once, believing half, and
not caring about the rest.

Because despite her deceptions, unknown and admitted, she was still one of the pleasantest things he'd almost
done in New York. And in all fairness, he thought, he'd
been known to adapt protective coloration himself. But
he couldn't help regretting the truth even as he was
pleased to hear her confessing it to him.

". . . so I can't make you promise. Because I've no
right. But please, please don't tell anyone, will you?"
she pleaded at the end of her confession.

"Why are you telling me now?" he asked as answer.

She shrugged. "I didn't want to lie to you anymore."

"Your secret is mine," he said. "Come sit down now."

"I can't," she said, and he felt a curious pang of regret
for the loss of the way she'd used to say "cahn't."

"I'm a man of my word," he said, stretching out his
long legs and patting the cushion next to him. "I won't
do anything you don't want me to do."

She could hardly say that was precisely the problem,
so said instead, in a nervous little voice, "It's awfully
late, I'd really like to go home."

"Fine," he said, rising to get her cape. "When shall I
see you again?"

"Oh," she said as she snuggled into her cape as though
it was the warmer embrace she'd lately escaped, "but
what would be the point? I won't . . . and you want to
. . . and I don't . . ."

"Oh, I still 'want to,' " he said, smiling, as he fastened
the clasp of the cape at her neck. As her eyes widened,
he restrained the impulse to kiss them closed, and went

on, still playing the game by the rules she'd set down, "But I meant what I said. I always do. I enjoy your company. And hope you like mine. You said you need to be seen about town, and I'm a man-about-town these days, playing at being a swell, just like your friend Mr. Skyler said. I could use the company, and at least you understand me, and I you. Why don't we take it as it comes?"

"I don't think so. I meant what I said too," she said, pausing as they reached the door. "So," she asked again sadly, "what would be the point?"

He looked at her woeful face peering from her hood, and it took all his restraint not to show her.

"Think about it," he said.

And as she left with him, she was even more frightened than when they'd arrived, because she knew she would.

11

NONE OF THEM had gotten much sleep the night before. They'd gone to bed at dawn, so even lying in until late afternoon hadn't banished the smudges beneath their eyes. Stage makeup did, and the spotlight always picked them up, and would, as Kyle encouraged his weary cast before the next night's performance of *Pinafore*, even if they were on the point of death and not just badly bruised by a night's dissipation. Dying onstage—literally, that is—was every actor's dream, after all. Except, of course, he conceded, to win their laughter as well as their best efforts, for the fact that it would be hard to give an encore.

They'd performed well enough. And one night early to bed and late to rise brought back the roses to their cheeks—all except for Ned, whose were the natural color of whey, and for Lucy, who was languishing more each day. She was well enough onstage, but an indefinable something was both missing from and added to her performance. It was fine for her sorrowing rendition of "Sorry her lot who loves too well," to bring tears to the audience's eyes. It was not too wonderful for her to perform her part of the rousing finale of "Oh joy, oh rapture, unforeseen . . ." as though she were Ophelia about to go for her final dip, as Kyle informed her.

"Admittedly," he went on to say as he paced in front of her in the parlor as he lectured, "portions of our little operetta are affecting. But *Hamlet* it is not. Brooding Danes ought not to be on the deck of the *Pinafore*."

He paused and looked to where she sat wide-eyed, watching him. He hesitated. He could speak about her performance onstage, but couldn't order her to stop sighing over her breakfasts and being so dismal at dinner too. Her reaction to life these days was as dispirited as it was unlike her. Even Lester's jokes failed to cheer her. He'd set the entire table laughing last night, but all he'd won from her was a softened look and a sadder smile, as though she were laughing at the folly of life, and not at the way he'd suggested she was mourning her mashed potatoes.

Kyle knew she was in love. Or thought she was, which was the same thing with women. And her loved one had left her. This much was clear, because Kyle hadn't seen tanned hide nor golden hair of her wealthy Western suitor since the night at Tony Pastor's. At first he was relieved, because the English Rose was his great gamble to rise from obscurity and he needed her full attention and cooperation, and because it was always trouble when an actress became entangled with an outsider—and because of a dozen other good excuses he made to himself for his concern. But now he was growing as alarmed as she was melancholy. Because if it affected her performance, it affected him as deeply as it did her.

So he told her. And won the first spark of liveliness he'd had from her in days.

"I am *not* in love!" she said defiantly.

"I see. You always pass September in a blur of tears, is that it? Come now, my dear Lucy. You were blooming, child, until you spent the night with him."

She leapt to her feet and started to speak, but he raised one thin hand and went on, "Now he's no longer here, and you barely are. Lovesickness passes . . . unless," he said, his dark eyes growing larger as the horrible thought occurred and grew plausible to him, "it's another sort of sickness? The morning kind?" he asked.

Her anger gave way to puzzlement, and she gazed at him curiously, so he prompted, "Nausea, indigestion . . . ah, the lack of one friend's monthly visits because of a surfeit of another one's nightly ones? . . . Damnation, Lucy, are you with child, do you think?"

Her gasp, he thought sourly, was enough to cause all the fern fronds in the overstuffed parlor to sway.

"How dare you!" she cried, even more unhappy as it occurred to her that she'd said that a lot lately. "I am not! I have never . . . He never . . . As if I would let him! Which is, I suppose, why he hasn't called on me again, will never call again, because I won't, although he wanted to, but I'm not that sort of girl, and so I told him. Why, I even told him all the truth about myself, I was that misled by his charm, but not so much as to . . . Oh, *never!* I never . . ." She paused in her defense because he was no longer wearing his sympathetic expression. Or any she'd ever seen directed at herself before. That long, thin, dark, and intense face was glowering at her murderously. She took a step back.

"You told him . . . all?" he asked.

She nodded. For once she didn't have to take a breath in order not to chatter. She had never felt less like speaking. But then he asked her, "Why?"

"As I said," she said quietly, hanging her head, "I thought he was . . . sincere. He promised not to tell a soul," she added with a little hope coloring her soft voice.

Her eyes were luminous and seemed to glow as much as glisten in her sad, pale face. He couldn't scold, the horse was stolen anyway, he thought on a sigh. But at least, he decided, his ever-present optimism rising, if she were to be believed, that was the only thing that had been. All wasn't lost. It didn't matter much to him if she was, as she implied, incredibly enough, still virginal. But he had the uneasy feeling it mattered far too much to her, and that she was every bit as staid, conventional, and bourgeois as she claimed to be.

He'd always thought that invisible bit of tissue only a bothersome barrier, better to be rid of early, exactly as so many women he knew also believed, or said they did. But he understood he was in a minority in society and that his was a different world from the great one around him—that was one of the reasons why he'd chosen it. She might have stumbled into his world only by chance, as she claimed. If so, then it was a problem. Girls from her sphere placed much weight upon that weightless veil to pleasure. For that matter, so did men from her world. They made a heavy burden of that gossamer thing. And so he feared that when she gave that tiny portion of her anatomy away, her whole heart would go irrevocably along with it. And where her heart led, she'd follow. In marriage, if she was wise and lucky, and he was not. In hopeless lifelong devotion, or even actual denial of life, if she wasn't.

If she gave it for love, and not for money, fame, or pleasure, he reminded himself. She was still young, younger than he'd ever been. And he was glib, growing more into the power of his persuasiveness each day. He still doubted the wisdom of attempting her seduction himself, no matter what his body clamored for when he gazed at her. Because if he failed to entice her, he'd frighten her away and lose her absolutely. But if she loved where he thought wise, and how—or, best of all, if she learned the thing didn't require love at all—she could be bonded to him just as firmly and far more safely. It was one of life's ironies that so long as she remained "pure," he could never afford to risk trying to have her, but once breached—only once—and he might be able to have her forever. Or for however long he decided forever ought to be.

He didn't believe a pure body bespoke a pure heart, and as he didn't believe in pure hearts either, he saw no problem in what to urge her to. The remnants of his conscience didn't so much as twinge. After all, the burden she carried was a useless one now. Her present occupation precluded her ever being accepted the way she said she wished to be. If she didn't know that yet, she would. The important thing was that there was still time.

"I can see your attraction to him. I'd make him a Marc Antony in a second," he said, and she frowned, wondering why he was no longer angry, "or a Mr. Rochester, or Enoch Arden. Why, I'd look no further for a Davy Crockett, for that matter. But not a Hamlet or a Romeo, because it's a ruined beauty. No, Mr. Sothern and Mr. Booth have nothing to fear from him," he chuckled.

He saw her frown, and realized she might feel sorry for the man, no matter how she'd said she felt about him. Then he realized she'd said a great deal, but nothing actually about how she did feel about him. Disparaging him might very well create a paradoxical effect. But praise could work where scorn failed.

"Nonetheless, it's a rugged sort of beauty," he said. "Have you been to the museum? The ladies promenade very slowly past one sculpture. However damaged Apollo's statue, it is still Apollo, and there are those who find that its defacement lends his beauty a humanity that perfection lacks. Mr. Dylan, no doubt, knows this and trades on it. And why should it not work with you? You, my pretty, have nothing to compare him to—not even in the theater—that's my point. Whom have you seen," he asked abruptly, turning on her, "except for him? And some absolute fools who let you put your little foot on their necks for the pleasure of being seen out with you? Eh?

"Why, child," he said as she bit her lip, "there's a world of men out there—actors and civilians, and many, many of them handsomer, finer, more trustworthy than he. Yes, yes, you do right to look doubtful. How should you know it, after all? Here. Jewel," he bellowed, "come down here."

Wherever he'd thought Jewel was, she came in so quickly Lucy realized she must have been leaning on the door. So she turned her flushed face to the window as Jewel came into the room Kyle had ordered everyone from moments before. It was just as well, because that way she didn't see Mrs. Fergus, Mrs. Fairfax, and Miss Hampton sidle in on her heels. The men of the house hung back by the open door. Even Duncan came to the doorway and dropped to the floor, nose to front paws, to listen.

"Jewel, my dear, before you decided to honor me with your gracious company, how many gentlemen did you walk out with?" Kyle asked sweetly.

"Really?" Jewel asked incredulously, shocked out of her usual bored expression. "You really want to know?"

"Ho," Ned said from the door. "Now she's got to take off her shoes and stockings to count."

"And all of ours too," Lester added in a bright stage whisper, ducking as Jewel turned to glare at him.

"Is nothing in this house private?" Kyle demanded with a great show of exasperation, but not much heat, because he decided that a majority of voices was exactly what he needed now.

"I don't know," Jewel said thoughtfully. "How do you mean 'know'?"

"Not just in the biblical sense," Kyle said, and then, when he got a blank look as answer, sighed and prompted, "Anyway at all, Jewel dear, just give us an idea of how many you walked out with, no matter what you did when you came in."

"Oh, dozens," Jewel said, resuming her usual expression, "dozens and more. I've been acting since I was a nipper."

"Just so!" Kyle said approvingly, and then turned to hear a stir at the door and glowed with pleasure as he saw the maid had let in Ada. "Ah," he said with delight, "you've come in on cue, my dear Miss Jessup."

Since Ada had never been his dear anything, she looked as apprehensive as gratified, but her freckled face broke into a complete grin as he went on, "We're trying to make our English Rose see there's more to my poor gender here in America than one straying Westerner."

"Then you have to get her better spectacles than I did," she said merrily. "It's what I've been saying, but she doesn't hear me. Weeks now, and all she does is wait for a fellow that never comes. My mother told me men are just like horsecars: miss one, catch the next one coming down the street. But it's weeks now, and all she does is—"

"It's been only eight days," Lucy protested, and then, sorry that she'd let them see how carefully she'd counted them, turned her last words into a cough. It was bad enough to have lived through those days waiting for a summons that never came, searching the audience each night for a face that never was seen. It was somehow worse to realize that all these well-meaning people knew it. And ill-meaning ones too, she saw, since even Bayard, who'd said nothing because he'd gotten into enough trouble with his impromptu performance at Tony Pastor's, let his smirk speak all he daren't say.

"Uh-huh," Ada said, nodding, "so I came to take her out for a walk in the park so she can see what's available."

"But she won't," Kyle said. "All she'll see in the park are loiterers and mashers, my dear. Not the kind of gents of quality she ought to be meeting . . . she could be meeting, if she'd only look up and live. Tonight," he said to Lucy, taking her hand, "this very night, after our performance, let me introduce you to some fellows who can make you forget that man."

"What man?" Lucy said loftily, drawing herself up to give her finest bit of acting yet, succeeding in becoming every inch the facile, sophisticated lady—every bit exactly what they all knew she never had been.

"Yes, the desk over there, near the window. If I have to be in the city, at least I can be in the clouds. Four stories up—it's like being on a mountaintop. Way above the noise and clutter. Thanks to you. Never thought I'd be camping in the same building the Commodore used to have his offices in," Josh said to the heavyset man watching the movers position the huge oak desk.

"Of course you did," William Henry Vanderbilt said on a laugh. "It was in your eyes from the moment you first laid them on Central Station, even then."

"Still, it's not often a man can make a dream a reality," Josh said softly as he ran his hand over the burnished wood.

"You don't seem to have much difficulty doing it," the older man said. "You've come far and fast, Josh. And it suits you."

"Fast?" he answered lightly, for all his eyes grew steely gray. "If you call herding and hauling and working twenty-six hours a day for most of my life 'fast,' why, then, sir, I believe I know what to get you for Christmas—a new timepiece."

"I meant that you've been in the city for a scant two months and you've already been admitted to the best homes and clubs. Sailing and spending weekends with the Van Horns? Keeping company with Miss Gloria? Sponsored by Jacob Van Horn for the Coaching Club? Why, Josh, will you speak to me when you pass my house to go to the Astors' fancy-dress balls, do you think?" William Henry asked with an attempt at a smile.

"I'll never go unless I can give you a lift there in my carriage," Josh replied idly.

"Loyalty, eh?" the older man asked wryly.

"Practicality, sir. I've got to have someone to talk to."

"Well, by that time I believe we'll both be too old to hear each other," William sighed.

"Why, I don't think so," Josh drawled, "but would you care to lay a bet on it?"

The other man stared at him, and then laughed.

"No, Josh. For all I doubt it, I never doubt you. And I've a desire to hold on to what my father left to me."

"If you're that leery of making bets you can't cover, I believe you will. Now, then," Josh said, turning to a slight young man who was sorting papers on another desk, "Mr. Whitbread, do you think you need me anymore today?"

The young man, who'd just been hired on as his secretary, looked up at his new employer through his heavy spectacles. "No, sir, I believe not. I'll have everything ready for you tomorrow. All the leases, transfers, letters, and permissions."

"Business as usual, eh?" William Vanderbilt said as he left with Josh.

"No, sir," Josh said, frowning, "as *un*usual for me. But I hear tell that a man can't work out of his hat here in the East. If I have to have an office, so be it. I don't intend to pass much time here—that's why I hired on a genuine Harvard graduate. Lord. To go in awe of your own help!"

As the older man was thinking there was no need for Joshua Dylan to go in awe of any man on the face of the earth, Josh said, brightening, "Just as well. I've got some work to do today that I don't think any college man is up to—except for my brother, that is."

"Another Dylan in the wings? Heaven help us. But what about play—is that all in the past now that you're a serious businessman?"

"But my kind of work is play to me," Josh said, laughing. "Still, don't worry, I've got my own plans for real fun too. All kinds of it."

Shaking his head as he shook hands, William Henry departed, leaving Josh to smile up at the gray sky as though the sun were brightly shining, before he turned on his heel and headed west, as he'd been yearning to do all day.

He heard what was happening long before he saw it.

And smelled it, he thought, grinning, soon after. By the time he rounded the corner and got to the dock, the scene was one of chaos. The steers were bent on getting into the street; the drovers, dockworkers, sailors, and policemen helping to act as herders were intent on getting them up the gangplank to the many-masted sailing ship. Neither side seemed to be winning. The cattle were balking, veering, crowding in all the wrong directions. The herders were shouting, cursing, and flailing all sorts of impromptu weapons in every other direction.

Josh stood in the growing crowd and watched for several entertaining minutes, smiling as he saw how gingerly the New Yorkers approached the lowing cattle, and how the animals took advantage of every awkward move. He wondered which species would go into the water first. Eventually they'd get the cattle on the ship. Mr. Darwin hadn't researched in vain; man could, given time, browbeat brute beasts into doing his will. But there was a better way. One, Josh thought, that was much more fun.

The spectators saw the tall, wide-shouldered, well-dressed gentleman approach one of the sweating policemen. A moment later they were surprised to see the policeman nod, swing down from his horse, and hand the reins to the golden-haired gentleman. A second later they saw him leap up into the saddle, dig in his heels, and give out a wild cry that curdled their blood. But it made the cattle pick up their ears and slew their white-edged rolling eyes around to see the direction the familiar sound had come from. Then the mad young man was riding into the herd, crying out, prodding some leaders he'd chosen with a long pole he'd had tossed to him by another drover. Shouting and yelping, clucking and whistling, the gentleman on the horse kept moving forward. As the other men followed his lead as neatly as the cattle began to do, miraculously the steers began forming into regiments to trudge up the long gangplank.

It took almost an hour, but finally the streetful of cattle had all been herded to safety aboard ship. Then the young man swung down from the horse, returned it to the policeman, and reclaimed his hat. The last of the crowd dispersed as the policeman shook his head in admiration.

"Good job," he said. "Nice of you to lend a hand."

The young man ran a hand across his face, begriming it further. "Not nice at all," he said, grinning. "Expedient. They were my cattle. Hello, Erie," he said, turning to the weathered, solemn older man in the dusty clothes of a drover, who'd come up to him. "How are you keepin'?"

"Tolerable. You?" the man he'd called Erie answered.

"Tolerable and better'n that. Looks like next time we have to send at least six more men. And trained horses."

"Looks like," Erie agreed. "Testy after all those miles on the train. Range-bred and pent too long. Restless. Got 'er done, though."

"Now we know, be easier next time," Josh agreed. "Need a place to stay the night?" he asked.

"No, sir!" Erie said with horror. "Goin' home straightly. With the boys. Probably have to put ol' Samuel Tee up, though. Says he's coming next shipload. Says he's looking forward to tearing the place up. Says to tell you."

"Tell him I'd be proud to. Now, take care, Erie. And remember, six more men and good working horses next time. That'll do it," he said as he shook hands with the drover.

"Should," Erie agreed.

"But," Josh sighed, looking up longingly at the ship where he'd stowed the last of his cattle, "it sure won't be as much fun."

"Be less when you start sendin' 'em in steaks in 'frigerator cars like you said you was goin' to do in time," Erie said slowly.

"That's progress," Josh sighed.

Erie spat on the ground. Just as Josh felt like doing. He agreed, some progress wasn't fun. Necessity seldom was.

Still, he thought as he headed back for his hotel to wash and change his clothes, there was, as he'd told William Henry, fun and fun, after all.

An hour later, cleaned and refreshed, he drove out in his new carriage, all the way down to Broome Street. An hour after that he was filthy again. But supremely happy. He rolled out from under the coach he'd been inspecting.

The man in a working smock who'd been there with him wriggled out too, grinning.

"Well, did I tell you?" the man asked, handing him a cloth to wipe his grimy hands on.

"Beautiful, Mr. Brewster. Just like they all said. Every one of them is a work of art," he said, sweeping one hand to encompass the rows of finished, half-completed, and just-begun coaches of every description in the huge carriage works. "But what I have in mind is somewhat different."

He took a set of papers from his inner pocket and spread them on a workbench for the other man to see.

Mr. Brewster whistled. "I never saw one like that," he said, "except in pictures, but I've never laid my hands on one. Talk about beautiful. You want it just like that?"

"I do. Just like that," Josh said. "Mahogany. Interior satin, and velvets. In black, with maroon doors dark enough to be black, and yellow wheels and trim. My grandfather drove a coach just like that in England. And my father learned on one of his. I doubt the Coaching Club has ever seen the like. Lord! I haven't, that's why I want it. They're said to handle sweet as a light phaeton, for all they're almost the size of a Concord. If they're built right. And I've faith in you. If you run into trouble, I'll be here every day. I've done my share of carriage work. I'll be glad to help out."

"I don't think we'll need the help, but since I doubt we'll be able to keep you out, I'll be glad of an extra hand," Mr. Brewster said, because if he'd ever seen a man in love, this man was he—he saw the adoration glowing in those grave gray eyes as they lingered lovingly over the sketches laid out on the bench. And as a man who loved coaching too, he was, as he immediately said, proud to share in such a project.

"An English stagecoach from the old high days of the Golden Road—from the days of the Prince Regent. Not even Mr. Havemeyer has one of those," Mr. Brewster said as he folded up the plans. "When do you need it?"

"Take your time," Josh said as he took out his wallet. "You've got a month."

Mr. Brewster's laughter stopped when he saw the amount offered him.

Play, Josh thought as he drove back to his hotel to wash and change once again—it had been a day filled with play disguised as work. His office was set up, with a secretary in place, his cattle loaded on a ship bound for England, his dream coach under way to being built— now that he'd found his footing in this city, he'd begun the race. He'd been moving and creating since he'd got back from his second weekend with Jacob and Gloria.

This time he'd driven Jacob's new coach for him, and in return for it had got the invitation, the offer for sponsorship to join the New York Coaching Club if they approved him. Or was it, he wondered, in return for partnering Gloria in the dance Saturday night? Or for riding with her in the early mornings? Or for sitting close with her in the evenings? No matter. She had both charm and correctness, and gave him every opportunity to see the former virtue and perhaps hinted that with him she'd rather not retain the latter. But he'd kept his kisses to gentle salutes, and kept his arms at his own sides most of the time. Time, he thought; he'd give it time.

Time would tell him when and if it was ever time to ask for or offer Gloria more. Or, for that matter, even to want more from her. For now it was enough that she'd told her father laughingly but firmly to find another lady to showcase in his coach at the next Coaching Club outing, because she planned to grace Josh's new carriage when he rode out in parade with them.

Business disguised as pleasure, followed by the joyful business of droving and coach-building. And now he'd an evening planned to take the shine out of all of that. It was time for pure play.

It had been fifteen days since he'd seen her, since that evening of incredible delight and exquisite frustration. Fifteen days and fourteen nights, and he'd thought of her every one of them—especially every night. But he was a master of time and knew the value of waiting for it to pass. Now it had been just long enough for her to have given up on him, but not long enough for her to have forgotten him. He'd planned to make it only two weeks, but he'd had to stay an extra day on Long Island. A day he'd begrudged. Because he found he couldn't wait a day longer to see her in person as he'd seen her in his imaginings every night. Now was the time to try for that again.

Now more fun, he thought, whistling as he dried himself after his bath; a man oughtn't to be allowed to have so much in a day. And so he wasn't too surprised when, only a few hours later, he discovered he wasn't.

He'd thought she'd been more than pleasantly surprised to see him in the audience, but with stage makeup he couldn't be sure. Now, backstage in her dressing room, her face innocent of paint, her eyes were just as wide and her cheeks as impossibly white. She was as lovely as he remembered, maybe more so, if that were possible. But he never remembered seeing her so distressed—no, not even when she'd torn herself out of his arms, even though he knew as well as she did that she longed to stay there.

At least he'd the meager joy of knowing now, as then, that it seemed to be the loss of him more than the thought of him that was upsetting her so.

"I wasn't here because I wasn't anywhere—I've been gone from the city for a while," he explained, which was at least a half-truth. "I just got back, and instead of sending word, came straight here. I'd hoped . . . I'd thought we could walk out tonight, have late supper, or whatever. It's been too long," he said, which was nothing but the whole truth.

"But I promised . . . that is to say, last night he came out with Kyle and me, and we all had tea and coffee together. Not all together, not tea and coffee mixed together, of course . . ." She stopped, and then spoke plainly. "I said I'd go out to supper with him tonight. He knows you," she added weakly, as though that would comfort him, because it had her—it was the only reason she'd agreed to go out with the man.

She'd been out each night for a week with a different man. Some were fine, some were undoubtedly trustworthy, some were handsome, just as Kyle had promised, but she couldn't remember any of them because of her remembrance of Joshua Dylan. There'd been a week full of late suppers at Delmonico's, ices at late-night cafés, carriage rides, and compliments. She'd listened while they told her all about themselves, refused their gifts without opening the packages, interrupting their other offers before they could finish making them. It had been a week of abrupt flurries of farewells at her boarding-house door, so she wouldn't have to linger in the darkness with them, waiting to repulse the advances they'd clearly begun to make.

She'd worried about the engagement she'd made tonight all day. Because she faced an evening alone with a man she'd never have allowed to take her arm to help her cross a street—if it hadn't been for the magic mention of Josh's name. He'd said he was Josh Dylan's friend. That had overruled the fact that she thought he was as unhandsome in spirit as he was in body. He'd seemed the epitome of all the older men who waited for the girls from the chorus in the alley behind the theater, their arms full of flowers, nothing but praise on their lips and lechery in their eyes. He'd been effusive in his compliments, and yet she'd felt he was patronizing her, never seeing beyond her face and form. He made her feel like an actress in every worst sense of the word.

But he'd mentioned his friend Josh Dylan. And in that moment there'd been an immediate small thrill of pleasure at the idea of Josh seeing them together and remembering all she couldn't forget. And a wild surge of hope that he might envy another her company, perhaps regretting all he'd given up. But that was fantasy, acted on impetuously in the night. This was reality. And it was turning out to be disastrous. Her little act of defiance, foolish hope, and spite had already netted her hours of unease. Now it turned on her entirely. Now Josh was here, and she was committed to someone else.

She stared at him helplessly, wondering if her reckless act had lost him to her for more than this one dreadful night. It wasn't just that she began to doubt he'd ever dispute a friend. She might have lost him even if he called on her again. Because, seeing her with that man, why shouldn't he believe her to be all she'd insisted she was not? She was behaving exactly like the woman he'd thought she was.

"A friend?" Josh asked, grinning. Trust Peter. Done with his fling with Ada weeks ago, now he'd tried for the English Rose. But he was a real friend. He'd see the game that was being played and step out of the way when he did. Josh was still smiling as the gentleman came to the dressing-room door. But when he saw who it was, his smile slipped.

Edgar Yates took off his high hat and took Lucy's hand as he bowed over it.

"Good evening, Miss Rose. Hello, Dylan," he said with real gratification. From the looks of things, rumor and what Kyle Harper had hinted were true. And almost too good to be true.

The English Rose was pretty enough, but Yates was never a man who sought simple pleasures. Actresses were plentiful. This one was different, if only for her associations. He had a score to settle.

Josh Dylan had refused his invitations from the first, ignored him at the club soon after, and now avoided him entirely. There seemed as little chance to sell or take anything from him now as there'd seemed ample opportunity when he'd arrived in town. He'd looked green as grass, green as all his obviously new-minted money was. He'd looked to be a prime example of Edgar Yates's natural prey. The moment the young Westerner had been introduced to him, he'd begun mentally sorting through his store of amusements to offer a newcomer to the city. He'd pondered about which bawdy houses, theaters, and gambling houses to take him to; and which insolvent railroad lines, defunct shipping companies, and sham mining interests to interest him in.

But Josh Dylan had been a surprise. An unpleasant one. Because even after Yates had conceded he'd have to find a new pigeon to pluck, he'd not been permitted to express the real admiration he'd felt, despite himself, for the resourceful young man. He hadn't been so much shunned as ignored as an insignificant nuisance, and that had stung more than would have outright hostility. Like most men who seldom earned compliments, Edgar Yates never forgot or forgave a snub.

But Josh Dylan had seemed to put himself above Yates's reach with stunning speed. He'd soon been hobnobbing with a class of people who seemed too high to touch. But "seemed" was a sometime thing. And Edgar Yates's need for revenge was always present, just as was his need for money. So he never stopped watching. Because he knew that so long as a man lusted after anything in this world, he was ultimately reachable. Crafty as he was cowardly, he was careful to find the methods that presented the least danger to himself. He'd waited. There was always more than one way to bring a proud man down. And since he'd been unable to have him at his side, he'd a yearning to see that untouchable young man at his feet.

Now he saw the way Josh looked at this actress, and was, in that one rare moment, satisfied. He would be, he guessed, judging from the spasm of fear he'd caught on the girl's face when she'd seen him, even more so later. He didn't know why she'd agreed to go with him, or why she'd fallen out with Dylan, but he never questioned gifts, whoever sent them.

"You're in blooming good looks tonight, Miss Rose," he said on a pleased sigh, "and I, alas, am only here on time."

12

"Ah, Edgar," Josh said immediately, with every evidence of pleasure, "hello. How good of you to keep her safe for me, my friend."

He put a long arm around Lucy's shoulders as he spoke.

It was as simple as that.

Edgar Yates hesitated for only a second. But that was a very long time for him to be dumbfounded. In that fleeting second, with the speed and clarity they said drowning men experienced, he rapidly reviewed all his options. He could hardly say, "No, I wanted her for myself," since that would give the lie to the claim that he was Josh Dylan's friend. There might be some advantage to clinging to the illusion of friendship; at any rate, there would be none to disputing it. He had no taste for trying to back up a claim to the woman; he had no facile way to even try. He was far more fearful of young Dylan. Then, too, for all that he was chagrined at being outmaneuvered, there was, as always with this young man, admiration to flavor his defeat. A man of admittedly strange tastes, this pleased him as much as it angered him. He laughed, and it was almost humor that he felt as he did.

"Well . . . then," he said heartily, "no thanks necessary. Anything for a friend, you know. Now, I just hope that little redhead in the chorus meant all those smiles I saw her showing me from the stage. Good evening, Dylan. Miss Rose. I hope you don't mind my taking my flowers with me," he said, as merry and easy now as a grandfather bidding them good night. "You'll have to get your own, Dylan. Some things I do not provide."

And as swiftly as he'd come, he was gone.

Lucy remained absolutely still. Josh felt her shoulders still rigid beneath his arm.

"Did you want to go with him? Is that why you're so silent?" he asked, but his lips grazed the top of her hair as he did, and his voice was low and vibrant.

"No, no," she said, more nervous now than she'd been before, but in a different way. She'd never known unease could be so blissful. "I never wanted to go with him. I said I would because . . ."

"Because?" he asked murmurously, turning her to face him, his lips at her forehead, his body very close, but not quite touching hers.

She looked up at him, fascinated by the fact that he had long dark eyelashes—she'd never noticed that—and spoke as absently as he had. "Because . . . because you never came again, and I . . ." He came a fraction closer, but that was all that was needful for them to touch, and his hand went to her hair at the side of her face, and the other encircled her waist, and she spoke without thinking, just to keep on speaking, so that he wouldn't do what she wanted him to do and what he was definitely going to do as soon as she stopped speaking.

"I . . . I thought he was your friend, and I thought I'd see you if I went with him, and that you'd see me, and maybe you'd remember me—"

"Tell me how to forget you," he breathed, and then didn't let her.

This time his lips touched hers so lightly, so barely, that it was she who eventually stepped the centimeter closer, and she who put her arms about him to bring him nearer. And then he helped her intensify the moment, and his lips were no longer gentle, but then she stopped thinking about all the particulars of their embrace as she began only to feel it.

Which was precisely what she'd been trained to be on guard against all of her life. It was as though the intense pleasure triggered some secret, hidden alarm system. Because after some long sweet moments, without knowing why, the pleasure abruptly changed to panic, and she pulled back before he could slip more than the second tight button on her dress out of its moorings. There were no words for it, but then, they'd been speaking only in emotions anyhow. Now she breathed hard and tried to recall her scattered wits. He didn't pursue her.

When she opened her eyes, he was looking down at her with an expression she couldn't read. She thought she saw desire, it might have been exasperation, but there was also definitely some humor lurking there too. That restored her. She might be well on the way to being compromised, if she hadn't been already—she was in no condition to evaluate how far she'd stretched morality, not right now. And, especially not, as she was always only too aware, after two months on the stage. She knew she was as infatuated as fascinated by him, if not far more. But she wouldn't be laughed at.

"I can't do that sort of thing," she said primly.

"Why not?" he asked.

It was a measure of how he affected her that with all her training, she couldn't answer at once, because at that moment, with him staring at her with his grave gray eyes, she didn't know why not. Or didn't want to remember. But then, of course, she did. And so her voice was more sad than offended when she replied.

"It's immoral," she said, for it was, for all it sounded too simple and dim to say. But he seemed to need everything spelled out, and she was distantly distressed to discover that she did too.

"And so," he asked lightly, naturally, "why not?"

She stared at him.

"I've done it any number of times," he said softly, "and I don't think I'm consigned to damnation."

"But you're a man!" she cried.

"And you're a woman," he said. "That's how it's done. I never did it by myself—at least, not since I was a boy—because they said *that* was sure damnation, and the low road to insanity. You'll note I'm many things, ma'am," he said, smiling, "but not insane."

She was too shocked to blush. Not because of what he'd asked her, but for the way they were talking about it and everything else they weren't supposed to. She didn't know what was worse, his embrace or his conversation—or, she thought, her own desire for both.

"I'm not like that," she said, now too sincerely bent on explaining herself to stumble more than she had to in order to get the thing into sayable words. "I'm not really an actress, I told you that. And someday," she said, gazing at him with entreaty, trying to explain without mentioning her dream of respectability and marriage, or anything else that might make him laugh, or flee, ". . . someday, I'll be nothing like one. And so I want to be . . . free from guilt, and free from shame."

"But you're the only one who will feel those things," he said with maddening reason, so reasonable she wanted to clap her hands over her ears, "and if you don't, you won't. You see? Think about it. But let's leave it now. Come, I'm starved for other things too. I had a busy day and no dinner. Let's go."

He held out a hand to her, as though he were about to take a child for a walk. She looked at it, and then up at him just as hesitantly as a child might. She might be, he thought, seeing the shadows darken her eyes, everything she said. She might not be. But two things were sure. She was an actress. And she wanted him. It needed only time to know, or achieve the rest.

"Ah, Lucy," he said, "come along. I won't do anything you don't want me to. You know that."

She placed her hand in his, even though she knew that all too well.

They looked only at each other as they left the theater; that might have been why Josh didn't nod to Edgar Yates as he brushed past him in the corridor. Or it might have been that he regarded him as a fool, unworthy of notice, Yates thought. Or it could have been that Yates felt something stirring when the two passed him by, oblivious of him, the tall, broad-shouldered Westerner as close to him as his own walking stick, and about as interested in him.

For whatever reason, Edgar Yates's lips tightened when they'd gone. He'd been about to try to find some chorus singer to give his hastily invented excuse some credibility. But now he decided to enjoy even more pleasant business—revenge. He turned and went back into the theater to seek out Kyle Harper.

Josh took Lucy to supper, and had her laughing by the time their first course arrived. By the time the sixth one was set on the table, the one that not even Josh, for all

he wore no corset, as he said, could not so much as
nibble on, they were at that state of exhilaration that
went beyond laughter to simple, transcendent joy. They
did more than flirt and admire each other or stare into
each other's eyes. They'd already discovered what that
could do. Now they were more daring. They talked. And
listened to each other.

She began to understand his love for coaching and how
his father had influenced him in so many other things,
and how much his family meant to him. She listened with
a smile on her lips, which slipped when she began to
realize how hard, however amusing, his life had been so
far. When he saw that, he left off discussing the past,
and took her only as far back as the day he'd just passed.
Then her only regret was that she hadn't been there to
see him herding the cattle, and she wished she could have
met Erie to ask him about the time Josh fell off the pinto
in the moonlight.

Then he urged her to speak. Soon he knew enough
about her grandfather to wish he'd had a chance to chat
with him, realized what a good job her grandmama had
done, and felt impotent anger at the way she tried to
forgive her parents and sister for their desertion. He
wished he could have spared her much of what had made
her what she was. When he understood the foolishness
of that, he only found himself wishing he'd the right to
meet Grandmother so he could show her what a success
her neglected grandchild had become . . . until the disturbing thought of what she'd actually become finally
occurred to him; then he abruptly cut off the conversation to order more wine and ask about dessert.

Because the truth was she was an actress, and might
be far worse. And if she weren't yet, she was still an
actress, and so would be soon, and he definitely wanted
to be the first one to make her so. It wasn't only this
that confused him, causing him to decide to go slowly,
changing his plans for the rest of the night. Unless she
offered more, he'd take her home after dinner, but not
to his home. He'd escort her back to her boardinghouse
as modestly as if she were the girl next door and he lived
next door to a church.

Because now he found that he desired more than what

he'd thought he most desired from her. Yet he knew full well it was something an actress could never give him. Unless, he mused, as she exclaimed over the flaming crepes, he decided to have both respectability and a less-than-respectable woman on the side. It was an alien and distasteful way of life to him, but he knew many men here had just that kind of arrangement set up. He'd already adopted ways of life that had recently been alien to him; it was a thing to think about. After all, he mightn't even like what she offered him when she did—and then he laughed aloud at that ridiculous thought as he gazed at her.

She lifted one arched eyebrow at his laughter.

"I'm happy," he explained simply. Because he was.

When Kyle Harper wanted his audience to know his feelings, they did. It was clear he was not happy. This pleased his audience of one enormously.

"Ridiculous, my dear sir," Kyle said loftily, and his disdain was as clear in his practiced voice as it was in his dark eyes and the way he looked down his long nose at his guest. "I've no intention of taking my troupe on the road as you suggest, thank you. Here is where our fortune will be made, and here we will stay."

Edgar Yates put on a look of chagrin, while his heart rejoiced. He'd suggested the tour, but it was only the suggestion that he could afford.

"Ah, but if Joshua Dylan steals her away from you—what then?" he asked, so that the idea he'd planted could sink deeper.

"He won't," Kyle said airily. "He'll hardly marry her, and what a gentleman wants from an actress will not affect her career onstage, except, perhaps, to her betterment if he's important, as it adds luster to her name."

"I don't know," Yates ruminated. "He isn't a New Yorker, and Western men have different ideas—they're sentimental, they don't know the ropes . . . except for the ones they use on cows." He chuckled at his joke as well as at the frown that had come to Harper's thin face.

But a moment later Kyle was smiling.

"Don't fret for me, my friend," he replied lightly, though he was just as distraught as he knew Yates wished him to be. It was natural for Yates to be consumed with spite; he'd expected it from the second he'd come to complain that Dylan had returned and swept out into the night with Lucy. Kyle had given a fine pretense of accepting the information philosophically, but it wasn't far from the truth. If his leading lady chose herself a lover, there was little he could do, after all. But *marriage?* He, who always envisioned every disaster as though by so doing he could prevent it, had never thought of that. That would, indeed, be the end to his plans. And given who Lucy was, and what the tall Westerner might be, it was just possible—unless he himself could step in, in time. But he'd be damned if he'd let Yates know it.

"I doubt a man who's come so far so fast will stop in his climbing now. For an actress? He's from another part of the country—not another planet." Kyle laughed at amusement he didn't feel.

But he was a very good actor. Edgar Yates grew cold as he heard the merry laughter. There was only so much frustration he could take in one evening. Instead of just planting doubts about the woman he'd been promised who'd gotten away, so as to make her way a little thornier, he decided to savor the pleasure of savaging his one-time ally, Kyle Harper, instead.

"I suppose it doesn't matter at that," he said comfortably, "since you'll be closing down soon anyway."

Kyle stopped laughing. He'd cultivated this unpleasant gentleman after he'd been approached about Lucy, because he never let any source of possible advantage slip away. He'd doubted Edgar Yates had money, but he had other assets that could lead to it—acquaintances in the right places and an ear where it could hear the right things. Now he wondered if he himself might have, incredibly enough, miscalculated. Could the fat gentleman have enough money to buy out his theater?

What he said was far worse.

"I hear . . ." Edgar Yates purred, "they say, and they're never wrong, that Messrs. Gilbert and Sullivan are coming to New York. Next month. To put an end to piracy, run their own *Pinafore*, and present a whole new operetta to their adoring public."

"So the rumor has been running," Kyle said on a yawn that hurt to counterfeit.

"So *they* say." Edgar nodded, smiling. "But the *they* I'm speaking of are never wrong."

Kyle knew this. And so, for once, he didn't have to act his perfect impression of the mask of tragedy.

"I don't know what's proper to wear for a football game, Lucy, but cripes! Why should you care? You look a God Almighty regular peach in that get-up!" Ada said.

Lucy frowned at Ada's way of praising her, wondering yet again if it had been wise to ask her along today. But that frown turned into a small smile of pleasure at Ada's very real compliment. And because she was as excited as she was anxious about the afternoon, and because Josh had asked her to invite some other girl to meet his younger brother, and particularly because she liked Ada very much, she let the matter drop down into the back of her mind with all her other doubts. It was a long drop, and the matter had a lot of company in those dark recesses where she'd stowed all her reservations about Joshua Dylan and where she was headed with him. And not just for this afternoon.

There'd been other outings on other days this week, and all those days had come one after another once he'd returned. Sundays came along too rarely for them now. So she'd gone with him Tuesday for luncheon, and Thursday they'd only just got back from the races at Brighton Beach in time for her to change for the performance. Friday they'd finally gone to the zoo to gawk at the hippopotamus. Since they'd not met on the weekend because Josh had to go out of town, they'd passed more time looking at each other than at the art at the National Academy on Tuesday.

Which was as well, because they'd passed a statue of Apollo that reminded Lucy of Kyle's comment about Josh and damaged beauty. She'd raised her parasol to cover her blushes because she'd seen more than the damage he'd mentioned. She'd been raised in Brooklyn, after all, where a girl never saw such things. But that was the only awkward thing that happened.

He was treating her with extreme propriety, just as

she'd asked. It was as shrewd as it was unfair, and it wasn't any better that she knew it. He was giving her no excuse to flee. Every day and night she saw him, she had to suppress her growing desire to ask him why he was being so entirely proper and treating her so respectfully. That, of course, was never the only desire she so firmly repressed.

Today was a Saturday, but they'd no matinee because the unexpected success of *Pinafore* had permitted the theater to be closed for a day for some much-needed repairs. And today, at least, was to be all out in the open air, with her friend and his relative as company, and so, she lied to herself, she was as safe as houses.

She twirled around for Ada's inspection. She'd put on a new walking dress of deepest yellow velvet, with a long bodice outlined by a mock-military marching line of rose velvet frogs. It had a "dress improver" under the draped fabric at the rear, only a delightful hint of a demibustle, and she was grateful that it was a collapsible one, because she'd be sitting for long periods today. The corset pitched her body forward at the waist, the little bustle made it seem to thrust out in back, and the narrow skirt forced her to walk with tiny steps. She hoped it made her seem to be promenading in the latest fashion, her body forming a perfect, graceful S shape, moving smoothly and regally, like a swan cresting the waters. But she secretly feared she looked like nothing more than a silly goose.

"That new outfit's a humdinger," Ada said, gazing at her. "You look like a little buttercup yourself today. Wish I could wear yellow, but it clashes with my hair," she sighed, patting the straw-colored tresses piled under her wide hat.

"You're wearing every other one," Jewel commented as she sauntered into the parlor where the two girls were waiting to be called on.

Almost every other one, Lucy silently corrected Jewel as she bit her lip and looked at her friend again. Ada had managed to squeeze into an extremely tight red dress, hobbled at the knee with maroon ties, and the bustle she wore was more than a hint, it was a proudly pink statement of fashion. Her hat was an assemblage of reds and greens, with the odd blue feather in among the garden of flowers there. She'd a coat of forest green over her arm, and a quantity of jewelry tacked on here and there. Anyone else, Lucy thought, would have looked a caution or a Gypsy. Ada looked delightfully rude. Which was charming onstage, Lucy thought guiltily, but not what she'd wanted Josh's brother to see.

But Josh evidently didn't agree. Because when he arrived, he looked long and hard at Lucy, and smiled and said, "Yes. Beautiful," before he looked at Ada and grinned.

"Now Gray will be in debt to me forever, Miss Jessup," he said. "You're just exactly what he was hoping to find in New York."

He'd called for them in a rented hackney coach, and when Lucy looked up in surprise as he held the door open for her, he whispered, "Easier this way. Gray won't be pleading for the reins to show off to the ladies. And there'll be room for them to ride with us, after, so we can chaperone them."

She giggled at the thought of chaperoning Ada, then sobered at the thought of introducing Ada to a young college man, then forgot all her worries as Josh swung into the coach, sat opposite them, and smiled at her.

The sun was shining, but there was a brisk breeze and a nip of early October in the air. The Polo Grounds were crowded and the spectators as enthusiastic as they were involved with what was about to go on in the field. They were well-dressed but loudly cheerful, and those who weren't merry with drink acted as though they were, so Lucy was relieved to see that in the press of people Ada wasn't so remarkable-looking at all. But Josh's brother didn't think so.

That young man, whose hair was almost the color of Lucy's gown, stood as though rooted in the aisle as they approached their seats. He was so spectacularly handsome, Lucy actually heard Ada gasp as they came close to him. He was tall and lithe and startlingly blond, with sky-blue eyes and finely chiseled features, and his smile was like the sun coming up in the morning as he caught sight of his brother. Although they looked very little alike on first stare, as they came into each other's arms and pounded each other on the back, Lucy could see the kinship in the long, lean lines of both men, and in their matching white-toothed smiles. And in the way Gray stared down at her when he was introduced, making her feel like the only woman in the world; his attitude was just this side of adoration, just that side of frank flirtation.

"So this is the English Rose," he breathed. "Ma'am, I can't wait to hear you sing tonight. This brother of mine has been doing nothing but singing your praises to me. Now I see he was holding back on me. Ma'am, I am purely enchanted."

"You are purely too late here, brother," Josh said, "so save your breath to cool your porridge. Or use it to better advantage. Now, make your bow to Miss Ada Jessup, Gray—she's kindly consented to be your nursemaid today."

"Oh, my," Gray Dylan said, looking at Ada with obvious delight as he took her hand and didn't relinquish it. "My, my, my. Is it my birthday? Miss Ada," he said with heartfelt sincerity belied only by his grin, "I am yours."

And so he seemed to be, Lucy thought, because Ada fastened on to him and sat down beside him, and hadn't a word or a look to spare for anything else for the rest of the afternoon. But Gray was as full of enthusiasm as the rest of the spectators, and he delighted in pointing out every aspect of the incomprehensible game that soon began. It was useless. So far as Lucy could see, the object of the game seemed to be for the players to leap upon whatever poor young man was unlucky enough to be holding the cylindrical brown leather ball that was being tossed around the field. Sometimes, it was true, they kicked it. Sometimes they threw it. But half of the time the young men in striped long-sleeved shirts were piling up on the young men in gold shirts, and the rest of it, the gold-shirted young men were grabbing the striped-shirted ones by the ankles and heaping up on top of them.

It seemed a frustrating sport, the way they never allowed anyone to run before they jumped on him, but when Lucy told Josh that, he was too busily cheering to hear, and the noise the crowd made drowned her words anyway. As the afternoon went on, it grew colder, and it seemed each separate stay in her corset was absorbing the chill, until she felt gripped in a frozen cage, each bar made of ice; and though the seats were nicely padded, she grew uncomfortable sitting on her small, not very collapsible, fashionable bustle.

At the intermission they called half-time, she rose gratefully, thinking it was all over.

"Be right back, don't stir stump," Josh said, and disappeared up the aisle with his brother.

"Oh, but he's a peach," Ada caroled when Gray had gone. "What a sweet boy," she said, her eyes sparkling, "so bright, so handsome, so—"

"Young," Lucy said repressively.

"—so . . . so what?" Ada replied, laughing. "And why not? What am I? An old lady?"

She was as right as she was wrong, Lucy thought, when Josh and Gray returned. Josh had brought a wool lap rug to place over her and a warm drink to put in her hand, and he put his arm around her and whispered, "You're cold, here, sit close, I'll block the wind for you." She sat very close, in the circle of his arm, and was acutely aware of the hard strength of him. She blessed the chill breeze for bringing him so near, so wonderfully, respectably, allowably near, and pretended to watch the game and care about how it came out, and never felt the cold at all until the game was over and he drew away from her.

They took the hired hackney back down to Ada's and then Lucy's boardinghouse, and said good-bye for just a few hours.

"The outing's put roses in your cheeks," Mrs. Fergus said admiringly as Lucy came in.

Lucy only smiled and raced up the stairs to change clothes as best she could with such numbed fingers. She was frozen to the bone, but too warmed to the heart to feel it. That night she sang for the two gentlemen in the fifth row, and she sang with a new joy that colored her voice in all the bright shades of the vibrant October day they'd given her. Even Kyle, pacing in the wings, had to stop to admire the sound of it.

"A word with you . . ." he said after she'd taken her bows and was racing back to her dressing room.

"Oh . . . but," she cried, "we're going out . . . he's waiting, and I've got to get dressed . . ." but she stood and waited for Kyle to speak, even as she protested she couldn't.

Her costume was the thin, insubstantial stuff of stage effect, all glisten and no warmth, and he could see her shivering in the draft in the backstage hall.

"Later, then," he said, despite himself, for he'd meant to call a meeting after this performance. "Go dress. We'll all meet tonight when you get home."

The restaurant was so warm most of the women dining there could sit in their low-cut gowns without a hint of gooseflesh to be seen. The food was served piping hot, and though the champagne was icy, it made Lucy's face flush. She had been so cold it seemed it would take far more to warm her now. When she suddenly realized she'd never be quite warm enough again until she was back in the arms of the man who sat so sedately opposite her now, she grew feverishly hot, before she grew icy cold at the realization of what that meant. But she couldn't worry about it, because Josh was smiling at her. Then suddenly he was on his feet.

Gray had decided to wait at the theater for Ada to finish dressing, telling them to go on, they'd catch up later. But it wasn't Gray or Ada that Josh greeted with every evidence of delight.

The newcomer was tall and gaunt. He wore fastidiously clean but ancient black evening clothes. He reeked of bay rum, and his long black hair was combed straight back and held down with so much macassar oil that Lucy could see the separate furrows the comb had made in it. That was also almost all she could see of his face at first stare. His hawklike nose jutted out from that forest of dark whiskers, and if it weren't for the pair of candid blue eyes she discerned, she'd have been genuinely alarmed at him. As it was, she fancied he looked a little like a child hiding and peering out at her from a thicket, and she was as amused as pleased by the look of awe in those wondering eyes as Josh introduced them.

"Lucy, this is Samuel Tee, an old friend from Wyoming Territory. He's blown into town with a load of cattle, and he's late because he's been washing off the evidence until now. Samuel, now that you smell like a flower yourself, may I present Miss Lucy Rose, the English Rose?"

"You surely may," Samuel answered in deep tones. "Honored, ma'am," he said, bowing slightly before Josh gestured for him to sit down.

"You look fine," Josh said.

"Sunday best," Samuel explained, looking around himself with evident awe.

"Samuel here," Josh said, "has known the Dylans since the dawn of time. He taught me a lot. Didn't you, Sam'l?"

"Sure did," Samuel answered, staring at a couple at the next table.

"He's been a drover, a cowboy, a coachman, rode the pony express for a while, didn't you, Sam'l?" Josh asked, to jolt Samuel from his wide-eyed perusal of the room.

"Did that," Samuel agreed as the woman at the next table laid her jeweled hand across the top of her exposed breast to deflect the heated gaze she found herself the object of.

"And carried a rifle in the late conflict between the states, and rode point in Indian Territory after, and was a homesteader on a railroad track for a few years after that," Josh said, beginning to wonder what he could do to divert the fascinated man's attention back to his own table, short of drawing a gun on him. But Lucy solved the problem and captured all of Samuel's wandering attention. It wasn't so much the question she asked as the voice that raised it. Samuel Tee wasn't used to hearing female voices.

"How could he live on a railroad track?" she asked.

"Why, little lady," Samuel Tee said, swinging around to study her, "easy. See, the gov'nment was a-givin' out land to any man who lived on 'er fer six months. So I made me a house on wheels and lived hopscotch on my claim—movin' off after I got it legal, to claim 'nother, then 'nother." He sat back proudly.

"Where do the railroad tracks come in?" she asked.

Samuel Tee convulsed with laughter, a circumstance which caused several chairs in the vicinity to scrape back as nearby diners tried to inch their tables away from the sound—which was something like a church organ being murdered.

"They come in after I sell off'n the claim, little missy," Samuel managed to say.

"He sells his claim to the railroad as soon as it's legally his, and then rolls his shack on to the next claim," Josh said, smiling.

"But that's . . ." She paused; "dishonest" would be insulting, however true. ". . . interesting," she said weakly.

Josh understood her face better than her words.

"Legal too," he said, "however devious it seems. That's how this country grows. The government reckons there's too many railroads—over fifty of them competing for land. So it passed the Homestead Act to bring out settlers instead. It forbids the railroads from buying up everything outright, so they buy it up out of sight. And maybe they're opening the West as much as settlers could do, too. Only kings can make laws men can't weasel around," he said softly, to ease her frown. "That's what a democracy is all about. Think of it this way: I couldn't have taken a train to New York with such ease if it hadn't been for dozens of men like Samuel . . . in every which way."

"Damn straight," Samuel said, wiping his eyes on his sleeve and so never seeing Josh frown. "Now," he said, placing two huge callused hands on the table in front of him and looking at Josh. "I et back at the hotel, so since you and Gray is hooked up so nice, can you tell me where I can go to get a gal? They all over the damn place. Point me where I can get me a nice ripe one who's yearning for a real man's lovin', a little honest belly-bumpin'. Nothin' too fancy, understan', but nothin' real cheap. No, I'll go a decent price, I ain't scrimpin', it's my vacation. No two-bit whore for this ol' boy tonight!" he said triumphantly.

Lucy's eyes flew wide as all the color drained from Josh's face. A second later it seemed to have been carved from marble. She'd seen him in many moods, but she faltered at the sheer murder reflected in his glittering ice-colored eyes now. Her own shock was forgotten at the evidence of his. In a movement too quick for Lucy to have comprehended it, Josh's hand shot out and gripped Samuel by the shirtfront. Samuel Tee stopped chuckling. He no longer seemed amiable as he looked down at the fist clutching his shirt in a death grip and then looked up to meet Josh's furious gaze. But he didn't move so much as an eyelash.

"I'm not wearing no gun tonight, Josh," he said slowly, too slowly for Lucy's comfort, "but I'll get one if'n you want. What's eatin' you?"

"Apologize to the lady," Josh said through clenched teeth.

"What lady?" Samuel asked, bewildered. "I don't see none. You tol' me she was an actress."

Lucy felt her heart skip, just one tiny spasm that told her she was still alive, as Josh said in low, insistent tones, "Damn you, Samuel, she *is* a lady. She just sings on the stage, like . . . like opera," he said desperately, not having the right words, for there were none to explain why Lucy wasn't just an actress, "but she's a real lady, hear?"

The transformation of Samuel Tee was so immediate and so drastic that Lucy blinked, unable to believe what she saw. One moment he'd been dangerous and arrogant; the next, that hairy face had crumpled, and his voice came agonized and low.

"Omygod. S'cuse me, ma'am. I didn't know. I thought you was an *actress*. Oh, par'n me, ma'am, I am so surely sorry. I'd crawl a mile on my belly like the snake I am to make up for it. Please say you forgive this ol' fool, Miss Rose, please do."

Real tears seemed about to spill from those anguished eyes, so Lucy mumbled something about it being quite all right as he went on begging for forgiveness. He ignored Josh, even though Josh's hand slowly relaxed and let his shirt go as he pleaded with Lucy for her understanding. It seemed, she thought, that insulting a lady was a step beneath horse-stealing and worse than cursing God in Samuel's humbly voiced opinion.

"It's quite all right," she repeated, though it wasn't.

After threatening to bow and scrape at her feet for another eternity, Samuel arose, made his good-byes, and Josh walked him to the restaurant door.

"I'll collect up all m'things 'n go," Samuel assured

him. "Won't be a trace of me in yor hotel when you get back, don't you worry, boy."

"Don't be a worse fool," Josh said bracingly. "It was an honest mistake. Listen, if you're gone when I get back, I'll hunt you down and call you out for the draw. Then there'll be two good men gone. Don't want that, do we? Now. You go out and grab a hackney cab and tell him to take you to Dave Allen's Dance House in the Bowery. They've got good liquor and bad women. Just keep your hand on your bankroll even when you're in bed. Have fun. See you later."

He clapped Samuel on the shoulder and then waited until Samuel offered his hand. After they'd shaken hands, Josh sighed as he watched Samuel go. He wondered what he could retrieve from the evening.

Gray and Ada's arrival should have helped, if anything could. Gray was young enough to be transparently happy and extremely vocal about all his joy because of his college's triumph of the day, his weekend in New York, his reunion with his brother, his pleasure at meeting Lucy, and his unbridled enthusiasm for Ada. Ada was glowing, and Josh was at his most charming, which was a considerable thing to see, Lucy thought, when she saw it. Because she couldn't leave off looking into herself any more than she could forget what Samuel had said. His casual vulgarity had changed him from a safe and gentle man to a leering, threatening one. Because it had been in her presence. And all because he'd thought her just like the woman he was thinking of buying.

But, Lucy wondered as she moved her food around her plate, where *was* the difference, except for the fact that she wasn't all he thought . . . yet? She was living alone, performing on the stage, out for the night with a man who desired her body, in the company of another actress who gave her favors as freely as her laughter. The only difference was that she'd not yet experienced that one act Samuel had mentioned. But she'd begun to think of it, and the more she had, the less impossible it seemed.

Lucy gazed at the slice of pheasant on her plate. It seemed she couldn't swallow another bite. Josh noticed that, as he'd noticed everything she'd done tonight.

"I do believe our songbird's caught a chill," he announced. "Lucy, I think I'd better take you home. Mr. Harper will have my heart if his Josephine turns into a frog by tomorrow night. Do you mind our leaving you alone with this galoot, Ada? We'd planned to be chaperons," he added, although he planned just the opposite, which was why he'd hired a closed coach, but remembered what he'd told Lucy.

Ada was too busy giggling at that bit of nonsense to try to answer, as Josh went on, "Mind your manners, then, Gray. Are you ready, Lucy?" he asked, concern in his softened gaze.

She looked up at him with gratitude. There was something the matter with her throat, but she didn't know if it was a cold coming on or simply new knowledge of herself that caused the blockage there.

"Tea with three lemons and three jiggers of what every landlady has in the cupboard, before bed," Ada advised as Lucy rose to leave.

"Add a dollop of black rum and some butter, and then get a heap of blankets over you, with a warming pan under your feet," Gray added before he bade her good night.

"And three stout men to get you on those warm feet in the morning if you take their advice," Josh said when he'd got her tucked into the coach and they were on their way home.

She didn't laugh, as he'd hoped. But then, he sighed, he'd hoped for a lot of things tonight before Samuel had opened his big mouth. This had been the night he was going to try for something very different from consoling a heartsick girl. Because whatever else she was, or would be, he'd no doubt she was sick to the heart. He could no more take advantage of her in her sorrow, taking her in his arms as he longed to do, than he could ignore her pain. And so he was astonished when he found her in his arms. And never thought to question who'd made the first move to put her there once he'd put his lips on hers.

But it was nothing like any kiss they'd had before. There was as much solace in it as there was passion. When the coach stopped in front of her boardinghouse, he laid his cheek on her curling, silken, scented hair, easily as shaken as she was.

He couldn't frame the entire question, because he wasn't sure of the answer he wanted anymore, not tonight.

"Do you want to go . . . ?" he asked, leaving it all up to her.

Although she didn't, because the only comfort she had was here in his clasp, she knew the paradox: there'd be less if she stayed. So she reluctantly drew away from him.

"I have to. Kyle wants a meeting with us tonight," she said, remembering the world again, "and," she added, because what Kyle wanted seemed unimportant now, "I do feel . . . strange. Maybe I did catch a chill."

In more than your heart? he wondered silently as he took her to the door.

He gave her a brief regretful, light kiss, and then saw her in, and then was gone.

"My dear child! You look so pale," Mrs. Fergus cried as she took Lucy's cape. "Are you feeling all right?"

No, not in body or spirit, Lucy thought, shaking her head and smiling weakly as she went into the parlor to see Kyle.

But she might have felt a bit better if she'd known how soon she'd feel worse.

13

KYLE HARPER had once been an actor—that was how he had learned to pitch his voice and wait for the dramatically right moments to raise and lower it. If he'd been able to hold his audience then as he held them now, he'd never have had to leave acting for directing others. But then, he reminded himself with the sort of realistic thinking that had been his ruination as an actor, his audience's future had never depended on what he was saying before. It was worse than reading them bad reviews. He was, he realized, pronouncing their death notices.

". . . and so," he said into the stillness in Mrs. Fergus' parlor, where the principals of his *Pinafore*—Ned, Lester, Bayard, Darren, Fanny, Jewel, and Lucy—listened so quietly he fancied he could hear their hearts racing, "it seems clear enough now that the rumors have substance. Messrs. Gilbert and Sullivan *are* coming to New York. In a matter of weeks. And yes, they are to present their own *Pinafore*, in November, with their own English cast. Most likely at the Fifth Avenue Theater. And yes again, they'll premiere an entirely new work for the new year."

The silence was absolute.

Then Ned spoke, and his voice was suddenly that of a man his age.

"How long will we keep our *Pinafore* going, then?"

The silence, Lucy noted nervously, was so complete now that she could hear her own blood rushing through her veins, and it was a thunderous sound.

"We'll keep going for so long as we have an audience coming," Kyle said on a shrug. "When it falls off, we shall fold our tents and steal quietly into the night. I hope you all will stay on until that unhappy hour," he added.

"Speaking of stealing . . . As to this new work . . . ?" Lester asked.

"That's why they're coming here," Kyle answered at once. "I'm given to understand they aim to make the copyright clear this time."

Lucy frowned in incomprehension. It had been a nightmarish night so far, full of alarms and diversions. She'd been shivering since she'd left Josh, and now she'd come home to this. Her face was eloquent. Lester explained it to her as everyone else mulled over Kyle's words.

"Your countrymen can't earn a cent from our production of their opera, or from any of the others in New York, or anywhere else in the world, for that matter, unless they take steps to secure their copyright. In New York they can't claim a penny unless the work's premiered here—that's the law. But if they open here, the rights are exclusively theirs."

"Indeed," Kyle agreed, "that's why they also say security will be maximum as they rehearse their new production. It certainly has been so far. All anyone's been able to discover, for love or money, is that it's probably going to be called *The Robbers*—perhaps," he said wryly, "in our honor. . . . So we wouldn't possibly be able to do it for at least a month," he added.

"Yes, I know I just said we're not supposed to be able to do it at all," Lester told Lucy, "but our English cousins haven't yet discovered how interesting the law is here. It might be an 'ass' in England, as your Mr. Dickens called it, but here, Lucy, it's a blooming patriotic idiot. We can't do Gilbert and Sullivan's *The Robbers*, true. But we'd probably be able to get away with Kyle Harper's version of *The Robbers*, or 'Kyle Harper's *The Robbers* Recalled,' or some such, if it's billed creatively enough."

"Exactly," Kyle said, "so I'll have Dr. Max and Mr. MacGruder on it immediately. Dr. Max can pluck a score out of the air and have it down note for note by the second encore. And Howard MacGruder can have the words done, line by line, by morning—if someone else doesn't get to him first: there are some very underhanded people in this business," he complained, to get them to laugh.

But then he grew sober again. "Still, it will take time to get it together," he said, "and I haven't the money to pay for your valuable time, my friends, nor can I ask you all to wait upon that happy day. So I will understand if you seek employment elsewhere."

There was no more laughter.

"Ah, well," Lester said, rising and stretching and looking longingly at the cut-glass decanter that Ned was unstoppering with shaking hands. "Nicely worded, Kyle. Don't know if I've ever heard a better farewell to the troops. But I've heard it often enough. It was a nice ride while it lasted, but every gravy train eventually comes into the station, eh?"

It was as if he'd freed them all from the spell Kyle had cast over them. Soon they were all up and chatting, comparing notes as to what new productions they'd heard were coming in with the new year, mentioning every new role and company that might need performers—every one, that was, except for the ones they intended to try out for themselves. Or so Fanny confided to Lucy as she took a glass of sherry and then a seat next to her.

"But you shouldn't have any trouble," she added when she saw Lucy's sorrowing face. " 'The English Rose' has made quite a name for herself. But, dear," she said, patting Lucy's hand, "let me give you a little advice. You're so very young, and you don't know our ways here in America."

She leaned closer so she could lower her voice even as Lucy lowered her lashes over the regret in her eyes. Fanny Gill was so kind, Lucy thought in embarrassment, she wished she could be as truthful as Fanny was with her.

"Kyle's a coming young man," Fanny said softly, "but if I were you—were I young and beautiful, with my career before me—I'd try to get into a company. That's the best thing for a young woman," she said urgently. "A company director will look after you, because he's thinking beyond this season's productions. He'll groom you and train you and advise you so that you can build a career. If Kyle forms a company, fine. If not . . . Oh, my dear, try . . . try for Lester Wallack's, or Augustin Daly's, or Mr. Palmer's theatrical troupe. They'll bring you along and keep you for the long run. *If*," she said with stress, "if you're wise enough to listen to their good counsel, you'll go far and they'll protect you. That's most important for a beautiful young woman. Beauty and youth don't last. But danger does. It's a difficult business, this life, a constant struggle, for all the joy of it. Think it over," she whispered as Kyle approached them, before she looked up and smiled as unconcernedly as if she'd been discussing the changeable October weather, the sudden chill in the air that had set Lucy shuddering.

"Come," Kyle said, "I only predicted the future. I don't really believe in fortune-tellers. If they were always right, they'd all be too rich to want to read our tea leaves, wouldn't they? At any rate, the future hasn't come yet, has it? We'll have weeks more together, maybe months."

The others quieted to listen; actors, he knew, lived on hope as much as praise. He raised his voice. "Why hold a wake before the corpse cools? Speaking of which," he said, taking out his watch, "it's a lively enough cadaver now. We've a performance tomorrow, people, and the clock's hands kissed each other good night two hours past."

He clapped his own hands together. "To bed, children," he commanded, "to bed, to rest, perchance to dream of continued triumph. We've beaten all the odds so far. Come. Go to bed so that we can keep our invalid ship sailing smartly across the stage tomorrow night."

Fanny took Lucy's two hands in hers and gave her a good-night kiss on the forehead before she left for her own room. Her murmur of surprise about the warmth of that forehead and the chill she'd felt in those icy fingers made Mrs. Fergus insist on sending Lucy to bed with a warming pan. That was after Kyle concocted some overly sweet and extremely alcoholic thing for her to pretend to drink before bed, and after she'd gotten complicated and differing advice from every performer in the room on how to forestall a cold's coming on. The best help, Lucy discovered, came from the most seasoned performer there. Because when he climbed into her bed in the middle of the night, she found his shaggy body the perfect thing to keep her toes from freezing.

So it was, then, that after taking all the advice and comfort she could from her fellow performers, Lucy found herself waking in the morning curled up tightly to Duncan, with fur on her nightgown, what seemed to be a ten-pound weight on her aching head, and the worst cough she'd ever heard issuing from her own sore throat.

In all the weeks that Lucy had passed at Mrs. Fergus', she'd never had any time alone. Even when she'd been in her room, she could hear the movements of the other lodgers. But tonight she was as good as abandoned, as though her fellow roomers had decided exile was the best cure for a cold. Mrs. Fergus was out to a card game with her cronies Mrs. Fairfax and Miss Hampton. The others were at the theater. As she should have been, Lucy thought with a wretched sniff. She was alone except for Duncan, at her feet, and Mr. Fergus, down somewhere in the basement, doing whatever it was he did there every night. And Mamie, the maid of all work, of course. All of which was much the same as a house deserted.

Lucy glanced at the clock on the mantelpiece as she huddled on a couch close to the fire in the sitting room, pressing a handkerchief to her swollen nose, and even she couldn't tell if she did so because of sniffles caused by her cold or by her self-pity. About now, she realized, Ada would be singing Josephine's first duet with Bayard. Ada and Bayard were as thrilled about it as Kyle wasn't. They couldn't disguise their elation, although for friendship's sake Ada had tried. But Lucy had read it clear in their faces when Kyle had made them rehearse at the house that afternoon so his star could give her friend pointers on how to fill in for her successfully. Ada was excited because it might mean a step up in her career; it wouldn't be the first time a replacement had become a star. Bayard was delighted because after he'd taken a look at Ada in her costume, and especially after he'd heard her sing her first line, he'd known the audience had no choice but to focus their attention on him.

Ada was charming, Lucy thought, and pert. But she'd no presence, and only a passable voice. And no English accent—as Kyle made sure to point out accusingly before he'd left for the theater, as though Lucy were staying home to entertain a lover, instead of a fever, tonight.

The only good thing, Lucy decided on a long sigh that turned into a painful cough, was that no one could see her now. Her face was dead white except for a rabbit-red nose, she thought, taking some small perverse pleasure from noting how low she looked and felt, and her swollen eyes were awash with tears. She'd wrapped herself in a long, old houserobe, belted in the middle like the sack of flour she thought she resembled without her figure-enhancing undergarments. Even her hair had lost its spirit, and so she'd dragged it back and fastened it up so that the ends of it wouldn't get trapped in any of the innumerable handkerchiefs she was using up, or trail in the basin of hot water on the stove that she had to trudge into the kitchen to inhale from every so often to clear her head.

And so she wondered if she could get up the stairs before she was seen, or if she'd have to hide, like an ostrich, with her head in the pillows of the couch, when she heard someone at the door. She wondered if she had time to slink under the couch, as Duncan did in a thunderstorm, when she saw that furry fellow rapturously greeting the caller the maid admitted to the sitting room without asking her.

She did the next best thing. She tried to cover her entire face with a handkerchief, talking through it as though it were a screen.

"I'mb bery infectious," she said immediately. "Go away."

"Only," Josh Dylan said as he laid his hat down on a chair and removed his long silk scarf from around his neck, "if you tell me who you are, sir."

"Oh," Lucy wailed, peering over the top of her handkerchief to see him looking as out-of-place as he was elegantly handsome in his evening clothes. "Josh, what are you doing here?"

"I thought we had a dinner engagement," he said gently, coming to sit beside her.

She held up one hand to ward him off.

"I'mb sick," she said.

"Thought you caught a chill at that blasted game," he

muttered, taking that hand and frowning at how icy it was.

"Go away," she said weakly. "No need for you to get sick too."

"You think I should go back and listen to Ada mangling your music again? That's even more dangerous. They're leaving the theater in such droves, I could be trampled. What are you taking for it?" he asked abruptly, looking at the bottles of the several remedies the people in the boardinghouse had left for her.

"Whatever you're offering," she giggled, delighted he'd fallen into one of Lester's favorite jokes.

He grinned at her. She looked terrible. But in a strange fashion he found himself pleased to see that even at her worst she looked better than most girls at their best. She'd pulled back that cascade of amber hair he loved, but it only emphasized the delicacy of her face and well-shaped head.

"Not dead yet, eh? But you will be if you take any of this stuff." He rose and went to the sideboard, took up a few bottles, and then strode to the kitchen.

"Hang on," he called as he went. "I'll mix up something special."

"I think you should go away," she muttered when he came back with a steaming cup in his hand. "I'm catching."

"Good, 'cause I'm pitching," he said, holding the cup out to her as he sat at her side again. "This here elixir is better'n snake oil, just like m' brother claimed," he said in lively country accents. "It fixes up sick steers, horses, hogs, and cowboys. They say it can make a dead man walk and move a mountain to tears. The Indians invented it, the white man stole it, and we all drink it, man and beast, when we want to chase the miseries away. It opened the West, so it ought to do miracles for one small girl's nose. Close your eyes and drink 'er down, Ma'am. . . . Trust me," he said more gently, as he offered it to her.

She hesitated after the first sip bit her tongue. It tasted, she thought, when she obediently handed back the empty cup, like fire in a spiceworks.

"Now, then," he said as he put his arm around her

and drew her head back to lie against his shoulder, "we'll just sit and chat, and when you sneeze or cough again, I'll fix you another."

"Dr. Dylan," she murmured. This would be wrong, of course, she thought as she relaxed and settled herself comfortably close to him, if she weren't so ill. But he'd have to be insane instead of just depraved to attempt anything with such a sick woman. She gave out a trembly sigh as she finally laid her heavy head upon his chest, discovering the unexpected joys of illness. She could sit close and try to fit closer, and feel as well as hear his voice vibrating in his chest, and yet never be in the least indiscreet. She hadn't felt so good in hours—no, days— and wondered how she could arrange to be sick forever as he began to tell her about what had happened when he'd got to the theater and found her off the program.

She chuckled at the way he described the audience leaving, even as she weakly put in a few "Oh, dears" where she thought they were needed. And she smiled to herself at more than his story as she felt his strong, steady heartbeat in counterpoint to the thrum of his low-pitched resonant tones. His hand was around her waist, and she could feel it even through the folds of her heavy flannel robe. But it was comforting, as was his warmth, and she hadn't felt so safe in years as they sat in front of the fire and spoke of drowsy, foolish things.

He noted her eyes closing against her will, and smiled. His remedy was famous for putting men to sleep faster than a mule's hind leg. He felt the tension ebb from her body, and the warm, sleepy scent of her rose up to meet him. It was just his luck, of course, he thought on a skewed smile, that he'd got her so close, discovered she'd finally left off that damned corset that it turned out she didn't need—just as he'd thought—and yet she was too sick to do more than take comfort from him. But he was pleased to give that. Because she needed him. And so for all that he couldn't take more from her than he could give her tonight, that pleased him too.

It was a weird way to spend an evening with a beautiful actress, he thought as he hugged her close and smiled down at her as she drowsed. Which was why it was stranger still when he heard voices at the front door and realized how many hours had passed, and that he'd have to leave her now, and yet didn't want to go—even though the slight but unmoving weight of her had put his arm to sleep long since.

The arriving actors paused in the doorway as he put his finger to his lips and nodded toward the sleeping woman. Then he put his arms beneath her and in one smooth movement lifted her against his chest and stood. She murmured something incoherent and he looked his question to them. Lester and the old man Ned understood at once and gestured to the stairs. Lester led the strange procession and opened the door to the first room on the right of the upstairs hall. After Josh had laid her down on her bed and drawn the covers up over her, he had a moment to look around the room.

It was neat and modest. The bureau held one framed photograph of a woman who must have been her grandmama; there were several magazines and a few books sharing the windowsill with a small potted fern. A few pots of creams and lotions, a hairbrush, and a subtle scent of flowers were the only other things he noticed that she'd lent to the rented room. For no reason he could fathom, the spareness shamed him—far more than the frown and glittering eyes Kyle fixed on him when he came down the stairs again.

He gazed back at the dark, slight young man. And so they stood looking each other in the eye, saying nothing, but understanding everything that went unsaid, until Kyle spoke.

"It was most kind of you to keep her company," he said, though no trace of any gratitude was in his face.

"Oh, well, now for once I can really say I sat up half the night with a sick friend," Josh answered lightly, though there was no humor in his cold gray eyes.

"I *am* charmed," Gray insisted in an undervoice, though the room was so crowded and the musicians played so loudly he could have shouted and wouldn't have been heard by anyone but his brother, and he only because they were standing face-to-face.

"I was charmed to meet Gloria," Gray went on in a goaded voice, "and charmed to meet her daddy and his friends and say howdy to the gaggle of young ladies you introduced me to. Charmed as all get-out, just like I said. So I will—get out, that is. Dammit, Josh, I'm *bored!*" he whispered fiercely. "And Ada's about done with work for the night, and I've only got this last night before I go back to school. Oh, come on," he said plaintively, before his eyes lit up and he said slyly, "Might as well let me go, 'cause I'm going to go anyway, and I don't think your fancy friends would care to see us wrestle, do you?"

Gray looked more than handsome and entirely adult in his close-fitting swallow-tailed evening jacket and dark formal trousers. Josh noticed most of the girls and many of the women covertly eyeing his brother. Most of them were worth noting too, if only for their names. Tonight the Van Horn ballroom was filled with guests from some of the finest, oldest families in New York; the men were captains of industry, the women, their wives and daughters. And Gray wanted to leave to sport with an actress.

Josh wanted him to see how childish it would be to leave now; how foolish to exchange limitless opportunity for instant gratification. But he knew it was important to keep light hands on the reins with both young horses and young men.

"All I'm saying is that some of these people could be important to you someday," he said reasonably.

"Well, I know that," Gray complained, "but I've met them, and it's not 'someday' for me yet. Damn, Josh, this is boring stuff. It's a fancy place, but so what? I've seen fancy before, and even if I hadn't, what's there to do with it after you see it? They got tons of food out, sure. But how much can I eat? They got music, but there's nobody I want to dance with. The girls are like the churchgoin' ones back home, plain as mud for all they're dressed to the teeth, and with about as much to say as a wood fence. I dance with them and they giggle. Or else they try to show me how much they know, which ain't much. God, Josh, they all remind me of Hank Jones's daughters, back home."

Josh smiled in spite of himself. Hank Jones ran a dry-goods store and made a bit of money from it. The Jones girls were richer than most in town. They put on so many airs, the joke was that they'd drown in a rainstorm, their noses were so high.

But these girls were debutantes, the pick of the season. And Gray, for all his youth, was already of a marriageable age. Josh stopped smiling. "You can always buy what Ada offers," he said bluntly.

"Oh, can I?" Gray asked belligerently. "Well, then you tell me, big brother, where can I buy laughter and a night of fun and then something even more fun, with someone who don't make me feel slimy or stupid for wanting it, eh?"

Josh paused, seeing trouble in his brother's blazing blue eyes. He silently cursed the boy's chivalry, curbed his tongue, and since he didn't want to say it badly, and there was no way to put it politely, tried to speak plainly,

"She's an actress, Gray, you can't take her anywhere but where you probably took her last night, and you can't bring a bed into a ballroom or any other decent place, however much 'fun' she is. She's just for fun, nothing else."

"Yeah. Like Lucy, right?" Gray said coldly, watching his brother's face as carefully as Josh had studied his.

What he saw spring up there at his words surprised him. But he didn't have time to put up his hands to defend himself from an attack that never came. Because Gloria had seen it too as she glided up to the two brothers and put her hand on Josh's arm.

"Heavens! Are you two all right?" she asked.

"Fine," Josh said, murder ebbing from his eyes as he turned to her and smiled and put his hand over hers. "But Gray was just saying good night. He's got another engagement tonight," he said quietly. "I hope you won't mind, Gloria, but he has only a few days here this time, and he's filled them solid."

"Oh, I don't," she said on a light laugh, "but I'm afraid my young lady guests will mind terribly. Next time, Gray, please do save some more time for us, will you?"

"Yes, ma'am," Gray said, looking down at her, his handsome face a study in polite gravity. Only Josh had seen one dark gold eyebrow lift at the casual mention of "next time."

"And next time," Gloria said, "you must come out to

our place on Long Island. That's where our best horses
are. Your brother loves my father's coach, as well as
riding along the seashore. But I hear that you are 'just
plumb crazy' about horses," she added coquettishly, to
Josh's surprise. It wasn't like her to abandon her cool,
reasonable air. She seemed to be going out of her way
to court Gray's good opinion, and Josh grinned down at
her for it.

"You can go play now, Gray," he said, though he still
looked at Gloria. "Just don't come home too late—
you've got a long ride tomorrow."

"Oh," Gray said softly, "but I won't. I know the difference between work and play, you see."

Josh looked at him sharply at that, and for the first
time saw something disquieting in his brother's eyes as
he gazed at him. But Gray bowed to Gloria before Josh
could call him on it, and was gone before it could be
seen again in his cold blue eyes. Then there was no time
to reflect on it, because Gloria was introducing him to a
man who wanted to know about Wyoming, and he had
a friend he called over who had interests in a copper
mine Josh was considering. Gloria drifted away then,
with a small smile on her lips, and Josh nodded as he
returned one to her. She was, he decided with admiration
coloring his amusement, before he began answering some
questions, a rare creature—a woman who understood
what a man wanted at a fancy-dress ball.

She danced well too, he discovered again as he led her
through a waltz. And fitted into his arms as lightly as
though they'd been dancing together for years.

"Josh," she asked as they danced, and she found herself studying his face for more than polite reasons, surprised at having to remind herself yet again that a lady
didn't step closer to her partner, "Father just realized he
has an appointment down in his book for tomorrow night
that he'd forgotten. If Gray's going to be gone, would
you like to come with me to a concert? I know," she
said quickly, "that it's a Sunday, and there's little likeli-
hood at this late date—but I thought I'd ask."

Gray would be gone, Lucy was probably going to be
in no condition to go out, or stay in, as he'd have preferred, with him. He looked into Gloria's eyes, never

noting their color or shape, only pleased, after Gray's anger, to see the hope springing up there.

"Ma'am," he said in a low drawl, borrowing his brother's phrase and setting it right, "I'd be charmed."

"Oh, good," she said, determining to get to her father immediately after the dance to tell him he had to find something else to do tomorrow night. He would be, she thought as she gazed up at the man who held her, just as pleased as she was—if that were at all possible.

It was late, but he hadn't been able to get to sleep. So he'd gotten up from bed and walked to the window to look down at the nighttime streets.

It was warm in the room, so he'd gone to bed wearing nothing, and now he stood at the window and noticed his nakedness and smiled as he thought of what Gloria's friends would make of that. The ones he'd met tonight at the Academy of Music looked like they slept in nightcaps and long gowns—and that was only the men, he thought, chuckling. Lord, they'd been a boring crew, with their chatter about the musicians and all the better concerts they'd heard, and when, and where. But Gloria had known it and apologized for it, which had amazed him.

He'd always been a perceptive man. But he knew himself far less well than he knew the world around him, because he thought of himself less often. As he stood and absently ran a hand across his wide chest, and the moon gave him the shadow of an inverted pyramid on the wall behind him, he never realized the enormous effect the long, trim, and hard length of him had on Gloria. Most women took to him, she seemed to be no exception, but he'd never traveled at such high altitudes before and was careful not to judge what he didn't know. She seemed content to wait for intimacies; he reasoned it was the correct thing in her circle, which suited him. He liked her well enough in turn, and was willing to let knowledge of her sensuality come in its own time—if it was to come at all. He guessed it was the novelty of him that attracted her. That and the fact that her father liked him so well.

Whatever the reason for her loyalty to him, he'd been

grateful for it tonight. Because he doubted he'd have been able to stay on at the concert after meeting those prattling friends of hers at the intermission if it hadn't been for her. He'd liked the music until then. They hadn't. They loudly had not, and seemed annoyed because he had. But he'd heard the education behind their opinions, and they let everyone know their opinions were based on traveling they'd done and the schools they'd gone to, until he wasn't sure it was anything but spite and jealousy that made him dislike them so much. But when Gloria took him aside and laughed into his ear, whispering she was sorry for inflicting such bores on him, it had eased his mind considerably. Enough so that when the thin fellow with the bored eyes asked what school he'd gone to after he'd been disagreed with, he'd been able to drawl, "Mrs. McKinney's eighth grade, and a damn fine teacher she was, too."

That had bought a moment's silence. They'd backed off, not knowing if he, or they, were being played for a fool. But knowing what they'd have done in his place, they were soon convinced they were being mocked. After that, they'd been more than civil, deferring to his opinion, almost begging for his approval. He liked them even less then.

But Gloria wasn't his enemy or a fool. And some things had to be made clear.

"It's true," he'd said when intermission was over and he sat next to her again. "I've no more schooling than that."

"I knew," she said. Only that. But then she put her gloved hand on his for a moment.

He stole a glance at her during the concert. She wasn't beautiful; she didn't pretend or need to be. Her face reflected her spirit; she was a strong woman. He admired that. He was comfortable with her. She'd turned to gaze at him in that moment, and he'd seen a thin smile on her lips. He'd chuckled. It seemed, amazingly enough, she was considering him just as he was evaluating her. They'd laughed together, and then turned their attention to the music. He'd wait. A man had to look until he was sure.

Josh went to his bed and lay down again, and thought

he'd surely get to sleep if that little song would only stop running through his head. It wasn't anything he'd heard at the concert tonight. No, he sighed, great music, like great thoughts, seldom haunted a man the way the trivial did.

It was a little tune he'd heard in the street while waiting after the concert for the line of hackneys and private carriages to pull up and take on their passengers. An organ grinder was clanking out the song that had then lodged in his ears for the rest of the night.

It was that tune he heard as he'd placed his lips lightly over Gloria's cool ones at her door. It was that melody that still danced in his head as he lay back on his pillow, and that same song that threatened to circle around in his weary head for the rest of the night.

"Poor Little Buttercup," he sighed at last, remembering it, accepting it, embracing it, because he knew he was unable to forget it. And only then did it sing him down to sleep in what was left of the night.

14

HERE SHE WAS, a young woman with twenty-one years
to her credit, pleading and whining like a child who
wanted a peppermint stick before dinner. No wonder he
was smirking, not even listening to her. Lucy straightened her shoulders and her resolve, cleared her voice,
and spoke up boldly.

"I'll be home by nightfall, time to get adequate rest,
and be in fine condition to sing tomorrow night, I assure
you. I've been locked up in this house for days. I feel
too stale to perform well. And . . . and Josh is only taking
me for a bracing carriage ride into the country, and . . ."

" 'And . . . and'?" Kyle mocked. "And what if you
catch another chill?" he asked dulcetly. "A cold at this
time of the year could lead to pneumonia. Ada's voice
doesn't carry to the tenth row, and the house is half-
empty. It isn't enough that the original *Pinafore* may
soon be bankrupting me. Are you contemplating suicide
to finish me off entirely?"

She glowered at Kyle. "No, but I'm going," she said
truculently, raising her chin.

She looked entirely recovered, Kyle thought. Her eyes
sparkled and her hair had regained its luster. She wore
a warm woolen dress of a deep rose hue, and a dashing
felt hat to match, tied beneath her chin with a contrasting
blue scarf. She had a warm cloak over her arm and a
determined look on her face. It was a mild day for the
season, and she was well-dressed, but then, it wasn't her
body, but her heart he feared for today.

Josh Dylan had sent her flowers for each day she'd
been ill, until Kyle had to compare the sitting room to a
wake-room to get her to stop sighing over them. But the
tall Westerner hadn't come back to see her, and that had

given Kyle as much hope as it had given Lucy anxiety. Now she was to go driving out with him, and there was, Kyle admitted to himself, nothing he could do but make her feel guilty and ensure her coming back before night. He frowned. Seduction itself usually took place at night. But for a girl like Lucy, the groundwork for it was best paved in the day. If he himself knew that, doubtless Josh Dylan did too.

"Where are you going, exactly?" he asked. It was none of his business, but she was too upset to remember that.

"He said the Village of Science at Menlo Park. His note said he'd made some investments with Mr. Edison and so we'd get a personal tour. There's a way to record a person's voice on a wax roll, haven't you read about it? He says"—she took out the note she'd read and reread to read aloud to him—" '. . . and maybe he'll let you sing "Buttercup" so we can have it down for eternity.' Wouldn't that be something?" she asked delightedly.

"Eternity, or until someone drops it," Kyle said sourly, thinking quickly. If she began to sing for others, even if that voice were only to be heard on one of those absurd cylinders, she might be lured away from him in more than body. His *Pinafore* might end soon, but he had other plans for other productions, and she figured largely in all of them. She figured *only*, in fact. Because she was the only thing that kept his *Pinafore* onstage, and everyone knew it but her. That was why he so seldom praised her. That was why, he kept telling himself as he gazed at her hungrily, he had to keep her heart-free, bodily near, and conscience-bound to him.

He'd have to be vigilant. He was a persuasive man, but so was Josh Dylan. He'd have to keep careful watch. This was a critical time for both men who wanted this entrancing, naive girl, for whatever purposes. And both of them, he thought as he saw her eyes light at the sound of someone at the door, knew it.

She glowed even more brightly when her caller was admitted. Seeing Josh, his face lightly bronzed, his dark gold hair shining in the early-morning light, his tall frame clad in close-fitting fawn-colored trousers and a brown jacket, reminded Lucy of everything she'd longed for these last days. His clothes, air of freedom, vitality—all of it was symbolic of all the wide autumn outdoors she'd missed as much as she'd yearned for him.

He nodded to Kyle absently, his eyes only on Lucy.

"You look wonderful. I've got a picnic basket," he said immediately, "and a team of fresh horses. Are you ready, Miss Lucy?"

"Oh, she is, but so, no doubt, is pleurisy, pneumonia and bronchial catarrh. She's only just out of a sick-bed . . . But pay no heed, pay no heed." Kyle sighed. "Pleasure must have its hour, even if it is only to be a fleeting one."

"I've also got lap rugs and blankets. It's warm as May outside, but I'm ready for anything," Josh said after a pause, looking at Lucy.

"I am too," she said determinedly as she stepped toward Josh to take his arm.

"And of course, since it is already ten o'clock, I've no doubt that a trip to another state is extremely advisable, if you want to bring a recently sick young woman home by evening—of course it is, of course it is," Kyle said, so much in his part, so completely the concerned parent, that even Josh had difficulty remembering the dark young man was probably younger than himself.

"It's only thirty-five miles—" Josh said, and Kyle immediately burst in with an astonished, "Only!"

Josh sighed. "We don't have to go to New Jersey," he said softly to Lucy, because all her indecision was clear on her face. "Mr. Edison didn't exactly save us the day, he's always there, and we're always welcome. We could take our picnic to Long Island, there's seashore there, *and*," he added as Kyle opened his mouth, "everyone knows how therapeutic sea air is for invalids."

"It looks to rain," Kyle said, drawing back the curtain and peering out.

"I've got umbrellas and a leather curtain to bring down if it does. I've got shovels if it snows," Josh said with steel in his voice, "and oars if it floods. Everything but wings, and I've ordered them for next time. Are you ready, Lucy?"

"Yes," she said simply, taking his arm and looking up at him, mirth and joy and something else in her shining eyes. Something that made Josh pause for a moment before he led her to the door. Something that made Kyle stand by the window watching after them long after they'd gone.

She was so silent when they started out and Josh picked up the reins and headed his team east to the river and the ferry slip there, that he tried to reassure her immediately.

"Harper's not altogether wrong. It wouldn't be the trip, it would be the destination that might've delayed us. Edison's got a whole lot of things to see and listen to at his barn. Well, it looks like one," he said, laughing at the look in her eyes, "and then too, I don't know if I'd want you to meet him just yet. He's a good-looking fellow, just about my age. And a genius. He's married, of course, but that doesn't stop ladies from swooning. What was it I heard?" He remembered what one of Gloria's foolish friends had said. "Oh, yes. They say he's got 'soulful eyes, and a poet's brow, and sensuous lips and masses of hair,' " he said, perfectly mimicking the throaty, exaggerated tones he'd heard. "I wouldn't go that far, but he is sightly. And if you sang for him . . . well," he said, as pleased by the smile he'd won as the way the sunlight spun gold from her amber hair, "well, now that I think on it, I'm purely glad we're just going to the seashore, because I can compete with a gull, but not a young and handsome genius."

She looked up at him and wanted to say that he could compete with anyone on earth or beyond, and so ducked her head and looked down at her gloves and said nothing.

"Still, he is hard of hearing, and so absentminded they say he forgot he'd got married on his wedding night and just worked in his laboratory till dawn. Now, that's a tragedy—absentminded, with a shy wife, to boot. I bought into a consortium that's subsidizing him, which is a fancy word meaning 'we'll put up the money, you supply the work and brilliance,' along with Mr. Morgan and some others, which is how I came to meet him. And I can go on talking about all my business deals, if you want," he said in the same light tone of voice, "but it'd be nice if you'd say something, you know."

She looked up guiltily, and, startled, spoke just what she was thinking.

"I'm so happy to be here. I've been so lonely. This is wonderful. Thank you."

His face grew still at her words and he looked at her without expression.

"Don't thank me yet," he said, and she wondered if that was a threat or a promise as he threaded his team on their way across town.

He knew the way from all the times he'd come to visit with the Van Horns this autumn. He'd found the grassy field that sloped down to the water's edge one day when he'd been out riding early. It was an hour away from their estate, far from any other homes. He'd seen it from a rise that overlooked the snaking shoreline he'd been following, and had stopped there for a long while, enchanted by it. He'd covered a lot of ground that morning, because he'd been alone. Except for his thoughts, and they'd all been of the woman who sat beside him now. Then he'd been amused to discover that his emotions toward her were equal parts lust, liking, and curiosity. He'd planned this day to assuage all three feelings. It was time.

"I'd forgotten it was autumn!" she exclaimed after they'd left the ferry and were riding further out into the long island that lay to the east of the city. "I mean, I knew the date, and saw the tree in front of the house turning, but nothing like this."

The roadside was ablaze with color, the forests beyond the road they traveled in full autumn foliage. When she realized that since Josh was from the West, he didn't know half the names of the trees they passed, she passed the time pointing out the most vivid ones, identifying them, chanting, "Oak and sumac and maple and . . . ah . . . well, anyway, very pretty, and maple and . . . another . . . anyway, very pretty, and oak . . ." as he laughed and turned the horses toward the smell of the sea.

"This," she said when the sun was past its zenith and he'd finally stopped, tethered the team, and was swinging her down from her high seat, "is grand. Just grand."

But she forgot whatever else she was going to say when

he didn't release her waist after he'd set her down. She only stared at him and looked away, and looked back up to him again.

"We'll spread a blanket here, do you think?" he asked when he finally released her abruptly, leaving her to stand, swaying, alone. "And now, because all this fresh air's made me hungry. Don't want Mr. Harper to accuse me of starving you too," he murmured as he went to the back of his curricle and brought out a straw hamper and a rolled-up blanket.

"Wine and cheese and meat and fowl and fruit and cake and bread and thou—now, that's my idea of a luncheon," he said as he shook out the blanket and took her hand so he could help her to sit down on it.

"Don't know how you managed that." He grinned as he saw her twist her body sinuously so that she could sit in her long tight skirt, coiled like a mermaid on a rock, without a glimpse of leg showing.

"May I take off my jacket, ma'am?" he asked politely as he stood before her. "It's warm, my shirt's clean, and there's nobody but us to see for miles around. It's up to you," he said, waiting for her answer.

She had the feeling he was asking for far more. Up to now, the day had been a delight to her. Now they sat on a grassy slope, before them a broad blue calm expanse of bay, around them nothing but low grass and shrub and wildflowers, beyond and past that, the trees all in gold and russet, with the sun shining down on it all. But at his words it seemed the setting shrank to the size of the blanket. He waited.

"Yes," she said breathlessly, feeling as foolish as frightened by her thoughts, while the sun shone down innocently all around them.

They ate in silence. It had been a week in which she'd thought of little else but him, and yet now that he was here, she hardly knew what to say to him. Because in her thoughts she'd said far more than she could in reality. And in that week he'd thought of her often, and the things they'd done in his thoughts were things he remembered vividly, looking at her now. He wanted her more than he could ever remember wanting any woman.

"I think we should leave the dessert until we've walked

off some of the rest. Come on," he said, rising and holding out his hand to her. "The way you have to sit in that dress, if you don't walk now, you might lose the use of those legs you've got curled up so tight under you."

He shouldn't have mentioned her legs, she thought with a touch of panic, but her breath was taken away with the thought when she stumbled into him on rising. But he only laughed, righted her, and led her down the slope to the rocky, pebbly shore.

"They say there's soft powdery sand and dunes and a roaring surf down on the southern shore, where the open ocean is," he said as he strolled with her. "Here it's like a bathtub, and the sand's all covered over with rocks . . . is that why you're limping? Lord, girl, how can you walk in those skinny, pointy, high-heeled things? I should have told you to bring walking shoes. Here," he said, holding out his arm. "Unbutton them and walk in your stocking feet. Good Lord," he said in exasperation as she hesitated, "no one will see except me, and I promise I won't leer at your toes," he added, to get her giggling, to get her to stop and hang on to his arm, undo the top buttons, and ease off her tight shoes.

He slipped them into his pocket, and they strolled on, he in his shirtsleeves, the sea wind tousling his gold hair, she in her rose dress, walking like an Oriental concubine as she held the hem of her dress and tried to negotiate the stony shore in her stocking feet and tight skirt.

"You know, I thought I'd never see anything as wide and free and yes—like we once talked about—lonely as the prairie," he said as they went on, "until I saw the sea. I keep coming back to it now. It suits me just as well, I think. Maybe better. This way, I'm halfway between where my daddy came from and where I was mostly raised. Maybe that's me, halfway between the two ways."

He stopped to gather up some stones, and flung them out at the sea as they walked.

"I lived near to the water . . . well, everyone in Brooklyn does, I suppose," she said thoughtfully, "but I never thought about it. I didn't see it very often. Grandmama dreaded the sun, her skin was so fair, you see. It's very beautiful. But so is the forest. I don't think I'm drawn to loneliness the way you seem to be."

"I'm not," he said, looking down at her. "I just know it best."

She bit her lip and looked out at the far horizon, where he said she could see Connecticut, and thought of something less intimate to say. It was astonishing how his presence and his words seemed to diminish all distances today.

"Halfway between England and the West, that's true," she said, and then blurted, "Were you very disappointed to find out I wasn't really English, then?"

"Then, yes," he said, stopping to look down at her. "Yes, I was. Not now. Then I was disappointed because I don't like to be lied to. Now I know why you thought you had to. So far as being English—I'm not English either. Once I was disappointed about that too," he said wonderingly, pausing before he shied another stone out to sea. "Can't remember why I felt that way either, now. Maybe halfway's a good place to be, after all." He smiled at her. "Anyway, even if I hadn't changed my mind, you can't become something by associating with it, can you? Or so you told me it was with you and acting, didn't you?"

"But I am an actress now," she said, and then wished she hadn't, as she realized what she'd said. And so she looked back to see how far they'd come and murmured, "I think we ought to be heading back now, don't you? I mean, my feet . . . my stockings . . ." She picked up one foot and looked down to see the hole the rocks had made in it, surprised to see that speaking with him had banished pain as well as distance, because there was blood on her sole and she hadn't known it until she saw it.

He muttered something and lifted her up in his arms immediately, doing it so easily she had no time to ward him off. He held her close, but not intimately, and then he made her laugh, so there was no reason to feel as nervous as she did.

"Now, that's good manners," he said as he strode back down the beach with her, "being willing to bleed to death so as not to interrupt a fellow. It's polite, but it's also amazingly dumb. If there were more girls like you," he added as she began giggling out of genuine amusement as well as uneasiness, "there'd be no more human race."

He was telling her to sit still while he got some water to wash off her foot, and she was arguing that all she needed was her handkerchief and her shoes, unwilling to even think of allowing him to hold her ankle and her foot, when they reached the blanket again and he deposited her on it. To do so, he had to go down on his knees so she wouldn't be jolted when he loosed her, and after he did, he stopped and stared at her. Then he brought one hand to her waist again, and the other to the back of her head, and he drew her near and kissed her. It seemed to be just what she'd wanted, because without knowing she wanted to, she brought her arms around him as he drew her down to the blanket with him.

There was something better and something worse about kissing him in the open beneath the sky rather than in the dim late hours of the night. Here she could open her eyes and see the look in his so clearly that she had to shut hers again. When she did, there was a lovely bright red pattern blazing on her closed eyelids that seemed to envelop her as completely as her feelings did. But when he took his mouth from hers and brought it to her neck, she could see only the gold of his hair, the side of his closed eyes, and his shoulder in his white shirt, and for all the pleasure at his lips, yet she felt alone again, alone and abandoned beneath the endless sky. So she closed her eyes to make her own blazing midnight again.

He felt so warm, so good and right, that she felt nothing wrong in anything they were doing, and the sun was shining so bright. That was why she still felt safe, believing there could be nothing wrong in allowing herself to respond to him for a few moments. She believed nothing could be done but simple affection here in the open, with both of them securely and respectably clad, and all in broad daylight. Everyone knew seduction was a secret act of the night. That must have been why, she was to think after—since she thought very little now— she let her feelings go as she never would in the dark, in the dangerous night.

He rejoiced at how she met him in his desires, and

found the little round buttons at the front of her gown simplicity to ease, each in order, from their several small slots. The skin at her shoulder and her breast was as pure white and fine-grained as night had hinted, even in the relentless sunlight they lay beneath. He didn't pause to savor the sight. He gave her no more time to think than he gave himself, because it was a time for feeling their way now. There was the scent of the sea and autumn and the earth all around them, and in the cool autumn sunlight the only real warmth in the world was each other. When he felt her tension growing, he'd only to kiss her lips again and murmur her name to get her to close her eyes and relax against him again.

She seemed as stunned by their pleasure as he was impelled by it. It seemed she now regretted the barrier of her undergarments as much as he did because she sighed in exasperation the same way he did when his hand found hard buckram and whalebone instead of soft flesh. But now he was wiser, and now she was compliant, and so now he found that the bow at the back of that corset could be loosed, and a strong hand slid under it to her skin beneath. And so he discovered that then each lace could be drawn, as slowly as her breaths beneath his searching lips, one by one from their proper place.

It was only when she lay in disorder, his hands and lips moving over the smooth skin of her body, the lacy cage of her long corset, though discarded, still around her, like the cast-off chrysalis of a newly emerged butterfly, that she finally understood where they'd got to. Because for all his delicacy and care, he had to leave her for a second then. He had to rock back on his heels to get the leverage to move what he'd removed from her aside so he could touch all of her; he had to move back to loose himself from his suddenly constricting clothes, so they could complete what they'd begun. This was too intensely pleasurable, too long desired, for him to finish completely clothed. Her pleasure was too important to him for him to try to grab his own quickly and furtively from her. But in that necessary second, when his lips left hers and his hands left her breasts, she opened her eyes to the sun, and the scene, and the truth, at last.

He knew it was over before he could bend back to her again.

Her eyes flew wide as she looked at him, and then down to herself. Then she sobbed, or cried out something, and shot upright, clutching whatever she could to her naked breast. She sat up in a welter of all the clothes he'd so patiently pried off her, and he could have laughed at the frustration of seeing all his slow work go for nothing, if the pain of his frustration hadn't been so great.

"I won't force you to anything," he breathed as he sat back on his heels and looked at her steadily, "but I surely would like to go on. And I think you would too."

"No," she said, shaking her head from side to side, her eyes very wide, "no, I would not."

"I don't like being lied to," he said on a sigh, "but it's worse when you lie to yourself. Think about it."

He bent to her and kissed her again, but after a scant second of surprise, she struggled away from him.

"That's enough!" she cried.

"No," he said, and for the first time with him, she felt real fear.

"No," he said again as he moved away from her, regarding her steadily with stone-gray eyes, "it isn't half enough, and you know it. But it'll have to be for now," he said as he rose to his feet. "I don't take without asking. I was brought up polite too. You can get dressed," he said as he walked away.

He stood looking out at the wide sea and fought with his desires, cooling them by thinking of the mass of contradictions that was Lucy Markham. She said she was one thing, acted as another, and convinced him of both. But then, she was an actress, after all. One thing she had said he would swear was true, however odd, whatever she'd doubtless soon become in her profession. It was damned strange for an actress to be an innocent, but he was fairly sure of that by now, if only because of the further contradiction of her eagerness in his embrace. Her pleasure had equaled his. There was no disguising that. And no experienced woman could have left off where she did, unless she'd a score to settle, unless she'd hated him, and he doubted that. Damn few experienced men would have left off there either, he thought with bittersweet amusement. He decided he deserved a medal, and then decided he wanted more than that. He wanted to know what she was as much as he wanted her, and that was a lot. For all that stopping their lovemaking had been difficult and unpleasant for him, it had been, even so, he realized, far better than continuing with any of the other actresses and whores he'd had.

He wasn't the sort of man to give up easily, and if she wasn't the kind of woman who did either, that would only make it better when she did. And she would. With all her protests and contradictions, her lips had told him that.

She scurried into her clothes as he stood with his back to her, looking down at the sea. She kept her eyes on his broad back all the while, because every look down to the discarded clothing she sat in struck her like a rebuke, and called out "Shame!" But she'd felt nothing but pleasure in his arms, and his touch had removed all her training as easily as his hands had stripped away the firm and false illusion of safety she'd worn. And her fear now was of herself.

The late afternoon was autumn-brief, and the sky was growing dimmer, darkened by clouds that might be bringing the threat of rain Kyle had invented this morning. But she still sat and struggled with her laces behind her back, because the meal she'd had and her panic made her clumsy. She was half-dressed and at her wits' end when he finally turned to face her again. Then he came back to the blanket and looked at her and grinned.

"Let me," he said, laughing, and kneeling behind her, he laced her up tightly, with all the passion he'd have shown to a saddle that needed cinching—as he told her as he did it.

That made her laugh too.

When she had everything on properly again, she helped him pack away the remnants of their picnic and they began moving down the long road back to the city. They'd done this all in silence.

Lucy stared at her lap. "I think," she finally said as they turned off the country lane that had taken them to the shore, "that it would be better if we didn't see each other again."

"No, you don't," he said.

"But I won't—" she began.

"Maybe I won't either. But you know we can't leave it at that," he answered calmly. "One way or the other, you know we have to see each other again. Aside from everything else, you like me," he said simply, "and I like you. We'd miss each other, and there's no sense in hurting if we don't have to. Now, if I didn't force the issue on a blanket, you know I won't in a curricle. It is getting colder. Now, come on, sit by me," he said, and wrapped his arm around her and pulled her close to his side.

When the sun began to set, he unfolded a lap rug and tucked it around her, and as her thoughts grew more tangled, she finally laid her head against his shoulder as he urged her to do. The bright day was ending, but the glow of sunset remained in the foliage around them. A late, brisk autumn breeze picked up; gusts of birds blew over the trees, as did the rattling, tumbling, falling leaves. Now and again eddies of wind-driven leaves raced out in single file across the road before them, beneath the horses' hooves. Dusk came as they drove on, and it grew darker still, but still their way was lit by the glow of the ragged yellow trees that stood on either side of the winding road like blowing candles.

They'd done too much to say more now, and they'd almost done more that they'd have had to talk about. But for now they rode silently, letting the evening fall over them with a curious sort of peace. She rested her head against him and wondered about too many things to speak of. He sighed.

"A man," he said softly, as if to himself, as he held her securely, "could get used to this sort of thing."

She looked up, even as her heart did.

"We don't have autumns like this back home," he said.

Everything looked better in the morning. She woke to a beautiful, innocent Sunday, and in its clean, clear light everything seemed blessedly simple.

It all came to Lucy as she washed and dressed, as though the solution were a thing she could slip on with her Sunday clothes. She never blamed him. She was an actress, she had gone willingly into his arms. If she were he, she thought as she raised a sudsy face from the wash-basin in sudden comprehension, she'd have tried to do the same to herself. She rinsed away the thought, sighing once again at the unfairness of how simple things like passion and release were for a man.

But he'd stopped when she had. He hadn't so much as argued about it, although his desire had been obviously, frighteningly clear. Which meant, she knew, that he cared for her. Which meant, as she'd believed when she'd gone into his arms in the first place, that she could trust him. She didn't know what he wanted from her aside from what she'd so vigorously defended yesterday; she'd never dare to think of marriage. That had been a dream reserved for the day she left the stage and took up a respectable life far from the fame of "The English Rose." But she'd met him now, and though she doubted any respectable man would want an actress as his bride, he knew she was respectable too now, and he was from the West, where they were less constricted by society's rules, and . . .

Anyway, she thought, brushing her hair and tying it up as she was doing with her hasty conclusions, in order to make it Sunday-morning-neat and proper again, she could trust him.

But since she obviously couldn't trust herself, why, then, she decided, as she prepared to go downstairs for breakfast, she'd just have to make sure she never put herself in a position where she could betray herself again. Just as the minister always said, she thought confidently, there were many things a person could do without putting herself in temptation's path. She'd just have to avoid being alone with him in the night, or the day, in a closed carriage, or his rooms, or her dressing room, or Mrs. Fergus' sitting room, or on a blanket beneath a clear blue sky . . .

She could do it, she thought angrily. Because she would see him again, she thought defiantly. And she marched down to breakfast with such a militant gleam in her eye that Kyle's spirits rose as he pulled out a chair for her at the table and asked how yesterday had been.

Something had happened; he knew that. She'd come

home late, he'd watched for her arrival from his window, and there hadn't been any lingering at the front door. Now she seemed angry, but at the mention of Dylan's name she flushed and dropped her gaze to her plate, smiling and flustered, the perfect picture of a girl in love. Kyle sighed and went back to his toast. Most of the other boarders were still abed, but Lucy had the habit of churchgoing, so he'd risen earlier than usual so that he could find out what was going on. Now he stared at his toast so as to avoid seeing Lucy's dreamy smile, and wished he'd stayed in bed.

She looked up in glad anticipation when there was the sound of someone at the door. No one ever called at this house so early on a Sunday, and though Josh had said he was busy, they'd both said a lot of things that had to be clarified today, she thought as she rose from her chair in eagerness. She sat right back down again when she saw who it was, pretending to be engrossed in her eggs.

"Good morning," Edgar Yates said. "No, no, don't bother, I've already eaten, I just came to see you, Kyle. How pleasant to find you another early riser, Miss Rose. If I could have but a brief word with you, Kyle?"

"I was just going," Lucy said primly as she rose again and sailed past him, on her way to get her cape and purse. Sunlight, she thought darkly as she did, was a great advantage in dealing with creatures of the night. Edgar Yates might look dashing in a world-weary way in the alley of the theater in the dark. But morning showed every evidence of that ill-spent life for what it was—dissipation—and highlighted every detail, showing on his face the nighttime soul he possessed. Which was why she was shocked when she came downstairs again and found both Kyle and Edgar Yates offering to accompany her to church.

"No, no, you're exactly right," Kyle chuckled at once, although she hadn't said a word, but only stopped and gaped at them, "I haven't undergone a conversion in the night. It's only that your church is on Fifth Avenue, isn't it? And Edgar and I are going that way. Shall we?" he asked gaily, offering her his arm.

She could scarcely say no, although his sudden elation confused her as much as Edgar Yates's barely restrained hilarity did. Their obvious pleasure warned her of something that had transpired in the blink of an eye, in the moment it had taken her to go upstairs for her hat.

They were promenading down the avenue with a springy step when Lucy began to realize there were many more people on the sidewalks than usual for this hour on this day. Edgar Yates noticed her reaction and grinned even more than he'd been doing.

"Ah, yes," he said loudly, "a perfect Sunday morning for a parade. Those chaps have all the luck. You're in for a treat, Miss Rose. I saw them as I was coming up to get Kyle here. The Four-in-Hand Club may be impressive, but all the swells yearn to drive with the Coaching Club on their Sunday outings. Look there, here they come."

They paused on the curb as the first of the coaches rolled by them, and Lucy had to admit it was a grand sight. It was pulled by two matched teams of cream-colored horses, their manes and tails plaited with gay ribbons, their heads held high, as were those of the beautifully dressed ladies and gentlemen who sat in the coach. A spanking black Victoria trundled by in its wake, festooned with ribbons, crowded with jolly young gentlemen in fine driving clothes. And then the growing crowd murmured their approval of a magnificent ark of a coach, all black and shining as the hides of the high-stepping horses who trotted it down the avenue.

"The high and the mighty, the top ten percent of the top ten thousand," Edgar said reverently as the long line of costly carriages rolled by them. "It's love of coaching and money that lures them here, but it's birth and breeding as well as money that get them here. Every blessed one of them could buy and sell us, Kyle," Edgar said, before he smiled at Lucy and added, "And that's all they think to do with us, too."

Lucy frowned at his comment; it spoiled the moment. Church had been forgotten, everything was forgotten as she stood on the sidewalk with all the other entranced New Yorkers, watching the parade of fine coaches and all their fine ladies and gentlemen.

She didn't have to feel Kyle's lean body tense at her side. Nor did she have to listen to Edgar when he spoke

again, and scarcely needed the tremulous excitement in
his voice to warn her of something pleasing to him—and
disastrous for her. But nothing could have warned her
against the sight that struck her to the heart. Because
just as the crowd gave a long low murmur of wonder, and
some impressionable souls forgot themselves so much as
to cheer—just as she was drawing in her breath at the
sight of the fine old English coach, all dark maroon and
black and yellow, with the frivolous legend "THE BRIGH-
TON THUNDER" picked out on it in gold, she raised her
eyes from its two matched teams to see what clever, elegant persons rode in it. And first among them, picked
out by the sun every bit as much as the trim of it, she
saw Josh Dylan driving it. He was done up as elegantly
as she'd ever seen him, in black clothes with a black high
hat on his glowing gold hair, with an equally elegant
young woman as close as his arm at his side.

"Ah, there's Peter Potter and his fiancée," Edgar
reported, moving close to her ear so she wouldn't miss
a word. "Quite the society wedding that will be. Hmm,
very sober he is too, not at all the gay blade he is when
he's disporting with you theatrical folk, is he? Oh, and
on my soul! Why, look who's driving! There's your friend
Mr. Dylan," Edgar cried in great mock surprise, "with
his lady, Miss Van Horn. She's from one of the oldest
families in New York. They say Jacob Van Horn's great-
grandfather lent Peter Minuit the money to buy the trinkets he offered the Indians. And charged twenty percent
interest on it—which he's still collecting. Clever lad, that
Dylan. Oh, here he comes," he cried joyously, "perhaps
he'll wave."

But Josh looked to his teams when he wasn't looking
to his lady, and the one time he looked aside, his gaze
swept over the crowd on the street and there was nothing
but tolerant amusement to be seen in his disinterested
gray eyes.

Or so, at least, Lucy thought, but then, her own eyes
were too blurred to see him all that well.

15

Lucy HAD NEVER known how good guilt could feel. But in comparison to the self-loathing, confusion, anger, and pain she'd been experiencing, being overcome with guilt was very like a vacation for her. It picked up her head and her spirits for the first time since the morning of the awful day she'd just lived through.

"Oh, dear," she said, her hand flying to her newly painted mouth. "Fanny's been sick? And you never told me? I must have given her my cold. She was so kind, visiting me so often, and I know she never misses a performance, and she's missed three since I've been out? Ah, she must feel awfully bad, I'll have to visit her tomorrow, first thing—because once you've had a cold, you can't catch it right back again," she said as Kyle was about to protest.

". . . and even if you could, I'd still go!" she muttered as she flounced past him to go to the wings to await her cue.

Kyle was more pleased than offended. At least she was speaking to him again. It was about time. She'd been silent and stricken since she'd seen her Western suitor with another woman in the parade of coaches. He could have killed Edgar for his prank, although at first he'd thought it a fine idea too.

With Fanny still out, Jewel would have to sing the part of Buttercup again tonight, and Ada would have to scurry into costume as Cousin Hebe. But at least Lucy was back as Josephine. She was furious with him, but her anger could only help her onstage, giving her eyes fire and her voice a ringing conviction.

Best of all, he wasn't the only one she was angry with. The stage-door porter told him that when she'd come to the theater tonight, she'd given orders that she was always to be unavailable to a Mr. Dylan in future. And she'd threatened that if anyone took a bribe from him to gain his admittance, she'd give that person a thing or two to remember for it that would prove more costly than the bribe. "And Miss Rose is always such a lady!" the porter had marveled.

Kyle paused, listening to Lucy's voice as it carried through the house as she sang her first solo. True, a love song oughtn't to be sung as if it were a call to battle, but at least the English Rose was back—in voice, and in person. And now she was dedicated solely to his own purposes again.

The only thing that ruined Kyle Harper's complete triumph, as well as Miss Lucy Rose's, was that Mr. Dylan never called that night so that he could be roundly rejected.

But for all her rage, bluster, and guilt, Lucy discovered that high emotions caused exhaustion of the soul, not the body or the mind. Because she didn't sleep very much that night. It was as well that Kyle was still sleeping when she rose early the next morning to pay a sick call on Fanny. She looked so pale, weary, and woebegone herself, he'd have been sure she'd had a relapse.

Lucy walked to the greengrocer's to buy some oranges and lemons and an assortment of sweets, and paused to pick out the most vibrant bouquet of flowers she could find. Then, laden with gifts and good intentions, she hailed a hackney cab.

She willed herself to think of pleasant things to say to Fanny. A description of Jewel's stiff rendering of "Buttercup" ought to do it, she decided; the only danger was that it might be enough to make an invalid fall out of her sickbed with laughter. Just rehearsing how she'd tell it made her giggle herself. But then she frowned as she looked out the window. Her luck was still running out. The driver obviously didn't know the way—the district they were riding through was grim and gray, the houses tumbledown and close together. Most of the shops were taverns; all other merchandise was being vended from pushcarts and open wagons. She was about to protest when the hackney rounded a corner, went down a street of shabby houses, and then rolled to a stop.

Lucy glanced at the address she held in her hand before she spoke. Then she held her tongue. Unless Kyle had got it wrong, Fanny lived here. The florid-faced woman who came to the door nodded when she mentioned the name. "Upstairs," was all she said.

Lucy signaled her driver to keep waiting, even though she'd come to the right house. After all, she thought as she mounted the dim and narrow stair, a sick call could be brief. And too, she decided as she finally came to the top landing and held her hand over her racing heart, it was the thought, not the length of one's stay, that cheered the invalid, wasn't it?

But she was appalled at how Fanny lived. Almost as shocked as Fanny was to see her. Lucy hadn't been expected, and for an awful moment, she wondered if she were welcome. Fanny looked more than sick with influenza. It couldn't have been only her recent illness that suddenly drained her face of color and left her speechless at her door. Her look of pain and helpless embarrassment made Lucy herself blanch and want to put down her parcels and rush down the stairs again.

Fanny recovered first.

"Lucy, my dear," she said in a soft, hoarse voice, "you're all better. Do come in—unless, of course, you worry that you'll be reinfected by me. You needn't. I'm on the road to recovery myself, as you can see, it's only that my voice isn't up to snuff yet."

"Oh, no. I mean, oh, yes, I will, thank you. Because I don't think you can get something back that you've given away. I'm so sorry for that, by the way, but glad you're feeling better," Lucy said too brightly as she entered Fanny's set of rooms, looked about herself rapidly, and then spoke up all in a jumble because she was as embarrassed as horrified by Fanny's living quarters.

The sitting room was scrupulously clean, but the furnishings were so old they looked as though they'd also been scoured of color and shape. It was as well that the windows faced another building, so that the sun couldn't show up more glaring faults. Even in the dim light, the carpet seemed faded, and the couch and chairs looked so ancient, Lucy remained standing so as not to stress them. There were few decorations, only some framed photographs on a table, and a china dog that looked wide-eyed at being left alone on his stand. There was a room beyond, and an open door showed another beyond that; the rooms seemed to run back in railroad-car fashion, as though endlessly replicated in a mirror, and there was neither color nor fashion apparent in any of them.

Lucy shifted from foot to foot, and decided to look at Fanny instead of her lodgings. Fanny was wearing a day dress, but her hair was down and she wore no makeup. She looked drab and much older than the polished actress Lucy was used to seeing, so much so that she wondered if she'd have passed her by on the stair had she met her there. Fanny might have been handsome once. Now, Lucy saw, she had only the illusion remaining of what had been, carefully recreated each night for the stage. Lucy called on all her acting talents, and was unhappy to find them not as extensive as she would wish. Still, she assumed a smile, and hoped it looked less artificial than it felt.

"Just see," she said cheerily, glad of the excuse to dig into her bag of presents, "I've brought you candy and lemons and limes for that throat of yours. And flowers—they can't cure you, but if you're like me, they'll make you not so sorry that you're home."

She'd come to gladden Fanny, but it seemed Fanny's smile was as sad as her own felt, and it was the older woman who set about cheering Lucy.

"It's very kind of you, Lucy," Fanny said softly, "and although I'm no longer ill, I can always use your company. Of all your gifts, I think that's the best. Do sit down."

Lucy sat on the edge of a couch gingerly, glad that the fashion requiring a demibustle made any other sort of sitting impossible. Fanny's color and usual air of calm had returned, and it was possible there was even a glint of humor in her mild eyes. She set about putting Lucy at ease by asking about how the *Pinafore* had fared in her absence. It wasn't long before Lucy forgot her dreary surroundings and was laughing as she told how Kyle had exploded when Jewel sang "Buttercup."

" 'No, no, no!' " Lucy mimicked his anguished tones. " 'She's a bumboat woman selling trinkets, not a Bronx matron vending fish!' " She chortled, and then added, "Truly, if you don't come back tonight, Fanny, his temper will get hotter, and then his bed will be colder. Oh, dear," Lucy said guiltily, her eyes growing very wide, "I oughtn't to have said that. But it was what Lester said, and it was so apt!" She giggled again.

Fanny's smile didn't reach her eyes. Nor did she join in Lucy's laughter.

"I won't be back tonight," she said instead. "My voice isn't ready. But I think I'll be well enough for tomorrow. In fact, I was going to go out today when the sun grew warmer. I'm eager to come back. After all, who knows how much longer there'll be a *Pinafore* for me to return to?" Fanny rose and walked to the window before she spoke again, and didn't turn to see Lucy's discomfort at how subdued and sad she seemed.

"I'm not used to being home alone in the afternoon or evening. I've another job, you see, as well as *Pinafore*. Sitting alone got me to thinking as I usually don't have the time to do. Of all things, I found myself thinking of you, Lucy. You remind me so very much of how I was, if not what I was, once upon a time. I don't know how much longer we'll be working together. I suppose if I hadn't got sick, I'd have kept my opinions to myself, but as it is . . .

"Lucy," she said, turning to face her visitor, "what will you do when Kyle closes the *Pinafore*?"

"I . . . I suppose I'll go home. . . . But, no," Lucy said, thinking of everything she'd tried to avoid thinking of since Kyle had announced the possibility of his closing the *Pinafore*, "I don't know if I'd be happy there now. So I'll look for another role, singing. It's not at all as bad as I'd thought it would be. . . . Well," she admitted, "I suppose I'll have to see."

"And what of Mr. Dylan? Does he figure in your plans? Everyone's been wondering. Some of us have been worrying too. Don't be surprised. Little goes on in an acting company that everyone else doesn't know. Maybe because performers need so very much love, maybe because we're so good at pretending, but when we're cast together we become almost exactly like a family for so long as it lasts—close as brothers and sisters or lovers. That's why so many of us so often fall in love with each other. And that's why such love so seldom lasts, too. Because at the whim of a critic or producer, we end our relationships and start the same ones all over again with others. I feel very much like your sister or mother now, Lucy. That's why I presume to ask: think now, what is it you really want to do when the *Pinafore* closes? It's to go with your young man, isn't it?

"I know," Fanny said at once, as Lucy grew silent, "it's none of my business. I won't be angry if you tell me so. But do you think he wants to marry you?"

"Huh!" Lucy said haughtily, recovering herself. "You've been away awhile, Fanny. I no longer see Mr. Dylan. Well, I'll no longer see him in future, that is. I only found out yesterday, quite by accident, that he has no intention of anything serious with me."

"But you knew that all along, didn't you?" Fanny asked gently. "And you're not over him at all, are you?"

Lucy bit her lip; her obvious discomfort was her answer.

"My dear," Fanny said, "that's just what I've been thinking about. It's not fair for you to be in this position and not understand what it all means. Wherever you came from, you're cut off from your own family, and you've no experience of the mock one you've found yourself in. Kyle will tell you what's profitable for him to tell you. Mr. Dylan will tell you what it profits him, in another way, to say. Ada will try to make you into her own image—friends always do. I'm not your age, and so, though I like you very much, I'm not your friend in that way. Nor am I your employer or your lover. But I've seen you change from what you were when I first met you, seen you accept what should be, and was, unacceptable to you, only because it's usual in the world you've entered. I worry for you. I don't want to see you become as I am."

Lucy looked aside as Fanny went on, "I won't lecture. I only want you to see. Have you an hour, Lucy? Will you come with me?"

It took Fanny only a moment to pin up her hair and

throw on a warm shawl, and they went downstairs to get into the cab that had been waiting for Lucy. The driver's eyebrows went up when Fanny gave him directions. They rode in silence, Fanny not speaking. Lucy afraid to. Because, only a short drive from Fanny's lodgings, Lucy gazed out the windows and suddenly felt like the alien she pretended to be, the foreigner she began to think Fanny had never really believed her to be.

"I know such districts must exist in all cities, across all the world," Fanny commented softly as she saw Lucy's expression, "but whether you grew up in London or New York, I think a girl like you never saw such before, did you?"

"No, oh, no," Lucy breathed, because she wanted to deny everything about what she saw now.

She didn't know where to look first. It was a Monday morning, but the narrow streets they drove through were more filled with people than any Lucy had ever seen, even when she'd been at a parade. The tenements were as crowded together as the people in front of them were, and the many rooftops obliterated the morning sky. Wherever they didn't, the sky was blocked from view by a network of lines of hanging wash that waved in the wind like the pennants of some weird ancient tourney. The festival atmosphere was strengthened because it seemed some sort of open-air market was in progress. But a closer look at the people showed that if there were any struggle to be enacted here, it was only an ongoing one against privation. And if it were a festival then it was a grimly ironic one, since the only thing these wretched people might celebrate was their continued survival against all odds.

Ragpickers with their panting dogs pulling their carts behind them trudged in the garbage-strewn gutters, avoiding the horse-drawn wagons and man-operated pushcarts that were being used to vend every sort of used merchandise. Even the bins of fruits and vegetables looked second-rate and secondhand. Yet still there was a crowd of customers picking over them, as there was at every cart and wagon.

Here, it was obvious, all merchandise was viable. The women wore what they could fit into, for warmth, not fashion. The children that weren't working as shoeblacks, newsboys, callers for vendors, or bearers of burdens, ran in ragged packs through the streets. The men who weren't working lay crumpled in doorways. And everywhere, men, women, and children showed evidence of every kind of deformity and illness the rich would have had cured or made otherwise tolerable, if only by disguise.

The hackney driver cursed and cracked his whip as much at the human traffic as at the horse-drawn sort, as, with only an occasional snarl, both slowly parted to give him his way. The stench of the streets found its way into the closed carriage, and the noise was so loud Lucy could scarcely hear Fanny's soft voice. But she did.

"This goes on for miles," Fanny said dully. "You see only the best face of it. The backyards, attics, basements, are where most of them work, the saloons are where they play. If the children are haggard it's because there's no childhood here, no, no boyhood, nor any maidenhood, it's too much a luxury. This is where those who first come to our country, without money, must live until they find their way. My parents came from here. Kyle Harper did too, though he'll deny it. He's to be congratulated, though he thinks it a shame. The only shame is that it's here. You must look at it and remember it, Lucy, if only so that you don't forget what happens to those without money in New York City. Because it's for those who have lost their way too.

"That's why so many girls here sell themselves and think themselves lucky to be able to. There are more prostitutes than ladies in New York, though ladies aren't even supposed to know what they sell. Their gentlemen do. My parents did too—that's why they worked so hard to leave here before I grew to an age for such despair. It's why I struggle to never return, whatever the cost. There are too many for any charity to feed and clothe, there are few enough charities, and more of these poor souls arrive with each ship every day. Enough," Fanny said sharply, and she rapped on the roof with her parasol, so the driver could pull out of the slow-moving traffic and head back uptown again.

"I wanted you to see the worst, so you'd understand

what's at stake," Fanny said. "I can't show you the two other extremes—the expensive houses of pleasure for gentlemen and the workhouses and prisons for those they've no use for, but, Lucy, a girl who's been unwise may end at either place, in time. Men want to marry pure women. With all your talent, being a wife is your best chance at happiness. There are hundreds of beautiful, talented young women in this city, and only a handful achieve successful careers. You may—but then . . ."

Lucy had listened with humble attention, but now she raised her head and stared at Fanny.

"This is all very interesting," she said as she lost interest in what Fanny said, because she'd been snapped out of her despondency by her last words. None of this, she realized with relief, really applied to her, after all. She didn't know whether to be bored or insulted now. As with all her other emotions, this showed on her face.

"Oh, dear," Fanny sighed, looking at her, "I should've remembered what it's like to be young. It's too removed from you, isn't it? You think I'm mad, or spiteful, or jealous. We're almost back and I've wasted your time and mine, haven't I? Then listen, my dear," she said harshly, sitting forward, "and learn from me. I was raised to try to be a lady even though I came from common beginnings. I was given an education, singing and dancing lessons. My suitors were numerous, if not from society, and the compliments they gave me made me decide none of them were worthy of me, and that I was wasted where I was. When my parents died, I dared to go on the stage. I belonged to a reputable company and remained a decent girl. But I met a wealthy gentleman, you see, and fell in love. Surely you understand that.

"He insisted I leave the stage, and so I did. He . . ." She paused and closed her eyes. "He gave me everything I wanted but his name, you see, and I loved him, so it was enough for me. I didn't understand then that a man doesn't want a mistress who's like a wife. No man wants two wives, no matter what they say in *The Arabian Nights*." She laughed bitterly before she continued, "But mine was a constant heart, and his . . . In time he developed an eye for younger women. I'd no recourse. I'd only his heart, not his name, and soon not even that."

The carriage stopped in front of Fanny's lodgings again. She sighed and then spoke quickly, as though she couldn't wait to expel the words, they tasted so bad in her mouth. "So I work in a clothing factory in the day. I was lucky to get a job singing at night. My voice isn't grand enough for concerts, I'm not a good-enough actress for better theater, nor young enough to compete with all the young women who can do as well as I can do at anything . . . but sewing." She laughed again, before she whispered harshly, "Go home, Lucy, wherever that is. Your Mr. Dylan is no different from dozens of other men who'd rob you of your only really valuable commodity, your virtue—your good name. Men place much reliance upon the first, society upon the second. Without either, you've nothing, believe me. And when men no longer want you, and that time comes quickly, believe it or not, the world won't protect you. Go home. And if you see your Mr. Dylan heading toward you— run for your young life.

"But whatever you do, my dear," she said as she swung open the door, "forgive me, please. Because, you see, those photographs in my sitting room are of my son and daughter. He's sixteen and works as a clerk, she's fifteen and works as a lady's maid. They can't hope for much better without a proper last name. Still, together we manage to keep out of those streets we just drove through. So you see, my love left me something of value, after all."

Her face twisted as she looked up at Lucy from where she stood in the street. "Run all the way home, Lucy," she whispered fiercely, "or at least think about it. And forgive me. Good day."

Lucy didn't run anywhere when Fanny left her dazed and alone in the carriage. She rode away. She took the hackney to the ferry slip, and took the ferry back to Brooklyn. Just to visit, she assured herself as she hugged her shaking hands to her bosom and pretended it was because of the light wind off the water. Just to see where there was to run to if she had to, she admitted when the trembling wouldn't stop.

* * *

She still had her key, but the door was open. Doors were never locked in the daytime in Brooklyn, after all. It was still morning, so Lucy walked into the kitchen. The murmurous conversation halted as she entered the room, and Grandmother and the other elderly lady stopped and gazed up at her as though she were an apparition.

"Grandmother," Lucy said, and paused, astonished to discover that after all her experience upon a stage before hundreds of people each night, she was still awkward in front of this one steely-eyed woman, "I've come to pay a call."

"Lucy," her grandmother said in the same tone of voice that she might say "Of course." "Well, look at you. Done up to the nines. Mrs. Briggs, this is my other granddaughter, the one I was telling you about. Mrs. Briggs is renting out your room, Lucy."

"Oh, my goodness," the plump older lady exclaimed. "I've heard so much about you, Lucy. Oh, my stars! Does this mean I must find other accommodations, Mrs. Markham?" she asked, ignoring Lucy to turn a worried face to her landlady.

"Oh, no, no," Lucy said at once, "I've only come to visit my grandmother, Mrs. Briggs, not to stay more than an hour, I promise you."

"Oh, well, then . . . then," Mrs. Briggs said, rising and tittering, "I'll leave you two together. A pleasure, Lucy," she said, and sidled from the table, and was gone from the kitchen in a moment, as though Lucy carried some contagion rather than just the threat of her eviction.

"Do you want some tea?" Lucy's grandmother asked as her eyes roved over her granddaughter, pricing every new thing she was wearing.

"No, no, thank you," Lucy said, perching on the end of a chair, more uncomfortable than simply sitting in her rigid dress-improver usually made her feel.

"So," her grandmother said, "still 'acting,' eh?"

But she smiled as she said it, and it was the sort of smile that chilled Lucy. She'd seen the same sort of knowing grin on the lips of the men in the alley outside the theater as they watched the girls of the chorus leave.

"Well, yes, of course. I told you. I do write to you. I tell you everything, don't I? I try to . . . well . . . well, maybe not," Lucy stammered. "I didn't tell you *where* I was appearing, because they were featuring me as 'The English Rose' and of course I'm not, and I didn't want to be discovered, but now it makes no difference, so I can—tell you, that is. I'm appearing at the Stratton Theater near Fifth Avenue. I sing Josephine in *HMS Pinafore*. You know it," she said desperately, because she hadn't wanted to say where she was appearing any more than she wanted her grandmother to see her there. But the silence and the small smile on her grandmother's face were making her frantic. "You know: 'For I'm called little Buttercup,' " she sang, " 'dear little Buttercup, though I could never tell why, but still I'm called Buttercup, poor little Buttercup, sweet little Buttercup, I . . .' " Her voice trailed off. The pretty little tune sounded foolish sung here in the silent kitchen, so she went on, "Only I don't sing 'Buttercup,' of course, but everyone knows it. Perhaps," she went on without wanting to, as she seemed to sit back and listen to herself say things she hated to hear, "you'll come to see me before we close?"

"I never go to New York," her grandmother said flatly.

"Maybe Gwennie will?" Lucy asked, although if there was anyone she wanted less to meet backstage, she couldn't think who.

"Gwennie never goes to New York either," her grandmother answered, her smile growing warmer at the thought of her other granddaughter's usual good sense.

"Oh, yes," Lucy sighed with as much relief as sorrow, as she remembered how most of the people she knew in Brooklyn thought of the city across the river as "New York" and never ventured there unless they had to.

"So," her grandmother said, as she stopped smiling, "I see you've done well for yourself. I suppose you've got yourself a wealthy gentleman friend, then?"

"No, not anymore," Lucy said, before she recalled herself and said brightly, "Oh, well, maybe not him anymore, but yes, many, many of them, in fact," she began bravely, before she paused as the possible other meaning of the question and her answer began to occur to her, as she saw the same pursed-lip knowing smile appear on her grandmother's face again.

The visit didn't last long. It couldn't, Lucy thought as she walked down the street to the church, not with that unspoken supposition between them, the one she'd lacked the courage to pursue further. It was all her fault, she supposed. The day she'd left, she'd told her grandmother what it was she'd be doing, if not where. Then she'd begged her grandmother's silence about it, because she'd feared the popular view of women who went on the stage, and had wanted the venture kept secret. But then she'd thought she'd return here when *Pinafore* closed down. Now she doubted she could if she wanted to. Aside from not wanting to dispossess Mrs. Briggs, she didn't know if she could bear living with the unspoken conclusion her grandmother had reached about her. Because, paradoxically, she realized, it would be even more difficult if Grandmother thought she'd failed at being as immoral and wicked as she supposed her to be.

The church was cool and clean and spare and chaste, and simply entering it made Lucy feel whole and cleansed again. It wasn't luncheon time yet, Miss Francis would doubtless be in the chorus room writing notes, noting music, industrious and dedicated as ever. She'd understand about *Pinafore*, Lucy thought, her spirits rising as the pace of her clicking heels on the stone floor picked up too. In fact, now she wondered why she'd ever been embarrassed to tell Miss Francis about her role. Now that she'd been doing it for two months, the girl who'd been ashamed to admit she was singing on the New York stage seemed as lost and ghostly as the memory of the lonely girl who'd come to this church to sing and escape her house every night.

Miss Francis' thin face lit up when she saw who was standing in her doorway. But a second later it fell, and she blinked and stared at Lucy forlornly. And her expression didn't change, no matter what Lucy said. In fact, she seemed closer to tears the more Lucy tried to convince her of her good fortune. When Lucy finally explained about "the English Rose" and then asked her to the theater, free, anytime she wished to come, Miss Francis stilled her invitation by placing one thin, frail hand upon her own.

"My dear," she said in her gentle, reasonable, well-loved and remembered voice, "I do understand. But although I might try, I doubt I could speak my heart on the matter as well as the reverend could. I fear he's already left this morning, to attend a meeting with other churchmen on charitable matters for the coming Christmas season. But he'll be back this afternoon. Oh, Lucy, as you've dared to come here again, as you've come so far already, please, please, wait and speak with him. He can help you further."

As what she meant began to occur to Lucy, and her face became a study in dawning horror after incomprehension, Miss Francis sighed.

"Your grandmother told us *all*, you see," she said, "how you left, and for where, and how you've been living on your own in New York City, appearing onstage and . . . But never fear, child, God forgives all. Although the path be thorny, sin can be washed clean. The congregation mightn't want you to teach their children anymore, but I'm glad you're back. I'm happy you've realized that money's a false idol, an unworthy goal, as is the promise of fame, as are . . ." Miss Francis hesitated before she said softly, dropping her gaze from Lucy's incredulous one, as she spoke of a matter she'd only heard about: ". . . the pleasures of impure love."

Well and well, Lucy thought, blinking back tears as she hurried down the street to the ferry slip again, a wise man had said, and truly, that there were none so deaf as those who would not hear. Miss Francis wouldn't even admit that she'd suggested the *Pinafore* audition in the first place. Only when Lucy had begun to cry had she hurriedly said that *if* she'd recommended it, it would've only been because she'd thought the audition to be for a chorale, certainly nothing else. The pure of heart, Lucy thought, stopping to blow her nose vigorously, found it easy to stay that way because of their empty heads, just as Lester, another wise man, had once said.

Lucy watched Brooklyn fade into the autumn mists as

the ferry drew her back to her lodgings. She didn't weep again. She was too busy trying to restrain herself from pushing a chance-met old suitor of hers overboard. Because though she'd distinctly heard her grandmother mention he was engaged to be wedded, he'd greeted her on deck with scarcely concealed glee. Because he'd heard of her new career, as it seemed everyone in the borough of Brooklyn had. When he began edging closer, murmuring about how he frequently went to the city on business, and how he'd a bit of money put aside, and was sure she'd know how he could spend it secretly and handsomely, she was only too pleased to answer.

"Oh, to be sure. Invest in a handsome shroud. Because if you come one step closer I'll push you overboard, and I'm sure the weight of your ignorance will sink you. If," she went on with continued fury, inventing obstacles with abandon as his face grew red, "my gentleman friend doesn't murder you first, that is to say."

Now, Lucy thought with painful satisfaction as the hackney took her back to Mrs. Fergus' house, even if the new bridge to Brooklyn wasn't finished yet, she'd surely burnt her own behind her. So she was delighted to be warmly greeted by Duncan, and then she gave Mr. Fergus such a hearty greeting he stared after her as she fairly danced up the stairs to her room in her joy at being back where she belonged. So she could have privacy to weep in until it was time to dress for the theater.

Stage folk, Lucy had discovered, were very superstitious. They never whistled backstage, mentioned the play *Macbeth* there, or wished each other "good luck" before a performance, and said: "All things come in threes." And so, even after her dreadful day, she shouldn't have been as surprised as she was when a despondent Ada came slouching into her tiny dressing room as she was readying herself for the performance.

Ada was obviously not ready to go onstage. She was wearing a handsome traveling costume of deepest blue silk, with a charming train behind it, and since she'd only decorated herself with a topaz brooch, a cameo pin, coral earrings, a rock-crystal necklace, and a silver belt, with a fringed floral figured shawl thrown over it all, she looked as unusually subdued as she sounded.

Lucy removed the cucumber slices she'd put on her eyes to reduce their swelling, and was scowling at her own image as she tried to paint over the remaining evidence of her recent bout of tears. She glanced at Ada in the mirror.

"Better get into your costume double-quick," she muttered. "Kyle's fit to be tied as it is. Fanny's not coming back until tomorrow."

"No, he's fit to commit murder now," Ada said as she absently picked up a pot of cleansing cream and put it down again, "because I told him I'm leaving tonight. Well, I am," she said as Lucy spun around and gaped at her.

"I guess I didn't have the gumption to tell him sooner. Or the heart to tell you until I was sure, and then I decided I'd better go as soon as I did. Well, I'm caught, Lucy," she said petulantly, wrinkling her freckled nose.

Lucy squinted at her friend and cocked her head to one side, as though to see and hear her better. Nothing anyone was saying today seemed to be making sense.

"I'm caught. I'm pumped. I've got a bun in the oven. I'm going to have a baby," Ada said glumly.

"Oh!" Lucy said, sitting back as though the wind had been knocked out of her. "Was it . . . Gray?" she finally asked fearfully.

Ada laughed.

"Gawd, Lucy, how long do you think it takes to know? I'm not a rabbit! And I'm not that good at telling. No, I was already thinking I was caught when I went with him."

Lucy's eyes flew wide, but miraculously, they opened further as Ada went on, talking to her own image in the mirror as she ran a gloved fingertip across her unpainted lips, as though the unaccustomed sight bothered her as much as her words disturbed Lucy.

"I thought of going and getting it taken care of—you know. But since they arrested Madame Restell, it isn't safe anymore. She did the best families as well as the poor working girls, until Comstock went and put her down. I guess I don't have the sand to try someone else.

I'd rather have it than end up dead trying to get rid of it."

There were some things Lucy wasn't ready to think of yet, so her mind stayed resolutely on the first thing it could comprehend.

"Do you think it was Peter Potter?" she asked.

"Coulda been," Ada shrugged. "But to tell the truth, it could have been a couple of others too. He knows that too, so there's no sense me trying to get anything out of him but train fare home. And I got that myself. Aw, Lucy, I'm sorry to go. It's been fun, but I always knew there'd be an end to it. Anyhow, now that *they're* coming next week," she said, "the famous Mr. Sullivan and Mr. Gilbert, we'd be closing up shop soon anyhow, and off down different roads too. So I'm just doing it earlier. I'm going home," she said on a sigh. "They'll be mad as hornets, but they'll take me. I don't think I'll be coming back to New York, though. Wouldn't be fair to leave the kid behind like it was an old flame. I'm twenty, after all, time to be thinking of settling down.

"After I have it," Ada went on more brightly, "I think I'll go west. Say I'm a widow and see what I can catch me for a husband . . . or a 'friend,' " she said shyly, with a look that was the roguish Ada Lucy knew again. "There's an awful lot of men and not half enough women there, Gray said, and if they look anything like Gray and Josh . . . Anyhow, I'm going now, tonight. You've been a pal. So I just came to say good-bye, Lucy, and wish you luck. Oops. Not supposed to say that, am I? Well, then, I wish you whatever you want, honey. Oh, Lucy, cripes! Don't cry. Not for me. I knew what I was getting into."

But Lucy wasn't crying for Ada. So she dried her eyes and gave Ada a last hug, and seemed to accept what she was told, because there wasn't anything else to do.

The overture was done. The brightly lit stage, the pulsing music, the crowded auditorium full of faceless people who'd paid, actually paid, to see her and hear her sing, caused Lucy's heart to swell with something more than sorrow for the first time that day. The music throbbed,

Lucy smiled, and happy to be where she belonged at last, she stepped out into her spotlight.

She was called back for five bows, and sang an encore. Even though Kyle had to shuffle Jewel around once more and improvise with a scrawny chorus singer as another poor substitute at the last moment, he smiled as he heard the reprise of "Ring the Merry Bells on Board Ship" that Lucy, Ned, and Lester gave to appease the audience's clamor.

Lucy was glad of the applause still ringing in her ears. It blocked all other thoughts when she got back to her dressing room. Then she stood gazing unseeing at herself in the mirror. That might have been why she only stared when she saw the reflection of the man standing in her doorway.

She didn't know how he'd got in. She didn't care. He looked more than handsome. He looked wonderfully strong and familiar to her after a bizarre and unfamiliar day had spun her world around her. He looked as eager to see her as she was overjoyed to see him, despite herself. She turned from the glass to see him in reality. There was tenderness and what seemed to be love—of whatever sort it was—in his eyes as he gazed at her. He was familiar, forbidden, dangerous, and enticing, and above all, she thought, he was Joshua Dylan, and he was really there.

She hesitated, thinking of her grandmother's spiteful wrongful conclusions, Miss Francis' horror at them, Ada's shame and dilemma; and above all, of Fanny's excellent advice given to her this very day. She remembered Fanny's words, exactly.

And so then she ran—right into his arms.

16

IT WAS THE last place she should have gone for comfort, and the first place she'd found it. His arms came around her immediately to hold her close, making her refuge as much of a trap as a sanctuary. Lucy knew that. But still she laid her head against Josh's chest. She didn't ask how he'd gotten in; he had a knack for making friends, and once, she remembered, she'd been one of them. So she shut her eyes and relaxed, unable as she was unwilling to examine the peace she felt, letting her silence say more to him than she could.

He was as much pleased as puzzled by her greeting. Nor was he fool enough to be completely flattered by it. She was obviously in some terrible distress, and the feel of her burrowed up against him, as fragile as she was substantially a woman, stirred him in several ways. He wanted to comfort her as much as make love to her, and the thought that he now might be able to do both made him lower his head at last to brush his lips against her silken hair. His hands, which had only soothed her, began to move in different fashion, and left her back to roam the curving length of her. That was when she stirred at last.

"I . . ." she said, drawing back to look at him through tear-beaded lashes. "I've had a difficult day, excuse me."

She couldn't tell him most of it. She could scarcely tell him about Fanny's warning about his intentions. Neither could she say that her grandmother and everyone else in Brooklyn already thought her a fallen woman, and she could hardly tell him about her best friend, who definitely was one. So she seized on the least of her distresses and told him about that.

"Kyle's told us that we'll probably close shortly," she

said, lowering her eyelashes and looking down so that she wouldn't see the warm look in his eyes and find herself back where she most wanted to be, in his arms, again. "Mr. Sullivan and Mr. Gilbert are coming to New York. As soon as they do, we'll be done for. Well, who would pay to see a copy when they can see the original?" she asked.

"I would, since there's only one original Lucy Rose," he said sincerely. He meant every word. Few things gave him as much pleasure as watching her onstage. He loved to see her step into her dance, to hear her sing, and never got over the warm glow of knowing, as he sat with the audience, that the girl who seemed a sparkling stage fantasy would soon be sitting next to him, looking even lovelier up close. Thinking of how much closer to him she might soon be made him smile.

"Thank you, but I doubt New York agrees. Anyhow," she said bravely, glad to remember something to distract her from his smile, and him from his fond scrutiny of her, "we're going out with a flourish. Kyle says we're going to hire a boat, as are all the other *Pinafore*s in New York, and we're sailing out into the harbor to escort the gentlemen from England into shore, singing all the way. He calls it going out in style. And it is. I suppose it's better to laugh than cry good-bye. I can invite a guest. Would you like to come?" she asked abruptly.

He drew in a breath, about to agree without thinking. Any expedition with Lucy was a pleasure, and the last time he'd gone with her to a theatrical party at Tony Pastor's, he'd enjoyed it hugely. But then he remembered other commitments. He hated himself for not saying yes at once, and for taking the light from her face by saying instead, "I'd love to—if I'm free. When will it be?"

"Well, of course, you don't have to," she said immediately. "It was just a thought, and I'd never—"

"Lucy!" he said sharply. "I meant what I said. I'd love to, but I made some promises . . . at least," he found himself saying without meaning to, "let me know the date so I can get out of them if I have to."

"Oh. Well. Next Wednesday. November the fifth."

"Oh, well"—he grinned, echoing her—"that's fine.

Just fine. I'd be proud to come, thank you. Now, would you care to come to a late supper with me?"

She ought to have said no, she realized later. For one thing, Kyle saw them leave together, and he looked as astonished as she felt at her decision to see Josh again. But she was weary and confused, and for all her reservations, ecstatic to be with him. Yet tonight she was tongue-tied because everything she wanted to speak about with him was forbidden. Ordinarily she'd be bubbling with merriment because she'd seen him unawares— as one of a couple who happens to catch sight of the other by accident always is, as if it were some incredible miracle, even if the two live next door to each other. But she couldn't mention that she'd seen him Sunday morning, because she'd seen him with the stylish lady he was rumored to be seriously interested in. So any thought of coaches or weekends rendered her mute.

She'd have liked to discuss poor Ada, but she didn't dare, and so any conversational gambit he tried that spoke of her theatrical company or the performance tonight caused her to fall silent. With the other unhappy events of the day hanging so heavily over her, she could scarcely speak of her plans for what she'd be doing after *Pinafore* closed, either.

"Are you getting sick again?" he finally asked when every topic he'd brought up was ignored.

"No, oh, no," she said at once. "I guess I'm just a little tired. But this is delicious!" she said eagerly, popping whatever it was that was on her fork into her mouth. And was happy to find that eating was a way to avoid talking, and that talking about what she was eating was even more effective. Until he spoke again.

"Yes, the water's delicious and the flowers are tasty too. You've mentioned every other thing that's been put on the table except for the plates and the salt. Now, do you want to talk politics? What's wrong, Lucy?" he asked seriously, too seriously for her to laughingly avoid answering.

"Well, it's been the most trying day," she began, and then chanced to look up, straight into his concerned dark gray eyes. She put down her fork. She seemed to have lost everything else today. It hardly mattered anymore; she might as well make it a clean sweep.

"Ada's left the company because . . . because she's going to have a baby," Lucy blurted, cheeks growing scarlet, "but don't worry, she says Gray's not responsible. And I saw my grandmother today and she thinks the worst of me, and told everyone else in Brooklyn about it, and nothing I can say will change their minds. Fanny told me to go home for my own sake, you see, but when I did, I found out what they all think of me now. And then there's this thing about *Pinafore* closing, of course, and I saw you Sunday morning, you looked very fine in your coach, but you never saw me," she said, and fell still, and then took a giant swallow of wine.

A man who spoke hastily didn't survive long where Josh came from. Both places he'd come from. He'd found himself in threatening situations east and west: whether in a poker game with desperate gents wearing sidearms or in on a deal of business with ruthless gentlemen armed with lawyers. It was as well that he knew how to play for time, because he was easily as confused as her speech was. He wondered if she could be asking for his protection, and decided she might be, but then couldn't be sure exactly what sort of protection she was after. He took her sentence apart word for word and answered as slowly as she'd spoken rapidly.

"Sorry about Ada. But I know it can't have been Gray. It's been only two weeks, and even so, Gray's awfully careful for a careless boy," he added as she gazed at him with perfect incomprehension, or, he thought, a perfect charade of puzzlement.

"As for Brooklyn—why, Lucy, people anywhere will believe the worst only because it's always a sight more interesting than the best, or so my mother always said. I don't know why Fanny told you to go home. I want you to stay. You know that. And I've the means to help you to do that," he said very quietly.

There was no right answer she could give to that. So she closed her eyes and brushed at the air between them as though there were cobwebs there that confused her.

"No, no, please," was all she said as she averted her head.

He was as pleased as he was disappointed by her reaction. Because he never wanted just more of the same sort of thing he'd always been able to buy. He treasured her air of innocence as much as he wanted to dispel it. When she came to his bed, he wanted it to seem as though it was because she couldn't help herself from doing it, for her sake, as well as his. Now he began to realize that that was odd, and further, began to feel uneasy, wondering just how he'd feel after he'd proved she was nothing but what all the other women who called themselves "actresses" were—or when he'd made her into whatever that was. So if her inchoate answer didn't please him, at least for now it suited him.

"All right," he said, "we'll talk about it some other time. Do you want to leave now?"

"Oh, yes," she said.

He hailed a hackney coach and took her home. For once he didn't ask if she'd like to come back to his rooms. Not in words. But when they stopped he took her in his arms and kissed her, and was astonished at the response he got. Because she clung to him as if she were taking some sort of sustenance from his lips, and his desire for her was touched with so much more than lust that he was shaken when their mouths parted. And so they met again.

"I must go," she murmured against his lips.

But she didn't move to the carriage door.

And so he passed the rest of a lonely, frustrated night trying to understand why he had opened his arms and then the door for her.

As she stayed awake, as grateful for his control as she was aghast at her own lack of it, remembering his words as well as his lips. And then sat up until the dawn, when, late in the night, she finally remembered that he'd never said anything about her having seen him with his lady.

It was a clear, cool, bracing day, or so Kyle shouted to his reluctant boatmates.

"My friends," he finally said, when it seemed that not only Bayard and Ned but also some members of the chorus, as well as of the orchestra, hesitated to step on board the swaying ship he'd rented, "there's no northern gale blowing. We're going for a pleasure cruise, not a whaling expedition. Come along. Think of how paltry it will look if the Stratton company remains onshore, when I can see that the Standard has sent not just one, but *two* tugs. And Chickering Hall's *Pinafore* is just out—there, see? Ah, and there's a boat from the Aquarium, and another from Lexington Avenue, and see, over there, just boarding . . . oh, look at their banners! All in German. And there's one with . . . a church-choir crew! Not to mention the boatloads of newspaper reporters. And you tremble onshore? When even choirboys and newspapermen dare the sea? Shame! Now, come along, step lively, we've got to show them a thing or two."

"By drowning?" an anonymous member of the male chorus shouted. "At least those vessels are seaworthy."

"And if you're worthy to see, you'll board," Kyle commanded, choosing to ignore the reference to the fact that the vessel he'd rented was older than any of the others, and from its scent, at least, more used to hauling fish than threatrical companies. But then, it was the best his budget could do.

"Of course," he added, as some of his listeners remained hesitant on the dock, "if this scow does sink, why, then, we'll be the ones to capture the biggest headlines of the day."

The boat was fully boarded within minutes. Then Kyle told the captain to set out from the dock and sail away to join the fleet of the other *Pinafore* companies as they prepared to greet the arriving liner *Bothnia* as soon as it came into sight in the waters off Sandy Hook.

On the open sea, the waters were choppy, and the boat rocked madly. But Lucy loved every minute of it. She wore a warm cloak and a flapping hat over her wind-tossed curls, and stood on the deck, warmer still because she was braced against Josh's hard body. There was so much noise and music they couldn't have heard each other speak, so they communicated with smiles and glances. Even that felicity was only a sidelight to the wondrous proceedings for both of them, and they stayed silent as they took in the sight. Because neither of them had ever seen another like it, and doubted they ever would again.

Every little tug in the flotilla they joined was festooned with bunting appropriate to the day. Each one sported an American and an English flag, and each one bore its own proud banner of origin as well. The musicians on every craft were all playing *Pinafore* music, and before long the several separate boats got into synchronicity and began to play the same tunes in order.

When the liner finally hove into view, the little boats converged upon it, bobbing and ducking their gay flags and pennants as though in homage to the great ship carrying Mr. Gilbert and Mr. Sullivan into their homeland. And then, all at once, one chorus in the improvised theatrical navy began to sing "Buttercup." Once the strains were heard, the song was taken up, ship by ship, until it seemed the music swelled out over all the harbor in one grand mellifluous musical welcome to the men who had written it.

The passengers on the *Bothnia* stood on deck to listen, astonished.

"A wonderful greeting," a hearty blue-eyed gentleman with an auburn mustache and muttonchop whiskers commented enthusiastically. "How charming, how very jolly!"

"Oh, yes," another English gentleman said wisely, looking out over the water, "so 'tis. But these charming musical natives are the very pirates we've come to do battle with."

"No! You don't say!" the heavyset gentleman responded. "Why, look at those brazen scoundrels! There must be dozens of them. I can feel the coins leaking out of my pockets just looking at them."

But they heard the music come clearer. Then despite what he'd said, the hearty gentleman began to grin, and then to laugh, as did the pale, soulful-looking gentleman who stood near him. The strains of their score drifted to their ears from the air all around the ship, as though they sailed through an inlet filled with clever merfolk, leading them on with their own beautiful music.

Even those that were singing grew wide-eyed at hearing themselves, like talented children astonished to realize that one and one and one golden voice multiplied by dozens made up a heavenly chorus. Those on the liner clapped their hands together in wonder as they listened. It was a raffish crew making an elegant, roguish gesture. Some listeners began to applaud as others grew misty-eyed at the unexpected loveliness of the moment. It was perhaps even more beautiful because it couldn't last.

Within moments a discordant clamor pierced the sweet music they were making. A tug with a bold banner proclaiming "NO PINAFORE" cut through the wake of the rest of the boats as the sound of banjos and tambourines rent the air. A chorus was singing with the rhythmic sound of it, but the singing was nothing like the lilting strains all the others had been harmonizing.

"What in God's name is it?" Kyle shouted, just as dozens of others were doing.

"Why, it's a black minstrel chorus," Lester said as he peered into the sun to make out the rogue tug coming up behind them.

"I thought I heard 'Ezekiel Saw the Wheel' before," Josh said, half-laughing, as Lucy stopped singing and blinked. "That's 'Dem Golden Slippers' they just sang, and now they're getting into 'Jump, Jim Crow.' I've heard that kind of music around campfires and on riverboats, as well as in New Orleans."

"Oh, damn them," Kyle shouted in his fury. "No wonder! They want their business back. They've been starving since *Pinafore* mania hit town. But they should face facts, their day's done. Never mind. Sing louder, drown them out, we outnumber them."

So they did, and so they all sang louder. But the steam whistle the black minstrels' tug began blasting was even louder than all the voices raised together, and soon there was a cacophony of sound instead of the score of the *Pinafore* surrounding the liner as it came into port.

The hearty gentlemen on board the *Bothnia* had to pantomime his words in order to be understood.

"Why are those black fellows doing that?" he shouted.

"You're taking their business away, William, they're minstrels, they play American music," another gentleman shouted back, and then smiled, because the steam whistle had stopped and he found himself shouting into a moment of relative quiet.

" 'American music'?" an amused lady asked. "Whatever is that?"

"Why," the gentleman answered, as the steam whistle began keening again, and he mouthed his shouted words in exaggerated fashion. "I do believe that . . ."—he jerked his thumb to the tug where the hellish whistle was screaming—"*that* is it. Why do you think they need us so much?" he added as it fell silent again. And then they all laughed so hard they could scarcely hear the black minstrels or all the sweet pirate voices singing to them.

Whatever the mishaps, Lucy was thrilled with the day. Because, she confided to Josh, she'd actually got a glimpse of Mr. Gilbert, she could swear she had. Kyle was beaming too, as were all the other "pirates" who'd come to dock with the liner bearing the famous pair who would soon be presenting a *Pinafore* designed, as Kyle put it, to blow them all out of the water.

"You may think it odd," he explained to his listeners before they left his boat, "to be so overjoyed at seeing the bread being taken from my mouth, but these are men of genius. And it may be, yes, it well may be," he said before he left his crew to their own devices until showtime, "that their advent may not mean an end of us. After all, have you ever heard an Englishman speak? Your pardon, Lucy, but the way many of your countrymen speak is absolutely incomprehensible to us. It could just be that the audience will prefer an American cast, you know."

"Yes," Lester said with an admirably straight face, "of course. But if we're to pay rent on that theory, remember that if you take it further, the German *Pinafore* may do even better. How many Germans can understand *us*, after all?"

Lucy passed up Kyle's offer to take her home to rest before the performance. And then promptly passed up Josh's offer to take her out to play before that time.

"Do you know what you want?" Josh asked her lightly, once he got her settled in the high seat next to him, before he picked up his reins again.

She knew, but couldn't say it, any more than she could

ask him why he'd taken her out in a light curricle instead of his elegant new English coach.

"I didn't want to hear Ned complaining about our closing, but I really don't have the time to go anywhere else right now," she said instead. "I promised to help Molly— the little dark-haired girl who was standing next to Bayard—she's taking over Ada's part," she explained, though Molly was helping her now by providing an excellent excuse to avoid Josh today.

Not that she really wanted to, but she knew what she had to do, she thought, stealing a glimpse at his strong face as he nodded and set the horses in motion. As always, she regretted as much as appreciated the injury that had changed the line of his profile. She didn't know if she could have borne the sheer beauty he must have possessed before his accident, and wondered again if he'd have been the sort of man he was if he hadn't come a cropper that day on the stagecoach. Whatever sort of man that was, she corrected herself. Because for all she admitted now that she loved everything about him, she still didn't know just who Josh Dylan was.

She knew he was capable of being gentle, she knew he was brave and clever, as humorous as he was perceptive, and often very kind. He loved his brother with the same intensity that he'd loved the rest of his family, and had a hard life behind him that had taught him the value of perseverance and tolerance. But she didn't know what his life was when he wasn't with her, or what his plans for his future were. Or what he really wanted from her.

Or maybe, she thought as she tore her gaze from him, she did know, and just didn't want to believe it. But it was almost impossible for her to accept that a man would go to all this trouble just for what she believed to be only a few moments—or hours (she'd never been able to ask anyone that particular question)—in a girl's bed.

"I'll be gone the rest of this week," he said, "but may I see you next week? Say, Monday? To start the week off right?"

"The way things are going," she answered softly, "we may not be here by then. We act on a day-to-day basis now, one performance ahead of the gate, as Kyle says."

"I don't think it'll be as soon as all that—their *Pinafore* doesn't open for almost a month. Even after that, it takes time to tell. At any rate, you'll be at Mrs. Fergus', won't you? You did say you weren't going back to Brooklyn. And even if you were," he added with a sidewise glance at her, "I'd find you."

She couldn't answer. It was a deft compliment; it might be more. She was very glad it was daytime and that they were riding in full view of the passing public, because again, against her will, and certainly against all her training and better judgment, she found herself yearning toward him. The trick of it, she decided, was to keep it light, and in the daylight, and in public, and wait to see what happened. Although, with all the restrictions that she had to keep adding on, soon it might not matter where they were when he looked at her like that and spoke the way he did. The idea of them embracing in plain view of the world on Broadway at the height of noon caused her to smile when she looked back at him. But the look he returned made her worry that her fanciful vision might be an omen.

He took her hand and not her lips when they parted, but his eyes told her all that she'd missed. And he didn't miss the regret and doubt in hers.

In time, she thought as she hurried to dress for the theater, surely in time she'd know what to do as clearly as she didn't know now.

Time, he thought after he'd left her, time was running out, just as she'd said. But for once, the old thief was on his side.

"In no time at all you'll be looking down on me," Josh told Gray, looking his brother straight in the eye as he took his hand when he met him at the door.

"I'm happy just to try to be your equal," Gray said with sincerity, "because I think I've stopped growing now."

"Late nights and liquor, tobacco weed and wild females," Josh said, shaking his head. "Old Erie was right—you've done stunted your growth, little brother."

"Wish I could've," Gray laughed, "but my late nights have been for studying, and my roommate smokes a pipe and I keep all the windows open. The liquor and wild females are in short supply—till I come to visit my big brother in the wicked city, that is. What Thanksgiving treats do you have for me?"

Josh shrugged into his long double-breasted coat and glanced at himself in the mirror before he spoke. When he did, he avoided Gray's eye.

"Gloria invited me out to her place on Long Island for Thanksgiving dinner and then for the rest of the weekend. The weather's closing in, they say, so they're shutting the house for the season and making a gala country weekend out of it. There'll be dancing and riding, and dozens of debutantes out there too . . . but," he went on, noting his brother's too-casual stillness, "remembering your thoughts on the matter, or rather, remembering how nicely and discreetly you never gave me your thoughts on the matter in your letters whenever I mentioned it—how do you feel about having Thanksgiving dinner with Lucy and her whole *Pinafore* cast at a humble boardinghouse today instead? They've decided to call it a holiday while they fix up the stage, and we've been invited."

The correctly dressed tall blond young gentleman let out a yip of the sort that was seldom heard in the Fifth Avenue Hotel, though it was a familiar sound on the endless plains, where it could call a horse or alert a man a mile away. "Whoo ha! Oh, say, that's a lulu! Yessir! I got nothing against Miss Gloria, but I'd rather share my turkey with Miss Lucy and her pals. Thank you kindly, Josh."

"Of course," Josh said lightly, "you remember Miss Ada won't be there, and I'd remind you of her fate when you meet any of Lucy's other young lady friends."

"I know," Gray said, looking uncomfortable for a moment, before he grinned and said, "You can skip the lecture. I know it by heart: I should always leave just before I pay my ladylove my final respects, or else send my love to her neatly wrapped in a French letter. Daddy really gave you a way with words, didn't he? I felt real bad about Ada," he said more seriously, "and I'm surely relieved it wasn't me. I learn fast. If I'm lucky enough to meet another like her, I'll take care, don't you worry."

"Since you're looking more like an Adonis every time

I see you, and you'll be meeting some new actresses tonight, I don't doubt you'll be lucky. Just be careful," Josh said wryly.

"I don't know—they're not all like that," Gray answered gravely. "Lucy's not."

Josh looked at him oddly as he went on, "Ada told me so. She'd no reason to lie about it. She was kind of jealous, though they were friends. She always said that if she had Lucy's looks and talent she'd use them better, but Lucy was held back because she was so straitlaced."

Josh grinned when he recalled how literally true that was, but grew more thoughtful as Gray added, "It's kind of funny. Because though it was Ada that landed in the suds, she always said she worried about Lucy, because Lucy was an innocent and just didn't know the score. I do believe that's true enough," he added, and his expression was as seemingly innocent as his words when his brother looked at him sharply.

Josh decided to ignore whatever Gray was hinting at. If it bothered him enough, Gray could be counted on to be more specific.

"But I have to go to Gloria's house tomorrow," Josh said.

"Well, that's okay," Gray put in quickly. "My friend George, from school, lives in New York. He wants to show me the town. I already told him to drop on over later tonight, when he gets through with dinner with his kin. I thought I'd stay here, and be able to go with him whenever. You don't mind, do you?"

"No, but now, come on, we've presents to scout out. A guest at a dinner for theater folk has to come well-armed. And that means arms full of food as well as flowers."

The flowers Josh and Gray brought with them filled Mrs. Fergus' sitting room with autumn colors. Considering that it was already stuffed with occasional tables, rockers, hassocks, spare chairs, framed autographed photographs, and knickknacks of all descriptions, as well as the holiday company, it should have been uncomfortably full. But crowded as it was, it was also filled with laughter, and that extra ingredient made it cozy, not cramped. After several of the bottles Josh and the other gentlemen had provided had been decanted, it grew even merrier, and though even the wallpaper's roses seemed crushed together, there seemed no need for another inch of space.

The table was even more crowded, and yet, with a glass at every elbow, even as another person's elbow was, it wasn't at all uncomfortable.

"Snug!" Ned insisted. And so it was, although it was clear the old fellow was charmed to find himself wedged into close proximity with young Miss Molly of the singing chorus and youthful Miss Nora from the dancing ensemble. Both of the girls were so merry with the festivities and the champagne, and so well-corseted besides, that it might have been they felt none of the tributes he tried to pay to them under the table.

Mr. and Mrs. Fergus reigned over opposite ends of the table; its tongue extended by so many boards that it required two cloths to cover it, so laden with food it resembled a medieval banquet. It reminded Josh of feeding time at the Zoological Gardens, because he'd never seen food disappear so fast—no, he confided to Lucy, who sat giggling at his side, not even around the campfire, after a hard day of droving, with sixteen hungry cowboys and one pot of beans. The fish, the soup, the turkey, the dressing, the several sorts of potatoes, the aspics, jellies, puddings, and breads—every dish the maid staggered out with went back to the kitchen as clean as if it had already been licked by Duncan. And Duncan himself would be hard put to find room for another bite, since he'd wisely positioned himself under the table. He wandered in the forest of knees and legs there, unseen, nibbling politely from fingertips, sharing in the feast at the hands of every person who thought himself the only one sly enough to slip Duncan some holiday offering.

Lucy sat next to Josh, and Kyle entertained her on his one hand, and Jewel on the other. Bayard had brought a lady friend, a plump blond from the Chickering Hall *Pinafore*. Lester invited an old friend, a gaunt prestidigitator who made his dinner vanish beautifully; Kyle asked a dim, bibulous gentleman, Dr. Max, to dinner, but all the old fellow did was drink it. Beside Miss Molly and Miss Nora, there was a trio of other young girls from the chorus, and a few equally charming, but far older, women friends of Mrs. Fergus'.

After every bite of food had been spared the indignity of being sent back to the kitchen, the company tottered back into the sitting room for more drink and "some light entertainment after a heavy meal," as Mrs. Fergus put it. And for all he'd gone to theaters across the West, and as often as he could since he'd come to town, Josh couldn't remember a better evening of entertainment.

The gentlemen began with songs and patter, and as subsequent bottles were breached, the older ladies showed they knew just as many music-hall catches, and with much warmer verses too. Dr. Max proved he could coax any tune out of the old piano, and humming three notes in a line could give him any whole song. The skeletal prestidigitator plucked coins from astonishing parts of the younger ladies' anatomies. As the laughter rose and the level of the bottles lowered, Miss Nora and the trio of dancers from *Pinafore* showed how a scandalous new dance from Paris was done, and Mrs. Fairfax had to be forcibly restrained from showing the same thing. Kyle astonished them all by enacting a scene from *A Boy and His Dog* that brought tears to even Jewel's eyes, and Duncan was then patted and hugged so much by all the company that he tried to escape to the kitchen. But that only brought him notice, and in a moment, at Mrs. Fergus' command, he was dying, suffering, mourning, and rescuing doll babies, to everyone's now hilarious pleasure.

It was way past the polite time to go when Josh and Gray realized it. The older celebrants were yawning, and Mr. Fergus had already slouched into the kitchen in search of leftovers for his before-bed snack. But the younger people were ready for more festivity. Bayard and his woman friend were off to a late-night club, and the trio of dancing girls left quickly, because they had another party to look in on. After conferring with Miss Molly, Gray announced that she and Miss Nora had agreed to go with him to meet old George. Then they'd go on to enjoy an evening on the town.

"But I can't go dancing tonight," Gray said, and as he rose from his chair they noted he favored one leg.

"There's a damp wind reminds me of a horse I once knew. Back home my leg hardly ever bothers me," he said innocently, though he watched his brother with a lurking grin, "but here in the East the wind comes right off the sea to my toes."

"Yes. And there's a fist that comes right from your brother to your nose if you don't stay here 'til you're done with school," Josh drawled. "So let's get on it," he said, smiling, "your vacation's wasting."

"You'll come along too, won't you?" Josh asked Lucy. "I'll get you home at a decent hour. I have to leave the city early in the morning myself—just going for the weekend," he explained quickly, when he saw the sadness spring to her eyes.

"I can't," she said, realizing how foolish the invitation was, because sooner or later the girls would go off with Gray and his friend and leave them, and being alone with him in the night would make any hour an indecent one for her.

She showed him to the door. But she lingered in the dim hallway after the maid had helped him on with his coat and left them alone there.

"I do wish that I could," she said wistfully as he stood staring down at her. It was true. But she wasn't like the girls who'd gone with Gray—although now she was dismayed at realizing how much she wished she were.

"But of course you can," he said on a chuckle.

His kiss was light, meant to comfort as much as persuade. And for all she meant to take it gracefully, and then gracefully leave it, the moment she felt his lips on hers, she forgot until it was too late to end it lightly.

"Ah, Josh," she murmured in a broken voice after she pulled away, only to hide at his chest. And because she trusted him as much as she feared him now, she asked him the unanswerable question she'd asked herself so often of late: "Ah, Josh, what can I do?"

He knew she meant more than what he'd asked her for tonight. He answered carefully. "You know by now," he said softly. "You don't have to ask me that. When you're ready you'll know that too, and then I'll show you what to do. But you know that too."

She raised her head. "I don't know that I'll ever be

ready. I truly don't know," she insisted, looking up to search his face for the answer she didn't have.

Even in the dark he could read the question in her eyes. He placed a feathery kiss on her lips, though when he spoke, his voice was deep with emotion.

"I'll wait," he said.

The wait would be worth it to him. It would be good to make love to a friend again. Time, he thought tenderly, as desire and impatience intermixed, she only needed a little more time. There was a natural evolution to all things, just as Mr. Darwin had written. She'd come to understand that. As she had already begun, so she'd go on, as would he. He knew very well where he came from, and where she'd been; who he was, and what she was; what she was becoming, and where he was bound and determined to be going. And so, too, he believed, would she. In time.

"You will know," he promised before he turned to leave her. "Soon."

It seemed true to her. And she didn't know whether to be glad or sorry for it.

17

THE GIRL EMERGING from the dark tunnel looked as fragile and incongruous in that setting as a mote of sunlight caught in the yawning maw of a whale. She stood poised halfway between the dark and the light, all in white, like some fanciful representation of spring hesitating to emerge after winter, but her look of horror was entirely human, and for a sufficiently trivial, mortal reason. She'd dropped her tray. The silver teapot lay on its side, leaking steaming liquid, the white napery was absorbing some of it along with the dirt on the brick floor, and the fragile cups and plates had splintered as if they'd been made of ice, not bone china. The girl was frozen in that instant, as though she were afraid that if she moved she too would shatter.

A moment later her face contorted and she wailed like a banshee. By then Josh had slipped from the saddle and was striding toward her. That seemed to terrify her even more. She held up her hands to stop him, gabbling something that sounded like: "Oh, Gawd, dinna come near, sur, oh, Gawd'nhiven, it's sure Mrs. Babbs'll have m'ears, oh, sweet mercy," and then, throwing her apron up over her head, she turned and pelted back into the long tunnel and rounded a bend into the darkness.

"Hard days for Sir Galahad," a not-too-sympathetic voice commented, and Josh turned to see Peter Potter silhouetted at the entrance to the tunnel. His friend was grinning.

"A New York gentleman doesn't notice servants," Peter said, gazing down at the remains of some other house guest's breakfast tray, "unless it's to offer them a better position, or at least a different kind of one. But I wouldn't bother. Some of them are pretty enough, but they're a dreary, pious batch this season—there's a whole new crop coming in from Ireland now, with the most primitive ideas about virtue. Joking, Joshua," Peter said a little anxiously after looking at his friend's face. He raised his hands and backed up a step. "Only a jest, dear friend," he protested.

"That's why she ran?" Josh asked.

Peter nodded. "The best thing you can do for her is to leave. She'll come creeping back to pick up the damage. They'll take it out of her wages, not her skin— we're not that medieval here. Old Jacob's a fair-enough employer."

"This tunnel looks like something out of the Middle Ages," Josh commented. "It's grander than a mine shaft, but twice as forbidding. To go to all that trouble to get guests hot coffee . . ." He shook his head, and began to stroll back into the weak winter sunlight.

When he glanced up at the morning sky, it told him the time of day as well as his pocket watch could have, and he gazed at his friend curiously.

"What are you doing up now? Didn't you go to bed last night?"

"In town I cavort, in the country I'm respectable. Have to be, my fiancée and her family are here," Peter said gloomily. "But three days is enough. This Thanksgiving weekend's already a year to me. Have mercy, good sir, just as the little maid begged. You said you were leaving today, I woke at dawn to find you, saw you out riding, and hurried into my clothes to flag you down. If you're still feeling gallant, I've got a capital errand of mercy for you: take me home—please! You may not mind the dancing and the charades and the piano recitals every night, you seem to be eating up all the amateur theatricals and social teas, but I'm losing my mind. I don't know how you can take it—all the sweet debutantes displaying their not-very-considerable talents, while their daddies hint about their considerable fortunes. I've been engaged to marry for a hundred years, so I can't even have the fun of choosing which fortune to take. And I'm promised to stay on for a week—unless a friend asks me along with him for company on the long, dangerous road back to the big city?" he asked hopefully.

"You're welcome in my carriage," Josh said.

"Ah," Peter said on a sigh, "now, let's see . . . yes. 'But, Elizabeth . . . dear Mr. and Mrs. Natwick . . . please understand. As much as I hate to go, Josh is a friend, I couldn't refuse him my company—he's a stranger to town.' Yes. That should do it, thank you. There are harder ways of making money than marrying it, I suppose. But I can't think of any just now," he added.

Josh smiled as he swung back up into the saddle.

"You have enough money, Peter. You don't have to marry it, you know."

His friend's eyes widened. He looked astonished, and it may have been that he was.

"What's *enough* money?" he asked incredulously.

It was an unanswerable question, as it was meant to be. Josh paused. Then he warned his friend to be packed and ready by noon, and headed his horse back to the stables. He'd been riding alone since first light.

He'd taken the shore route for miles, and it was only the shape of the land that finally showed him the spot he'd sought, the place where he'd picnicked with Lucy. Weeks had passed, and autumn's splendor had burnt out, leaving skeletal tangles of shrubs and the bare bones of trees to sway in the winter wind. The water echoed the sky, so even the sea was slate. The year was running out. He'd taken the dawn ride to escape that knowledge, but the land itself reminded him of it again.

But there were ways to make time linger, he thought with rising spirits as he turned the horse over to a stableboy. He was headed back to the city. The weekend had been as agonizingly dull as Peter had complained. And too, he'd begun to feel a vague disquiet. He'd started to wonder, from the way he was naturally assumed to partner Gloria in the dance, at the table, and during the day, if he really had any choices left in the matter. But that was here, in the country.

He was bound for the city, where winter was said to be the most exciting time. There were new theater productions and dress balls, concerts and exhibitions, lectures and sporting events and entertainments everywhere to attend. The clamor of the city would give him a distance and objectivity that the quiet of the countryside couldn't. Living in a girl's house with her, her father as constant a companion as she was, with her friends and family watching his every move, was like living in a small town again. It could get a man to feeling an urgency to settle matters that wasn't realistic.

Josh was whistling under his breath as he strode into the front hall and prepared to take the stairs to his room. But the tune died on his lips as the butler intercepted him.

"Ah. There you are, Mr. Dylan. The master would like a word with you," the butler said. "If you would . . . ?"

Jacob Van Horn's "den" was very like a real one, Josh thought. Darkened by heavy draperies and wood paneling, it was soft underfoot with Turkish carpets.

Josh took the goblet of brandy proffered him, and then a seat in one of a pair of leather chairs facing the blossoming fire in the huge fireplace, as Jacob settled himself in the other.

"Forgive me for summoning you, Josh, but it's hard to get hold of you any other way," Jacob said. "You and Gloria are busy every minute. But I wanted a private talk with you before you left. By the way, are you sure you don't want to stay on for the dancing tonight?"

"Thank you, Jacob, be delighted to, but I've got an appointment in town," Josh answered, feeling uncomfortably like Peter for a moment, until he remembered that he did have an engagement—and that he was looking forward to it, and to seeing her again.

"Ah, too bad—it's such a big party, and the last one here for the season. I'd hoped . . ." Jacob's voice trailed off and he fell silent.

There was an awkward pause as Jacob stared into the liquid he was swirling in his goblet. Josh wondered what he had on his mind, but had no intention of breaking the silence. He let it grow, appeared to relax, and stared into the fire as he sipped his brandy.

There might have been admiration coloring Jacob's voice when he finally did speak, but what he said was so riveting, Josh forgot to analyze the way he said it.

"I don't know how these things are done where you come from, Josh," Jacob said at last, putting his glass down on a side table and placing his hands on his knees, "but I believe in plain speaking. She'll have you. Gloria and I agree on many things—she should have been my son," he said, before he chuckled, adding, "Fat lot of good that would do you, eh? But it's true. I've never given my consent before because I've never been asked for it. She's twenty-two, and about the most eligible girl in New York, but she's as careful as I am. She said her choice would be worth waiting for. So it is—you've got brains and grit, ambition and breeding. I've studied you, and I know you won't take it wrong if I tell you I've had you studied too. It all looks good. You don't have an old New York name, but your breeding's good enough. Half of New York's buying foreign titles for their daughters, and they're getting castoffs and weaklings. You've got the background *and* the backbone. I'd be proud to have you in the family, my boy."

It was Josh who paused now—for breath as well as words. When he finally spoke, his voice was warm and amused, everything he was not.

"I'm flattered, Jacob. No, much more than flattered. But the thing is . . . I hadn't asked yet."

"I know that," Jacob said imperturbably. "She may have my head on a plate for it too. But, shall we say . . . I anticipated you? I think it's my right. She's no common girl, I'm not just a fond father. She's my one child, she'll get all I have one day. That's considerable . . . *very* considerable. I won't talk numbers now, but my lawyers will meet with you whenever you want. I've got even more than you know, and with what you have, we can have the running of a lot of things, Josh. A lot of things. So it's a matter of business as well as the heart. In the old days, you know, these things were all business, and I'm not sure it wasn't better that way—but either way, I approve of you and want the best for her, so I decided to have it out on the table. Now."

"I see," Josh said. Then he raised his eyes. Jacob was a powerful man. But Josh had learned that in a tight spot you tell the truth, unless it will get you hanged. His truth might get him barred from the exclusive circles he aspired to—had gotten used to—it might hurt him financially, and could even upset his plans for a stay in the city he'd staked out as his own. But it wouldn't hang him. Jacob wasn't that powerful, yet.

"She's everything a father could want. I expect everythin' a man could want in a wife too," Josh drawled, as a smile spread on Jacob's face, only to slide away as Josh added, "But I hadn't asked yet, Jacob. Or talked to her about it. It's true I don't know how things are done here, but where I come from, a man decides his own life or he don't really deserve it. You'll excuse me, I know it's business as well as pleasure to you, but it's my life, and I have to insist on orderin' it for myself. I think I'd like to go have a talk with Gloria now, if you don't mind."

There was a flash of something in Jacob's reserved expression, a hint of a thing that turned his mild blue eyes cold and thinned his smile, that told of how he'd gotten his palatial house and grounds, and exactly how he'd paid for the elegant room he sat in. But how quickly that sudden look vanished was an equal indicator of how he held on to it.

"If I don't mind—or if I do, I suspect," he said blandly. "Of course. That's what I like about you. I respect a man who doesn't put up with pushing. I'll speak with you later, Josh. You don't leave until noon, do you?"

Kyle Harper's eyes closed in pain fifteen minutes into the first act of *HMS Pinafore*. Only an act of sheer will kept him from sobbing aloud after a half-hour. He'd never heard anything like this production of the operetta that the original English company was giving. He'd never guessed the witty dialogue they had between the first and second numbers, never imagined how he and everyone else in New York could have got the words wrong at Sir Harold Porter's entrance, never guessed how the music would sound played right, sung right, and acted perfectly. He knew he'd be weeping publicly by the first intermission, and so he stumbled from the theater before the lights went up. It was beautiful, it was superb, he was out of business.

Not immediately, of course, he reasoned as he walked back to the Stratton, where his company was giving their abortion of a version. No, it would take time for the public to hear about the difference, because with all his connections, he'd had to move heaven and earth to get a ticket for himself tonight. But when they finally did, it would all be over. He wandered into a tavern and ordered something bracing, and thought that it would be one of those tragic, lingering theatrical deaths—the ticket sales would ease off until they found they couldn't afford to pay a stagehand to open the curtain on another performance. Even so, he doubted it would take more than a month. After the surge of Christmas business, he'd enter the new year without a source of income. Without a company, without a production, without an idea—except for the fact that he always did have an idea.

His company was expendable: Lester, Ned, Fanny, and the others were as replaceable as they were forgettable. They weren't what the audience came to see. Neither was *Pinafore* itself. There were better ones—none like the one he'd just seen, but superior to his own. But none had what his did. He'd created a star. A minor one, to be sure, and perhaps only a meteoric one, fated to burn out as quickly as she'd lit up the stage. But she did light up the stage. It was true that Blanche Roosevelt, the Josephine he'd just seen, was altogether a more polished professional, and a far better singer, actress, and dancer. But talent wasn't altogether necessary for stardom. The English Rose was intriguing. She was lovely, talented, and even more important, she had that lovely imaginary and imaginative history that the public adored. She pulled in business, and business was what the theater was all about. *Pinafore* or not, he needed to keep her by his side until he could decide what to do with her next, what new vehicle could best help them make a quick fortune together.

But she posed a problem. She was naive, loyal, and virtuous. All bad things for his purposes. Still, if a man couldn't make something good out of the bad, he didn't deserve to be in the theater, did he? Kyle thought, draining his glass. He slammed it down on the bar and stalked out into the night again. As he walked, he planned.

First, Miss Lucy Rose must never see the original production of *Pinafore*. She'd be even more devastated than he'd been, because, he conceded, she had a sense of shame and none of his defenses against it. But for the next few weeks she'd be onstage whenever her competition was, and so that posed no immediate problem. He could hide the reviews or ignore them; all actors did. Second, she must be made to see that whatever production he mounted next was right for her and wrong for her fellow actors. She'd formed a sentimental attachment to them and had no experience, as they did, with the usual lot: the brief encounters, sudden deep emotional involvements with each other, and the even more sudden fracturing of their relationships—the estrangements brought about by fortune that all actors learned to deal with. But he could talk her around anything, he decided, especially something she'd soon see the others accepting. And so even that was a minor difficulty.

The third thing he thought of loomed largest—because he hadn't wanted to face it first. There was another attachment that posed the biggest threat to his plans. Unless that attachment made a misstep . . . But that was unlikely, Kyle thought ruefully, since Joshua Dylan was fully as devious and talented a salesman as he himself was, and was definitely as determined too.

But, Kyle mused as he walked, and he thought best on his feet, he did have one advantage the tall Westerner did not. He, he thought with pride, was of the theater. And that was what the theater was all about, wasn't it? Persuasion. Kindly deception. Illusion. The ability to blur the line between fantasy and reality until it no longer mattered if it existed at all. He, Kyle Harper, was an actor, producer, and director, an artist, a man in a profession with a heritage he respected more than anything else in the world, except money. If he couldn't persuade her, manipulate her, and win her to his side, he decided, he didn't belong where he was. Or where he was determined to go—with her. He hurried to the theater.

But it wasn't until they got home that he spoke to her.

By then Lucy was relaxed, happy, and at ease, Kyle saw as he came into the kitchen and studied her as she sat at the table feeding the last scraps of her midnight snack to an appreciative Duncan. It was time to act, Kyle decided as Lucy rose to leave for bed, pantomiming a contented stretch. He raised one long finger and said sweetly, "Ah, Lucy. A moment of your time, please."

He closed the kitchen door. It was seldom closed unless there was company in the house, so the others would stay away, and to ensure it, he'd also had a word with Mrs. Fergus. It was perfect. The parlor would put her on her guard. A kitchen was an unthreatening, homey sort of place for friends to chat in. It was only too bad, he thought as he came back to sit at the table with her, that she looked as though she were about to be burned at the stake.

Well, of course, he'd been to see the real *Pinafore* tonight, Lucy thought wretchedly. She'd been expecting this chat, everyone had; the only question was when he was closing them down, and the only other ones were where she'd live, how she'd eat, and what she'd do when he did. She was so consumed with her own dreadful thoughts that she didn't hear what he said at first. He repeated it patiently.

"I saw Mr. Sullivan and Mr. Gilbert's own production of *Pinafore* tonight," Kyle said easily, turning an orange around and around in his long-fingered hand, as though wondering what it was. "A good production," he said, digging a fingernail into the orange. "Yes, very well done, I'd say," he added as he began to peel it.

"Everyone says it's wonderful," Lucy said softly.

"Oh?" Kyle asked, pausing with a half-peeled orange in his hand. "Who else do you know who's seen it?"

"Well, the papers . . ." Lucy said, as Kyle chuckled. "Oh. The *papers*. If it was from Britain, the papers would give raves to the plague, you know. Their *Pinafore* was good. But it was not so good as all that."

A wild surge of hope began to thrill through Lucy's tense frame, until she heard him say laconically, "Of course, it will mean an end to our little endeavor anyway. And most of the others here in New York. Snobs, pretenders, the social few who make the successes—*they* heed everything the papers say."

"Oh," Lucy said, because there was nothing else to say.

"But it won't end our association, of course," Kyle said, and then said again, until the returning life in Lucy's great brown eyes assured him she was listening, and actually understanding his words at last.

"You see," he chuckled, "I went somewhere else after the show."

She didn't see. Her absolute silence encouraged him.

"I had an audience with Mr. Sullivan and a brief encounter with Mr. Gilbert backstage," he said, and the enormity of the lie silenced even him for a second.

He could hear her swallowing in the quiet kitchen. It seemed he could also hear her rapid, shallow breathing, until he realized it was Duncan's; she didn't seem to be breathing at all now.

"They've heard of you. Yes. 'Pray tell, who,' they inquired, 'Mr. Harper, is this "English Rose" Mr. D'Oyly Carte told us of? She sings, she dances, she is supposedly magnificent to look upon, and most important, she is rumored to be English, and titled, at that Mr. Harper,' they said, 'We've some talking to do.' "

He sat back, enormously pleased with himself.

"Who said that?" she gasped.

"Now, now," he said, wagging his finger so that the scent of orange wafted beneath her nose. "Greedy creature. I am not at liberty to say. Strictly sub-rosa. Suffice it to say it was said, and heard, and so what do you think?"

"I hardly know what to think," she said, rising from her chair and pacing in such agitation that Duncan opened one eye, wondering if he ought to move out of her way. "I . . . I can't imagine . . . do they want me to sing in *their Pinafore?* Here? Or in their new production? Do they want me, really?"

"Really," Kyle said casually, "they do. But not, of course, in their *Pinafore*, it's already cast. Nor, I'm afraid, in their new production—there's too much security around that one," he grumbled, forgetting his mission in his annoyance. "Armed guards in the hotel corridors, it was impossible to even get our Dr. Max in an adjacent room with a water glass up against the wall. . . . So, naturally," he said, remembering her, "wonderful as they believe you to be, as they don't know you, they can't very well cast you in this new production I hear is to be called *The Robbers.* They trust no one new. No, they want you to eventually perform in England for them. They'll bill you," Kyle said, his imagination soaring as he, as always, began to believe his own inventions, " 'The English Rose—Returned After Her Triumphant New York Experience.' "

It grew very quiet in the kitchen.

"I can't," Lucy said in a pinched voice. "If it was hard to pretend to being English here, only think of how impossible it would be in England! I couldn't. I made so many mistakes," she sighed, "and you know? Now I think no one I know believed me at all, not really."

"My point exactly," Kyle said blithely. "Did it make any difference? The English will think you're making mistakes because of this secret past you're covering up. Either way, don't worry. All you have to do is trust to me, we'll see it through together. I only ask that you keep it entirely, absolutely to yourself, and when our *Pinafore* closes, you stay on here, with me."

He sat back, triumphant, and watched her face. It was, as always, an exact indication of what was going on behind that high, white, and flawless brow of hers. First she seemed stunned; then her eyes opened wide with excitement percolating in their amber depths. But then, slowly, her gaze turned inward and her smile faded.

"And the others—Fanny, Lester, Ned, Bayard . . . ?" she asked, as he'd expected her to.

"They'll go on to their own new triumphs," Kyle answered, and seeing no dawning smile, sat forward. "Lucy," he said, "that's an actor's lot. Many of them won't even tell you where they're going. Or if they do, be sure they'll tell you a fabrication, for fear of your telling someone else and ruining their chances, or getting the role for yourself. True. That's true," he said as she cocked her head to one side, looking so adorable he was glad that this, at least, of all he'd said tonight, was probably true.

"Oh," Lucy said, subsiding, mulling that, accepting it, until her eyes sprang wide again as at last the thought he'd waited for all this time finally occurred to her.

"Kyle," she said nervously, "I'd have to go to England?"

"Yes," he said bluntly, with none of the anxiety he

felt, because that was the crux of it. If he could get her to accept that kind of separation in the cause of her career, he could get her to accept anything—from waiting until such time as he really had a project for her to appear in, to staying with him until his fortune was made.

"I couldn't," she said, sitting down abruptly. Her eyes filled with tears. "Oh, Kyle, I'm so sorry, but I can't leave the country."

"I applaud your patriotism," he said wryly, and she grinned, until he added, "except that I believe it's really that you can't leave one of your countrymen, isn't it? And why?" he asked gently as he arose from the table, tugging his vest down carefully, for it was now time for his greatest performance.

Her eyes followed him as he paced; he moved restlessly, his long thin frame personifying agitation in every part, and when he wheeled around to face her with his dark and burning eyes, she wanted to hide her own.

"He will never ask you for more than a few months of your time," Kyle said harshly. And immediately knew he'd begun wrong, because of the mutinous set of her lips.

"He can't," he said more gently, and she looked at him with more curiosity than anger as he continued, "Let us say it right out: your Mr. Joshua Dylan can't. Only he's not yours. That's the point. Where is he tonight? Everyone knows. He's with Miss Gloria Van Horn on Long Island. A wealthy, socially correct, and very unmarried young woman. And why so, do you think, if he admires you so?"

She'd lowered her lashes, but snapped them open when his voice came harshly, "Face it. If it isn't to be her, it will be another like her. Lucy, you are an *actress*. You can't afford to forget it now. Oh, I know you may, one day. But you've not met him 'one day'—you know him now."

It was a good point, and they both knew it, but she, he realized, was very much more in love than he'd thought, because he could see from the sudden upward tilt of her chin and her swollen breast that pride was obscuring the truth. She was, he knew, defending her man's love in the time-honored way of all women—by lying to herself about it. She believed her love was, despite all outward appearances, noble, fine, and honorable. There was no way he could compete with Cinderella, Kyle thought as he ran his fingers through his hair and stared up at the ceiling. But she wasn't the only seductive female he knew. There was always Lady Macbeth to be considered; a man's ruin brought about by a woman's ambition was an enchanting theme.

"Oh, yes, well," he said, "so imagine he does throw over his millionairess, and all the others he's so assiduously courting. Imagine then that he proposes marriage, and actually takes you to the altar. Imagine beyond your wedding night, my dear," he said coldly, and she jumped in her seat, because, in truth, in all her daydreaming, she'd never thought further than the events of that unknown, deliciously frightening night.

"What does he get? A wife who is a known actress. He'll have to give up half the invitations he's gotten, half the friends he's made, half the business opportunities that only association with equals can bring a man. Or, of course, he can always leave New York and go back west with you. It's a vast place, plenty of room to hide in," Kyle said easily.

He waited while she thought about that, until the dawning fear on her face gave him his cue to begin again. "A fine wedding gift—a wonderful reward for a man who has worked hard all his life to achieve success—you'll be bringing him, won't you, Lucy? And all," he said with a perceptible sneer, "because he made the human but honorable error of loving you—or," he added lightly, very lightly, "of wanting you."

Timing was everything in the theater. He waited until he judged she'd reached the depths of her self-dislike. After all, being accused of trying to wreck one's true love's life was no easy thing to bear. He reasoned she'd soon be searching for some way around that terrible thought, some way to justify herself. Knowing Lucy, Kyle understood it was harder for her to absolve herself than anyone else. But however good a girl she was, she was a human one. And however decent she was, she was, even though she might deny it, an actress. He'd no doubt of that. She wouldn't have lasted a day in the profession if she were not, at heart, an actress.

He gave her quiet time in which to loathe herself, knowing that like every other sane person, she'd eventually grow sick of it and seize on any excuse that would deflect all that self-disgust and guilt. She needed a reason to turn it around so that it was someone else's fault. He'd give it to her.

"And what will you give up?" he asked softly, as her wondering eyes fastened on his lips, "because, be sure, you will give up something too. Why, Lucy, you'll give up your career. Entirely and forever. You will sacrifice your brilliant talent, your opportunity, your entire chance at fame, at fortune"—her doubting expression showed he was losing her until he added—"your chance to realize your true worth."

She grew still again. His words hung in the night. His deep and dramatic voice went on, almost exultant because he'd found the key at last, as she stared up at him. "Lucy. Think of it. Do you think he'd let you go on tour? To England? Anywhere? Or allow you to stay out every night, night after night, singing and dancing and acting on the stage? No, he'll want you in his bed, or in his kitchen."

He hurried on, because he realized from the flicker in her eyes that he'd made another mistake; the mention of Josh Dylan's bed was a hindrance to his purposes just now. Soon it would be imperative, but not just now.

"Yet, there's a need for you—there's always a crying need for talent in this sad old world," he said, wishing it were true so much that his voice broke a little on the words, giving them poignancy and stress. "You could be bowing to the Queen of England," he said, reaching out his hand to her. "To her consort. You could be taking their applause. You could travel to your grandmama's home in England, in jewels and furs, to tell them all of what a great woman she was, this woman who raised you up to be the great success you are."

His voice soared. His words became her tune, his hand her lifeline; without knowing what she was doing, she arose and stood with him, never seeing the kitchen before her, but instead the unknown glory of the world beyond the footlights that awaited her. His next words opened her eyes to the reality of the small kitchen and the lateness of the hour.

"Marriage? For him: exile. For you: lost opportunity. And for what? My dear, my sweet, my lovely innocent Lucy—forgive me, but I must say it. It's too important to bury for propriety's ignorant sake. After all, what is it that he has most wanted from you all this while? What is it that you yearn to give him? Why, child," he said sorrowfully, as though he were a hundred years old, "you don't even know, do you? What a crime, what a waste, to sacrifice everything for a thing you don't even know. And what does he sacrifice for it? Time. Only a very little time.

"It's the work of a moment, child," he said softly, as she avoided his eyes, "over so quickly, and not even very pleasant for a well-brought-up girl, whomever she engages with—husband or lover. There's really nothing to it, a few embarrassing, panting moments, then an inexplicable relief on the gentleman's part. Only an ache for you."

Shocked, she turned her head abruptly. But didn't speak. She should, she knew, stop him; it was all that was improper to discuss. But in truth, she didn't know the facts of the matter beyond the biology of it, and she wasn't entirely sure she knew all about that. Obviously he did. Most of all, he seemed to care. She needed that above all else. Who else, after all, was there for her to listen to? She'd no family, few friends. She'd felt Josh was her friend, but he frightened as much as comforted her. And now he was gone—to a place that hurt her to think of. Ada was gone, too, and Fanny was no ideal model.

At least Kyle cared enough to speak with her, however improperly he did. And, she thought as she stayed silent, eyes downcast, she was only listening; how much of a sin was it to speak of sin, if you only listened? Anyway, she couldn't ask him to stop, no more than she could leave the room until he'd done. Because the more she heard, the more she understood that he was only speaking of all the things she'd tried not to think about.

Kyle looked at her downcast head and saw the way

that averted cheek blushed, then paled at his words. It would be harder to win her to his own bed after what he'd said, he knew. But then, it would be difficult anyway, after she'd had her heart broken by Josh Dylan. He hadn't lied about that. She was well-brought-up and innocent; it would surprise him very much if she would have any joy the first time she fell. Or the second. But by then it wouldn't matter anymore. If she fell, she'd be, whether she ever fell into his arms afterward or not, forever his. Because if she gave herself away without wedlock, and renounced the idea of it, she'd never love that way again. She was far too pure ever to forgive herself. Dylan, like any other man in his position, would take what he could get without questions, and be glad of it when he did. And be bored, of course, soon after. Purity, honor, and shyness were acceptable in a wife, but Kyle knew that girls like Lucy made terrible mistresses.

"Such a little thing it is that makes a woman's purity," Kyle whispered. "Weightless, but it weighs so heavy on your mind; weightless, but heavy enough to change your life. But not if you don't want it to. An actress can take everything that happens to her—tragedy, heartbreak, betrayal, or rejection—and change all that dross to purest gold upon the great stage. If she loves in vain, the world will love with her another day; every artist needs a broken heart to draw on, nothing's lost when experience is gained," he said hoarsely, his face close to hers, cheek to cheek, as they stared at nothing in the quiet kitchen.

It was almost too dramatic for a matinee. But it was effective in their dim refuge from the night. She was very weary, tired of fighting against so many things she couldn't seem to change, and Kyle was so convincing.

And now, thought Kyle, the finale.

"What if you give in to Josh Dylan and stay with him for a night of love? And give him your virginity?" he asked, so softly the words seemed to come from within her own head and so didn't shock her as they should.

"Why, I'll tell you," he said. "He'll take it and leave you. Why, do you imagine he'd marry you, then?"

She shook her head slowly. She was a good girl, well-brought-up and virtuous. She couldn't imagine anyone wanting to marry a girl who wasn't pure.

"And yet," he asked, with a certain laughter in his voice, "you'd give up virginity in marriage, only to find yourself a slave? Without worth of your own? Without a career? All for a man who wouldn't want you if he could get you, although all he's tried to do since he met you is have you? Lucy," he said, drawing back from her, but holding her shoulders as he gazed into her eyes, "why should you sacrifice anything for that sort of man, much less everything? Better, far better, to give in, to get him out of your system, but give nothing more than your body. I swear, the stage is a truer lover, it cares for nothing but your heart."

She looked up into his dark eyes, close to him alone in the night, the tension in his body communicating to her, the forbidden things they'd spoken of still revolving in her head. He gazed at her hungrily. Everything about him, she understood now, was hungry, a hunger that went beyond any man's she'd ever known—beyond any appetite for food, or drink, or even lust. He seemed to have been born starved, his life an intense search for fulfillment.

"The stage," he repeated, "cares only for your true heart," and then he added, very quietly, "as do I."

He looked down to her lips, his thin hands shaking . . . and then he drew back and released her.

"But as for me," he said solemnly, "what I want isn't so important as what you need. And remember, whatever that is, whenever you decide to avail yourself of it, I'll always be ready to help you. But, Lucy, however I feel, though it break my own heart, I almost urge you to discover it for yourself so that you can be free. You can be. There's a new world for women coming. For brave women. Throw away convention, it is for conventional girls. Because, don't be misled. Few girls who give up all for love have as much to give up as you do."

He'd spoken all the truths he knew, as well as all the lies he had to. Her face showed she'd ponder them. There was nothing more he could do; he knew when it was time for the curtain to fall. He let her go entirely then, and she tried to smile at him, and then, backing up, she went to the door. She looked back once, with a tremulous smile, before she left him alone. Then he wheeled and pounded his knotted fist on the table, causing Duncan to spring up in alarm and slink away to a corner of the room.

It would be damned difficult, Kyle thought, angry with himself for the thought, to see her go to Dylan's bed. Far harder than urging her to it had been. But however difficult, he'd endure it. Because he wanted her, and he was very used to hunger, to doing without so that he could have what he wanted later.

18

HE WISHED it were early morning, so they could ride to the sea and talk as they walked along the beach. There the wind could whip their words away and their expressions might be read as reactions to the sun or the spray. But instead, Josh had to meet with Gloria in a quiet sun-filled morning room, because time had run out. It was almost time for her to perform as hostess at luncheon, past time for him to have been on his way. It was also the worst time for what he had to say, even if he'd been entirely sure of what this was. Always gracious, she made it easier.

"I understand my father proposed to you this morning," she said.

He heard no laughter in her voice, and saw none at all in her eyes, and so the hope he'd had of joking it all away with some foolish "But this is so sudden . . ." died on his lips.

She looked good this morning, the sun lending a glow to her hair; her eyes—a blue so light they seemed to be only reflecting that color, he saw now—gravely searched his face. She seemed more fragile too; the fussy, frilly high-necked apricot morning gown she wore made her appear more delicate than the highly colored, fashionable embroidery-encrusted brocades she usually wore. He thought he might tell her that, because he couldn't think of any other thing to say at once. He wasn't used to being courted, less accustomed to hurting women's feelings, and still unsure of his own, for all he'd thought he'd known what he was doing all these weeks.

"I asked him not to," she said, "but he was insistent. He's impatient, concerned. You mustn't blame him. Please understand that I don't ask for an immediate decision, as he does."

"But once a question's been brought up, it's like hitting a volley over the net in tennis—like you taught me. There's got to be a return, or the game can't go on," he said, as much to himself as to her.

She bowed her head. This woman never had to hold her breath to bottle up her feelings; everything she said was clear, cogent, and carefully considered before it was ever spoken. It was impossible for him to know just how much her feelings were involved. Her slender neck was bent, her head was down; he turned his hat round and round in his hands, feeling awkward and crude, like some rough beast who'd offended her. When she raised her face again, he could see nothing of what she was thinking.

She was disappointed that he hadn't leapt to the bait. But not devastated. She'd never been in love, and even now didn't know if that was precisely what she felt for Joshua Dylan. But she wanted him as her husband. It wasn't just his looks; they thrilled her, but that actually wasn't so very good, since she'd been taught that thrilling things were impermanent and perhaps not for her. But she knew she'd never be ashamed of such a clever man; he'd never squander her fortune either, and she felt, as her father did, that he'd give her strong and clever children. If her father had no son, this would be the next-best thing.

Gloria had no illusions, those who believe they have everything are not in the habit of daydreaming. She knew she was neither beautiful nor enticing. But she also knew she didn't need to be. She'd always gotten what she'd wanted, but was enough her father's daughter to realize that to do so now she might have to compromise, taking him on his terms, not hers. That was acceptable. The acquisition, as her father always said, was more important than the manner of it.

"It would be terrible if Father's well-meaning interference made you hesitate to see me again," she said calmly.

"Worse if you thought I didn't care for you—at all," he added hastily, threading his way through his answer, feeling foolish for the way he had to watch his words lest he commit himself unawares, "because I do—it's only that I haven't been thinking along those lines yet."

A slight frown crossed his face, because as soon as he'd said it he knew he was lying. Of course he'd been thinking along those lines—from the moment he'd been introduced to Jacob's daughter. Now that he knew her, he no longer thought of timber, steel, mines, railroads, and the "Four Hundred" when he looked at her, because if he hadn't been able to get past the fact of her material wealth and social standing, he'd never have continued to see her. But he had, and had begun to enjoy it too.

Josh gazed down at her and couldn't understand why he just didn't laugh now—take her in his arms and say the hell with it, kiss her, and leave the room an engaged man. She was bright and handsome, well-bred and charming, the empire she brought with her wouldn't take up much room in the marriage bed. Some stubborn impulse held him back. He told himself he didn't have time to investigate it now. He told himself it was his pride. He'd bought enough women to know that it was hard to respect anything you paid for as much as something you'd won. And he'd a notion to be more than respected by his wife. Or so, at least, he told himself as he stood in the morning room growing impatient with himself.

"Is it that actress?" she asked softly, so placidly that he didn't understand at first. "Everyone knows about her," she said on a little sigh as she turned to the window. "New York's huge, but never big enough to hide yourself in if your face is known to those who watch for it. She's said to be beautiful. I understand what's happening," she went on with a slight frown, "although I don't really understand why it is that men require, sometimes, that which respectable women, even their beloved wives, can't give them. Sometimes I think they prefer that respectable women *not* give it to them—it adds a certain quality to the thing that gives it savor—or so, at least, I've been told."

She turned back to look at him with a small tired smile and shrugged. Her narrow apricot-draped shoulders rose in a helpless little motion, and he stepped forward, moved to put his arms around her to comfort her, reassure her, and make her smile again. But he froze in place as he realized that was exactly *all* that he was tempted to do with her, and so dared not, not now.

"Please understand. I don't condemn you. It's common enough," she continued sadly. "Even Father has his interests. They've never touched us. Those of us who understand about these things, that is to say. Mother never has. She has headaches and spends her life on her couch, remembering her youth instead of accepting her adulthood. I'd rather you didn't have to resort to such . . . women," she said softly, "but there it is. Men sometimes do. I don't complain now, and so long as you never flaunted it, I'd never complain in the future. What I don't know will never hurt me, and if it helped you, I'd be content."

Josh was as appalled as angered, and so was incapable of answering her immediately. He'd never seen her so vulnerable, or felt so much so himself. He didn't know whether to defend Lucy first and absolve himself after, or to just turn on his heel and walk out. But now, at least, he could see that in some way Gloria ached, whether she knew she was revealing it or not. For all he was almost as furious at her estimate of Lucy as guilty because she'd so very nearly been right about him, he couldn't hurt Gloria now.

But he also couldn't take her as his wife. Suddenly he knew that, and knew it absolutely. It wasn't just because he realized he'd been thinking of Lucy long before her name had been brought up. Or because of the painful tangle of emotions he'd felt when it had been. It was simply because when he came right down to it, as this moment had forced him to do—it was simple. But then, for him, rare as it was, love always was.

Jacob's daughter was everything he'd come to New York to win; she embodied everything he thought he'd ever wanted in a wife, and was exactly the sort of woman he ought to marry. But that had been in his dreams of a wife. Now he saw he needed a whole lot less—and much more. He could be very happy with her. That was certain. But she'd used the word "content" just now. And all at once he understood. He might be very happy with her, but he doubted he'd ever be content.

"You should be greedier," he finally said softly, sadly. "You should want more, you deserve more. I wouldn't want to keep my 'interest' after I got married, any more than I'd want my wife to keep hers. And I don't know about that extra 'savor' either—appears to me marriage has enough savor just as it is—don't think I could stand more. I've been looking for sharing, myself. And more," he added gently.

She didn't answer. He knew all his time had run out now. He felt a pang, quickly suppressed, and it wasn't just for her sake, because he knew the taste of regret. For all he'd only acted on his honor, as he'd always done, he knew what he'd given up, and he was only human. He wondered if Jacob would ever recognize him in public again. It would be damned uncomfortable next time they met. Even so, unaccountably, his spirits were already rising. He marveled at himself. He'd just thrown away a fortune; that must have been why he felt so light.

She looked at him consideringly, and he braced himself.

"Shall we see you at the Anderson's soiree next Friday?" she asked politely, and he knew then that he'd made the right decision, because he didn't understand her at all. She should've slapped him. Or at least walked out on him in actuality, as he'd rejected her by his words. He wished she would.

But he took her hand, gave an indeterminate answer, and fled. He knew where he was going at last, and why, and couldn't wait to get there now.

Her neck ached, her arms were numb, and she'd smiled for so long her mouth felt permanently cramped. But Lucy was exultant. The photographer had been a perfectionist. There'd been times in the past two days that she'd wanted to scream, drop her pose, and stalk off his platform, right out of his studio. But Kyle said he was a genius, and that one should be prepared to suffer for art. She wondered how much art it was to wear low-cut gowns and show so much ankle, but her mind had eventually grown as numb as her limbs, because she'd allowed it. Publicity, as Kyle said, got you everything. And flattery, he knew, achieved everything else.

He'd arranged for Lucy to have an abundance of flattery. So far, most of it had come in the form of photographs. The famous photographer Kyle had hired had considered her very closely. So closely, she was newly fascinated with herself. Now she knew her left side was superior to her right; her nose looked best with a little shadowing, and her hair cried out for the print to be hand-colored. Now, even before the finished prints had been shown to her, she lingered at her mirror, assessing her face as she never had before.

She pouted at herself in her mirror. And then giggled, because she'd never studied herself pouting before yesterday. Then she grinned, because Mr. Gerard, the photographer, had said her pout was ravishing, but her grin was "sunshine." If she hadn't heard Mrs. Fergus call her from downstairs she might have gone on posing for hours. But she did, so she raised her head and after giving a conspiratorial nod to her reflection, hurried downstairs. She wanted to be on time to say goodbye to Bayard, who was leaving them to go on tour with Beck's Players.

The company was breaking up, abandoning the sinking *Pinafore*—or trying to. But as yet only Bayard had gotten himself a new position. The others in the company were very spiteful about it, both to Bayard's face and behind his back. Or at least Lucy thought so. But then, she'd never experienced the way people who lived in each other's pockets for weeks coped with change, and the threat of more.

"Ah, my Josephine, come to say farewell," Bayard said when Lucy came down into the hall where he stood, his packed bags all in a heap, his fellow performers in a ragged circle ranged around him.

"Sweetheart, I will miss you," he said, catching her up in his arms and kissing her, chuckling when he felt her fury and embarrassment as he deepened the kiss, knowing she'd never dare to kick him or bite his tongue, because then the others would know what he'd done. It was only good manners that kept her civil when she staggered back from him.

"I'd rather shake hands, if you don't mind," Lester said, eyeing Lucy with sympathy.

Bayard clapped on his hat and patted it as answer, before saying, as he drew on his gloves, "Anyone who wishes to correspond with me while I'm on the road may do so through Beck's New York offices."

"Ah yes, the 'road'," Ned said with a nasty grin and a wink.

"It may not be New York," Bayard said sweetly, "but we end our tour in San Francisco, and then play there for a guaranteed two months."

The others fell silent. A guaranteed two months was too enviable to jest about.

"Good luck to you, Bayard," Fanny said quietly, kissing his cheek, and then stepped back so that the other players who'd come to see him off could give their own subdued farewells.

Bayard's hackney came, collected him, and they waved him off.

When Bayard left, the gloom dissipated. He may have gone off to months of regular meals, and they might be left with a production on its last legs. But he was gone now. And they were here, and they were, after all, actors. So they cheered themselves and would have gone off in high spirits to face the day, if Kyle hadn't spoken again.

"Oh, Lucy," Kyle said, "by the way, Mr. Gerard wants you back in his studio again this afternoon. Some nonsense about how he thinks he can improve on that pose with you on a swing. Can you be ready after lunch?"

"Franklin Gerard?" Ned asked, before she could answer.

"*The* Franklin Gerard?" Jewel asked as Kyle nodded and said quickly, "Yes. I only hope he's half as good as his prices. Oh! My feckless tongue!" he exclaimed apologetically, as though someone had protested, although no one of his audience breathed, much less interrupted him. "I'm at a loss. I hadn't meant to bring it up, not that I'd tried to keep it a secret, but I didn't think . . ." He spread his hands helplessly. "Since it is out . . ." He sighed. "Ah, terribly sorry, but when we're dealing with such as Gerard, my budget can stretch for only one of you. Lucy has no portfolio at all, you know.

Just reviews and handbills. She needs . . . Oh, but you're all professionals, I'm sure you understand."

"Oh, perfectly," Lester said quietly at last, as the others nodded, shifting in their places, some darting little looks of dislike at Lucy, others ignoring her as pointedly as if there were something distasteful to see where she stood.

"Well, then," Lester said, smiling as gallantly as a soldier going off to war, "I've some errands before curtain time to see to. See you later, friends."

The others didn't look like Lucy's friends as they left. Most continued to ignore her. Ned brushed past her, head high; Jewel marched upstairs without so much as a backward smirk; only Fanny stood looking at Lucy's confusion. When Bayard's replacement stopped Kyle for a question about stage placement, Fanny came to Lucy's side.

"I see. You're the only one staying on with Kyle. My dear," she said, taking Lucy's hand, "I thought a place in a true acting company would be your only salvation . . . but then, how good is my advice, after all? I've not turned out so very well, have I? But oh, my dear, be careful—be very sure—if not of the wisdom of what you do, then of your comfort in doing it. That's the thing you must live with long after, the only thing no one else can advise you on. I'll see you later," she said hurriedly as she saw Kyle bearing down on them, frowning.

"Jealousy," Kyle said on a long exhalation when he was left alone with Lucy. "Yes, plain jealousy. Don't look at me that way, child, as though you'd stubbed your toe and believed yourself too big to cry. They behaved abominably. I oughtn't to have slipped and mentioned it, but I erred, and did. Now they know you're bound for greatness, as they're not.

"Jealousy," he sighed. "It's epidemic in the theater, like ghosts and backstage mice. Be glad you won't have long to put up with it," he said bracingly, giving her rigid form a brotherly hug before releasing her, for all he yearned to draw her closer in less comradely ways. "In truth, and this is just between us, I don't know how much longer we can keep *Pinafore* going. I've been struggling to keep it afloat for their sakes, but seeing how they treated you, I don't know why I bother. Now, go put on your best hat: Mr. Gerard, and fate, await thee."

She bit her lip, wavered, and then flew up the stairs to do his bidding.

Good, he thought, relaxing, a good beginning. Ada was gone, and now he'd just severed Lucy's connections to the rest of the *Pinafore* company in a relatively painless fashion. Some doctors might believe in the theory of counterirritation—causing a blister on the cheek to take the mind off the pain in a tooth. But Kyle believed in a pleasanter remedy for a hurt—to outbalance it with pleasure. Attention and flattery were, for an actress, sheerest pleasure. Under his tutelage, she was at last beginning to behave as what she was, an actress. She'd hesitated to obey him. After a pause, she'd hurried up the stairs. But first, he'd gleefully noted, she'd glanced in the mirror to see how she was taking all this.

Now there was only one more obstacle.

19

HE'D SEEN IT too many times to count, but tonight it was as if he were seeing an entirely different operetta. It was true that some of the words had been changed since Josh had seen it a week before, but even so they were familiar enough and couldn't account for this new sense of strangeness he felt. The cast had changed too. Bayard Skyler was gone, as was the old man, Ned, and Josh saw several new faces in both the male and female choruses. Yet even these things could have been accepted had there not been something else, some other, intangible alteration. Because when Lucy came gliding out on the stage, for all he relaxed and rejoiced to see her, there was something different about her, though for the life of him he couldn't place it.

Her costume was the same, her voice as unerringly sweet as ever, her face as lovely as he remembered it to be. But maybe, he thought uncomfortably, it was that she knew it as well as he did now. Because as her song went on, it seemed to him that the difference was that she played with—and not to—the audience tonight. What was missing was her shy, innocent pleasure in their enthusiastic reaction to her. What was added was her sly, amused acceptance of it. And when her eyes met his, in that one sparkling instant, she didn't smile and glance away, as she'd always done in the past, but smiled in triumph, he thought, before she turned away. That, he decided, smiling to himself at last, had to be just his own imagining. No one in the world knew why he was here tonight, or what he planned to do; he himself was still astonished by it. So he sat back, half-attending to this revised *Pinafore* as he allowed himself to imagine the rest of the coming night.

There was, after all, little reason to watch the performance when Lucy wasn't onstage. He didn't even bother to judge the new players, and not just because of his preoccupation. He'd seen the real *Pinafore* last night.

It wasn't so much that it was better than this one. It went beyond that. The sets, the sights, the sounds—there was no comparison at all. Even the burlesqued version he'd seen had been better, because it had been blatant satire. This production, he saw now, wasn't even as honest as a mistake or as flattering as an imitation. Neither fool's gold nor silver, it had no value at all because it was dishonest. It was the cheapest kind of imitation: the kind that ignores the source it copies from while pretending to be as good as the original.

All of it was so inferior as to be shoddy . . . all of it, he thought, except for Miss Lucy Rose. Last night he'd seen the performances of Blanche Roosevelt and Rosina Brandram, acknowledged flowers of the English theater. It was true Blanche Roosevelt's Josephine was a revelation; it wasn't only her style and accents that were perfection; her voice and acting were suited to the role as perfectly as her costuming. She was a true professional; watching her had been a delight. And yet, and yet, he thought, as he saw Lucy before him now, he wasn't a complete fool; it couldn't be only his own blinded heart that made him feel that for all their talent, none of the English ladies of the stage had been as lovely, graceful, and compelling as she was. The audience around him seemed to agree, and he heard, with proud pleasure, how their applause interrupted the performance after her solo.

But for all its enthusiasm, it wasn't a very long pause for tribute, because, he noted, turning and frowning, it wasn't that large an audience anymore. For the first time, he saw vacant seats in the dim theater. Those empty spaces disconcerted him as much as a beautiful woman with a gap-toothed smile would have done before he'd taken such a proprietary interest in the Stratton's *Pinafore*.

At least the night passed quickly. With fewer pauses for audience laughter and cheers, the *Pinafore* sailed along unimpeded, and so was over long before it had

ever ended before. Josh regretted it for Lucy's sake, but
for his own, he was delighted to be admitted to her dressing room at such an unexpectedly early hour. Now she
had no excuse to refuse his company for a late dinner.
Not only had he sent word before the performance to
prepare her, but now the night lay out before them for
their pleasure as if it were a blameless Sunday, as if it
were the holiday he felt it to be.

"Josh!" she cried, coming out from behind the dressing-room screen, her hand held out to him as limply and
gracefully as a handkerchief, her face all smiles, every
inch the delighted actress receiving her devoted fan—
every bit nothing like she'd ever been with him before.

It was a game, he decided; he'd been gone less than a
week—even the weather couldn't change so profoundly
in that short a time. A game, or maybe not even that.
Maybe he only saw it as such because he hadn't seen
anything remotely like her in days—no woman at Jacob
Van Horn's house had been so vibrant, glowing, and,
yes, theatrically beautiful. Add the further fact that he
was brimming with his own secrets tonight, and he wasn't
surprised to find his perceptions so heightened and distorted. He grinned. He was no actor, but he appreciated
theater too.

He took that extended hand in his, and then, running
his hand up her arm, drew her close, enveloped her in
his embrace, tilted her backward, and kissed her most
dramatically. Not being an actor, within seconds he'd forgotten the effect he'd been going for, and was lost in
the warm, spontaneous reaction he'd surprised in her.
Moments later, she struggled free. When she looked up
at him, it was the familiar Lucy he knew and delighted
in that he still held lightly. Her face was pink, and she
bit her lower lip as he smiled down at her. She was
breathless when she was able to speak, but his smile
faded when she did, because her words surprised him
again.

"I'm so glad you came," she said.

He'd expected a protest, a denial, at least an excuse
for her enthusiastic participation in his greeting, and was
prepared to soothe her and explain it away, as always.
But a fellow had no right to complain about getting what

he'd asked for, so Josh put the niggling doubt aside and celebrated their successful reunion instead. He held her hands and grinned back at her.

"Dinner, Miss Lucy Rose," he said emphatically. "A long, delicious dinner at 'Monico's, and then a bracing ride in my new carriage, and then . . . you have to agree on someplace we can go to talk in private, because I have to talk with you alone . . ."

He was about to add lightly, ". . . but after you're fed properly." He was going to continue by saying, ". . . if you can keep everyone out but Duncan, your place is as good as mine," and he was prepared to promise to leave his hotel-room door open and pay the whole hotel staff of chambermaids or a German band to stand in his hall for propriety's sake, if she wanted, if she'd only come with him. But all the words died before they were spoken.

"Oh, yes, I'd love that," Lucy said gaily as she snatched up her cape and smiled up at him, "and since the new lodgers at Mrs. Fergus' have no sense of privacy at all, I guess we'll have to go to your hotel."

"It's amazing, you know," Lucy said, continuing with her bright chatter as the first course was removed, "but I've never liked oysters. I may be the only New Yorker that doesn't. You, after all, are from the West, and yet you obviously love them," she said, watching the waiter remove his plate full of empty shells, "but I can't swallow them, and it isn't just their squishiness, I don't like them fried or steamed or—"

"I came from New York originally, remember?" Josh began, only to be cut off immediately by her trill of laughter as she cried, "Oh, yes! I'd forgotten. Well, then it makes sense . . . Ah, but how lovely—soup. I like every kind of soup, or at least I can't think of any I don't," she went on as he gazed at her across the table, as troubled as she seemed ecstatic at the thought of soup.

But she didn't seem to enjoy her food so much as she was inspired to new heights of garrulousness by the menu. Because she ate very little and talked incessantly. She prattled through the hors d'oeuvres, reported on the new players in her *Pinafore* over the fish, made commentary on all her fellow diners through the beef and lamb, and the entrées of chicken wings, lamb chops, and stuffed artichokes were accompanied by three wines, several sauces, and Lucy's unrelenting bright conversation. Monologue, rather than conversation, Josh corrected himself, because she didn't seem to need any sort of encouragement or reply in order to keep it flowing.

She was upset; he knew that. He could only sigh and watch her animated face, and feel a nagging guilt, because why shouldn't she be ill-at-ease with him? He'd done nothing but stalk her under the guise of befriending her, and now that he realized that, it was a wonder to him that she'd put up with him for so long. The least he could do, he decided, as she fell silent at last as the waiters brought out some sorbet to cool their palates in preparation for the duck and quail to come, giving her a chance to rest her tongue, was to tolerate her nervous chatter, since he deserved to suffer every bit of anxiety she displayed.

Anyway, he thought, it was enough for him to watch her, for now. She wore a deep amber patterned velvet evening dress, cut low enough so that each time she drew in breath for another interminable sentence, he could console himself by watching the effect on a tantalizing expanse of her exposed white breast. The gown fitted so snugly he thought it little wonder she couldn't do more than move the endless parade of food around on her plate, and he realized, with as much amusement as shock, that for the first time, he wanted to see her out of her corset, if only so that she could eat and breathe freely.

He was very quiet tonight, Lucy thought as she swallowed down another glass of wine. But then, she hadn't given him much chance to talk, and she wished she could stop so that he could say something. But she was so nervous she found that Kyle's trick of breath-holding didn't work tonight. Every time she glanced across the table and saw his thoughtful gray gaze fixed on her, saw that perfectly imperfect strong and uniquely rugged face so somber as he studied her, her heart rate picked up, her palms grew cold, then warm, and the words began to spill out once more. It wasn't only that she was staggered at how wonderful it felt to be with him again. That alone would have been enough to set her babbling. It was that she knew what she was going to do with him later tonight, and was as terrified as she was determined to go through with it, and yet didn't know how she could bear to, or not to, any longer.

She peered over the top of her water glass at the glittering diners around her. She wasn't thinking of dinner at all—she was musing about what all these elegant men and women did with each other when they were alone after dinner. Everyone in the restaurant, she decided, bar none, had done it. All the waiters, and every exotic woman there, and all the men, of course. She'd bet she was the only one who hadn't, so obviously, she reasoned, it was as simple as it was commonplace, and left no permanent mark. She brooded, grateful that the waiter was serving just then, as she realized that no matter how hard it was to read or hear about the subject, it was how the human race got on and had always done, so obviously everyone did it and knew it, even if it wasn't polite to talk about. The thought of such a vast conspiracy of silence on such an important matter humbled even as it chagrined her. It frightened her more. But she was determined.

Because Kyle was right. She couldn't go on the way she'd done any longer. She'd thought about Kyle's advice constantly since he'd spoken with her, every lonely day and disturbed night that Josh had been gone, courting his proper young society woman. Lucy accepted that she couldn't go home to Brooklyn anymore. Nor could she attract any proper gentleman as yet. Not because she hadn't the financial resources to strike out on her own, away from the theater. That had been a pleasant lie she'd told herself; she saw that now. But because she knew she'd never find anyone who enthralled her the way that Joshua Dylan did. She loved the way he spoke—the way he did, she corrected herself, when she gave him a chance to, that was. She liked his sense of humor and his graciousness, as well as his obvious strength and strength of character. She agreed with most of his opinions, and respected his education, for all he belittled it. She liked that lack of bragging in him too. She loved to

look at his face, his form; she felt complete when he was
with her, and absolutely lorn when he was not, for all
she was as frightened by his attraction as she was thrilled
by it. She supposed she loved him. And that was that.

But she knew what he wanted from her, and now knew
where she was bound, as well as where he was. And they
weren't going in the same direction. She could either stop
seeing him or give in to him. In either case, she'd not
see him for much longer; she understood that. Although
she might hate him for it, she couldn't blame him for it
either. Or stop feeling the way she did about him, for
that matter. Kyle was right in so many ways.

Ordinary rules no longer applied to her, she was no
longer an ordinary person, that was true too, just as Kyle
had told her and as she kept telling herself. She was an
actress; that would be her life in the foreseeable future.
It was as much her salvation as her sorrow. And her
virginal state held her back in many ways; fear always
did. Kyle had spoken nothing but truth. She had to know
about it so she could be done with it and get on with her
life. And so if she had to be initiated, it had to be Josh
who did it, and not some other man, some other years
from now. So it might as well be tonight. She was as
unhappy as she was excited at the thought of it, and
determined to get on with it, and all those contradictions
had set her tongue on wheels.

"It's an amazing way to dine," Josh commented at last
as he watched another untouched plate being taken from
her. "It's like you're some kind of food critic, here to
approve the style of the dish before they take it away to
give to someone else. It's to eat, Lucy, not judge. Won't
you try some pastry, at least?" he asked, gesturing to
the tray of miniature minarets and towers and elaborate
fantasies of cream and cake that had been put out for
their approval.

"Or mousse, or petits fours, or ices . . . Lucy," he said
in exasperation, "you have to eat something. Or the chef
will come out of the kitchen with a cleaver to find out
why not. At least, that's the way any cook worth his salt
would handle it back home if any of the hands just
looked and didn't taste a thing."

"Well, the hands didn't wear corsets, did they?" she

asked haughtily, very much the great lady, ruining the
effect by the way the warm color crept up her throat and
tinted even her earlobes when she heard what she'd said.

Then he laughed, so she could. And that, after all the
wine and mindless gabbling she'd done, was the thing
that relaxed her at last, and made her feel better about
everything that was to come.

His guest looked about as relaxed as a woman sitting
on tacks, but from what he'd seen that one time he'd
pried her from her gown, she was probably sitting in
worse, Josh thought. He sighed, crossed the room to give
Lucy her glass of champagne, and then seated himself on
the couch next to her. He hoped it was his hotel rooms
that made her so uneasy, and not himself. He eyed her
thoughtfully. Not for the first time, he wished he could
free her from all the restrictions surrounding her—from
her absurd underpinnings to the foolish cage of convention that society forced upon them both. He wanted to
speak with her the way he yearned to hold her again,
heart to heart, stripped of all impediments, in absolute
honesty. Her first words gave him such hopes that he
stopped sipping his champagne and stared hard at her.

"I've missed you so much, Josh," she said softly, looking up at him and then down to her glass again, "I know
you had to leave, but I missed you so."

It wasn't poetry, but it stirred him more than elo-
quence could. She said nothing after it, didn't so much
as hold her breath. He let out all of his in one exhalation,
put down his glass, reached for her, and took her, unpro-
testing, into his arms.

"You can't know how much I missed you, no, Lucy,
oh, Lucy, you can't know," he said into her hair, and
then, because there was so much more to say, he kissed
her.

The astonishing thing was that he'd always thought he
was a man of some intelligence, and more control, and
yet it took him almost five minutes to realize something
was very wrong, and even after that, a few more to stop
what he was doing. But her lips were warm and her arms
went around his neck, and if she didn't hold his head
down to hers, she didn't hold him back. Her mouth was

yielding, and though she flinched, for a second, at first, she never protested when he eased the top of her gown down, no more than she did when his other hand slid up from the bottom of it. Her scent was springtime, and her skin was as soft as he remembered, although it stretched delightfully taut over those parts he treasured that were a wonderful combination of soft and firm together. She didn't initiate anything, but neither did she resist anything, and he would've gone on doing whatever he wished—and he wished for more and more—if he hadn't, somewhere in the last functioning part of his reasoning brain, realized this dream of lovemaking was actually reality.

That was when he drew back, his arms trembling with the effort of doing so. Looking down at the glorious disarray he'd created, the tousled and rumpled beautiful woman in his arms, half-out of her gown, and then down at himself, half out of his mind, he spoke again, at last.

"What in God's green name are you doing, Lucy Markham?" he roared.

She'd just gotten to the point where she'd been able to forget what she was doing. His lips and hands and body had taken all her doubts away. Her fears remained, of course, but they were as though outside of herself then, like abandoned waifs looking in through a window at what their owner was doing with the handsome man on the couch. Then he'd stopped and sat back. Now he was staring at her. And shouting at her, and she didn't know what he wanted anymore, although she'd just begun to realize what she really wanted. So of course, she felt shame to equal her confusion.

"I wanted . . . what you did," she said. And fell silent, amazed at how well the truth sounded.

"Oh, Lord. I'm sorry, Lucy, my love, I am," he said, closing his eyes, taking her back into his arms, covering her state of undress with himself, though he held her gently, compassionately, and in no way the same way he'd held her moments before.

But now she found that upset her even more, and she wriggled in his clasp, as though to remind him. He remembered, but he sighed, put her at arm's length, tugged up her gown, ran his hands over her hair in a futile attempt to arrange it, before he took in a breath himself, and eased away from her.

"I meant this to be memorable, Lucy. But not this way." He smiled again, but it was such a rueful smile, she reached out to him. He took her hand and held it firmly.

"Lucy, honey. I want you to remember this as something fine. Somethin' very fine," he said, his drawl returning, his voice slowed with emotion. She nodded, because she agreed, as he went on, "Because in the years to come, no matter how good those years may be, maybe there'll be regrets anyhow, we're only human. I think it'll help if you can always remember that it was a decision you made without coercion, freely, and with your whole heart and mind."

She closed her eyes to feel tears prickling behind her lids. How well he understood; no wonder she loved him. She'd made the right decision, whatever came of it; she could never go wrong giving herself to this man, and she began to feel her fears evaporating as she opened her lips to say yes, to begin in joy what she'd begun in doubt before.

But his next words made her eyes fly open as her mouth did, although she was too astonished to speak.

"I've given you a hard time, my love," he said softly. "But comfort you, 'cause I gave myself a harder one, I think. I saw what you were, despite what you were, and yet I tried to lie to myself about you. No more. I want you too much. It's too important. First, I want you to forgive me, Lucy, for trying so damned hard to believe you were less than you were so I could have you and not have you too, with a clean conscience. But I found there's only one way I want you—every way. 'I want you to marry me, Lucy. I'll try to be the best husband in the East or West, or whatever direction you look in. Just say you'll marry me."

But she said nothing, only stared at him, amazed.

"I . . . I'll be faithful, if that's what's bothering you, I can't help it, it's in my bones to be, not just because I'd never hurt you," he said, wondering what it was that made her eyes so wide and startled. He was newly uncomfortable because he'd fully expected to have her back in his arms by now, only stopping long enough to put the ring he'd bought on her finger, willing to let whatever happened happen after that, after he'd honorably staked his claim in the most traditional way he knew.

"I thought you wanted to marry her—that Miss Van Horn everyone talked about," she said, saying the first thing that came into her mind after the silence had gone on too long and impelled her to speak.

"No, no," he said, taken aback. "I might've had some ideas along those lines . . . but you sure changed everything I was thinking," he answered, laughing at the truth of that.

"I thought you wanted a society wife, someone with a long pedigree, someone at least respectable. I'm an actress, Josh, remember?" she asked, watching him closely.

There was something stirring at the edges of his mind that worried him more than the bizarre way she was answering his proposal, but he saw her pallor. His heart filled, and he answered her as he'd answered his own last lingering doubts in the nights since he'd made up his mind.

"Lucy," he said tenderly, "how could I know what I wanted until I saw what there was to want? As for pedigrees . . . I still don't know much about society, but I know nature. I know all purebred lines start out with a matched pair of mongrels. It's *lasting* that makes them thoroughbreds, Lucy. Nothing else. My father came from a country that worshiped pure bloodlines, but if he'd believed in that, why, he'd never have come here, and I wouldn't be here. I hope I'm not less than he was. He said this was a good place to live because a man could make his own life. Make mine—marry me. You're an actress, but now I know why you're that, and what you are aside from that, and you're respectable enough for me. You're a lady. Almost too much of one," he added, grinning, "because I think you trusted me too far. I'm glad I'm here to ride herd on me."

He sat back, smiling, and his hand went to the small fob pocket over his heart, where he'd put the ring so he'd have it ready for her. He'd only gotten two fingers thrust into the top of the pocket when his hand froze there.

"Ah, Josh," she said, biting her lip, looking aside, "I . . . I didn't expect this."

And then he remembered the puzzle he'd tried not to think about moments before.

"What did you expect?" he asked quietly, but his voice had grown colder, and his eyes were gray as sleet.

"Well . . . you know," Lucy said, shrugging, causing her gown to slip down, glad of the chance to pull it up so she could speak as if to her shoulder and not have to meet his eyes. "I thought you only wanted . . . what you've wanted all this time."

It was very quiet in the room. Never able to bear silence, any more than she could bear to look at his still, impassive face, she went on at once, "I never thought you'd propose. And you kept after me, so I thought I'd . . . well, Josh, I thought I'd take what I could get before I had to say good-bye. I didn't want to leave with nothing," she said, her voice breaking.

"Oh, Lucy," he said gently, pulling her close, his voice as soft as the wide, beautifully shaped mouth she focused on as it came so near to her own, "I'm so sorry. I've been selfish. But I'm glad of it now, because that's what made me see the light. That's just it. I realized you leave me with nothing when you're not with me. No more problems, love," he said against her lips. "Forgive me, marry me, never leave me again."

She could have gone on for the moment, only responding to him, without another thought or word. She wanted to, sensing she wasn't far from what she'd wanted to discover, and a great deal more. But she'd convinced herself of many things in the last lonely nights; she'd decided on her course in life. With Kyle's help, she'd built new dreams to take the place of the ones she'd thought she had to give up. And they were very sweet. Now she was unable to turn her thoughts, reconcile her doubts. It would be even harder to lose them altogether in his embrace, as she always lost herself there.

She thought it was her honesty that made her speak just as his lips touched hers, but it might have been her lingering fears, or even the last tattered remnants of her

conscience flailing against her Sunday-school memories
that forced the words from her. But she did speak, and
her words stopped everything as soon as he'd heard and
comprehended them.

"I'll stay with you tonight, Josh. I want to. But I don't
think I can marry you."

He pulled back and stared at her.

"I'm grateful to you," she said, looking everywhere
but at him, flustered, even more uncomfortable with herself than she'd been at that final second when she'd
resolved to let him make love to her, "but," she said,
plucking at a loose thread on the arm of the couch that
she'd just almost laid herself down on to accommodate
him, "I don't think I can. Maybe before, but now . . .
I'm an *actress* now, Josh," she said, drawing herself up
as though she drew courage from her words.

She raised her head, and even though her hair was
mussed and her lips swollen from his kisses, she seemed
regal, dignified, and inviolate. "I have a career to think
of now," she said. "You wouldn't let me marry you and
then go on performing, would you?" she asked quickly,
her confidence in what she was saying rapidly fading
beneath his growing incredulous stare. "I mean, to go on
tour to Britain and the Continent and such, would you?"
she added before he could answer the first part of her
question.

She paused, unable to read anything in his closed face.
He shook his head.

"No," he said calmly after a moment's thought, "I
wouldn't. I wouldn't marry you and leave you for months
at a time. I wouldn't pass my nights in the arms of other
women, even in pretense, much less travel the world with
them without you if I could help it. And I wouldn't want
you to do that to me."

"But you see?" she cried triumphantly, sitting up
straight. "There it is! That's just it! *You* wouldn't have
to. But *I* have to give up my chances for happiness just
so I can make love to you—is that fair?"

"I see," he said softly, though a faint line appeared
between his eyes as his dark gold brows swooped down.
"You don't love me?"

"Oh, I do, Josh, I do, with all my heart," she said,

wondering why he couldn't see the whole of it as clearly as she did, the way she'd thought it and rehearsed it over and again in her own mind since she'd first heard it. "But why should I be the one who has to sacrifice for love?"

"But you were willing to go to bed with me?" he asked, ignoring what she said, as though he were still reasoning out what she'd said before.

"Yes, don't you see? Kyle said . . ." She hesitated, because his head snapped up at that and his lips tightened. "But it's true enough," she said proudly. "My life's different now. You yourself thought I was no better than I should be when you met me—and after you met me, actually, up until just now, right? Just because I was an actress. I wasn't like that, but it's true that those in the theater don't mind that sort of thing, because they understand every experience we have can go to creating our art." She paused; it had sounded better the way Kyle had put it, but it still sounded like music to her—even better, like applause.

"If I . . . stay . . . with you," she said in a more subdued voice, avoiding his eyes, "it will be because I love you. And I want to learn what love is like with you— only you. But if you love me, you can't ask me to give up my dreams, any more than I'd ask that of you. Not all girls who give up everything for love have as much to give up as I do," she explained, remembering Kyle's words, and savoring them.

She began to fidget again, because she couldn't tell what he was thinking from his face. But she saw his hands. She'd often admired their grace before, the way they could hold the reins so capably, the way that he could touch her so gently that she'd never have thought it had been a caress from one of those strong, veined, work-shaped hands. Now she saw they'd curled into tight fists, so tight that she could see the knuckles whiten in stark contrast to the rest of his tanned skin.

He struggled to conquer his rage before he could answer. That was his way. His own fury may have been the only thing on earth he really feared. She'd spoken of sacrifice, and the first thing he'd thought of was what he'd given up for her just the day before. But he'd never tell her about that. Why should he? She hadn't asked it of him; that had been his own sacrifice. He'd given up a fortune for her hand, and it wasn't her fault that she didn't have a fortune to offer in return. But then he thought of what else he'd sacrificed in his life for love, and that he knew he had to tell her, if he never told her anything else again.

"Sacrifice?" he asked, willing his voice not to shake in his anger. "What is love if it isn't sacrifice? Not any kind of love worth a damn at all. I never had an education, because I loved my family. I never thought of raising my own family until I could take care of the one I was born to. I never stopped working to do it. And if it was a sacrifice, I'd no choice, and didn't look for one. It was what I had to do for love, what any man should do for love."

He grew cold as he thought about it; he'd be damned, he decided, if he'd lay all of his life out for her to reject, as she had his offer. He spoke instead, in a clenched voice, of what he'd have done for her.

"If I'd married you," he said, "do you think I wouldn't have sacrificed anything? I'd never have touched another woman again, and I'd never have hated you for it. I'd have worked for you all my life, and never blamed you for it."

"But . . . your career," she protested.

"Oh, yes, true," he said slowly. "That's true. I've never thought of it before. I wouldn't give up my career and let you work for me, I don't know a man who would. I'd ask you to be content to be my wife and the mother of our children. That's true. That's the world the way I know it. I wouldn't want to be married to an absent wife. I don't know any man who is—even married actresses are married to men who travel with them, if they're working at being married. And what would become of any children—would you drag them with you or leave them to me? No," he said, "I don't think the world's ready for that—at least, I know I'm not. Maybe someday . . . no, not me, not ever, I guess. But you're ready now, huh? I see.

"Then, all right, come on," he said after a moment's silence, "let's get on with it. I withdraw my offer, but

I'll take you up on yours. I'll take what I can get too. Come on, make love to me."

There was a bitter humor on his hard face as he shrugged out of his jacket and began to unbutton his shirt.

"Come on," he said, nodding to her, his gold hair falling over his brow as he did, "it's better when you're naked, like bathing. Come on," he said as she gaped at his lightly gilded bared chest and he took her in his arms, pulling down the flimsy low shoulders of her gown again. "I'll help. That's fun too."

She would have been able to slap him, or at least slip away from him, if he hadn't kissed her. But then she thought, when she could think, that he was only doing what she'd asked, and what he was doing felt so right and wrong that she was paralyzed by the complexity of it. As well as by the shock of the feeling of his warm, hard, fuzzy chest against her breasts, the feel of the thunderous beat of his heart vibrating against her own, the taste, the scent of him; the remorseless gentleness of his hands, and the leap of her answering response. But it was wrong, now it was altogether wrong, and her desire fled before her confusion. She trembled, but not with desire, and began to weep, but not for any reason she wholly understood.

He'd thought he'd discover if she'd been lying. He'd thought he might be able to crack that facade of innocence once and for all, as he moved her onward past where they'd been before, to find out how far she'd been without him before. But although she let him do anything he wanted, he began to see she didn't know what he wanted, or, for that matter, what it was that she wanted from him. He knew women enough to know inexperience, and fear and trembling when he found it. So for all he yearned to go on and ease himself, and he knew he could, he paused. And wondered if it wasn't really punishment, and not love, he was after now. Once he wondered what it was he wanted, it ended it for him.

He stopped entirely, only holding her close, gathering himself together, getting his thoughts and his body in order again. At least he knew he'd done the decent if not the most comfortable thing for them both, when he

saw she stayed still in the circle of his arms, obviously
not knowing what he was doing now, or how to go on.

But after a while she understood. She could feel him
fighting for control. When he drew back, she could see
his chest heaving with the effort of it. She didn't dare
look at his face, or anywhere else but straight ahead, at
his chest, because she dared not discover what else he'd
uncovered, and she'd imagined she'd felt a great deal
more when they'd been pressed so close. When she saw
his hands go to his buttons, doing them up again, she
looked down at herself at last and shuddered at what she
saw.

"It's all right," he said. "You're an actress, all right.
I'm convinced. We removed everything else, but you
were ready to keep your corset on through it all. They
all do. Bravo. I'll take you home now," he said, rising,
tucking his shirttail into his trousers. "I find I'd rather
not give you what you wanted. I don't like to be used,
either," he said, and then, relenting when he saw her
wince, added, "and I think I'd only disappoint.

"Because it's really not very good the first time," he
said conversationally as she turned her head, her hands
shaking as she tried to do her gown up again. "At least
not for women. So you haven't missed much. But don't
worry. It's easy. And it gets better each time, too. You
can get Kyle or somebody else to teach you what you
want to know. I was going to try to show you something
else. Goes by the same name, but it's something entirely
different. Now I don't care to anymore. My problem,
not yours. Thanks anyhow."

They didn't speak on the drive back to the boardinghouse. She was too confused, angry with him and herself,
as well as deeply shamed by what she'd done, not done,
and wanted to do. It hadn't been simple, as Kyle had
said, as Josh had said—it had been every bit as personal
and profound as she'd been taught it was for all these
years, and Josh had said they hadn't even done it all.
Even if everything else she'd thought and done tonight
had been right and true, neither Josh nor Kyle had been
right about that. She was so shaken she didn't even know
what to say to herself now, so she didn't have a word to
spare for him.

He hardly noticed. He was thinking that it was a good thing, after all. Now that he'd had a taste of grand passion, he'd a lovely disillusion to show for it, and a nice broken heart to coddle. It would protect him from such stupidity again. He was through with illusions; it seemed he'd created the woman he thought he loved—a cowboy Pygmalion, he thought ruefully, now able to laugh at himself. It was the only thing to do. But now, at least, he knew that later he'd be able to marry cold-eyed and clear-thinking, the same way an intelligent man conducted any serious business, and so get the very best for himself.

When they passed beneath a gaslight near her boardinghouse, he looked at her and saw her bowed head, and noticed how she seemed to have folded up on herself. He sighed. She was young, and alone in the world, and what did he know of her dreams? Turned out he hardly knew her at all, anyway. How could he? He nodded to himself, through with all illusions tonight, and, he hoped, forever. He knew he was just a roughneck in gentleman's clothing, an undereducated drifter from out of the West, naturally shrewd and lucky in business, trying to get by in the big city.

A lot of what she'd said made sense, even though he'd never thought of it before, and knew just as surely that he could never live with any of it either. But that wasn't her fault. Maybe a more cultured, educated man could accept that kind of a marriage. He only knew himself, and was glad of it, and determined to never lose sight of that self again.

That's why he was glad he hadn't taken her, as much as he'd wanted to. He was old-fashioned, he guessed. Just as he was also a victim of sacrifice, as he'd said. He didn't think he could have stood the guilt after he'd done it.

He drew the carriage to a stop in front of her door. She looked up to him, white-faced and hesitant, not knowing how to say good-bye any more than he did. But he had been raised to be a gentleman, and he was as glib as he was polite.

"Good-bye, Lucy," he said. "I'm sorry it didn't work out for us. But maybe someday I'll see you on the stage and remember how I used to know you a long time ago, before you became so world-famous and admired."

She turned her head abruptly. It was worse, she thought, because she didn't know if he was being sincere or not.

"Only, Lucy," he added softly, "for your own sake, make sure you know what you want, because I think you can get whatever that is. I truly do. Good-bye, girl," he said.

Then he kissed her cheek as he held out his hand to help her down, because her head was down, so she couldn't see what she was doing, and she was about to tumble from the high seat in her haste to get away from him.

He waited until she'd gone in the door, and only then sighed, picked up the reins, and drove back through the night, thoughtful and weary. And curiously glad it was over, at last.

20

SHE WALTZED into his arms before the music started. He'd never seen her dance that way before. When Josh put his arms around her, he heard her sigh, looked down, and couldn't mistake the look on her face. She was radiant, relaxed, entirely satisfied. He felt the first chill intimation of dread as he swung Gloria into the dance.

He hadn't come to the Havemeyer ball to partner Gloria. He'd come because it was a great social event. All the powerful men he knew in the city would be here tonight, along with a great many others he wanted to know. It wasn't as grand as an Astor ball, but the Astors were here. As were the Vanderbilts; it was that democratic an affair. The price of admission was only money. And since it was given for men with money, there was money to be made by attending it, and so, though it didn't impress the highest sticklers of society, they could literally not afford to miss it.

Josh had dressed in his best evening clothes and come on time, resolved to be as charming as possible with the ladies but to keep company more with their men. He was done with courting anything but business for a while. Which was why he was as horrified as he was angry to find that everyone expected him to partner Gloria, especially Gloria. He had the uncanny feeling that maybe nothing he remembered had actually happened that last weekend on Long Island. Not by word or gesture did Gloria or Jacob refer to it, and if it weren't for the fact that everything about that past week still stung so badly, he'd have doubted himself.

But it hardly mattered what games the Van Horns were playing. It might be that they were only being amazingly polite. Or, like robber bridegrooms, they could have decided to have him whether he was willing or not. He realized it was possibly only that he didn't have the background to appreciate such exquisite manners. It made no difference. Josh was resolved to be nothing but himself from now on. But since he was always polite, he began to see there'd be a problem with that.

Gloria said nothing at first, but just as he'd begun to relax with the music and the motion of the dance, she spoke.

"Will you be in town for Christmas?" she asked.

"I likely will," he answered, careful to keep his voice light and his words noncommittal.

When they'd made the circuit of the floor once more, she spoke again, just as he was beginning to enjoy himself again.

"Then will you be going to the grand opening of Mr. Sullivan and Mr. Gilbert's new opera on New Year's Eve?" Gloria asked. "Everyone will be there," she added.

His muscles tensed so suddenly he was sure she could feel them bunching under his evening jacket, where her hand rested lightly on his shoulder. Clever, he thought with admiration, forcing himself to calm. Get a man off-balance if you want to know the truth.

He'd been told that New Year's Day was the big day in New York City. It was when all the socially prominent wore themselves out going from house to house, from morning to dusk, to pay calls. But New York couldn't be that different from the world he knew. He'd bet New Year's Eve was a big night too—it was a sentimental night, and a long one. A night when a man wanted to be with someone he cared for.

He supposed she expected him to ask her to accompany him then. And he decided that if he did, it would be just about the biggest mistake he'd made since he came to New York . . . the second biggest, he corrected himself quickly, frowning.

She saw the frown, and he felt her slender frame grow taut. There was no reason to hurt her, he thought.

"I've promised to take my baby brother around that

night," he answered, deciding that wasn't such a bad idea, at that, as he did. "We may show up there."

But he had hurt her; that was unavoidable. And he was almost pleased to discover that the calm, immaculate lady had teeth. Almost.

Because, "Oh," she said after a pause, "I hope you do. We'll be there, Father and I. I'd worried that you might not. After all, everyone's noted how you've suddenly given up the theater."

No decent man ever hit a woman. But that didn't mean he had to keep dancing with her. He waited until the music was done; that much breeding he had. But then he bowed, and thanked her, and took himself off to find a friend. Only to remember, when he got across the room to the punch bowl, that all his friends were in Wyoming Territory, or Chicago, or New Orleans, or New Haven, and that this evening and this city didn't have anything to do with friends—only money. And since he didn't want to think of one friend in particular, the one he damned himself for missing most of all, the one that probably had never been his friend at all, the one that was still in this damned city, he looked over the company, searching for any substitute he could find.

He'd looked too high. He felt a tug on his sleeve, and looked down to find Peter standing right by his side. Odd that he hadn't thought of him, he thought, some of his tension easing, feeling warmth from more than the rum-laden punch he sipped as he smiled at his friend.

"Ha. Old Jacob's smarter than a fox," Peter said with a smirk. "You turn him down and he turns the other cheek. Look out, Josh, he'll keep turning till he spins, and you'll get so dizzy watching, they'll have you before a minister before you get your balance. Don't look at me that way. Of course I know. Everybody does. But I don't know everything. Where have you been lately? They changed practically the whole cast over at the Stratton. I found the sweetest new little soprano there last night, blond, and all over too. And there's a redhead . . ." Peter put two fingers to his lips and kissed them. "Just up your alley—that is, if you haven't given up on actresses forever."

Josh's warm glow cooled to chill annoyance.

"Dry up, Peter," he said calmly, and looked into his cup of punch, remembering why he hadn't thought of Peter when he'd looked for a friend. It was hard to be friends with someone so completely different, almost as hard as it was for him to remember why they'd been friends in the first place. Peter never worked at anything but whoring and gossip. He didn't give his allegiance to any man or woman. He told tales about everyone he knew of both sexes: announcing his triumphs with women as soon as he'd got up out of their beds, and trumpeting every man's secrets—the more depraved, the better. And yet still, once, and not so very long ago, Josh realized, he'd found him delightful company, very amusing.

"Everybody's asking where you've been—except Miss Lucy Rose," Peter persisted. "I know for a fact that Gloria had her daddy escort her to the Stratton the other night. She spent the first act watching the audience, and then, when she decided you weren't coming, at least not to the performance," he chuckled, "the second act, she studied Miss Lucy Rose. I guess she was taking notes. Beware, Josh," he laughed, "the Van Horns are determined people. Almost as much as the English Rose is. She won't go out with anyone, not even me. And I asked her so nicely, and used your name too. Or is that why she wouldn't? Oh, I . . . ah," Peter said, backing away from the look in Josh's eyes. "I only asked her because I thought you were done with her. I'd never trespass, believe me, ah . . ."

"Shut up, Peter," Josh said, and said it so coldly that Peter was only too glad to do that, and scurry away from him, as well.

Josh talked business with some men he knew, but was surprised to find himself almost as bored with them as he was with himself. He soon left them to take up a post by a window, and stood there watching the company. There were many men and more women who saw him and thought to approach him, but there was such a still, dangerous look on his face they thought better of it before they did. He remained alone amidst all the company, locked in with his lowering mood.

He was edgy and irritable tonight, at a loss to think of

what to do to lighten his spirits. Back home, he'd have
gone for a gallop or a long solitary walk, or gone into
town to drink himself into submission, or at least have
wandered over to the bunkhouse to gamble and talk trash
until the morning light. Or, he remembered, he'd have
driven to town and gotten himself a woman. But he
didn't even want to think about women tonight. He
couldn't ride faster than the traffic here, it was almost
impossible to walk alone for very long in this teeming
city, and though there were a hundred places to gamble,
he'd had enough of the vagaries of fate to last him a long
time. And there was no one to relax and be foolish or
fond with.

Maybe, he thought, watching the well-dressed men and
women swirling around him, just maybe he'd ride to New
Haven tomorrow and visit with Gray. But then he
decided that would be an admission of defeat, and he
wasn't done with this city yet, or if he was, he refused
to admit it.

The entertainment he loved the most that he could
think of was one that he refused to think of. He'd rather
go to a hanging, even his own, than to a theater tonight.

A voice cut into his brooding.

"Josh," William Henry Vanderbilt said as he gave him
his hand, "I was just leaving when I looked over and saw
you here. But *are* you here? You look like you've already
left."

"I expect I have," Josh said. "I'm not feeling very
festive tonight. You're going so soon? I guess it isn't just
me, then."

"Ah. They snubbed you too? I'm surprised. So far as
I knew, you were a great success."

Josh's look of puzzlement caused the older man to gesture, only the slightest inclination of his head and eyes
to the left, behind him. "There," he said softly. "Mrs.
Astor and Ward McAllister. They're wonderfully good
at not seeing you right in front of them if they don't want
to. It galls me, Josh—it's nonsense, but I'll admit it galls
me. So I'm leaving."

Josh looked at the small, magnificently dressed woman
standing by the short, plump, balding, and rumpled light-
eyed man, and saw how they looked out over the ball-

room in turn. And how everyone in the ballroom gazed back anxiously, every so often, at them.

"*That's* McAllister?" he mused. "He asked me if I was going to the Natwicks' Christmas ball. I thought he was looking for a handout. Seedy-looking gent. I've seen her before. Not bad-looking, but back home, if you get dressed up to your ears, they say you look like her pet horse. I think her horse probably looks a damn sight better tonight. I never saw so many feathers on anyone's head but an eagle's or an Indian's."

William laughed loudly before he said, low, "Josh, keep your voice down, you're talking social suicide."

"Am I?" Josh answered, smiling, looking genuinely pleased for the first time that night.

"That just may be why you're such a success, that devil-may-care attitude of yours. I know you don't understand it," the older man said heavily, "but every man's got a goal. I *will* have my rightful position for my family and myself before I'm done."

"Oh, I understand about goals," Josh answered quietly, and added, "and if the talk I hear about the palace you're building is true, you'll have those two happy to eat out of your hands when it's done. Every time I pass, I see another crew hauling marble down Fifth Avenue to it. Is it a pyramid or Xanadu you're about erecting there?"

"You'll see, you'll be one of the first we ask in when it's done. But wait until you see what my boy is putting up nearby. Alva has plans too. Clever girl. No one will be able to overlook it, or us, then," William promised with grim pleasure.

"No one should now, sir, no one with any sense, that is," Josh said sincerely, before he gave his hand in farewell.

The idea that he was socially acceptable didn't appease Josh; instead, he found himself growing even more annoyed. These weren't the sort of people he wanted to please. He may have hated snobbery because he'd seen his father waste his life trying to amass riches to show his noble family how he'd measured up to their expectations. Or it could have been the egalitarianism of the West that he'd got used to that accounted for it too.

But there was no doubt it could also have been the slow-growing and smarting realization of his own recent folly. Because now he could see that the way he'd begun that sundered relationship had ensured its ending in disaster. He'd violated his own principles when he'd refused to believe what his heart told him all those weeks he'd only tried to seduce her. He'd been too busily entertaining his own preconceived notions to see what was right before him, too. By the time he'd realized that, it was too late, he'd lost her trust and her interest, and he could hardly blame her. The theater, as she'd said, was a more flexible lover, or at least a more honest one.

For all those reasons, it was no honor to think that the greatly feared Ward McAllister, the cold-eyed, world-weary arbiter of New York society, had accepted him.

That was why Josh was so instantly and thoroughly delighted when Edgar Yates came up to him and said what he did.

Edgar grinned his greeting, and then whispered a few words in Josh's ear. He was laughing as he did, but was unwise enough not to step back when he'd done.

The dancing, the chatter, the entire ball stopped at the moment Josh's fist connected with Edgar's jaw. By the time Edgar lay sprawled on the floor, the only sounds came from the musicians still playing in their secluded arbor, making eerie background music to what looked to be a murder. But Josh did nothing more than stand over the man he'd felled. When he saw that Edgar lived to lie again some other day, and seemed to want to do nothing more than crawl off in peace now, Josh unclenched his fists and strode away himself, across the floor, through the path the astounded partygoers immediately made for him.

Edgar had been a satisfactory last straw. What he'd said about his plans for Miss Lucy Rose now that Josh was done with her would have made Josh do the same thing to any creature on his earth. Hitting Edgar had felt very good, and despite the fact that it probably meant the end to many of his plans for triumph in this city, the thought was the second thing to please him tonight.

"Young man! Mr. Dylan," his host cried as he hurried

into the hall after him. "Wait! You can't just leave, not after that!"

Josh tensed and turned, ready to take whatever abuse he must before he could go. He reckoned a fistfight in a Fifth Avenue mansion must have earned him other penalties than mere social ostracism.

"What a splendid thing!" the man crowed, clapping him on the shoulder. "That bounder's been asking for it for years!"

"A bang-up job! Hoorah, sir! How straightforward," a bewhiskered gentleman agreed vigorously.

"And gallant. I understand it was a lady's honor in question," a woman whispered.

The crowd of partygoers that surged into the entry hall seemed all in agreement. Peter took advantage of his knowledge of their new hero, striding forward to shake his hand, as did several other gentlemen, as their avidly interested ladies begged to be presented to him too.

It took a while for Josh to disentangle himself from all the well-wishers, and by the time he'd managed to convince them that he really had to go, his mood was blacker than ever. Jacob didn't improve it.

"Before you leave, Josh . . . the Coaching Club's holding a special outing next Sunday if it doesn't snow," Jacob said. "Can we count on you? Gloria will likely desert me again, if you ask her, but I'll manage to bear it. You're the new man of the hour, as well as an excellent whip, after all."

Josh wondered how far he could be goaded. But decided not to test his limits. His excuse was on his lips, when he paused, a wonderful idea occurring, full-blown, to him. He'd have everything on his terms, or he'd have nothing at all. And tonight he'd rather have nothing of any of these people. Edgar deserved no one's sympathy. But they'd called him friend and put up with him until their fancy turned and they applauded the stranger who'd struck him down. This wasn't the world he'd envisioned when he'd come here. They'd no loyalty or honor he could see. He was tired of their herd instincts, their sudden veering interests, their unshakable belief, even the best of them, that what they thought counted more than what other, poorer men did. He was weary of being manipulated too. He eyed Jacob and Gloria's barely concealed eagerness as they waited for his answer. A man should be taken at his word, even if it was the word they cared for least: no.

Josh smiled, a warm, friendly, altogether winning smile.

"Be pleased. Be proud. Next Sunday, did you say? Hope I can get my new rig together by then," he answered.

"Another one?" Gloria asked, visibly pleased.

"Oh, yes, just wait till you see it," Josh said, and said good night before she could decide whether that was an invitation to ride with him or not.

It would serve her right if she decided it was, he thought as he climbed up to the driver's seat of his carriage. He smiled broadly at the thought all the way home. He only stopped to send off a telegram, and only stopped grinning as he wondered if he could get the answer he wanted by Sunday. Soon he was laughing to himself again. Given his amazing ability to wreck his dreams these days, he decided there was no doubt the message would be received in plenty of time for his purposes.

They waited along the avenue, sometimes two deep, all the way up to Central Park, so they could see all of the coaching parade as it went by. Few of the spectators could afford such glorious vehicles as they saw drive past; most would simply like to have been able to afford the time they wasted just watching them go by. But few resented the members of the Coaching Club. Because a man could dream, that was what America was all about, and these vehicles and their passengers were what those dreams were all about.

There were phaetons and town carriages, formal drags and private road coaches, all polished wood with silver and gold and painted adornments outside, and as they passed, the curious could catch glimpses of the lavish use of silks, velvets, and satins within. They cost as much as a man's house and were the sum of most of their ambitions. They were drawn by horses got up finer than most of the people in the crowd. High-stepping thorough-

breds, heads held, or forced, up higher, brushed until
they shone like the lacquer on the vehicles they drew,
they paced on thin and graceful legs, alone or in tandem
or double-team style. Their fittings were silver on
leather, embossed and shining like their own glossy
coats.

But none of these trappings were half so fine as what
the ladies ornamenting the coaches wore, since they were
magnificently dressed, and their gentleman drivers and
escorts no less so.

Curricles and gigs, vis-à-vis and coupés rolled by, all
manner of grand vehicles, some occasioning comment,
most greeted with silent respect as they rolled down Fifth
Avenue. Toward the end of the revue, as though the best
had been saved for last, like at a fireworks display, there
were indrawn breaths at the sight of a gleaming mahogany coach filled to the roof with a collection of lovely
ladies and a full complement of aristocratic young men.
But the usual hallmark of the members of the Coaching
Club was absent, because the passengers didn't wear
faintly bored expressions, nor did they ignore their surroundings. In fact, they looked terrified. They craned
their necks to gaze in apprehension at what was coming
up behind them, just as their high-stepping white-eyed
teams did, as they shivered and strained trying to gallop
down the avenue to get away from what followed them.

There was no sound at all as the spectators first saw
what brought up the end of the parade. It wasn't until it
had almost passed them that they responded. Because it
wasn't like anything they'd ever seen before.

The wagon was pulled by three teams of beasts that
well might have been horses. But they were as unfamiliar
as pagan war-horses to the citizens of New York City.
Great deep-chested brutes with long shaggy hair and rolling eyes, they were buckled together with leather and
steel; their strong legs were the width of the necks of the
thoroughbreds they pursued, their own necks as broad
as the chests of the men they were pulling. They didn't
step lightly as ballerinas, as the other horses in the grand
procession did, but charged down the avenue, powerful
and purposeful as a wind from the north. But then, no

graceful and mannered beasts could have pulled what they did.

They towed a heavy wagon. A huge long and scarred Wells Fargo coach, the sort most New Yorkers had seen only in newspapers or in penny novels about the West. It was high, wide, and plain, painted Wells Fargo red, with a yellow underbelly. Canvas within, its windows were open, their canvas lashes rolled up. Atop, it held a few rough-looking men, the sort that looked as if they knew how to handle the teams that pulled them. No well-got-up gent drove it. A buckskin-clad, high-booted man handled the reins, a kerchief at his neck, a wide and slouching hat atop his golden hair. There was an older, bearded, intense, and travel-stained cowboy at his side.

As they neared the parade's end, as ever since they'd begun their wild ride, the spectators' shocked silence turned to cheers, and they left a wildly enthusiastic, applauding crowd in their wake.

" 'Pears they love you," the cowboy commented.

"But they don't count, Erie. Keep your temper, friend," Josh said, "because I do believe the leaders of the Coaching Club are going to have some harsh things to say to me for trying to bring their fancy parade down to solid, dirty old earth. And I don't mind, Erie, so just don't draw, okay?"

A cluster of wide-eyed gentlemen awaited them on the pavement near the Fifth Avenue Hotel. Josh drew his teams to a stand with a jerk on the reins and a wild cry they recognized as a command. The great horses stopped as one, and stood, blowing heavily. The sound of their breathing was the only sound as Josh handed the reins to Erie and climbed down. In that same moment, he almost regretted what he'd done. Except that it had made him feel better than he'd done in days.

"Dylan," a top-hatted gentleman began, but was interrupted by a younger one whose eyes never left the wagon or the horses. "By God, Dylan, what a getup!" he said reverentially.

The older gentleman froze the upstart with a glance. Then, having maintained his position and asserted his superiority again, he turned to Josh.

"Yes," he said. "Just so! Splendid! Bully! Well done! A credit to the club, sir."

"A salute to the American people," a gentleman cried.

"You, sir, are an original," another young man put in, as he noted every detail of Josh's dress and resolved to have the same thing made up for the next masked ball he was invited to.

"Can I take the reins?" a man cried, and was drowned out by others clamoring for the same treat.

"I understand why you didn't want me up there with you," Gloria said after she'd won her way through the throng to his side, "but I think you underrated me. I wouldn't have been frightened at all."

And then the mass of gentlemen and ladies converged on Josh, surrounding him, engulfing him with praise and compliments on his daring, his originality, and his cleverness. Erie relaxed, only troubling himself to order his men to keep the horses from tearing off the odd arm or hand that came too close to them.

"Harsh words, all right," Erie commented as they drove the wagon back to the stable they'd rented for the weekend. "Was all I could do to keep still when they started in lynching you," he added. "Glad you warned me."

"I wonder if I'll have to murder one of them to displease them," Josh said moodily.

"You could dance in your long johns in Madison Square and they'd pat you on the head," Erie said.

Then he fell silent, and only watched Josh's closed and angry face. He wasn't a loquacious man. In the past he'd spent whole days with his young employer without saying more than he had to, and he never had to say much. But when they got to the stable, he spoke again.

"What's eatin' at you?" he asked. "You got what you wanted, didn't you?"

"Yes," Josh said, "so I did. Just what I wanted. Didn't I?"

She didn't like sitting by herself, but she didn't want to see anyone else, and as she couldn't even bear the sight of her own face in the mirror any longer, Lucy was very grateful for Duncan. He was excellent company. He asked for nothing but petting, and when her hand grew tired, he was gracious enough to rest his chin on her knee and wait for her to remember her duty again.

It was her night off, and she had the house to herself. All the other occupants of Mrs. Fergus' roominghouse seemed to have gone out for the evening. Now, as the evening wore on, Lucy was no longer sulking or brooding, she'd gone beyond that to some gray and empty place.

It was much better to be alone, Lucy decided. Otherwise someone might ask her why she felt so badly, when, after all, her future looked so rosy and everything was going so well for her. And she couldn't explain what she didn't know. She began to understand the merits of having a companionable dog instead of an inquisitive human with her when she tried to explain it to herself. She'd just discovered that dogs were better than humans to weep on too, because they didn't have to offer you a handkerchief, only an ear, when her companion slewed his head around and stared at the door.

Lucy startled, she sat up straight, and ran a finger under her nose. But then she relaxed. It was only Mr. Fergus, emerged from his basement workshop, probably come looking for something to cart down to repair. He gave her a quick look from under his bushy gray eyebrows. She expected him to do the usual—nod and then wander away. But instead, he stopped, looked at her directly, and spoke.

"All alone?" he asked.

It was a simple-enough question, but she couldn't answer right away. She was too surprised. Mr. Fergus had never spoken to her; in fact, she couldn't recall ever having heard him speak. He seemed to live in, but not precisely with, the house. He ate at the dinner table, was usually to be seen roaming about the house at night, but the rest of his time was passed tinkering with pipes and such in the basement, or so she thought someone had said. He was small, gray-haired, and he usually wore shapeless gray sweaters and loose-fitting trousers. When she thought of him at all, Lucy wondered why a theatrical sort of woman such as Mrs. Fergus had married him.

"Oh, well, yes. But I've got Duncan," Lucy said as brightly as she was able, surprised to find herself defensive as those suddenly keen brown eyes watched her.

"Not seeing that Western fellow anymore?" he asked.

She was too surprised to be offended. It was as though the chair she sat in had suddenly begun discussing philosophy with her.

"No," she said. "Well, he didn't understand. Not from the theater, you know," she said loftily, and it sounded entirely right to her as she said it.

"Uh-huh," Mr. Fergus said. "Then, want to come down and see what I do? Better than nothing."

There was a time when she would have said yes, without pause or question. He was elderly, she was well brought up. But she'd lived in Manhattan for months and had been on the stage all that time. The lecherous millionaire she'd slapped and abandoned all those weeks ago had been Mr. Fergus' age, or older. So were many of the men who waited for the chorus in the alley after every show. She hesitated.

"If I was thinking of something underhanded," he said with what might have been a glint of humor, "I wouldn't do it in my own house. No, Mrs. Fergus is about all I can handle at my age, but then, she always was. Coming?" he asked, as he began to shuffle toward the door.

The basement steps were wooden and wide, and seemed to go on forever. Mr. Fergus led the way, and Duncan, pressed against Lucy's ankles, almost sent her tumbling several times in his attempt to be companionable.

"Dog," Mr. Fergus commented as he walked down, "is useless for anything but the theater, but he means well. Hang on to the banister."

When she reached the bottom step she looked up at the room before her. It was more astonishing than any stage set she'd ever seen. It must have been illusion that made it seem as big as the whole house, so brightly lighted and cluttered with odd objects, too many competing to catch the eye to pick out any immediately. It looked, to her dazzled eyes, to be a huge and sparkling wizard's cave.

There were, Lucy began to see as she wandered into the room, all sorts of plans and papers atop almost every one of the many tabletops. Some also held ornate and miniature sets of wonderful exotic places: palaces and promenades, gardens and gargoyle-encrusted cathedrals, all perfect, and all in tiny, faery scale. There were paintings on canvas tacked on the walls, all backdrops to any drama she could imagine, and some she couldn't. Statues and plaster busts, armor and skeletons, bird cages and machines of incomprehensible purpose—the room was sheer confusion, and utter magic.

"My job," Mr. Fergus explained, sitting down on a high stool, watching Lucy's enchantment as she roamed the room, discovering ever new treasures to exclaim over. "I make sets. I worked at Booth's awhile, the Olympic, Wallack's. I work for Niblo's, all of them, in fact. It's what I do."

"I never guessed, I didn't know . . ." Lucy breathed, touching a tiny swing that hung from a minute tree, and watching how it swung, as though in an absent spring breeze.

"You wouldn't. You have to know the words and music and the moves. We're the ones who make the place for you to work in—what would you know about hydraulics and flies, rigging, traps, and platforms? You have to speak about Birnham wood, we have to make it come to you. You have to convince the audience you've drowned yourself, Ophelia, and we have to never let them doubt that's a real grave Hamlet's trying to jump into after you. You supply the play, we'll do the work. But our work's our play too, you see."

She looked up. He had a deep, clear, modulated voice, as unexpected as this room of his.

"That's how you met Mrs. Fergus!" she exclaimed, everything making sense now.

"Well, no," he said, humor evident in his voice. "Here, look."

She came to his side and looked down at the scrapbook he'd opened on the table. It was covered in beautiful red velvet, and filled with yellowed clippings.

"Don't look for 'Fergus,' " he advised. "She was Eleanora Atherton then."

But even with the right name to guide her, it took Mr. Fergus' blunt fingertip to finally show Lucy the way to a mention of his wife. Because in each review, the only mention of her was in the listing of the cast.

"This," he finally said, turning the page, "was her last and greatest triumph."

It was a review of *Romeo and Juliet*, and following his finger, Lucy read, at the bottom of the article, ". . . Mr. Grimes was a fine Benvolio, in a supporting cast that included Mr. Small as a compelling Prince of Verona and Miss Atherton as Lady Capulet."

"But look . . ." Mr. Fergus said, before Lucy could find an appropriate thing to murmur, and he turned the page to show her a fading ambrotype of a smiling young woman in an ornate low-cut gown.

It was Mrs. Fergus; Lucy could recognize some of her features. But it was a Mrs. Fergus gone to heaven: young, shapely, with the clean clear lines of youth on her face and body, charming, innocent-looking, vulnerable, and absolutely enticing.

"Aye," he sighed, "and so I see her still. She could've perhaps been famous. But she never got the right chance. It's all a matter of timing, you know."

"And you did the sets?" Lucy asked, because he seemed to have forgotten her.

"Not then," he said, absently turning the page back to where the review of *Romeo and Juliet* was.

And that was when Lucy's gaze fell on the top of the review and she read what was there.

"Mr. Fergus' Romeo is surely one for the ages," it read. "It is a pleasure to see a performance of such style, such grace, such understanding of the finer emotions. He is like the wind in his fencing scenes, like an orator as he speaks of love, like a lion . . ."

Mr. Fergus shut the book.

"They spoke more flowery back then," he said. "It was only a production down at the Cooper, in the Bowery. Burned down ten years ago, and good riddance, not much of a house. I was very young."

"But you were an actor?" Lucy gasped. "And a good one, and if so, why . . . ?"

"Because she said she'd marry me," he said softly, with a smile, as though the words still gave him pleasure, "and then she was offered a part in *East Lynne* with a touring company. They had no part for me, and it was too good an opportunity for her to pass up. I wouldn't let her pass it up. It could've been her chance. But I didn't want her leaving me for six months either—that's eternity for a pretty young girl on her own in the theater. So I married her and went with her, and found work backstage. I was always good with my hands."

"But . . . when you came back?" Lucy asked.

"Theater's a gamble. We had to eat. Better chance of regular work backstage if you're good, than on."

"You sacrificed your career for her?" Lucy cried, as astonished as she was upset.

"Of course not!" he said, his brows snapping together. "It isn't sacrifice if you want to do it. It's no sacrifice doing something that makes you happy. Or something you'd be miserable not doing. I gave up something I loved for something I loved more. That's no sacrifice, my girl. Now, if Joan of Arc loved going up in flames because she knew it was such a lovely saintly sacrifice to make, would she really be a saint?" he mused. "You should have seen it, at that," he said dreamily. "It was something. Kitty MacGuire played her that way once at the old park. She was so happy to go to the stake, the audience cheered when they lit her pyre. Wonderful effect. A red-and-orange isinglass globe over a footlight, and then—snap!—a flock of yellow and red streamers blowing up from a fan under the trap. Gorgeous," he sighed.

"But . . . you could have been a great actor!" Lucy wailed.

"Don't know about 'great,' " he said with a shrug. "That's part of it. If I'd been sure of 'great,' " he said, smiling now, "maybe I wouldn't have done it. I'm no saint. But you can't be sure of anything in life, and nothing at all in the theater. I knew I could be paid for what I did backstage, and knew I could be good at it too. And I am. Close one door, open another."

It may have been Lucy's expression that made him say what he did then, because, as always, everything she wondered was there to see on her face.

"How would it have been if I had gone for the blue ribbon my way, and lost it, and her? I've got her," he said with satisfaction, "and I've never been sorry. You find what you want in life, my girl, and you go after it. Some people make sacrifices to get it, some can't help making them, and don't get anything. All I know is sometimes it hurts more not to make a sacrifice. Most of the time you won't know if you were right or wrong for years," he said more quietly, "and sometimes, not ever. But if it feels right, you do it. And if it feels right, it's no sacrifice."

Lucy pondered that. She couldn't have answered him immediately even if she'd known what to say. Because at that moment she heard faint voices and looked around to see where Mrs. Fergus, Miss Hampton, and Mrs. Fairfax were. It sounded as though they were coming into the room. But then she cocked her head, as Duncan did. Because the voices grew louder, even though no one else came into the basement room.

They were indistinct, but recognizable voices; she could almost but not quite make out what they were saying. They were obviously coming from upstairs, carrying through the registers, because she could hear them moving—as Mrs. Fergus and her homecoming friends moved from room to room, from the hall to the kitchen. They'd be clear, Lucy thought, if she laid her ear against the wall . . . and then was instantly ashamed of her unworthy thought—until she glanced at Mr. Fergus and saw his rueful, apologetic expression, and was staggered by the implications of it. Then she stood still, understanding, not knowing just what to say, as the voices and the footsteps seemed to approach the stairs, and then finally faded away.

She understood more than what he'd told her now too. She thought she knew why he'd told her. Curiously, she wasn't upset or uneasy at finding out how much he knew about her life from what he'd heard and seen without her knowing. Because she realized he'd guessed more, and the thought that he'd cared enough to care overweighed all else.

Mr. Fergus gazed at Lucy, looking a little worried and a lot more embarrassed. But then, she thought, he was a fine actor.

"I've got my work," he finally said, "and we only keep

this house to keep the theater close for her. But I like to keep myself informed too. I won't say I snoop, but I hear things. I can't say I spy, but I see things too. You remind me of her, the way she used to be."

"You've been very kind," Lucy said, tears growing in her eyes again. "I've got a lot to think about. Well, you know that. I still don't know what to do, but even though it wasn't precisely fair of you, you've tried to be helpful, and just when I needed a friend. . . ."

"Don't fool yourself," he said, alarmed. "I did it all for Duncan. He's a very old dog. If you got him all wet with tears, then when I let him out for his nightly walk, he'd catch his death of chill, or worse."

"Dear Mr. Fergus," Lucy said when she was able, "we lost a great actor when you left the theater, a *great* actor, I do know that."

"Gained a better engineer," he answered. "Look here. This is going to be a set for *Uncle Tom's Cabin*. See how we're going to make the angels fly?"

And she thought she did.

21

JOSH LOOKED fierce enough, he hardly needed the scowl he wore. He wore fringed leather clothing and a thunderous frown, and he stormed out of the small elevator cage after it arrived at his floor, like a bear who'd burst its bars in a break for freedom. He'd finally detached himself from the clots of newfound friends he'd made with his wild ride down Fifth Avenue, rejecting their offers to dine and drink. He'd passed some time with his old friends from the West before he'd seen them off to the diversions they'd promised themselves in the city, leaving them to the beer gardens and brothels of their choices. Now it was late, and now, at last, he was entirely free, just as he'd wanted to be. And he'd just begun to realize that whatever else he was, the one thing he was not was free.

Too soon to leave, too late to go back, he was, he decided, trapped here by his success, caught by what he'd sought, like a fly mired in a dish of honey—left to die of disastrously fulfilled desire. There was no reason to stay, and none at all to leave.

He could stay and marry Gloria, or someone just like her; he could go and go to the devil with himself in any way he chose. He'd thought of himself as burdened all his life, and only now realized that the freedom he'd worked for made him even lonelier than he'd been when he'd been fettered by responsibility. At least then he'd had his dreams. And the illusion of being needed. He'd been alone most of his life, but never felt it so keenly as now, and that made him angrier, because he hated self-pity as much as he did fear.

He was striding to his door when he noticed a movement in the shadows of the hotel corridor where the arcs

of gaslight didn't reach, and he felt a surge of wild joy.
A figure unfolded in the dim light, stepping out of the
shadows, and his muscles tensed. He hoped, no, he
prayed, that it was some villain, slipped into the hotel
looking for easy prey. He braced himself. And then
gaped in wonder.

It was Miss Lucy Markham.

His second surge of joy faded as abruptly as it had
arisen at the sight of her. He braced himself again. He'd
no desire to open old wounds, much less ones that hadn't
healed over yet. This, he thought, eyeing her with disfa-
vor, was exactly what he hadn't needed tonight.

"What do you want?" he snapped, at the end of his
patience at last.

She blinked. He was dressed like a frontiersman; he
looked as unfamiliar as he did furious.

"I . . ." she said.

"Oh!" she said.

She drew in a deep, gulping breath. And let it all out
in tears.

"No, no," Josh said wearily, insisting she take the glass
he handed her, "drink it first, talk later. There. That's
it. I didn't mean to startle you. My mind was sixteen
other places."

Lucy sipped the fiery liquid he'd poured for her, her
throat and heart unknotting. When she'd made up her
mind it had been late and the house had been dark.
She'd written and torn up two letters, and then composed
three more in her head before she'd lain back in bed to
dream of what she'd do in the morning. Only to sit bolt
upright again, realizing she'd never really be brazen
enough to do any of those things once morning came.
She'd only wait for fate to bring them together, the way
a proper girl should.

But fate had never brought her anything so good as
what she'd gone out and gotten for herself. And she'd
met him and then lost him by not being a proper girl.
And she really didn't know what kind of a girl she was
anymore, except for a miserable one. Further, she told
herself as she scurried into her clothes, she owed him
an apology, and there was nothing improper about that.

Holding that flimsy excuse before her eyes like a shield, she left her room and hastened to his hotel with the courage of the dark of the night still upon her.

It was an enormously improper thing she was doing. She almost hoped she'd be punished for it. It helped her to find the courage to hail a carriage to envision a dozen dreadful things, from finding him with another woman, which would have freed her entirely, to finding him cold and reserved, which would have served her right. She'd not expected to find that he was out. But she'd waited, hidden in the corridor, entertaining herself with a thousand excuses for not flying back home at once, or even, after the hours dragged on, knowing that if she left now, she'd never come back again.

And then, finally, he'd come and frightened her to tears. Before she could reflect on that, he almost did it again.

"Do you know what time it is?" he asked, settling on the arm of the couch next to her. "What is it that couldn't wait until morning?"

It had been a stupid idea. She saw it now, and saw it with brutal clarity. What was she doing in this hard-eyed stranger's rooms in the night? When something was over, it was done. Her eyes were bright with tears of anger— at herself this time. But anger was easier to deal with than shame.

"I . . . couldn't get to sleep. I was thinking of how rude I'd been to you, and I found that guilt distressing. I came to apologize for my behavior the other day— night—and so I have. Well, then," she said, rising and putting down the glass, "I must say that feels entirely better. Good night."

He stood too, and put one hand on her shoulder.

"No," he said, and she swallowed hard. "Not good enough."

"But it's true," she said obstinately. "I didn't realize what time it was. My goodness, it's late!" she exclaimed, looking down to her lapel watch, which she obviously didn't read. "Good night."

His gaze softened. She was flushed and she looked everywhere but at him. Her amber eyes were pink with weeping. Her hair looked dreadful; it was snarled, rather than curled, as though she'd combed it with her fingers in the dark. Her skin was white with tension, where it wasn't blotchy from recent tears. Her entire face was blurry with exhaustion, her gown looked as though it had been put on backward in a closet, and he thought she looked more beautiful than ever. He didn't know why she'd come to him, but looking at her seemed to melt away the hard knot of rage within him, and warm up all the empty places. He found that he was as tired of being noble as he was of missing her. However much he might know it was wrong for him, or her, this time, he promised himself, he wasn't going to let her leave so soon.

"You've buttoned your dress all wrong," he said.

"Oh," she said, looking down, relieved to find that they were at least all done up, except for the last one, no matter how oddly that made her gown fit. "So it is. But if you give me my cloak, it won't matter."

"Lucy," he said gently, quietly, his two hands on her two shoulders now as he bent his head down to try to see her downcast face, "why did you come here, now, in the night?"

"I was sorry for what I said," she said stubbornly, because that was true, and even so, the way she said it, it wouldn't hurt her pride.

"Oh, Lucy," he said, smiling slightly and shaking his head, his voice suffused with gentle merriment. "Try again. You're supposed to be an actress, remember?"

She jerked her head up, but before she could tell him that she was, and a good one too, his lips were on her own, so she couldn't speak, and he gathered her close, so she couldn't think of what she could say if she could.

"Lucy," he said after long moments had passed, as he rested his cheek against hers, and his hands finally came to rest on her waist. "Ah, Lucy."

"Well, but I love you," she whispered in answer to the question he hadn't asked in words, as he grew still, hoping he'd heard what he had, "and I missed you, and it isn't a sacrifice if you must do it, or if you'd be miserable if you didn't. It's only a question of finding what you want and going to get it, like Joan of Arc, and . . . Oh, Josh, is your offer still open? Or have you changed your mind? Oh, how I wish it was last week again, so I could answer everything right the first time."

She'd said a great many things he didn't understand, but he knew that was her way, and one thing he did understand was enough for him. He was as devastated by her kisses as she'd been by his, but he was also a shrewd man of business. He'd grasped enough to know the essence of the rest of what she'd said, even if he hadn't already discovered most of it, unspoken, on her lips.

"Will you marry me, Miss Lucy Markham?" he asked helpfully.

"Oh, yes, Josh, I will, please," she answered, resting her forehead against his chest.

"And your career . . . ?" he asked, because he had to. For all his joy, he didn't want them back where they'd begun again, and he'd been doing some thinking on his own.

"There's no way I can have both," she said softly. "It's not possible for us, not here, not now, not yet. You were right. Unless you want to become a set designer?" she asked with a muted giggle.

"We could try," he said, craning his neck to look down, trying to get her to look up to him. "I mean, I can't work in the theater, but maybe you could here in New York, and I could try to arrange things so that I could go with you on tour if you had to go. We could try," he insisted as she shook her head back and forth against his chest.

"No," she said, and there was finality in her voice. "Bad enough to marry an actress; you couldn't do that, Josh, and you know it. You'd look foolish to your friends and associates . . . and . . . and even to mine. It isn't done. If actresses marry out of the theater, they retire. And that's that. I don't mind. No. Much more than that. I want to. None of it matters without you. That's all there is to it."

When she raised her head from his vest there was no reason to speak, and a very good reason not to. When he let her go again, there were several misbuttoned buttons undone, and although his big hands were uncommonly deft, it was painstaking work. But, sleepy and abandoned as she was, she suddenly realized what was happening.

"Josh, you're friends with people in the highest places. Oh, Josh, this is a mistake. How can you marry me?"

"It seems I can do whatever I want, Lucy," he answered, "because I've got money. Sad to say, that's all I need to win their approval. We really have to get us some new friends when we're married, you know," he said, his hands covering hers, encouraging her to resume her work on the tiny buttons that he yearned to simply tear apart.

"Speaking of which, honey," he said in her ear as he bent to her again, "how does Wednesday sound?"

"Hmmm?" she asked, bemused, because the soft leather of his jacket felt so luxurious against her newly exposed skin.

"Well, because it'll take Gray a day to get down here after he gets my telegram," he explained, driving his words from her mind as his hands showed her what else felt delightful against that newly uncovered skin, "And there's no sense waiting until next Sunday. No sense at all."

"What?" she asked a moment later, as he paused, sighing with gratitude at seeing the last of the interminable row of pearl buttons undone.

"Because you're staying here until we do get married," he said. "There is no way on earth I'm going to let you go and let someone else change your mind again. Lucy," he said, "you don't have to 'stay' with me tonight, like you once said. But I'm serious. You are staying here until then."

He sounded forceful and determined. She felt a moment of sheer panic, until she saw his eyes and all the worry there—until she heard him ask very softly, "Okay? I'll send a telegram to Gray, and write instructions to my secretary to set the thing up and send invitations to anyone else we want at the ceremony," he went on, as though he were asking, watching her face carefully. "I'll send a note to Mrs. Fergus—and to Kyle Harper too," he added, to get the dangerous name out and said to see if it would end everything, "so they won't worry where you are. All right?"

"All right," she said, because she didn't want to leave him or let herself think of any other reason to destroy her hope of happiness now, any more than he did.

"Good," he said, and left her, to walk away and lock the door.

"Now, then," he said as he turned back to her and saw how her hands went up to pull her gown together, and he cursed the simple facts of mundane life that had taken him from her side and gotten her to worry again. "We'll be married in a few days, and I'm not letting you out of my sight until then, and it's very late. You can go to sleep alone, if you like. I'll take the settee here, or . . . Lucy, would you rather . . . ? Do you . . . ? Would you care to make love to me now?"

She was too wise to speak. She only nodded violently, and he stopped her by holding her head in one hand and kissing her answer away.

"Are you frightened?" he asked, unnecessarily, when he'd gotten her into his bedroom and onto his bed.

"Yes . . . no," she murmured into the hollow of his neck.

But he knew her rapid shallow breaths and racing heart were caused by more than his kisses and his touch. As much as he wanted her, he also knew how hard it was for her to allow herself this. For himself, he'd played the role of seducer for so long he wanted to be entirely free of it in his heart and her mind; and so he knew they both needed more than the gift of her body before he took it.

"You *certain* sure, Lucy, love?" he asked, shivering with the effort of pausing to hear her answer.

"Yes, yes," she whispered, blindly seeking his mouth with her own again, thrilled with him and terrified at herself, afraid to stop for fear she'd be too cowardly to continue if she thought about it.

And then her lips told him so much more that he forgot his reservations. He forgot more than that, he realized with dismay only moments later, when, dazed with desire, he paused to free himself from the last of his own restraints. He rose and quickly slid from his trousers before turning back to come into her arms again. And saw his mistake at once, of course . . . because she did.

Every story he'd heard from other men, and the one

much-fingered medical book he'd found as a boy and read, agreed. When it came to initiating marital relations with young brides, they all cautioned against letting them see what was up, literally, as their husbands began their married lives. But tonight there was light from a full moon, and though he'd spared the time to put out the lights, he hadn't remembered to draw the curtains. Careful as he'd been, he was very anxious to get the mechanics out of the way so he could love her. He'd been careless in that moment, and she got a glimpse of him, entirely naked, as he began to get into bed.

She stared, grew rigid, and looked away, one hand to her heart, just at the top of the hated corset that he'd finally been about to peel away.

He angled himself away from her, but it was too late. For once, he, who'd done this same thing more times than he could count, or cared to, was totally at a loss as to how to proceed. He loved her too much to go on if she was upset, but was too experienced to doubt that stopping now wouldn't be a bigger mistake.

"It's how I look," he said as casually as he could, "it's how every man looks," he added, knowing it was a stupid thing to say, but playing for time. He could scarcely apologize for it, could he? he wondered.

"It's not how the men in the museum look," she said in a tiny voice.

"What men?" he asked, totally confused now.

"The statues. Apollo," she said softly, "Mercury—you know."

He didn't, and was racking his brain trying to think of what Greek gods had that he didn't, aside from perfect noses, when she spoke again, tracing a pattern on the sheet with one finger as she did, even as she averted her head.

"They all had five-pointed, ah . . . like this," she said, showing him the design, hideously embarrassed, but brave, because she was as confused as he was. More so when he started laughing.

"Oh, Lucy," he said as he fought for control, "oh, my lovely Lucy, someday you'll think this is as funny as I do. Dear, lovely, beautiful Lucy, mine," he said, drawing her into his arms, "those are leaves. Grape, or fig, or acanthus, or something. To cover up what you saw. Real men don't have leaves," he said, and roared with laughter again. It was all of it absurd, he thought—her idea of what men were like as well as what they were in fact like, as he realized how her closeness and her distance were affecting him.

"But why should they want to cover that?" she asked, as honestly puzzled as she was embarrassed by her foolishness for not recognizing leaves and inventing new terrors. "It's much easier to think of men having what you . . . what I saw . . . than those sharp and pointy things, isn't it?"

"Oh, yes," he said. And then he sobered.

"Lucy," he said. "I love you, and you can't believe how much I want to make love to you. But I can see the way a good girl is brought up is going to make that very hard for me tonight."

Privately, he began to think the reason that old men were the ones who liked to seduce virgins the most was that they'd started when they were young, and hadn't finished yet. He was exhausted before he'd begun, and strung out thin and taut as a washline, terrified of beginning. But he did love and want her very much, so he sighed and said, "I want you to love what I do as much as I do, and there's nothing wrong with that, believe me. Do you?"

She nodded.

"All right. Then maybe we'd just better lie here together and get to know each other, and take things as they come, even if that means they have to come later, tomorrow, or the next day, or our wedding day. Or even later. Okay?"

She nodded again, and went into his arms.

"Do you think you can take off that corset?" he asked wistfully a few minutes later.

But when she had, with his help, he was the one who had to look away, and, suddenly dry-mouthed, draw in his breath, and make believe he was fully in control.

"Lucy," he said softly, lying apart from her, addressing the night, because after one yearning look, he couldn't trust himself to turn to her again. "Now, you may think I look funny, and I confess, I may. Especially if you've never seen the like. But just think of how hard it is for young men when they start out. A man needs powerful faith to put such an important part of himself in such a dark mysterious place. Women manufacture babies too. If they don't, something else happens every month to show they're not—talk about strange! It's been known to make brave young cowboys turn green at the thought, much less the sight."

She was too shocked and titillated to answer. She was trying to understand how she could be as frightened as she was excited, when he spoke again, and made her forget herself.

"Lucy," he said into the stillness, "does the look of things matter so much? Can't you forget, and remember that you said you love me?"

"Oh, Josh, I do," she cried, and came into his arms.

Then it was too much for all his experience and patience together to withstand. As it was for all her ignorance and fright. Because although his body was strange, his hands were familiar, as were his voice and his lips and his arms. And though he knew he should move slowly and take less than he wanted this first time, it seemed she wanted to offer him everything and more. It was late, and they were both weary with waiting, anxious to please each other, each astonished in turn at how beautiful the other was, and bent on pleasing. They were very much in love, and that was the thing that equalized them; making him as unsure as a raw, untutored boy; making her as wise in the ways of pleasure as a courtesan.

They came together, finally, as equals, until he realized that with all the best intentions and care in the world, they were not.

"Sorry . . . oh, Lucy, honey, I'm so sorry," he whispered when they were firmly joined at last.

But she was not.

Because if it didn't feel wonderful just then, it still felt wonderfully right, and so she told him, to encourage him. Her hand went to the back of his head, the other to his back to hold him against her, despite the discomfort it caused her. It was loving trust which soon ended what he'd begun, and he was glad of it for more than the joy of it, because he wanted to give her relief as much as he needed a different sort for himself. She could see and feel how extraordinary it was for him then, and that was something that filled her heart, if not her body, with as much delight as he'd wanted for her.

When his shuddering had ceased, and his lips left hers so that he could drag in breath again, he spoke.

"No," he said as he held her close, "being happy for me is *not* enough for you. But you'll see, it's only a beginning. And we've got that now, haven't we?"

The doubt in his voice brought her as much pleasure as his tenderness had done, and she was quick to agree. But then she froze his growing smile.

"You were wrong," she said musingly. "It's not easy. It's not so much difficult as complicated. And you were right. Oh, Josh, I wouldn't want to do this with a lot of people. I couldn't. Stop laughing, you know what I mean. Don't you ?"

"I do," he said seriously. "Now, at last, I do."

He left her soon after, only for a moment. When he came back with a dampened towel, to lessen her embarrassment as much as her discomfort, he asked, as he persuaded her to relax for him, "Lucy, do you know how lucky I am?"

"*We* are," she corrected him with feeling.

What happened next, because of what she'd said, she announced drowsily when they were done, was worth everything that had happened since the day she was born.

"*I* was born," he corrected her as he hugged her close, and meant it too.

Fanny was fussing with the last flower she was anchoring in Lucy's hair.

"A bride needs white roses, a great many of them, and with your hair . . . There, now, Miss Lucy Rose—never has a name been more appropriate!"

"You're supposed to cry at the wedding, Fanny," Lucy said after she'd looked in the mirror to see the many white roses caught up in her curls, and looked beyond to see her matron of honor, behind her, tears rolling down her cheeks.

"During, before, and after," Fanny said softly. "My

dear, I am so very happy for you. Now, then, do you have everything?"

Lucy gazed at herself. She wore the gown Josh had ordered sent to the hotel, the new pearl necklace and earrings that Josh had had his secretary deliver; her bags had been packed and sent to her from Mrs. Fergus' house. She'd not left Josh's side since the night she'd arrived at his rooms, except to wash, except for the last hour, when Fanny shooed him out of the room so as to dress the bride. And she was still surprised at how the time had slipped away when this morning had come. But, as he'd promised, everything was in place and readied for their wedding. Everything, she thought with sinking heart, except for perhaps the most important thing to him.

"Yes," she said with a sudden solemnity that alerted Fanny as she went to open the bedroom door, "everything—but for the best man."

"There's still fifteen minutes—more than enough to spare," Fanny said too brightly. "A late entrance is so much more dramatic."

"Ah, but it's a wedding, not a play," Lucy answered as she got up and went to the half-open door to look out to see her fiancé crossing her line of vision as he continued pacing, consulting his watch the harried way a man does when he's looked at it ten seconds before.

When the knock came, Josh sprang to open the door.

He felt a stone roll off his heart when he saw who was standing there; he was so relieved that he didn't note his brother's expression as he took him into his arms to give him a quick and energetic hug.

"Gray! Thank God. If you'd left it much later, I'd be the oldest living groom in America. What did you do? Walk down? It doesn't matter, you're here. Now everything's set. I wanted you to come with us—the boys are going to meet us there. Do you think you could force yourself to say hello before we go?" he finally asked, as his brother's grim expression and cold demeanor registered and began to dissipate his eagerness.

"I'd thought," Gray said with quiet emphasis, "that you might've said something else to me before you'd invited me here today. I'd thought," he added, as Josh's eyes grew as cold as his younger brother's voice, "that I might've got some warning of what was to come, not just a command to come to the festivities. But then, I s'pose times have changed, haven't they? This city does that to people, I guess. How should I know? I'm just a country boy. But I know my duty, I'm here."

Josh's eyes were narrowed, and he stood so tall and rigid it seemed to Lucy that he was in his fancy black-suited best in order to attend a funeral, not a wedding. Gray stood up to him, tall, blazingly fair and patrician, his distaste as easy to see as his anger. They faced each other, toe to toe, in a silence that grew too profound.

Lucy froze, and watching them, felt her foolish idyll ending. She wasn't surprised—no, not even now, at this last minute. It had been fated to fail, from the first. Because joyous as it had been, it had been immoral, and she'd known the rules even as she'd defied them. Now she was to know, just as she'd always been taught, what happened to bad girls. She supposed she deserved it. But she didn't want Josh to share in it.

Staying with Josh every minute until this hasty impromptu wedding day had been as terrible an idea as she'd surely have thought it was only days ago, before she'd abandoned her good sense and allowed herself to come under his spell. Because now she could see that Gray personified the world they'd have to face when they left these rooms. The world that wouldn't think it amusing, or romantic, or even decent for an eligible, handsome, and wealthy gentleman to marry an actress. The world that would belittle him for it, just as Kyle had warned.

It wasn't too late, she thought, as with a panicky gesture of pride she slipped Josh's dressing gown over her wedding dress, so as not to shame herself further. She raised her chin and prepared to enter the room to step between the two brothers before they did each other an injury, it was never too late to end something that might start too much pain. Even if it pained her. She might be fallen, but she wasn't lost. Or at least she hadn't lost her dignity or sense of honor, or love for him. She'd think of something to save him and something to save her own face as she did.

Because now, at last, and suddenly, she understood the true meaning of sacrifice. And knew that because she loved him, she was capable of it, since she loved him more than herself. Armed with her new wisdom and all her old talents, she put on a calm face, opened the door, prepared to give up her life if she had to, for his pride and his family, and his future.

Gray's face froze when he saw her. He didn't speak to her, even to greet her; he only spun around to confront his brother, his eyes blazing, his rage barely contained.

"How could you!" he cried, his voice, in his pain and fury, very much a young man's, cracking under the strain of his disillusion and sense of betrayal. "I knew this damned city had changed you, I saw it happening. I was prepared to take it, but dammit, couldn't you . . . spare her this? What's Lucy doing here, you bastard?"

Josh's fists were at his side. In that moment the only thing that kept them there, aside from the pain that seemed to weigh them down with his spirit, and his last lingering unwillingness to hurt this boy, his brother, was his absolute surprise.

"She's here," he said through tightly clenched teeth, "because it's customary for the bride to be with her husband on her wedding day."

"Bride? Lucy? Oh, my God, Josh," Gray said, embarrassment, relief, and joy chasing across his vivid young face as his sky-blue eyes searched his brother's face. "I didn't know . . . I thought you were marrying that other . . . Glor . . ." He lowered his voice. "You know. Well, hot damn, Josh," he cried, "you just wired me to come to your wedding, you didn't say to whom—and that the reception would be at William Henry Vanderbilt's house, so what was I to think? Damn!" he said as his arms went around his brother. "You don't know how happy I am. Oh, this is nothin' short of wonderful!"

"And you, baby brother, don't know how close you came to acquiring a lovely new nose, just like mine," Josh said, weak with relief.

"Oh, I know you'll find some excuse to do it someday. Lucy!" Gray said, abandoning his brother after slapping him on the back. He walked up to her and took her two hands in his. "He doesn't deserve you. Look at you!

You're beautiful in every which way, and I'm grateful to you for taking him. Damn. Excuse me, Lucy, but I am plain old happy!"

They drove to the church, with Gray exclaiming over his happiness all the way. He only quieted when the service began. At that, his lips quivered and quirked with swallowed smiles as he stood beside his brother as the minister spoke. But as soon as his brother had kissed his new wife, he started talking about his delight again, and his voice only faded away when Erie and Samuel Tee carried him off bodily with them to their coach, to follow the bridal pair.

The occupants of Mrs. Fergus' boardinghouse seemed not at all as impressed with William Vanderbilt's great house as they were with the buffet he'd set out for them, but then, they were actors, and good ones too. A great many gentlemen from Josh's club didn't realize that they were talking business with men who didn't know a stock from a share, but Lucy's new friends were too gifted to let them know it, and too polite to be contemptuous of them for not knowing a cue from an exit line. The groom's friends from the West were not half so taken with the gentlemen from the East that kept priming them with questions, but once they started talking about horses, geography faded away.

In all, it was a wildly successful affair. All the guests mingled happily; even Kyle Harper seemed pleased and charmed to be present. But then, he was, after all, the best actor there. Only Lucy's grandmother, sister, and brother-in-law were stricken to silence by the circumstances and their surroundings. They were the quietest there—they, and the politest guest of all, a fellow named Duncan, but he was by far the more popular.

For all it was successful, it was a strange sort of wedding, and a more bizarre reception, but when word of it got out—about how that daring young Dylan was up to anything—there wasn't a soul in society who didn't wish he'd been there. Except for the Van Horn family, but they were too wise to ever let that get out, and too practical to allow themselves to remember it after another day.

The guests pelted the departing newlyweds with rice and roses. Gray let them get away only after being assured they'd meet on New Year's Eve again, at the grand opening of the new operetta.

"I thought we'd have to drag him behind us like the ribbons and other things he'd tied on the back of the coach," Josh commented as he drove his bride uptown.

But Lucy was too happy, too moved and proud to speak at once. She only gazed at her husband's profile as he drove up the avenue, delighting in reminding herself that he was hers and she was his. But she noticed when they stopped, far uptown, on the avenue alongside the park. Then a man came up to them and touched his hat. Josh handed him the reins, and turned to his wife and offered her his hand. She looked to him in confusion, but placed her gloved hand in his. He helped her down, and then immediately up and into the closed carriage he'd pulled his own coach alongside. When the carriage turned and began to drive them back downtown, he sat back and sighed with relief.

"I decided the best place for us to go at such short notice was back to the hotel. Well, we have to be back in a week anyhow for New Year's, and I thought you wouldn't mind staying there until we find a house or build one or two—until we can make plans for a real good honeymoon too. Do you mind?" he asked, troubled by her silence.

"No, no, it's fine, but why such secrecy?" she asked.

"Ah, well," he said, relaxing, holding her hand tight in his own, "back home, you see, we've got this practice called a shivaree—the fellows like to carry on when a friend gets married, banging pots and pans outside the bedroom window, making jokes and singing certain sorts of songs all night long. I didn't think New York was ready for that, and I didn't think you were, and I know I'll never be."

"I married a very clever man," Lucy said, shivering at the thought of her narrow escape, but not for long, because then he took her into his arms and it was impossible to shiver with anything but delight.

He sighed against her lips.

"Maybe I ought to ask the driver to stop," he finally whispered, in an effort to get himself to stop, because for all he loved coaching, there was only so much a man

ought to do in a carriage on such a short trip, especially
with his so lately innocent, properly raised, and newly
legal wife. "I'm a respectable married man now. Since
we're so near the park, maybe I ought to go out and get
me a leaf. What do you think?" he asked as he nuzzled
her ear.

"Josh," she said breathlessly, "I think you'd better get
a tree."

He lit up with laughter, and when he could, thanked
her for the compliment, warning her that he was cor-
rupting her. She thanked him kindly for it, and he took
her lips again to end her wicked laughter, and then the
carriage stopped.

And so Josh Dylan was even gladder than he'd ever
imagined he'd be, when he realized that after all his wandering, he was finally home.

22

December 31, 1879

IT WAS TO BE hoped the Fifth Avenue Theater was as fireproof as it claimed. Because there was some question as to whether even a roaring blaze would have persuaded anyone in the audience to leave the seats they'd paid so much, in money and influence, to get. They were blissfully content to simply be there, even though they hadn't known the name of the production before they'd been given their programs. But now they knew they were seeing *The Pirates of Penzance*, and now they were enjoying the show; almost as much as the fact that they were part of the privileged few who were.

They looked forward to the intermission as well, because it was clear this audience thought it was as gratifying to see itself as the show. The members of the select crowd glittered and shone as brightly as any set or costume on the great stage. Tonight it was even simpler than usual for Mrs. Astor to ignore Mrs. Vanderbilt, since there were so many notable others sitting between them. The cream of New York society was here to welcome in the new year and the new Gilbert and Sullivan operetta. The cream of the New York theatrical world as well, Kyle Harper thought smugly, and it was never the famous performers in the audience he was thinking of. The talented few he was concerned with weren't sitting in the best seats, covered with jewels and furs. But some of the best in his business, even if it was a slightly different facet of the business, were also in attendance, and had come just as well-equipped for their own purposes.

Dowager queens of the Four Hundred and merchant

princes from the ranks of the Ten Thousand might be studying each other, noting every dollar that went into the makeup of a gown, and estimating every cent each tiara cost. But in the less expensive seats there were men who could note every note that they heard as fast as the musicians could play it, and as many who could copy each word in shorthand as it flew from the mouths of the cast.

Kyle Harper nodded in satisfaction. His own Mr. Mac-Gruder had a seat and a notebook, Dr. Max was in the balcony with a bottle, a pencil, and a pad. Their peers, he saw, were salted everywhere throughout the house. Let the Four Hundred exclaim and applaud the play and each other. He'd pay tribute to this singular night in his own fashion, as would several other theatrical entrepreneurs he recognized in the crowded theater. The security that had been thrown up around the production of *Pirates* was like the moral training that had protected his former star: it had merely delayed, not prevented, theft of virtue.

Thinking of the English Rose made Kyle frown, and he hadn't frowned often tonight. He'd seen her arrive, even as he'd heard the admiring whispers that accompanied her walk down the aisle with her tall, handsome husband. Then he hadn't looked her way again. Business came before regret, even as it came before pleasure. And now his pleasure was all business. Because Kyle Harper, like his minions Dr. Max and Mr. MacGruder, was working tonight.

Mr. D'Oyly Carte doubtless thought he'd been clever premiering this production on the same night here and in England in order to establish a New York copyright, maintaining leakproof security until parting the curtains to present the operetta, full-blown. He had been, Kyle admitted, giving him his due. But he was also, regrettably for him, British. And so, didn't understand the situation at all.

A copyright meant that no one could open *The Pirates of Penzance* across the street next week, true. But as Kyle gloated to himself, he could open, for example: *Kyle Harper's Memories of "Pirates of Penzance,"* or *Reminiscences of "Pirates of Penzance,"* or *Scenes and*

Songs from "Pirates of Penzance," or such like and similar, as early as tomorrow morning, and right next door. And never pay a cent for copyright, so long as his production wasn't exactly the same as the original, and the title admitted it. Because that, as he knew, and Mr. D'Oyly Carte obviously didn't, was legal and New York City law.

Kyle smiled luxuriously, sat back, and watched the first act of *The Pirates of Penzance* with a professional as well as an appreciative eye.

"Bravo! Encore! Encore!" the voice cheered softly. But the only reply was a muted giggle.

The firelight played over the two figures on the wide bed, making them gilded statues of human beauty as they relaxed together at last, forming a representation of perfect human love such as was never seen in a museum.

"Do you think they noticed? Or wondered why we left so soon, before the intermission?" Lucy asked drowsily, with only a hint of worry, as she stretched.

"They didn't notice," Josh said as he admired her movement with hand and eyes, "and if they did, I hope they knew why, for their sakes. If they can't remember why they'd have left on their own honeymoons, poor folks, then—"

"But, Josh," she cried, all languid grace vanished, as she finally remembered the other reason why they'd left so soon now that the first one had been temporarily satisfied, "how could you have let me deceive myself so! What a fool I must have looked. 'The English Rose'? 'The American Weed'! I was an amateur, a caricature of the sort of performances I saw tonight. I never knew—until I saw light opera done the way it ought to be," she grieved once more, "and I thought I could've made it my career. How good of you not to tell me, even when you wanted me to give it up. Oh, how noble! How I love you for it!"

"Good. But I hope not for that. Because it's not true," he insisted again, realizing that the way he'd stopped her protests when they'd got back to their bedroom wouldn't work again. She needed words. She always would. And he had them for her.

"You were wonderful, and would've been in this new production too. Or any other. Never doubt it. I didn't. You know I would've done anything to convince you to leave the theater and marry me. But I wouldn't have lied, and didn't," he said, and meant it. "You were wonderful."

"Well, no," she said, but left it, only to whisper low, suddenly thoughtful, suddenly shy, even so intimately pressed to him as she was now, "But even so, if I *ever*, someday, years from now, because I'm only human, get mad at you and say I gave up my splendid career for you—remind me of what I found out tonight, Josh, will you? Because I don't want to deceive myself again, even though I love it when you do."

"Do what?" he teased, sorry that she couldn't believe him, determined to convince her someday, but just now humbled and honored simply because she was thinking of someday, years from now—with him.

There was silence in the room for several moments, except for the sounds of sliding sheets and limbs and the chuckling of the fire in the grate.

And then a husky voice implored, "Encore! Encore!"

"Oh, all right. What I won't do for my public," Josh pretended to grumble.

"I hope not, this is a private affair," Lucy giggled, before she could only murmur again, "Oh, yes, that way . . . Encore!"

There were three good solid numbers, Kyle decided when the final curtain finally fell. That "Modern Major General" recitative—Ned could do that well, and would be glad to leave his revue for a chance to; the amusing "Tarantara" policemen's chorus, and the "Policeman's Lot" number. It would require essentially the same cast as the *Pinafore* too: an ingenue, a handsome hero, two older men, and an older woman. Add one chorus of men, one of women, and Presto!—another Gilbert and Sullivan opera, another chance at fame and fortune. A good night's work, Kyle thought, rising, as the audience rose to its feet to applaud.

After the bows had been taken, and the seemingly interminable cries of "Encore!" had faded, and the count of seconds to the new decade was done, the champagne corks began popping and Kyle looked for an exit.

He had patiently made his way from his seat to the aisle, when he was intercepted there.

"Row Q, seat number six? Mr. Harper, sir? Message for you, sir," the page boy said, handing him a slip of paper.

He stood stock-still, and let the other theatergoers flow past him, like a standing stone in a current of swiftly moving water, until he finally accepted what it said. Then he took in a breath, just as he'd taught Miss Lucy Markham to do, before he straightened his shoulders and sought out the backstage door.

Backstage after a good performance was always a pleasant place to be. After a wild success on a New Year's Eve in New York City, it was very like Kyle Harper's idea of heaven. The rich stood side by side with the famous, but the rich paid tribute to the theater, and fame meant nothing unless it was theatrical. He drank in the sights and sounds, and it gave him courage and honed his cleverness, so that by the time he'd found the door he sought, he was as prepared for battle as he was for surprise. But for all his training, he wasn't prepared for what he faced.

Still, he recovered quickly. By the time all the gentlemen had been introduced, and he'd assessed them as narrowly as they had him, and he'd subdued the always-present chill of excitement at meeting up with the famous, he was ready for whatever they had to say. He recognized two of them from their pictures in the papers, as well as from the bows they'd taken this night. Another, from all the descriptions he'd had of him. And the others, he imagined, must have good and sufficient reason to also be admitted into the company of the authors of the opera and their manager.

"Ah, Mr. Harper," the small, dark, immaculately dressed man said in his scrupulous English accent, "you're younger than we'd thought, that's a decided advantage we'd not considered."

Kyle smiled, and waited, since there was nothing else to say. The advantage was theirs, and they knew it.

"I understand you've closed your production of *Pinafore*." the gentleman said.

"I am honored," Kyle said in his best and deepest mellow voice, "that of all the productions of *Pinafore* in our fair city, you noted my poor effort." Then he smiled again, pleased with how neatly he'd evaded the question.

The tall, big-boned, bewhiskered gentleman with the bright blue eyes seemed very amused at that. The other man that Kyle watched from the corner of his eye, the plump, melancholic one, betrayed no new expression.

"Yes. Just so. But we have," Richard D'Oyly Carte answered. "Mr. Harper, we've not much time tonight. Duty calls and friends are thronging. But still . . . as you are, at the moment, at liberty, so to speak, we wondered if you'd be interested in a little project of ours."

Kyle assumed a polite expression, though his heart was pounding wildly and his mind teemed with possibilities too exciting to give voice.

"There are, and were, dozens of *Pinafore* productions here in New York City. That was why we came here, you know. Likely you also know what we've just discovered. We've lately been made aware of the fact that our opening here tonight is merely a stopgap measure. Ah, yes. What creative laws you have, they've quite enchanted Mr. Sullivan, but they have, I'll admit, vexed me. Our new production's extraordinarily well-named, given the circumstances, is it not?"

A polite quirk of the lips, with only a hint of triumph in it, was Kyle's reply.

"Yes, well, to proceed," Mr. D'Oyly Carte said. "I saw your production at the Stratton, Mr. Harper. It was singular. You'd the least adequate theater, the most meager sets, and with some notable exceptions, the most meager talent, as well. Yet you did as well as, if not better than, better versions of our opera. We're suitably impressed. You've an expression here: 'If you can't beat them, join them.' Excellent idea. We're going to be sending *authorized* touring companies across your land very soon. We need someone to organize and oversee them. Someone who understands our sort of theater, as well as his sort of country; someone with the ability to make much of little would suit our purposes very well. In short: would you be interested in the position, Mr. Harper?"

Kyle remained still, the small smile fixed on his long face, as he said with admirable calm, "I would be interested, yes—if the terms are as advantageous as the offer."

"I think you'll find the financial benefits very much to your liking. The position would also involve traveling, and the experience gained and contacts made would be valuable to a man of endeavor, as we do believe you to be. Our man of business will have the details drawn up, and if we meet, say, in a week or two, when this present hubbub dies down, I think we can come to terms. Here's my card, and my direction. If you would be so kind as to leave us yours?"

They named a day to meet again, and shook hands solemnly all around. Kyle was about to leave, so that he could be alone with his whirling thoughts, when he heard the tall, robust gentleman cough, and Richard D'Oyly Carte said, "Ah! Oh, yes. One other thing, before you go . . ."

Kyle froze in place; he'd been doubting his good luck since he'd heard of it.

"Mr. Sullivan, here," Mr. D'Oyly Carte went on, "had the notion that an American production of *Pinafore* might amuse . . . ah, charm our own audiences. Do you think you could reproduce yours for us in London, in the foreseeable future?"

"I cannot see why not," Kyle said, astonishingly calm for one whose worst fears had just vanished.

"With the same cast? Splendid," Mr. Sullivan exclaimed.

"Ah . . ." Kyle hesitated, now remembering something he'd been trying to forget for a week. "With *almost* the same cast. Circumstances do change, you know."

"Let's have the truth with no bark on it," Richard D'Oyly Carte said. "The one ornament of your production was 'The English Rose.' An extraordinary young woman. Beautiful, graceful, with a hint of intelligence and humor not often found in ingenues—the model of what we'd envisioned as Josephine. Interestingly, her apparent lack of formal operatic training only enhanced her performance. If some of the others have moved on, so be it. But you must be aware that she was the heart of your *Pinafore*."

Kyle gathered himself up. He closed his eyes for a moment, and then opened them to what he knew would have to be his finest performance yet, or ever.

"Gentlemen," he said in his smoothest, lowest voice, "Miss Lucy Rose is, in actuality, Miss Lucy Markham, no more English than I."

"It makes no matter, Harper," Mr. Sullivan said impatiently. "Neither is our prince consort. It's theater, after all."

"But," Kyle said slowly and thoughtfully, although he was thinking frantically, "I thought you were interested in my opinion as well as my productions. Gentlemen," he said more forcefully, as it came to him, "I thought you wanted an American production for London. I'm sure my ersatz 'English Rose' would amuse your countrymen—she's a talented little creature, isn't she? But I'm sure they—as I—would be more interested in seeing something unique.

"Doubtless," Kyle said as he paced, and the gentlemen in the room stared at him as he drew them in with his words as well as with the magnetism of his barely contained restless energy, "handbills saying 'Direct from New York, HMS Pinafore, starring "The English Rose," ' would attract some interest. But just envision . . ." he said, stopping and staring at them with brilliant eyes, gesturing with his thin and shaking hands, his voice growing louder as he announced thrillingly, " 'Direct from her New York triumph, the American Beauty Rose in HMS Pinafore.' "

"Is she . . . is this new 'American Beauty Rose' so talented, then?" one of the gentlemen asked, as the others still seemed to be staring at the invisible headline Kyle had written in the air for them.

"Why do you think I no longer have 'The English Rose' in my employ?" Kyle asked sweetly. "She is beyond lovely," he said passionately, "her voice is so pure it sounds like prayer, but the glint in her eyes is all amusement at the folly of men, even as her eyes hold compassion for us all. Her grace is without measure, as are her resources and her boundless attraction: she is, in essence, America, embodied, to me. I cannot say more—or less. In truth, I cannot," he concluded, his voice breaking.

"Well, then, certainly . . ." one of the gentlemen said, as Mr. Sullivan smiled wanly and Mr. Gilbert nodded with content.

"Do you think you might bring her with you when we meet in a fortnight?" one of the gentlemen asked, like a boy requesting a treat.

"But of course," Kyle said amiably as he shook hands all around. Then he bade them all a good night and a happy new year, and stepped out into the corridor, and then into the new year's first night.

He walked in silence for a block, seeing none of the merrymakers thronging the pavements. He walked on for some streets more, never noticing the direction in which he was bound. He was far from where his feet were leading him, lost in deepest thought. He'd the greatest opportunity of his life before him, and whatever the obstacles, if Kyle Harper was in the habit of passing up opportunity, he'd not have gotten to this age in his life.

Two weeks wasn't enough time, but in a pinch, two days would do, he thought. There was only one Lucy Rose, and she was Lucy Dylan now. But there must be more where she came from. Remembering where she came from, Kyle paused in his steps. For once, his heart, that always hopeful organ, grew cold. She'd come from another world; she'd come from a church choir in Brooklyn. But he didn't deserve success if he couldn't do something with something even as hopeless-sounding as that, he thought. And he never doubted he deserved success. He walked onward.

In time, when his thoughts had focused and formed, he permitted the outer world entry again, and so he heard a merry cry.

"Hey, chief!" a boy from a ragged roving pack of jolly young newsboys shouted to the top-hatted, well-dressed gent striding along, alone in the night. "Happy New Year to yiz, captain!" the boy cried, hoping for a coin, tossed in the spirit of the night.

Kyle reached into his pocket and sent a copper spinning toward the boy, but on hearing the happy, "Thanks, sport!" he paused and called back to the boy, "Here! For another of the same, tell me something. Which way is Brooklyn?"

"Hey, what?" the boy exclaimed. "Brooklyn! Why, walk east till yer hat floats—that way," he gestured, laughing, helpful as he was impudent, because he was close enough to catch a coin, but not a beating from the gentleman's walking stick, "or take the ferry, and yer there!"

"Good enough," Kyle said, and tossed another coin.

He'd never been there, but they called it the city of churches, after all. There must be dozens and dozens of church choirs to see and hear. And so somewhere, certainly, Kyle decided, there'd be someone who could be his "American Beauty Rose." The dawn that was coming was New Year's Day, and there'd be services all day. And it was never too soon to start searching; he'd only two weeks, after all.

He headed east, his spirits rising as he finally allowed himself to indulge in thoughts of the night he'd just passed, as well as the hopes for the day that was coming. Then, best of all, he had a good omen. Because for all of his hardheadedness, he was of the theater, where portents were taken seriously.

As he passed an organ grinder, out late to entertain the roistering crowds this New Year's Eve, he heard the familiar "Captain of the *Pinafore*" being cranked out. He flipped a coin. Very free with his coins he was tonight, he thought happily. And then, as though he couldn't help it, and he couldn't, he did a sudden lively little sailor's hornpipe step, right out of the first act.

Some passersby laughed at the drunken gentleman, and the organ grinder, encouraged, picked up the pace.

Kyle bowed, flicked his opera cape around himself, turned a corner, and strode on toward Brooklyn, alone and determined in the gaslight-studded dark. But the music played on in his head. Suddenly his head rose, as his heart did. He'd thought he heard a voice from far away crying: "Encore! Encore!"—the most glorious words he knew.

No one was there. But he was. And he knew what he'd heard, however it had come to him.

Then, always the actor, alone as he was, he obligingly executed a few more steps of the hornpipe. And so danced off alone, into the night.

About the Author

Edith Layton has been writing since she was ten years old. After getting a degree in creative writing and theater arts, she worked for a motion picture company, a television production company and in the newsroom of a radio station. She has also written publicity and worked as a freelance writer for newspapers and magazines. But history is both her hobby and her delight, and so she was naturally drawn to writing her own versions of it. She has three children, and lives on Long Island with her physician husband. She collects antiques, books and large dogs.